King

of Bombs

A Novel About Nuclear Terrorism

Sheldon Filger

authorHOUSE™

1663 LIBERTY DRIVE, SUITE 200
BLOOMINGTON, INDIANA 47403
(800) 839-8640
WWW.AUTHORHOUSE.COM

This book is a work of fiction. People, places, events, and situations are the product of the author's imagination. Any resemblance to actual persons, living or dead, or historical events, is purely coincidental.

First published by AuthorHouse 4/6/2006

ISBN: 1-4208-6055-0 (sc)
ISBN: 1-4208-6054-2 (dj)

Library of Congress Control Number: 2005905530

Printed in the United States of America
Bloomington, Indiana

This book is printed on acid-free paper.

Table of Contents

Lake Abitibi

An estimated thirty million Americans watched the Tom Scanlon Show each evening. It was the most popular nightly talk show on television, lauded for the celebrity personalities it presented in a lively interview format. As the year 2006 drew to a close, Scanlon featured, as one of his guests, a balding man in his fifties, with disheveled, thinning hair and a slightly rumpled suit. His face was not recognizable, unlike virtually all the other participants on the show. To a typical viewer, he represented anonymity rather than celebrity.

"My next guest, ladies and gentlemen, is Dr. Mark Grill," Scanlon said, as he made his introduction of the man seated next to him. "You probably have never heard of him, at least until recently, let alone seen him. He is not an entertainer or Hollywood celebrity. He is a physicist on the faculty of Yale University."

Scanlon then held up a book briefly, waiting for the TV camera to focus on its cover. Continuing his introduction, he went on to say that Dr. Grill was the author of a new book entitled, "Will The Next 9/11 Be Nuclear?" It having been just over five years since the traumatic events of September 11, 2001, Scanlon told his audience, it was timely to sit down and talk with Dr. Grill.

Turning to his guest, he began with a provocative question. "Doctor, as you know, your book has been harshly criticized by our government as being wildly speculative, massively exaggerated and loaded with fear-mongering. How do you respond to those charges?"

Unused to the glare of the studio lights, Dr. Grill squinted briefly, giving the impression that he was struggling in the process of constructing a response. However, he spoke with spontaneity, exuding the courage of his convictions.

"I well understand those critical comments. Being an academic, I prefer to deal with facts and not illusions. The undeniable facts are these: in the five years since 9/11, nuclear proliferation has grown by leaps and bounds. We know that the father of the Pakistani nuclear bomb, with the probable connivance of his government, ran a veritable black-market department store in nuclear weapons technology for rogue states, with strong connections to Al-Qaeda. In the former Soviet Union, fissile materials are poorly protected and vulnerable to theft, while unemployed scientists and technicians from their downsized nuclear weapons industry are peddling their skills and craft to the highest bidder. And what has our government done to address this threat? As I prove in my book, virtually nothing."

"You pull no punches, Dr. Grill," Scanlon retorted, "but the government disputes your charges, claiming America is much safer. What have you got to say about that?"

"In my book, I have plenty to say, I'll just paraphrase a few key points," Grill responded with more than a trace of indignant ridicule. "Almost all of the homeland security investments have been made in preventing aircraft hijackings. If a nuclear weapon is smuggled into our country, it is most likely to come by ship, truck or railroad. Last year, almost 51,000 foreign ships entered our waters with minimal scrutiny. Our 361 ports received nearly eight million shipping containers, with a mere four percent being inspected. That means 96% of all foreign cargo enters the United States without our having any idea if there might be a nuclear bomb hidden in one of those containers. Over two million foreign rail cars and eleven million foreign trucks cross our land borders each year, the overwhelming majority receiving nothing more than a superficial glance. Given these facts, I don't see how the government can maintain the fiction that we as a country are safer. With regard to terrorists using weapons of mass destruction, especially a nuclear device, we are as vulnerable as if we were stark naked."

The audience sighed with concern, displaying far more interest in the subject. Or perhaps fear rather than interest. The talk show host sought to inject a note of calm into what was an entertainment program.

"Dr.Grill, so everyone can sleep peacefully tonight, won't you at least agree that groups like Al-Qaeda lack the technical knowledge and access to necessary materials, such as plutonium and highly enriched uranium, without which they can't build a nuclear weapon? Maybe a dirty bomb is within their capability, but not something like the Hiroshima bomb. Would you agree with that statement?"

Grill now looked directly into the camera, as though he felt connected with every television viewer. His jaw appeared firmer, his demeanor more stern. "It is said that the terrorists succeeded in attacking us on September 11 because of a failure of imagination on the part of our leaders," Dr. Grill said in a voice conveying a hint of anger, subdued by sadness. "To my everlasting sorrow, I see our government officials repeating the same mistake. Whatever we may think of the terrorists, we should not doubt their motivation and determination. Osama bin Laden has made it very clear that he considers it a religious duty for the Islamist radical movement to obtain nuclear weapons. Please be fully aware of what the implications are. If Al-Qaeda or its sister groups were ever to acquire a nuclear weapon, there is not the slightest doubt in my mind that they would use it, on American soil."

❖ ❖ ❖

Patches of snow covered the desolate landscape that enveloped the small mining town of Timmins, in Northern Ontario. From a distance, the topography resembled a ragged salt and pepper beard. In the center, the scars on the terrain evoked large open-pit copper, gold and uranium mines. Nearby were the small, detached homes of the miners and their families. Closer to the center of town were located larger homes belonging to the town's merchants, lawyers, doctors and civil servants. The buildings in the center of town were small and nondescript, with icicles dangling from eaves troughs. One of the indistinguishable buildings was a small, two-story office building on Orchard Street. The ground floor housed the office of one of the handful of local dentists in town. The top floor, as proclaimed by a small sign ostentatiously hung from below a window, was home to The Weekly Current, the sole newspaper in the town of Timmins.

The only newspaper in town had exactly four employees. One was the owner and publisher, Robert Burton, a retired local businessman who had grown tired of retirement. He bought the newspaper as a hobby more than a business, and was quite content that the paper usually only just broke even financially. He had a secretary, Lucy, and a circulation manager, Jane, who was responsible for making deliveries to vendors in an old van. Finally, there was Vincent MacFarland. Vince, to those familiar with him, was in his late thirties, with a full head of red hair that frequently covered his brow, of medium height and slightly paunchy. He was fair skinned, wore glasses, which somehow did not disguise his light blue eyes. His face was a contradiction, boyish in appearance, except for his brow, which often looked strained, indicative of a focused, reflective mind.

MacFarland was a coup for Burton. Vince had been a reporter for the Toronto Star for 12 years, starting right out of Journalism School. He had an excellent reputation as a serious journalist, and yet, one day he packed it all in to move from the big city to the backwoods of Northern Ontario. His wife, Judy, was from Timmins. When they decided to get married they also migrated north, leaving Toronto for her hometown. They made the decision to forego money and professional advancement for small town life, less stress and, they hoped, a healthier environment to raise a family. They had a young daughter, Rebecca. Judy was a science teacher, and taught part-time at the local elementary school.

Vincent MacFarland was the editor of The Weekly Current. He was also the newspaper's only reporter. He liked the ability to edit his own news. He also enjoyed wearing many hats: lifestyles, business, local politics, and crime. Not that there was a lot of crime in Timmins. There was the odd break-in, a small number of armed robberies each year, a few dozen auto thefts. Perhaps more than anything else, it was the diversity of MacFarland's work at The Weekly Current that gave him the greatest enjoyment. Compared to the stratification, petty competitiveness and tight editorial control he experienced at a large city newspaper, MacFarland found his career at the small weekly to be liberating. He enjoyed getting up in the morning and preparing for work, feeling a level of fulfillment that had been totally lacking at The Toronto Star.

On this particular winter morning, Vincent arrived at the office at around 11:00 AM, having returned from an interview he had conducted with a local official on the construction of a new highway. As he entered his office, he removed his fur hat and hung up his old blue winter coat. Still clutching a beat-up leather attaché case, he turned to Lucy, who caught his attention.

"Vince, Mr. Burton asked that you speak with him as soon as you arrived."

"O.K.," he replied matter-of-factly and he walked directly into the publisher's office.

"Hey Vince, how did the interview go?" asked Burton.

"Same B.S., Bob." He answered in his familiar high-pitched voice. "They're going to appoint another planning committee to examine the creation of the new feeder road to the Trans-Canada highway."

"Well, Vince," Burton responded laconically, "I won't see that feeder road in my lifetime. But I'm hopeful that you will."

Burton pulled out a written message from his desk and handed it to MacFarland.

"This message is from Constable Stevens. He said it was important you call him right away."

Vincent grabbed the note and merely responded with an "O.K." His face, however, betrayed a hint of bewilderment. As he left Burton's office and headed towards his own much smaller office, he wondered what could be so urgent. Constable Michael Stevens, with the Timmins detachment of the Royal Canadian Mounted Police, was a regular contact of MacFarland's for the crime beat. He fed him information on arrests for break-ins, domestic disputes and whatever other crime statistics could be obtained for the newspaper. In MacFarland's five years with the newspaper, he had yet to cover a crime that even came close to being labeled remarkable and noteworthy. As he sat in his chair and reached for the phone, his feeling of bewilderment transformed into one of marked curiosity.

MacFarland vigorously pounded the buttons on his phone with finger movements resembling the artistry of a pianist. He heard the familiar voice on the other end say "This is Constable Stevens."

"Mike, this is Vince. I got your message."

"Hello Vince. I thought you would want to know this as soon as possible. It looks like we have a homicide."

This was indeed newsworthy. In five years, Timmins and the nearby communities had not recorded a single murder. MacFarland's interest was certainly piqued.

"That's unusual. What are the details, Mike?"

"The body of a deceased male washed up on the south shore of Lake Abitibi this morning. I'll be heading out there in about an hour. I thought you might want to join me."

"Of course, but what makes you certain at this point that it's a homicide?" MacFarland was being the skeptical reporter in responding to the Constable. "Could it be an accidental drowning, or suicide?"

"Well, I don't think it's likely to have been a suicide or an accident," responded Stevens. "You see, the body has no head."

"What!" replied MacFarland.

"The corpse is missing its head," the Constable explained. "Apparently, the deceased was decapitated."

The Lion

In a small cubicle on the eighth floor of the Central Intelligence Agency's headquarters in Langley, Virginia, a young woman peered diligently at her computer screen. A petite brunette, barely more than five feet tall, she had dark hair tied in a bun and thin wrists made conspicuous by the ornate silver bracelets she wore. She was Amelia Baldwin, a junior translator in the Arabic Translation Division at the CIA. Barely a year out of Georgetown University, her job was to monitor and translate the content of numerous Jihadist websites. Since the events of September 11, 2001, the CIA had continuously monitored Arab-language websites that advocated terrorist attacks against the United States, either at home or against its interests abroad.

Amelia scribbled frantically on a notepad as she absorbed the contents of the website. She clicked on various pages of the site, then continued her rigorous note taking. The expression in her eyes gave evidence of the deep concern she was internalizing. She let her pen drop from her fingers as she thought for a moment. Then, prompted by an inner impulse, she lifted the receiver from her phone and dialed her supervisor.

"Mr. Dobbs, I believe I have a time-sensitive matter involving one of the websites I have been monitoring."

Philip Dobbs, Director of the Agency's foreign languages translation department, supervised the small staff of Arabic-speaking linguists as part of his duties. A small man with thinning hair, a limp moustache and thick glasses, he listened attentively to his subordinate.

"Amelia, which website?"

"Sir, it's the Al-Assad El-Islamiya."

"Come to my office, Amelia," Dobbs said brusquely. He turned to his own computer monitor and quickly entered the website address. He had its homepage on the screen just as Amelia stepped into his office.

Dobbs glanced briefly at Amelia, then turned his gaze back towards the website on his monitor.

"Amelia, it seems to be the usual catalog of threats and dire predictions of our doom. What have you found that distinguishes today's message?"

"Over here, click on that," Amelia said as she pointed to a box on the homepage.

Dobbs looked at a box that he translated as "News for Believers." He rapidly moved his mouse over his mouse pad, clicked and brought up on the screen a page saturated with blood-red Arabic script on a green background.

Dobbs, whose language specialty was Russian, dating from the priorities of the Cold War, had only a rudimentary knowledge of Arabic, especially in written form. Turning to Amelia, he told her she would have to help him translate the page, mentioning that his Arabic was not so good.

"The first four paragraphs pretty much mimic what's on the home page, using more flowery rhetoric. It speaks of the retribution of Allah's that will soon strike America, and that the next attack by the martyrs of Islam will make the world forget 9/11, as it will be inconsequential compared to the catastrophe that is about to become America's fate."

Dobbs listened carefully as Amelia spoke, however, his demeanor betrayed no evidence of concern.

"Amelia, this is no different than the usual apocalyptic pronouncements we have monitored on virtually all the Jihadist websites. For years, since September 11, 2001 there have been literally thousands of predictions of attacks worse than 9/11 that were about to occur. It reminds me of the forecasts of the Jehovah's

Witnesses about the imminent end of the world. I fail to see what is unique about this message."

"It's the final paragraph in that message to believers, Mr. Dobbs, that is alarming."

Dobbs asked her to translate that paragraph for him, word for word. She looked directly at the computer monitor as she spoke slowly and deliberately.

"The Lion calls on all believers in religion to avoid being in the United States in the middle of March of this year if possible, and to definitely leave New York City, the new Rome of the unbelievers, at that time. In the name of Allah, the merciful and compassionate, a martyrdom operation that will be the mother of all martyrdom attacks against the infidels will be conducted. This one act, Allah permitting, will bring about the annihilation of America."

The look on Dobbs's face changed. Amelia turned towards him, their eyes locking.

"Amelia, did it in fact say annihilation, or could the words be interpreted as devastation or serious damage?"

"No, sir," she replied emphatically. "The Arabic word that is used is *fana*. In the Arab language, it has a very specific meaning, which is annihilation or total destruction in a cosmic sense. It would suggest an event of apocalyptic proportions, and nothing less."

Dobbs began to perspire from his forehead. He pulled out a handkerchief to wipe his brow, using the interval to ponder for a moment.

"Amelia, I appreciate your concern. However, other websites have also made similar predictions about the downfall of America."

"But Mr. Dobbs," Amelia forcefully interjected, "there is a critical distinction. This website has always been right. It predicted the terrorist attacks in Bali, Madrid, Casablanca, Iraq and Chechnya. It has yet to make a prediction of an upcoming attack that was factually wrong."

Dobbs nodded in agreement.

"Close the door, Amelia," Dobbs said in a soft voice. He then asked her to sit down.

9

"What I am about to tell you is highly classified. I am sharing this information with you for strictly operational reasons, and you must not tell anyone else about this. We have not been able to identify who the Lion is, but through interrogation of Al-Qaeda and other terrorist prisoners, we are convinced that he is the single most important operative that Osama bin Laden has in the field."

Amelia listened attentively as Dobbs continued.

"We think, Amelia, the Lion has orchestrated the most violent terrorist attacks in Iraq, and has himself personally beheaded many of the hostages. However, for the past four months, we have detected nothing from him in Iraq, or anywhere else for that matter. It would appear that he has gone completely underground, as though he has vanished from the face of the Earth."

Amelia glanced briefly at Dobbs, than focused again on the News for Believers on her boss's computer screen.

"Could it be," she said slowly but with trepidation, "that the reason the Lion is no longer in Iraq is that he has a new mission, an attack on America that will be a super 9/11?"

Dobbs reflected for a moment, then told his subordinate what he planned to do.

"This calls for consultation with people above my pay grade. I'm going to refer this matter directly to the Director of Counter-Terrorism."

◈ ◈ ◈

The blue and white RCMP cruiser slowly pulled off of route 169 at a point about 70 kilometers east of Timmins, not far from the Quebec border. It being winter, the numerous birch trees enveloping the dirt path the police vehicle was slowly proceeding on were bereft of any foliage. Their forlorn appearance combined with a graying January sky created an atmosphere that was somber and melancholy. At a point where the tree line ended was the rocky shore of Lake Abitibi. There was already another RCMP cruiser parked on the shoreline, next to an ambulance. One RCMP officer was photographing various points around the lake. Another Constable turned towards the oncoming cruiser, while two paramedics unfolded a stretcher they had removed from the rear of the ambulance.

Inside the cruiser was Constable Stevens, a strapping, tall man with dark hair and a strong face, who was at the wheel. Next to him was Vince MacFarland. Stevens parked the car, and the two men exited as one of the other RCMP Constables on the scene approached him.

"Hi Jack," Stevens said in a voice familiar to his colleague.

"Hello, Mike," the other officer said in response.

Stevens introduced MacFarland to the other officer, who pointed to a spot near the shoreline. "There's the body," he said.

MacFarland and Stevens looked towards an object clumped conspicuously near the waterline, covered by a green blanket. The other officer who had been photographing the crime scene approached the group.

"Pretty gruesome, Mike," the officer said, clutching his camera, dangling from a neck-strap. "Why don't you have a look, you'll see what I mean. The two ice fishermen who discovered the corpse couldn't stop throwing up."

The paramedics had just lifted the covered body onto the wheeled stretcher. An officer told them to wait just a moment before loading the corpse into the ambulance. The three Constables walked towards the stretcher, joined by a nervous and somewhat apprehensive MacFarland. In his seventeen-year journalism career, he had yet to see a dead body, though he had covered a couple of homicides during a brief stint as a crime reporter at The Toronto Star.

As one of the Constables lifted the blanket, the others present looked upon what appeared to be a bloated torso with arms and legs looking almost diminutive, covered with waterlogged fabric. The fabric was from what had been a winter coat and flannel pants. Intermixed with the water-saturated fabric were dark black blotches on the upper torso, suggesting congealed blood. At the top of the torso, where there was no fabric, shreds of decomposing skin emerged to suggest the stump of a human neck. As MacFarland took in the scene with a horrific look to his face, he thought for a moment that rusty pipes emitting dark smoke were emerging from the victim's neck. His sense of horror was only compounded by the realization that he was looking at the remains of a human

11

trachea, blood vessels, savagely ripped muscle fibers and other tissues, cauterized by thick blood clots.

Stevens looked at MacFarland, noticing his appearance of extreme discomfort. He told his colleague that they had seen enough. The blanket again covered the corpse, which the paramedics then loaded into the ambulance.

Several minutes later, MacFarland and Constable Stevens were on their way back to Timmins. As Stevens tightly gripped the steering wheel of the police vehicle, MacFarland stared straight ahead, ashen faced. The RCMP officer briefly glanced at his passenger's face, noticing his shaken appearance.

"Pretty hard to take it in, eh Vince?"

"I don't recall as a reporter ever seeing anything so horrific. What about you, Mike?"

"Oh, about eight years ago," recalled the Constable, "I had to pull the remains of a family, including two small children, from a Cessna that crashed in the woods just west of Timmins."

MacFarland asked the Constable how the investigation would proceed.

"They're taking the body to Sudbury for an autopsy. They first need to establish the cause of death."

"That seems superfluous," responded MacFarland.

"Well, Vince, in determining the precise cause and manner of death, the coroner may also uncover forensic clues that might aid our investigation. Our greatest obstacle will be identifying the deceased, without a head. That's where you can help. We'll check our recent missing persons reports, but perhaps you can print something in The Weekly Current inviting citizens who may have useful information to come forward. We may be able to pull together fingerprints, body hair and DNA that can match a missing person. Without the victim's head, we not only lack a face, we also can't use dental records."

Later that evening, Vince MacFarland arrived home. As he entered the foyer of his house, the family dog, an energetic Labrador Retriever named Ironside, barked mightily at his feet.

"Come over here, Ironside," called Rebecca, his daughter. His wife Judy, a small woman with curly brown hair and wearing wire rimmed glasses, emerged from the kitchen, wearing an apron. "Hello, dear," she said as they exchanged a kiss. "How did your day go?"

MacFarland was silent for a moment, arousing his wife's curiosity. "Well, Judy," he said, "something out of the ordinary did happen. The RCMP found a headless body that washed ashore at Lake Abitibi. It looks like I have my first homicide story since we moved here five years ago."

Rebecca, who was nearby, looked at her parents with an inquisitive glare in her eyes.

"Mommy, Daddy, what's a homicide?"

A Strange Tattoo

In a small conference room at CIA headquarters, Dobbs was briefing the Director of Counter-Terrorism, David Cole, on the latest message contained on the Al-Assad El-Islamiya website. Cole, a tall, big man with a weather beaten face and sparse, graying hair, listened attentively. At the front of the room was a monitor displaying the homepage of the Jihadist organization.

"However you assess this, Mr.Cole, I want you to know that I have total confidence in Amelia Baldwin's interpretation of the Lion's warning."

Stroking his chin, Cole looked downward momentarily at his notepad, reviewing bullet points he had made during the course of the briefing. He then raised his head, looking directly at Dobbs.

"I have a bad feeling in my gut about this, Dobbs," he said. "From intercepts and e-mail monitoring we have conducted of suspected Jihadists around the world, there are growing indications that something spectacular is in the works by Al-Qaeda and their supporters."

He reflected for a moment, then continued.

"Our problem is a lack of human intelligence. We have zero human sources within the Lion's organization. We are left with wiretaps and phone interceptions and other spurious sources, all open to manipulation by our adversary. I have no doubt they are deliberately planting misinformation to throw us off their tracks."

"Even with the intercepts, we lack the ability to fully translate all the data, sir. Our resources are severely strained," responded Dobbs with concern.

"I know," Cole replied with empathy. "It wasn't my idea to ship nearly half of your Arabic translators to Iraq. I fought that tooth and nail, but I was overruled by the boss."

"You mean the President?" said Dobbs.

"No, I mean Dick Darnell. But I'm sure he was acting in what he thinks is the President's best interests." Dick Darnell was the current Director of the CIA.

"My department can interpret virtually every point of data in Russian, and all the other East European languages, for that matter. I have a surplus of people with those language skills left over from the Cold War. But when it comes to our number one language requirement for our counter-terrorism mission, I lack highly capable people." Dobbs explained. "Even before I lost many of my best interpreters to redeployment in Iraq, I had insufficient capacity. Now I'm down to a handful of fully qualified people. Many of the interpreters we have on staff are contract employees with Middle East backgrounds. That means they don't have a sufficient security clearance to translate data from classified sources."

"I understand your point, Dobbs, but that is a problem outside of our control. Let's focus our limited resources on what we can prioritize. That Al-Assad El-Islamiya website does interest me. And you agree with Ms. Baldwin's interpretation?"

"Yes. Based on the track record of the website, and her translation of the message, I think we have been given a warning of something in the planning stages that is at least on par with 9/11. It also strongly suggests New York City as the target, around the middle of March."

"In that case," Cole said, "we need to go over everything concerning the Lion. Tell me about Ms. Baldwin's background."

"Well, sir, she has a masters degree in Arabic from Georgetown, and has been with us for about a year. She has a superb grasp of contemporary and classical Arabic, understands the nuances of the language, and is very thoughtful in her interpretations. One other thing about her is the level of motivation. I don't think I have any other linguist with her degree of commitment."

"How do you explain her motivation?" inquired Cole.

"Mr. Cole, Amelia Baldwin's older brother was a bond trader. He worked for one of the largest trading firms in the country, which had its offices on the 95th floor of the south tower of the World Trade Center. He was there on the morning of September 11, 2001. They never found a trace of him."

Cole's hard face softened as his eyes displayed a hint of sadness.

❖ ❖ ❖

It had been three days since the decapitated corpse had been discovered on the south shore of Lake Abitibi. Friday afternoon, while sitting in his office, MacFarland received a phone call from Constable Stevens. He was passing on news from Sudbury.

"Vince, Dr.Davidson, the coroner in Sudbury, is here at the detachment. He has a daughter in Timmins that he's visiting, and decided to provide us with the autopsy results in person. Why don't you join us?"

MacFarland did not need much persuasion. "O.K., I'll be right over," he responded. In less than twenty minutes, he had joined the Constable and coroner at the RCMP detachment.

Stevens introduced Dr. Davidson, a man in his sixties with white hair and a gray moustache. They shook hands and then MacFarland hung up his winter coat as Davidson removed a file folder from his briefcase.

"Dr. Davidson, please share with Mr. MacFarland your findings."

Davidson cleared his throat, then proceeded to explain what his autopsy had uncovered. The deceased was a Caucasian male, probably about five foot eleven assuming normal head size, slightly overweight with an age range in the mid to late sixties. He appeared to have been in good health for a man of his age. "There is a scar on the right groin of about 18 mm, most likely from a hernia operation," Dr. Davidson added. "The deceased also has a tattoo on the left bicep, kind of an odd one."

The coroner pulled out an 8 x 10 glossy black and white photographic sheet, with two images of the tattoo. The top photo image showed the bicep with the tattoo, with the lower photograph providing a close up view. Pointing at the images, Davidson said, "You'll notice a design with letters or numbers underneath. The design is quite clear. It's the classic symbol for nuclear physics or atomic energy, the elliptical lines with dots representing electrons circling the atom's nucleus. It's what's underneath that is strange."

Both MacFarland and Stevens stared at the photographs with intensity. "It looks to me," said MacFarland, " like *U6*."

"Hmm, U6," responded Dr. Davidson, "could be the German U-boat that sank my father's corvette in the Second World War."

All three men laughed briefly. Taking another look at the photographs, Constable Stevens pointed out that what appeared to be the letter U had a discrepancy, as though a tadpole was sticking out of the bottom.

"Do any of you gentleman have any idea what this tattoo might represent?" inquired the coroner. Both men shook their heads.

"I might be able to find someone who can make some sense out of it," volunteered MacFarland. "I know the guy who runs the local tattoo and piercing parlor in town. I'll drop by on him on Monday and see if he can shed some light on this."

Constable Stevens asked the coroner to share his findings on the cause of death. He answered that, as would be expected, decapitation caused the death of the victim.

"There were no other injuries or indications on the body to suggest other contributing causes. There were only some lacerations around the left ankle, probably from a rope attached to some form of weight to anchor the body to the floor of the lake; the rope must have been torn by rocks on the bottom. I have therefore concluded that traumatic amputation, in other words the severing of the head, was the cause of death." Continuing, the coroner added, "it was not an easy death. No guillotine for this gentleman. The uneven cuts of the various tissues and blood vessels in the neck suggest that a knife was used to slowly cut through the throat of the deceased. Rather than decapitation, I would describe this as butchering."

The Constable asked if there was any additional information he had to share.

"I pulled some tiny metal shards from the victim's neck, probably microscopic fragments from the killer's knife. I forwarded them to the RCMP laboratory in Ottawa. They have the equipment to do a spectrographic analysis of the shards. This may help us identify the type of knife used. I have also sent a sample of the victim's tissues and blood so the lab can conduct a complete toxicology analysis. Among other things, it may tell us if the victim smoked, was taking a particular medication or anything else than can help us ID him."

❖ ❖ ❖

Amelia Baldwin stepped into David Cole's office. This was the first time she had been invited to meet with the CIA's Director of Counter-Terrorism. Cole, who was standing, motioned for her to sit in front of his desk as he closed the office door. Amelia looked directly at Cole as he now sat at his desk, looking intensely at her.

"Ms. Baldwin, I presume that Mr. Dobbs told you why I wanted to meet with you."

She said in response that Dobbs had told her of Cole's interest in the Al-Assad El-Islamiya website.

"That is correct. By the way, how would you literally translate the name of the website?" inquired Cole.

"The Lion of Islam," Baldwin replied.

"Hmm, the Lion of Islam," Cole repeated. "Is there any significance to that nomenclature?"

Baldwin explained why there could be. "In the 78th sura of the Koran, a sura being similar to a chapter in the Bible, there is a revelation to the prophet Mohammed from Allah concerning the Day of Judgment and the fires of hell that await unbelievers. There is a specific verse, I think verse 51 or 52, that refers to the lion as an instrument of Allah's from which the unbelievers and infidels will flee in terror into the abyss of the fires of hell."

"I think I can see the connection," Cole replied in a taciturn voice. Continuing on, he said, "Ms. Baldwin, this Lion of Islam

18

may be the most dangerous man on the planet. And we in the American intelligence community haven't a clue as to who he is."

Cole pulled out a DVD from a drawer and placed it on his desk. Amelia looked at the label on the DVD, noticing its description of the contents, "Beheadings of hostages."

"I have an important assignment for you, Ms. Baldwin. It will certainly be difficult and unpleasant."

Cole handed the DVD to Amelia, explaining what he needed her to do.

"The DVD contains unedited footage of ritual killings of foreign hostages taken from videotapes captured by our troops during raids on terrorist safe houses in Iraq. It is far more complete and graphic than the edited versions displayed on Jihadist websites. In every case, the man reading, or shall I say, pontificating and then cutting the throats of the hostages, wears a black hood covering his face. We believe the masked executioner to be the Lion. I need you to watch and listen to everything he does on this DVD. Listen to every nuance in his rhetoric, every inflection of his voice. Report back to me on Monday with anything you discover that can help us understand who this man is."

As Amelia left Cole's office, a worried Director of Counter-Terrorism repeated to himself what she had told him moments before: "...flee in terror into the abyss of the fires of hell."

A Matter for CSIS

On Monday, late morning, MacFarland parked his red Ford pickup in front of Tony's Piercing and Tattoo parlor on Ames Street in the center of Timmins, not far from where The Weekly Current office was located. He entered the establishment carrying his briefcase. Bells jingled as he opened the heavy steel and glass door. As he heard the door close behind him, MacFarland surveyed the intricate tattoo designs that saturated the parlor's walls. "I'll be there in a minute!" a loud voiced boomed from behind the curtains in the rear of the establishment. In a moment, a large arm covered in tattoos pulled apart the curtains, drawing MacFarland's attention. Instantly, a small man with large, muscular arms appeared in front of the curtains. He was Tony Moskevitch, who owned the piercing and tattoo parlor. He had greasy, unkempt black hair and a long, shaggy gray beard, giving him the appearance of a warlock. He had the sleeves of his plaid shirt rolled up, exposing the myriad tattoos on his arms that seemed to match the baroque looking earrings that hung from both of his ears.

"Hey Vince, good to see ya!" shouted Tony.

As they shook hands, Tony added, "So you finally decided to bite the bullet and have that nipple piercing."

MacFarland gulped.

"Not quite, Tony, I think my wife would divorce me if I did that."

"Oh women, what do they know. If you ask me, I think you'd be happier with a piercing or nice tattoo."

20

"I think there are some men who might agree with you," MacFarland responded as he pulled an 8x10 glossy sheet out of his briefcase.

"I need help, Tony, identifying a tattoo."

"You came to the right place, Vince."

MacFarland showed Tony the images of the tattoo from the body that had washed ashore at Lake Abitibi.

"You ever see anything like this before?"

There was an inquisitive glow to Tony's face, which MacFarland took note of.

"I've seen thousands of tattoos, but not one quite like this."

Tony kept staring at the images.

"Well, the top part of the tattoo, that's the symbol for atomic power," Moskevitch said. "I remember doing a tattoo like that for a couple of guys that worked at the nuclear reactor outside Toronto."

"Are they still alive?" asked Vincent.

"Oh, for sure," said Tony. "One of them was in recently to have me do a hood piercing for his girlfriend. You know what a hood piercing is, Vince?"

"I'm not sure I want to know," MacFarland said, seeking to keep the conversation on topic. Continuing, he asked about what was under the electrons circling the nucleus of an atom.

"That looks like U6, to me, at least," MacFarland said. "What could that mean, Tony? Could it be something biker oriented?"

"Oh, no," replied Tony. "I've seen just about every biker tattoo around, Hell's Angels, et cetera, you name it. Let me have another look at that."

"Hmm," uttered Tony as he looked again at the image, this time more carefully.

His response surprised MacFarland.

"I don't think that this is U6, Vince."

"What makes you say that?"

"This doesn't look like our typical English script. I think this is Cyrillic," Tony said in response.

"Cyrillic?" MacFarland replied with bewilderment.

"Yes, Cyrillic, Russian. I'm not sure what these letters are, because I really don't know the language. But my grandmother was Russian. I remember as a kid visiting her house, all her books were in Russian. I'm sure those two letters are Russian. You just need to find someone who understands the language to tell you what they are."

◈ ◈ ◈

Amelia Baldwin sat alone in a small room watching horrible scenes on a video monitor. They were from the DVD provided to her by David Cole. She listened attentively as the masked man believed to be the Lion chanting menacingly in front of a large Arabic banner, with other masked men gripping automatic rifles at his side. In front of him was a frightened man in an orange jump suit, kneeling on the ground with his arms tied behind his back. As the Lion stopped speaking and pulled a sinister looking knife from his belt, Amelia shielded her eyes. Screams of agony ensued as her body tightened and quivered. It seemed that the excruciating cries from the victim lasted an eternity, yet in thirty seconds they were silenced. The Lion began to rant and rave once more, and slowly Amelia withdrew her hands from over her eyes, her body still twitching with fear and horror. Though feeling disgust at viewing the Lion holding the severed head by its hair as though a sporting trophy, his words sparked her attention. She grabbed her notepad and began writing impressions that she thought were important.

◈ ◈ ◈

From his office, MacFarland put in a call to Constable Stevens. He relayed to him the outcome of his conversation with Tony Moskevitch at his tattoo and piercing parlor.

"Mike, he doesn't know anything specific about this tattoo, but thinks the letters underneath the symbol are Russian. The paper goes to press tonight, so we'll mention that in our notice about the body. Maybe one of our readers can help us make sense of this."

"Good idea, Vince," responded the Constable. "We have no leads here, so I'll be grateful if you can contact us as soon as you hear anything from your readers…that's if you hear anything."

"O.K., will do," MacFarland replied in his typically cheerful manner.

❖ ❖ ❖

David Cole sat stiffly at his desk as Amelia Baldwin proceeded to brief him on the gruesome DVD she had been reviewing. Cole's normally diffident facial expression mellowed somewhat as he observed Amelia's body language and detected her severe discomfort.

"I know what I asked you to watch was awful, Ms. Baldwin. I hope you understand that I felt it was very necessary."

Amelia took a deep breath, steeling her composure.

"Sir, it was very difficult to watch how human beings can be so cruel and barbaric towards other human beings. But it was important that I saw that DVD."

Cole's expectations were raised, as he leaned forward on his desk, looking directly at Baldwin.

"Then, you did pick out something significant from that DVD?"

"Yes, sir," she said quietly. In a low tone of voice she continued. "I don't believe that the Lion is an Arab."

Cole was intrigued by her observation. "That is interesting," he said. "Very interesting. But what makes you think that?"

Amelia offered her explanation. "This was the first opportunity I've had to hear him speak at length. His Arabic vocabulary is excellent, however, he speaks with a dialect and uses certain expressions that are only taught at Islamic religious schools in northwest Pakistan. I am almost positive that the Lion is of Pakistani origin."

Cole was even more intrigued. "This is indeed significant," he told her. "This may be the first indication we have of the Lion's nationality. Anything else?"

Amelia referred to her notes before responding.

"Yes, just one other thing. After he killed one of the hostages and held his head up to the camera the way a fisherman might display a prize catch, he made a sarcastic reference to how easy it was to kill infidels by splitting heads from bodies, and he would kill many more by splitting atoms."

"Splitting atoms?"

"Yes, splitting atoms. He said it in a way that was not common, but scientific and technical. In the manner he expressed himself, he gave the impression that he has some form of scientific background."

Cole was perplexed. What Amelia had observed could mean nothing, or everything. He thanked Amelia for her work and dedication, and suggested she take the rest of the day off. Escorting her to the door, he then called her Amelia for the first time.

"Amelia," he said, then hesitated for a moment. "Amelia, I know about your background, and that you lost a brother on 9/11. I just want you to know how greatly appreciated you are at the Agency, and that the work you are doing to protect our country is damned important."

"Thank you," she said in response, noting for the first time the strength of Cole's face.

Cole closed his office door, and immediately dialed the most important extension in the CIA directory. As soon as a secretary answered, Cole wasted no time in making clear what he wanted.

"I need to meet with Dick Darnell as soon as possible."

"But Mr. Cole, the Director is over at the White House briefing the President on Iraq," the secretary brusquely replied.

Exasperated, Cole attempted to negotiate time on the CIA Director's calendar.

"Can I see him after the briefing?"

"Not possible, Mr. Cole. The earliest I can put you down for is tomorrow at 10:00 AM."

❖ ❖ ❖

At a busy truck stop cafeteria just outside of Timmins a swarthy looking man loaded his tray with his breakfast order. At the checkout counter he picked up a copy of The Weekly Current and placed it on his tray. After paying the cashier he picked out a solitary table far from the other truckers so he could consume his breakfast in privacy. As he began munching on French toast and poached eggs, he quickly scanned the front page of The Weekly Current. He was about to turn the page over when something caught his eye on the front page. It was a one-paragraph item on

24

the bottom right hand corner, with the headline, "Body Discovered at Lake Abitibi." The man's facial muscles tensed and his eyes betrayed a sensation of panic as he read the item:

"A headless body of a man believed to be in his sixties was washed ashore along the banks of Lake Abitibi last week. So far, the identity of the man has not been confirmed. He is believed to have been five foot eleven, slightly heavy build, and had a distinctive tattoo on his left arm consisting of an atomic symbol with letters or numbers underneath, which may be U6 or possibly Russian letters with a similar appearance. Persons with information which may assist in the investigation are requested to contact the RCMP."

The man abandoned his breakfast and immediately ran outside the cafeteria to a secluded spot. Using a cellular phone, he made a quick call, then spoke excitedly into the phone in Arabic.

❖ ❖ ❖

David Cole sat outside the office of Richard Darnell, whose closed door proclaimed him to be the Director of the Central Intelligence Agency. His appointment was scheduled for 10:00 AM, but it was nearly 11:00 before Darnell's secretary called him in. As he entered, Darnell greeted the Director of Counter-Terrorism in a jovial mood. He invited Cole to sit next to him around a small table far from his office desk. As he seated himself, Cole observed the walls of the office, filled with plaques, awards and photographs of the CIA Director posing with prominent political and public figures. He had seen these testimonials to the Director's ego before, but looking at them once more served to remind Cole that his boss, unlike him, was not a long serving intelligence professional, but rather an obscure Congressman who had been plucked by the President to fill a vacancy.

"David, the President was in an extremely good mood when I briefed him yesterday."

"What's the explanation, Dick?" a puzzled Cole replied. "I wasn't aware of any dramatic improvement in the situation in Iraq."

"Oh, it's not any change in Iraq," Darnell said. "It's just as murky as before. It's the progress the President has achieved on his two key pieces of legislation before Congress; privatizing social security and new tax cuts for entrepreneurs."

"New tax cuts?" an exasperated Cole interjected. "With the annual deficit approaching a trillion dollars and the value of the American dollar in free fall?"

"That's not your worry, David. The Agency's budget is intact, that's all we need to concern ourselves with," Darnell replied with self-confidence.

David Cole pointed out to the CIA Director that even with an intact budget, the agency lacked proficient Arabic translators.

"I disagree with you," Darnell said defensively. " I think we have plenty of Arab translation specialists."

"Even if we do, most of the best ones are in Iraq!" a frustrated Cole said.

Temporarily taken aback, Darnell replied in a more conciliatory tone. He suggested that things in Iraq would be calming down in the near future, so it could be expected that the CIA's Arabic language specialists would be returning to Langley. Then, glancing at his watch, he indicated his understanding that Cole had something important to discuss.

"Dick, one of our translators, who has been monitoring the Lion's website, has brought to my attention some disturbing indications that he is planning a mass casualty attack on the United States, possibly New York City, sometime in the middle of March."

Darnell, fiddling with a pen, stumbled in response to Cole's warning. After a moment's silence, he gave his reply.

"David, I really think our people place far too much stock in these websites. You and I both know how many times, practically on a daily basis, they utter threats that turn out to be meaningless. These websites, if you ask me, are set up to spread terror by propaganda. I think we would be ahead of the game by simply ignoring them, and by the way, freeing up the translators you say you need."

Cole was surprised at the response. He had requested the meeting because he was firmly convinced of the urgency of the message on the Lion's website.

"Dick, I would agree with your characterization applying to most of the Jihadist websites. However, this one is much more credible. It is the online newsletter, if you will, that the Lion uses to communicate with his followers. For the past three years, at least, the Lion has made specific predictions of upcoming terrorist events to his followers that, in every case, have come to pass. If nothing else, this website should have some credibility with us."

Unable to contradict his Director of Counter-Terrorism, Darnell reluctantly conceded to him that he did have a valid point.

"However, David, the center of gravity for the terrorists is Iraq. It must be there that the Lion is planning something, if anything at all. Not in the homeland, of that I am certain."

"With all due respect," responded a determined Cole, "I believe the warning points to an accelerated threat level here, in America, and not overseas, especially Iraq."

The CIA Director seemed unmoved by Cole's argumentation. "David, you're a good man, and I value your work. But your judgment on this matter is flawed. Not a single analyst in the Intelligence Directorate agrees with you. They all point to Iraq as where we need to deploy the agency's assets, and not Main Street USA. A vague boast about the future is not a sufficient reason to go against their consensus."

❖ ❖ ❖

On Wednesday morning, in the parking lot behind the small building housing the office of The Weekly Current, Jane, the employee responsible for the newspaper's distribution, parked her delivery van. She stepped out of her van and closed the driver's side door, unaware that she was being closely watched by a dark skinned man with sunglasses, pretending to read a newspaper folded atop the steering wheel of a late model blue Chevrolet Malibu. Once Jane had disappeared through a rear entrance to the building, the man placed the newspaper on the front passenger's seat, scanned through the front and rear windows of the automobile and then, satisfied that the coast was clear, exited the vehicle. He looked deliberately at all points of the parking lot, noting five other cars parked, and that no other persons were present. Clutching a small duffel bag, he looked intensely at a red Ford pickup. Slowly and carefully, he approached the pickup, stopping just in front of the left side door. Twisting his neck, he glanced rearwards one last time to ensure the lot was still devoid of any other human presence. He pulled a leather-covered fob from his coat pocket, which held several different keys. He tried two of them, without result. With the third key, he was able to gain entrance into Vincent MacFarland's pickup truck.

❖ ❖ ❖

It had been an unusually long day at The Weekly Current. Around 6:30 PM, MacFarland and Burton were the last to leave. Burton locked the office for the evening, and joined MacFarland as they exited the rear of the building and proceeded towards their parked vehicles.

"Bob, I think my battery is running on borrowed time," MacFarland said. "I barely got my truck started this morning. Can you wait a moment to make sure I get her started?"

"I'm happy to wait, Vince. If you do have difficulty, I have jumper cables in the trunk."

MacFarland climbed into the driver's seat of his truck, his breath creating a miniature fog within the cold confines of his parked vehicle. He grasped for the ignition key, inserted it into the ignition and turned, but only received a lazy, struggling noise in response. He tried turning the ignition several times, without success. "Shit," he softly uttered.

He jumped out of the vehicle and informed Burton that he would indeed need to take up his offer of a boost for his battery.

Vincent lifted the hood of his Ford open, exposing the engine and battery. Burton brought his car over to the side of the pickup truck. In a moment, he had shut off the engine and retrieved his jumper cables. With the hoods of both vehicles now open, the two men quickly connected the cables to the terminals of their batteries.

MacFarland stood by Burton's car, waiting for the publisher to turn his engine over. Once Robert Burton's engine was running, MacFarland assumed he would be able to start his engine without further difficulty. Burton turned his ignition on, heard the engine start followed by a huge bang.

Burton looked startled. He thought something was wrong with his engine, until he realized through the motor's noise that his engine was running properly. It was only when he glanced towards MacFarland's pickup truck that he noticed something was terribly wrong. The cab was filled with thick smoke, which also was pouring out of a rupture in the truck's roof.

"Shit!" cried out Burton.

MacFarland just stood still, unable to say a word, his eyes transfixed on the flames and smoke now devouring his vehicle's interior.

Several minutes after the explosion, Constable Stevens arrived on the scene, joined by another RCMP officer. The red strobe light atop the police cruiser's roof provided most of the illumination amid the dark winter night, the flames from the explosion having died out. Now, only a thin stream of grayish smoke was emitted from the cab of the pickup. Soon, a tow truck with a flashing dome light added to the illumination.

Constable Stevens looked at a shaken MacFarland and startled Burton. "You think the gas tank might have exploded?" inquired Burton.

"It sure doesn't look like it to me, Bob," the Constable said. "The gas tank is located in the rear of the truck. Look at the bed and rear wheel well. It's totally intact, not even a scratch."

The Constable looked at the engine compartment as his colleague shone a flashlight. "And nothing here. No scorch marks under the hood," Stevens added, as he now peered into what had been the interior. He noticed a strange smell.

"Something in there, Mike?" a nervous MacFarland asked.

"It smells like ammonia nitrate."

"Ammonia nitrate?"

"Yes, Vince. It's a substance used in manufacturing explosives. It looks to me like somebody wanted to blow you up."

Several minutes later the carcass of MacFarland's red Ford was towed out of the parking lot. Burton placed his arm around

MacFarland's shoulder, seeking to comfort him. He asked his editor and reporter if he needed a ride home.

"That's alright, Bob. I'll call Judy."

"You'll have to tell her what happened, Vince."

"I know," he responded sadly. "She's going to freak out. I can't blame her, I'm freaked out myself. And how do I explain to my daughter why I no longer have the red pickup truck?"

Constable Stevens approached the men, his face grimacing with concern.

"Vince, you know anyone who would want you dead?"

"No," he replied. "Not a soul."

The Constable still had questions.

"Bob, is there anything the newspaper has been investigating, or recently published, that might have upset some folks?"

The publisher pondered only briefly before replying.

"The only thing remotely controversial we have been covering are the delays in approving funding for a new feeder road to the Trans Canada Highway," he said.

"I hardly think I deserve to be killed over that," added MacFarland.

The Constable reflected for a moment before weighing in with his own speculation.

"Vince, Bob, I can think of one thing your newspaper published, at our request, that might have upset somebody. It's the notice you printed on the body we retrieved along Lake Abitibi. It might be that the killers saw the notice, and reacted."

"Reacted!" MacFarland said with indignation.

"Yes, reacted, but not in an impulsive way," said Stevens. "If someone had taken a shot at you with a rifle, that would be impulsive, yet what one could expect from a sole individual acting alone. However, a bomb, that involves planning, and some level of sophistication. Vince, I'm treating this as a terrorist incident."

MacFarland asked what that meant in real terms.

"What that means," Stevens responded, "is that this is no longer exclusively an RCMP investigation. This is now a matter for CSIS."

"What is CSIS?" asked Burton.

"It's the Canadian Security Intelligence Service," Stevens responded.

"That's Canada's CIA," added MacFarland.

Embassy Row

The ornate building on Metcalfe Street in downtown Ottawa had a gold plaque at its gated entrance identifying itself in English, French and Farsi as the embassy of the Islamic Republic of Iran. Across the street, near a bus stop, a tall man with blond hair, neatly parted, and wearing an olive trench coat, gave the appearance of waiting for an express bus. Periodically, and in as inconspicuous a manner as possible, he would glance obliquely at the embassy's front entrance, noting who entered and left. He was Pierre Dextraze, an intelligence officer with CSIS, on a stakeout. Originally from Rimouski, Quebec, he had eleven years of experience with CSIS, which he joined after completing a masters degree in political science. Sophisticated and highly analytical, he patiently waited until a person of interest left the embassy. Carefully, Dextraze pulled a cell phone out of his coat pocket, utilizing its built in zoom camera and video recorder to obtain images of his quarry. The person he was observing was short, stocky and had a dark complexion with tufts of black hair enveloping his balding scalp. In a moment, the dark skinned man hailed a cab. Dextraze immediately pressed a red button on his cell phone, which instantly connected him with another CSIS agent, Henry Littlejohn.

Littlejohn was seated in the driver's seat of an off-duty cab parked near another embassy, on Slater Street, belonging to the Democratic Peoples Republic of Korea. He was of Aboriginal background, originally from a small town in Saskatchewan. He had

32

the demeanor of a cab driver in his late thirties, with a muscular build, face chiseled with toughness and long black hair tied in a ponytail. He was also, like his colleague, very well educated, with a bachelor's degree in chemistry and fluent in several languages. The radio in his vehicle came to life, and he heard his colleague report in from the Iranian embassy. "Henry, our visitor just departed, over," Dextraze said in his thick French Canadian accent.

"Roger, Pierre. Let's see if he does his usual game of embassy swapping, over."

Littlejohn folded a newspaper over his steering wheel, giving the appearance of looking over the day's sporting news. A few minutes passed and then he noticed the stocky dark skinned man emerge from a taxicab. As the man under observation proceeded through the entrance gate of the North Korean embassy, Littlejohn activated his radio.

"Pierre, our visitor continues his pattern. He has just entered the DPRK embassy."

Later that day, Dextraze and Littlejohn entered the office of Alex Dunlop, Deputy Director of CSIS's Operations Division, at the spy agency's headquarters. Dunlop had a military bearing reflecting his 20 years experience in the Canadian Army's defense intelligence section. Distinguished looking, in his mid-fifties, he also spoke with care and refinement.

"Sir, Khan's visit with the Iranians was only for twenty minutes," Dextraze reported.

"His time at the North Korean embassy was even shorter, no more than fifteen minutes, I would say," added Littlejohn.

Stroking his chin and appearing pensive, Dunlop reflected for a moment before speaking his mind. "We know that Dr. Pervaz Khan is the leading figure in the Pakistani nuclear bomb program and a key player in the international black market network of nuclear materials and technology smuggling. He enters Canada on a tourist visa for 30 days, supposedly to visit his daughter here in Ottawa. Yet, he spends several hours each day since his arrival in the embassies of two countries that are separated geographically by thousands of kilometers, but united in their nuclear weapons ambitions. What is his game? Why does he do this daily dance on embassy row?"

"Whatever it is," Littlejohn interjected, "it must be close to being wrapped up, if today's embassy visits were only for a few minutes."

"You're probably right in your intuition," Dunlop said. "That still doesn't answer the fundamental question: what is Khan doing in Canada?"

"Could it be that he is attempting to smuggle nuclear items from Canada into those two countries?" Dextraze said.

Alex Dunlop indicated that this might be a possibility, but that there were other avenues to explore. He directed Littlejohn to continue the surveillance of Khan and monitoring of his phone and e-mail communications. After Littlejohn departed Dunlop's office, Dextraze was informed by the Deputy Director of another matter that required investigation.

"Pierre, there was an incident in Timmins yesterday, the attempted assassination of a newspaper editor. It appears to have all the hallmarks of a terrorist act. I'd like you to investigate."

Dunlop passed a file to Dextraze, asking him to review it in preparation for a trip to Timmins the next day. "It appears to be an act of domestic terrorism," he told his agent, "but do keep an open mind."

The following day Dextraze arrived in Timmins. After meeting with the RCMP detachment and looking over MacFarland's heavily damaged Ford pickup, he briefly stopped by at The Weekly Current, meeting with the publisher and other staff, and looking over the parking lot where the bombing had occurred. MacFarland was at home that day, recovering from the trauma of the previous day's event.

In the late afternoon, Dextraze dropped by on the MacFarland home. Since the events of the previous day, new deadbolt locks had been installed in the front door, which Dextraze could hear being noisily disengaged after he rang the doorbell. A chain lock allowed the door to open just a crack, enabling Judy MacFarland to peer at the visitor, who presented his credentials while identifying himself. As he entered the MacFarland home, he noticed the worried look on Judy's face. Ironside, the family dog, ran up menacingly towards Dextraze, barking loudly.

"It's alright, Ironside. He's here to help," said Judy. Ironside drew back, the dog's loud breaths revealing only slightly diminished suspicion. "My husband's in the living room, Mr. Dextraze," Judy said, beckoning him to follow her.

"Honey, the man from CSIS is here."

MacFarland rose weakly from his armchair, and limply shook the hand of Dextraze, as Judy departed, leaving the two men alone. The CSIS agent noted how deeply anxiety was sculpted into the facial expressions of Vincent MacFarland. He sought to reassure Vincent.

"Mr. MacFarland, I am here because the government of Canada takes seriously its obligation to protect its citizens from terrorism. I know what happened yesterday was a shock to you and your family. However, you can be sure that we will do whatever it takes to ensure your family's safety and apprehend the culprits."

MacFarland looked directly at Dextraze, wanting to believe him but feeling sadly skeptical. "You know, Mr. Dextraze, Judy and I moved here five years ago from Toronto, to escape the hustle and bustle for a quiet town. This is not exactly what I had in mind."

"Well, Mr. MacFarland, Timmins is still a quiet town. What happened here the last few days is totally out of character for this area. Some outside influences are almost certainly responsible for these acts, the incident with your truck and the body found at Lake Abitibi."

"So the two are linked?" inquired MacFarland.

Dextraze explained that all other possibilities could be ruled out. Other than the short item on the front page of The Weekly Current, nothing else had appeared in the newspaper in the time MacFarland had served as its editor and sole reporter that could even remotely antagonize anyone. He also explained that a preliminary investigation had determined that the bomb that was planted in his vehicle was of a degree of sophistication requiring an infrastructure to design and manufacture that could not possibly exist in Timmins.

"The detonating mechanism was quite sophisticated," Dextraze said, "and ironically, it is that sophistication which probably saved your life." Dextraze could tell from the look on MacFarland's face that he was puzzled.

"Let me explain," Dextraze continued. "The way the bomb worked is that is was planted under your seat, so that when it exploded the full force would travel upwards, meaning you would have been literally blown through the roof. The intent was to ensure that the driver of the vehicle was killed. The detonator required two things to happen before the bomb exploded: the ignition had to first be engaged, than a full force of electrical current required for turning over the starter motor flowing from the battery. You set the first step in motion when you tried to start the motor, but the battery was run down so it would not start. When you attached the jumper cables to Mr. Burton's car and he started his engine, the detonation process was completed, and the bomb exploded. Presumably, the bomb makers were not familiar with our Canadian winters and the difficulty of starting an engine in cold weather."

MacFarland was quiet for a moment, though his body language manifested his inner knowledge of how close he had come to death.

"One other thing," Dextraze said. "The bomb used a very specific type of composite explosive, a variation of triacetone triperoxide with a mixture of ammonia nitrate, that is manufactured only in Iran."

Dextraze told the editor he should lay low for a few days, and if possible work from home. Under no circumstances should anything further be published in The Weekly Current regarding the body found at Lake Abitibi. He also instructed MacFarland that neither he nor his colleagues at the newspaper should comment to anyone about the bombing of his Ford. It should be explained as some type of mechanical defect with the fuel lines, at least for the time being.

"As a journalist, it will go against my instincts to sit on this, especially as it involves me," responded MacFarland.

"I well understand your professional journalistic instincts," replied Dextraze. "I only hope that, for the sake of you and your family, your instinct for self-preservation is stronger."

❖ ❖ ❖

The following day Amelia Baldwin was again called into David Cole's office. With the door closed, the Director of Counter-Terrorism had another assignment for the Arabic language specialist. He handed her a cassette tape, then explained what was on it.

"Amelia, this is a recording taken two days ago during a sermon at the Al-Shaheed mosque in Hamburg, Germany. This mosque is known as a nest for Islamic extremists in Western Europe. The recording is of a sermon given by a gentleman named Mahmoud Yantissi, one of the most radical Moslem clerics in Europe. We have reason to believe he has links to the most dangerous terrorist organizations, including Al-Qaeda and the Lion's group. Translate his sermon, and get me a verbatim transcript ASAP."

❖ ❖ ❖

Dextraze had returned to Ottawa and driven to the RCMP headquarters for a scheduled meeting with the head of the forensic laboratory, Dr. Taylor. He was shown into Taylor's office. The doctor, wearing an immaculate white coat and thick glasses, presented Dextraze with highly relevant findings.

"Pierre, our laboratory has completed its analysis of the samples sent to us by Dr. Davidson from Sudbury. Very peculiar."

"In what way?" inquired Dextraze.

Taylor's findings were indeed baffling. He expected to find the victim's blood on the metal shards from the killer's knife. What he did not expect to find were traces of blood from at least eight other persons.

"Are you sure?" a baffled Dextraze said in response.

"No doubt about it, Pierre."

Dextraze wanted to know if Dr. Taylor had any leads on the other victims. Taylor informed the CSIS agent that he had had the samples run through the RCMP's database of persons in Canada killed or injured in knife assaults, and there were no matches with the DNA on the metal shards.

"That could mean, Dr. Taylor, that these other victims resided overseas."

In response, Dr. Taylor indicated he would be contacting both Interpol and the FBI to find out if they had data that would match the DNA samples. "Please let me know as soon as you hear back from either Interpol or the FBI," Dextraze requested.

"We found something else that would tend to reinforce your supposition of an overseas connection," Taylor said. "The alloy composition of the metal shards is of a type used in manufacturing knives and swords in only one place on Earth; the Northwest frontier province in Pakistan, along the border of Afghanistan."

"Holy mackerel!" exclaimed Dextraze.

"One other thing, Pierre, that could be significant in trying to establish the victim's ID. Whoever he was, this was an individual who must have worked with radioactive materials," Taylor added.

Dextraze could feel his pulse rate accelerate, as though his body was anticipating the implications of Taylor's analysis faster than his mind. Attempting to form a cohesive picture of what the laboratory results were pointing towards, he asked Taylor to elaborate on his findings.

"We found in the tissue samples trace elements of a variety of radioactive isotopes, cobalt 60, strontium 90, uranium 238. Also, we discovered much smaller traces of uranium 235 and plutonium. Not enough to have harmed him, but measurably more than what a typical human being would accumulate from normal background radiation. In other words, a level of exposure commensurate with a person working with medical isotopes in a cancer ward at a hospital, for example. Or a technician at a nuclear power plant, working on the reactor."

"Any other possibilities come to mind, doctor?" asked an anxious Dextraze.

Taylor hesitated for a moment, then added, "there is only one other possibility, Pierre. He would have all these trace elements in his tissues, especially uranium 235 and plutonium, if he was involved in manufacturing and assembling nuclear weapons."

One Way Ticket

At one of the most exclusive restaurants in Washington, Richard Darnell was recognized by the maitre'd, who escorted him to a table set aside for maximum privacy, where the person who invited him for lunch was waiting.

"Mr. Vice President," said Darnell as he reached out to shake his hand.

"Dick, please sit down, and join me for a martini. Two martinis!" beamed the Vice President to the waiter standing in expectation, who quickly produced the drinks for the two luncheon guests.

"So, Dick, anything new at the Agency?"

"Oh, fairly routine. As you know, we are making a special effort on the Iraq problem."

The Vice President indicated how pleased he and the President both were that the Agency was finally mobilizing for a full effort in addressing the longstanding Iraq insurgency.

"Let me tell you, Mr. Vice President, it was not easy to change our focus. There are too many old shoes at the Agency all wrapped up in September 11, as though it happened yesterday, and not five years ago."

"We know that," responded the Vice President. "That's why we put you in charge of the CIA. And you're accomplishing things, getting the Agency on board with our administration's program."

"Well, thank you Mr. Vice President."

Darnell then explained that too many CIA senior staffers were thinking in terms of another 9/11, instead of focusing on winning the war in Iraq. He used David Cole as an example.

"Our Director of Counter-Terrorism and his staff are spending too much time surfing the web, and getting the shit scared out of them. They think that because we have lost track of the Lion for the past four months and also the threats on his website, something is going to happen again in America."

The Vice President pulled out a cigar, which he slowly lit and then inhaled and exhaled, leaving a halo of smoke floating over the table.

"Dick, the President and I think the reason that the Lion has been invisible for the past several months is that we've got him on the run. If you ask me, he's hiding in some hole in the Sunni Triangle, just like Saddam Hussein was before we nabbed him."

"I couldn't agree with you more, Mr. Vice President," said a beaming Darnell.

The Vice President then explained that David Cole's influence would soon diminish. The post of Secretary of Homeland Security had been vacant for six months, but was finally to be filled. Within days, Congress would confirm the President's nominee for the post and once at his desk, his power and influence would supersede Cole's in counter-terrorism matters. His name was William Mendik.

❖ ❖ ❖

Back at CSIS headquarters, Dextraze and Littlejohn were meeting with the Deputy Director. Dextraze updated his colleagues on the strange initial findings from the attempted murder of Vincent MacFarland. He drew attention to the use of an explosive that originated in Iran, the radioactive traces in the tissue samples from the headless corpse, and fragments from a knife suggesting other victims who were not Canadians, and a foreign killer.

"This is my assessment," Dunlop said. "The retrieval of a radioactive corpse, a bombing with apparent foreign connections and Dr. Pervaz Khan's shuttling between two embassies of rogue states here in Ottawa is somehow connected. I'm not sure precisely how, but that is the assumption we must now operate under." He looked sternly towards Littlejohn and Dextraze, adding, "It is imperative that we ID that corpse, and soon."

Dextraze added that he expected to hear back from Dr. Taylor at the RCMP forensic laboratory once he had received from the FBI and Interpol a response to his inquiries. It was at that moment that Dunlop's intercom buzzed. Dunlop responded, and was informed by his secretary that there was an urgent phone call that had come in from Judy MacFarland.

Dextraze's face tensed up as Dunlop passed him the phone. Though only hearing one end of the conversation, both Littlejohn and Dunlop could sense that something bad had happened.

"Mr. Dextraze, my husband is missing!" Judy cried. She explained what had happened. The knowledge that the explosives used in the attempt to kill him had originated in Iran had prompted MacFarland to contact the Iranian embassy. His reporter's instincts had gotten the better of him. He had scheduled a two o'clock appointment with the Iranian ambassador. Judy had begged him not to go, but he assured her everything would be alright. He rented a car, and drove to Ottawa. He told Judy the appointment was for half an hour, and he would call her immediately afterwards on his cell phone. It was now 5:00 PM, and Judy had neither heard from her husband nor been able to reach him on his cell phone. Dextraze could sense her deep anxiety.

"Mrs. MacFarland, I appreciate your concern. Whatever you do, do not contact the Iranian embassy. Let us handle this."

Upon hanging up, Dextraze muttered a single word, "Merde."

"When Pierre swears in French, it means things are really fucked up," Littlejohn said.

"Indeed they are," Dextraze replied, as he added details to the part of the conversation Dunlop and Littlejohn could hear.

Dunlop reached for the intercom, asking that he be patched in with intelligence officer Turner right away. "Turner is doing the watch on Metcalfe Street," he informed his colleagues. In a moment, Turner was on the line. "Pierre is going to give you a physical description of a man we believe entered the Iranian embassy earlier today. Tell us if you noticed him," Dunlop told the agent.

Upon hearing Dextraze's description of a red haired man with glasses and blue eyes, Turner said, "An individual matching exactly that description entered the embassy about five minutes before two this afternoon. He has not yet left the building."

Dunlop acknowledged the answer and directed Turner to report the moment any cars departed the embassy's parking lot.

"The poor fool," Dextraze said in frustration. "How the hell are we going to get him out of the embassy?"

"I'm certain that the Iranians will do that for us," responded Dunlop. "Someone in their government is obviously concerned that he, number one, is still alive and, number two, possibly knows much more about the body from Lake Abitibi than is actually the case."

Dunlop paused for a moment, then continued. "They obviously want to interrogate him, and then dispose of him in some manner. But not at the embassy. Not even the Iranians would stoop to that. No, in my judgment, they'll try to smuggle him out of the country, and bring him to Iran. They know once he's in their custody over there, there is not a thing we can do for him."

Littlejohn suggested that the RCMP enter the embassy.

"You know they can't do that, the embassy is the sovereign territory of the Iranian government," Dextraze interjected.

"I know they can't go in with a search warrant," Littlejohn replied, "but maybe they can inform the ambassador directly that they know a Canadian citizen is being held by them."

Dunlop shook his head in the negative. "If it were anybody else, that would be the correct course of action. But MacFarland is a different matter for them. For whatever reason, they apparently cannot afford to release him, or otherwise they would not have gone to this extreme. They could deny holding him, or even kill him and claim he was an intruder."

Dextraze asked if there were any Iranian airlines flying out of Ottawa.

"No, not Ottawa," replied Littlejohn, "however, there is a nightly IranAir flight that leaves Montreal each evening at 11:00 PM."

Dunlop asked Littlejohn to check if any special aircraft had been charted by the Iranian embassy. Within minutes, he reported that a charter company based in Montreal had been hired on short notice to send a Learjet to Ottawa to pick up two Iranian diplomats and their baggage and immediately return with them to Montreal to catch the IranAir flight to Tehran.

"Then that's it," Dunlop said. "They are going to put him on that plane, probably in the luggage. When is the Learjet expected to arrive in Ottawa?"

Littlejohn, looking at his watch, told his colleagues that the plane would be landing in about half an hour.

"We must not let them catch that IranAir flight at any cost!" Dunlop said with determination. "This is what we will do. I'll make an emergency call to the minister of transportation. He'll instruct the control tower at the airport to divert the Learjet to another airport for whatever reason they can construct. You two will go to the airport immediately. Keep your eyes on those Iranian diplomats and especially their luggage."

Within seconds, Littlejohn and Dextraze departed the Deputy Director's office and were racing for the airport.

◈ ◈ ◈

In Frankfurt, Germany, it was late evening as a Mercedes taxicab pulled up in front of a dingy building located in the heart of the city's Turkish quarter. There were four men waiting along the curb, one of them opening the rear door while another assisted the passenger in stepping out of the taxicab. The man being escorted into the building in a reverential manner was of medium height, somewhat obese, with a narrow pockmarked face, short, frizzled black beard and wearing an Islamic clerical robe with a white cotton cap covering the top of his head. One of the men inside the building warmly greeted him. He was embraced by a younger looking man who said, in an obsequious manner, "Praise be onto you, Sheik Mahmoud Yantissi."

The sheik noted two men at the entrance of a small meeting hall inside the building carrying AK-47 assault rifles. One of the admirers, seeking to prevent the cleric from being unduly worried, explained the situation.

"Sheik Yantissi, we discovered that a traitor, a CIA agent, had attended our meeting in Hamburg. We have had to take additional precautions. Everything here is under control, I can assure you."

"I am reassured," replied the sheik, who added, "I trust the traitor has been punished."

"You may rest easy, the traitor is a head shorter. Of course, we first made sure he talked. We know who he was working for."

Yantissi strode into the hall, warmly greeting individually each of the twenty men present. He then stood in front of a lectern, stretched his hands in front of his face, and led the group in chanting a short Koranic verse in Arabic. Clearing his throat, he then began his sermon.

"My talk this evening will be brief, yet nevertheless of unprecedented importance. I first send my greetings to each of you, the holy warriors of Islam, who have had to make the supreme sacrifice of living among the infidels here in idolatrous Europe, amidst the spiritual poison of Western Civilization, so that the cause of jihad against the enemies of Islam may be advanced mightily. Our prophet Mohammed, may peace be upon him, instructed us that the world is divided between two houses, the House of Islam and the House of War. It is in the House of War that the unbelievers, the rejecters of Islam and the holy Koran, dwell in their degeneracy. It is the sacred duty of all Moslems to turn the House of War into the fiery inferno that will consume all of Allah's enemies.

"Now, I want to touch on a topic that has been widely discussed by Moslems since the glorious events of September 11. There are some sincere but also misinformed Moslems who think that what we did to the World Trade Center was wrong because along with heathens and infidels, innocent Moslems were also killed. They say that for Moslems to die during an act of jihad is wrong, because they knew nothing and were sent to their deaths in ignorance of the great cause being served. This is an incorrect interpretation. The Koran and Sunna and Hadith, as interpreted by the most pious of scholars, leaves no doubt that committing jihad is the most sacred single act for a Moslem to commit. You all know my own theological credentials, and it is with that foundation that I offer

44

you this commentary and legal ruling or fatwa. If any opportunity to destroy infidels in very large numbers should also lead to the deaths of a few Moslems who are not involved in the operation, they are still viewed as martyrs in the jihad and you are actually blessing them by assuring that they enter paradise. My fatwa is directed particularly at America. If we can destroy the infidels there by the tens of millions, the Moslems who fall innocently shall praise us on the day of judgment, for Allah will be pleased, and they shall lie with virgins under the shade of palm leaves for eternity!"

The men in the hall had listened attentively to the sheik. There was brief silence, then spontaneously all present yelled out in unison, "Allahu Akbar", repeating the chant with exuberance.

❖ ❖ ❖

At Ottawa's international airport, Dextraze and Littlejohn sat in the VIP lounge, wearily eyeing the two burly Iranian diplomats, who were arguing with an employee at the information kiosk. Dextraze looked at his watch, and noted it was nearly 10:00 PM, as Littlejohn gently poked his arm with his elbow. "There's our backup," he whispered in Dextraze's ear, as three uniformed RCMP Constables entered the lounge.

Another hour had transpired before Dextraze had again checked the time, prompted by the two diplomats being called to the kiosk. Both Littlejohn and Dextraze overheard the diplomats being informed that their Learjet had just landed. Dextraze pulled out his cell phone and reported the news to headquarters. Their reply was disturbing.

"Henry, headquarters reports that the IranAir flight that was supposed to depart Montreal about now is being held until these two gentlemen have boarded the aircraft."

"Then let's move now," Littlejohn responded, followed by Dextraze discretely signaling to the three RCMP officers. Dextraze and Littlejohn walked slowly towards the Iranian diplomats, who both had small carry-on baggage. Behind them stood a large trunk covered in diplomatic stickers and seals. They appeared to be preparing to place the trunk on a trolley for loading.

Politely, Dextraze identified himself and Littlejohn as officers with the Canadian Security Intelligence Service, the two men displaying their ID badges. The Iranians appeared stunned, one of them demanding to know what was transpiring. "Just routine," said Littlejohn, "we are assisting Customs in checking for contraband being exported from Canada."

Not amused, one of the diplomats made known his displeasure. "We are employees of the Embassy of the Islamic Republic of Iran. We have diplomatic immunity. There is no Customs jurisdiction with diplomats."

"May I ask what are the contents of that trunk?" inquired Dextraze, ignoring the claim of diplomatic immunity.

"Absolutely not!" yelled the other diplomat. "This is diplomatic property of the Iranian embassy, and none of your business!"

Dextraze pulled out a stethoscope. With the earpieces in place, he put the receptor on top of the trunk.

"What is the meaning of this, you imbecile!" shouted one of the diplomats, who angrily pounded the top of the trunk with his fist. At that exact moment, a series of muffled but distinct moans emerged from inside the trunk. Dextraze removed the stethoscope as the three RCMP Constables slowly approached.

"Gentleman, what is the source of that noise from inside the trunk?" Dextraze asked the diplomats. The two men appeared to be in a panic, and looked at each other befuddled, one hoping the other one could formulate a quick explanation.

"It's a pet dog!" one of the men said.

"Sure doesn't sound like a dog to me," Littlejohn said. "Besides, keeping a dog in a trunk is not a proper way to stow a pet animal aboard an aircraft."

"This is diplomatic property, it's none of your business what's inside," said one of the diplomats by rote.

Dextraze at this point made it clear that the Iranian ruse had run its course. He informed them that they had reason to believe a Canadian citizen was inside the trunk, and that they were going to inspect its contents.

"You can't do that, stupid Canadian! We and our property have diplomatic immunity!" shrieked the diplomats, as Dextraze began removing the diplomatic tags from the trunk.

"Gentlemen," said Dextraze, ignoring the rudeness he had been subjected to, "the rules of diplomatic immunity in no way give you any right to kidnap and detain a Canadian citizen and attempt to smuggle him out of the country, against his will."

Dextraze was about to open the trunk when one of the diplomats pulled out a revolver, demanding that Dextraze stop, while waving the gun wildly. Littlejohn executed a quick judo kick, which knocked the revolver out of the diplomat's hand. The three RCMP Constables immediately approached the diplomats, guns drawn. Dextraze proceeded with unshackling the trunk's locks with a pair of pliers he pulled out of his coat pocket.

As the two diplomats nervously watched, Dextraze opened the trunk, noting the air holes on the cover. Inside, a moaning MacFarland, his mouth gagged with tightly bound cloth, was seated horizontally on a leather saddle seat affixed to a pole connected to the right side of the trunk. His wrists were secured to one end of the trunk with leather thongs, with his head held in place in a padded clamp, which formed a helmet fitted with a chinstrap. His feet had been placed inside slippers fixed to the other side of the trunk.

Dextraze removed the gag from a an obviously groggy MacFarland, who asked in a weak tone of voice, "What happened, where am I?"

"You are at the Ottawa international airport," replied Littlejohn. "The Iranian embassy bought you a one way ticket."

"For a journey no one is expected to return from," said Dextraze.

Interpol

Dick Darnell's intercom buzzed. His secretary informed him that David Cole was on the line.

"What is it?" Darnell said in a tone of voice that revealed his impatience.

"Dick, I've just received the translation of a sermon Sheik Mahmoud Yantissi delivered in Hamburg a few days ago. In it he seems to be addressing the concerns of Moslems who are fearful that a mass casualty terrorist attack in the United States will also kill innocent Moslems."

"So..." replied a disinterested Darnell.

"Yantissi is a revered Islamic cleric and spiritual leader to Al-Qaeda and other Islamist terrorist cells in Europe. His sermon provides religious justification for an attack using weapons of mass destruction, even if Moslems are among the victims.

"Hmm," was all Darnell could respond with, initially. He waited a moment, than said, "Well, let's discuss this later. I have to leave immediately for the White House for the swearing in of the new Secretary of Homeland Security." Before Cole could say anything, the CIA Director had hung up.

❖ ❖ ❖

At CSIS headquarters, Dunlop was meeting with Dextraze and Littlejohn. They first discussed the ramifications of the incident at Ottawa International Airport.

"I just met this morning with our Director. He told me that the Iranian government lodged a formal complaint with the Department of External Affairs. Tehran is protesting the expulsion of the two diplomats we have declared persona non grata. They also demanded we return their property, specifically that very interesting trunk."

"They have real chutzpah, the Iranians," Littlejohn said.

"I can actually understand why they want that contraption returned," replied Dunlop. "The RCMP forensic laboratory found sweat and blood stains inside the trunk, suggesting it had been used before." Dextraze pointed out that the luggage stickers on the trunk were evidence that it had been used throughout Europe, the Americas and Asia. "Apparently, they drug the victim so he is unconscious until the trunk is loaded into the cargo bay of the aircraft. Fortunately, we detained the Learjet the Iranians chartered long enough for the drug to begin to wear off," Dextraze said. He then distributed file folders on the Abitibi corpse.

As Dunlop and Littlejohn thumbed through the material in the folders, Dextraze updated his colleagues on the investigation of the body's identity. "Dr. Taylor heard this morning from Interpol. The blood samples matched the DNA from two Turkish truck drivers and a South Korean engineer who had their heads cut off in Iraq, over a two year period."

Dunlop and Littlejohn looked towards each other in bewilderment, then looked back at Dextraze.

"Are they sure of the match?" Littlejohn asked.

Dextraze replied that they had told Dr. Taylor that they were 100 percent positive. He added that Taylor expected to hear back from the FBI within twenty-four hours.

"Were those decapitations videotaped and broadcast on the Internet?" inquired Dunlop.

Dextraze confirmed that this was indeed the case. It was believed that the head of the Al-Qaeda offshoot, Al-Assad El–Islamiya, the Lion, was the executioner in each instance. He always wore a black hood and no facial photograph of the Lion was known to exist.

"This is indeed significant," Dunlop said. "I don't want to believe that the Lion is now operating in North America, however, if his weapon of choice has been used here in a murder, that is a distinct possibility. We still need to identify that headless corpse. Interpol and the FBI can't help us with that."

Dextraze referred to a glossy photograph in the folder displaying the tattoo located on the victim's left arm.

"You will notice the two letters under the atomic symbol. It looks like U6, but MacFarland told me that they may be Russian letters," Dextraze said. Turning towards Littlejohn, he continued. "Henry, you're fluent in the Russian language. Does this mean anything to you?"

Littlejohn replied immediately. "They are from the Cyrillic alphabet. It's the Russian letters tseh and beh. They're both consonants, and sound like that."

"Do those two letters hold any special significance?" inquired Dunlop.

"Nothing I can think of at the moment," Littlejohn said.

"In that case," Dunlop said, "I'll contact the FSB liaison at the Russian embassy. Let's find out if they have any missing persons that might match our stranger from Lake Abitibi."

❖ ❖ ❖

The President entered the briefing room at the White House to make a short statement to the media who had gathered there. To one side stood the Vice President, CIA Director and other administration officials. On the other side was a short, stocky and balding man with a bushy moustache, huge nose and small forehead. His hair was sparse on top and his eyes betrayed a touch of shyness, though his chin projected the strength of a bulldog. He was William Mendik, and was about to assume the duties of Secretary of Homeland Security.

"Mr. Mendik has had a distinguished career as a military policeman in the army, as a highway patrolman in Ohio, and then Chief of Police in Cleveland for fourteen months before moving to the private sector as a consultant. He will bring new energy and vision to the Department of Homeland Security."

Mendik spoke briefly, emphasizing his devotion to the administration and determination to carry out the President's policies, which were the best way of guaranteeing the security of the American people. He then shook the President's hand, and the swearing in ceremony was concluded. Among the reporters present, one whispered to another, "Mendik isn't qualified to be the night watchman at a warehouse!"

❖ ❖ ❖

That evening, Dunlop met Major Petrov from the Russian embassy. He held the post of embassy consul, but was known to be the resident officer for the FSB, the Russian Federal Security Service. They had drinks at the Chateau Laurier Hotel near Parliament Hill, where they had met many times before.

"Alex, I assume that when I meet with the Deputy Director of CSIS, the topic of conversation is not wheat sales to Russia," Major Petrov said in a forthright manner.

"As usual, your intuition is correct," replied Dunlop, who pulled out of his attaché case a large envelope, which he handed to the Major. Petrov removed its contents, observing a series of grisly photos.

"My apologies for the distasteful images. However, they belong to a deceased person whom we have not been able to identify. We believe it may be possible that the victim of this murder was a Russian national."

Petrov lifted his gaze from the photographs, and looked directly at Dunlop.

"Alex, what makes you think this is the body of a Russian citizen?"

"This," replied Dunlop, pointing to the photograph of the victim's tattoo.

"Hmm, tseh and beh," Petrov said, looking and sounding puzzled.

"Major, it might be a long shot, but that is all we have to go on at the moment. We can also provide you with DNA samples."

Petrov nodded affirmatively, telling the Deputy Director he would make inquiries with Moscow and see what he could learn.

❖ ❖ ❖

Cole was in his office when he was informed that Darnell was on the line. Picking up the receiver, he expected to finally be able to brief the CIA Director on the Hamburg sermon.

"Dick..."

Darnell cut him off.

"David, the President has made an organizational change, to help things run smoother. From now on, any overseas intelligence that suggests a domestic threat is to be reported to the Secretary of Homeland Security instead of me."

"But Dick, it doesn't make sense to take you out of the loop on a matter of such vital importance!" said an exasperated Cole.

Trying to sound conciliatory, Darnell told Cole that the President required him as CIA Director to be more focused on the Iraq insurgency, so he had less time for other matters. However, he would be meeting with Mendik periodically, so he would not be entirely out of touch.

After the conversation concluded, Cole slammed his phone down, yelling "Jesus Christ!" His body language manifested the deepest level of frustration.

❖ ❖ ❖

The following day Dextraze was at his desk when Dr. Taylor contacted him by phone.

"Pierre, we finally heard back from the FBI on those DNA samples. The remaining DNA on the metal shards definitely matches five Americans who were killed by terrorists in Iraq..."

Three days later, Dunlop was driving in his Buick when his cell phone rang. He pulled to the side of the road and took the call. It was Major Petrov.

"Alex, Moscow informs me that they may be able to identify the body you found. Due to sensitive matters of Russian national security, they cannot share any information by cable or through the embassy. However, if you were to send a representative to Moscow, the FSB is willing to assist you, on a strictly unofficial basis."

"Tell them I accept their offer, with appreciation," Dunlop instantly responded.

The following morning Littlejohn was called into Dunlop's office for a meeting.

"Sir, you sent for me", Littlejohn said as he entered. He didn't even have a chance to sit down.

"Here are your airline tickets and briefing packet," Dunlop said perfunctorily. He then noticed the surprised look on Littlejohn's face.

"Sorry, Henry, for the short notice. My contact at the Russian embassy suggested that the FSB might be able to help us ID that corpse, but for their own reasons they will only share information with us on their territory. We're going to put your Russian language skills to good use. You're leaving this afternoon for Moscow. As soon as you arrive you will be meeting with Colonel Ulanovsky with the FSB. They'll have a car waiting for you at the airport. Have a pleasant flight."

Arzamas-16

David Cole had arrived at the office of the Secretary of Homeland Security to brief him on his growing concern regarding the Lion and his possible plans for a major terrorist incident on American soil. Escorted into the Secretary's office by a young female assistant, Cole was warmly but glibly greeted by Mendik, who offered him a chair.

"Mr. Secretary, I don't know if you have been previously informed, but I have grave concerns, serious worries that our nemesis, the Lion, has shifted his focus from Iraq to the American homeland…"

Cole briefed Mendik on what he knew: the threats posted on the Al-Assad El-Islamiya website, the sermons of Sheik Yantissi, and a growing body of anecdotal evidence. As Cole spoke, he noticed that Mendik's facial expressions swung like a pendulum from abject disinterest to passivity. After only five minutes, Mendik looked at his watch and apologized to Cole, telling him he must leave immediately for another appointment, but that Cole should keep him informed.

After dismissing Cole, the Secretary left the office building where he was situated, and entered the rear of a Lincoln Town Car that was waiting for him. The limousine driver knew exactly where to convey his passenger. After about ten minutes navigating Washington D.C.'s traffic, the Town Car pulled up to an ornate apartment building. Mendik looked at the wedding ring on his finger, then silently slipped it off and into one of his pockets. Before leaving the limousine, he instructed the driver to wait, telling him he thought he would be about two hours.

He entered the building, took the elevator up to the twelfth floor, swiftly exited and strode to apartment 1214. He knocked on the door twice before being warmly invited in by a tall, sophisticated looking blond woman wearing a black dress, her peroxide hair tied tightly into a bun.

In a brief moment, they embraced each other warmly, their hands rubbing vertically along each other's backs.

"Bill, what took you so long to get here?" the woman said with a soft, suggestive voice.

As his fingers began loosening the buttons on the back of her dress, he whispered, "Some clown from the CIA was wasting my time."

◈ ◈ ◈

The Air Canada flight landed at Moscow's Sheremetyevo airport in the early morning. The aircraft traffic was light that morning, and within minutes the airplane was off the runway and parked at the tarmac for unloading.

Passengers disembarked and headed toward Customs clearance and passport control. As soon as he left the aircraft, Littlejohn was approached by two well-groomed men in business suits, who politely asked to see his identification, which he swiftly produced.

"Mr. Littlejohn, there is no need to go through Customs. Just proceed with us."

Within minutes, Littlejohn was being driven through downtown Moscow. He noticed St. Basil's distinct onion-shaped dome as they traversed the area around Red Square. In less than half an hour, he arrived at the FSB headquarters, and was escorted into the office of Colonel Ulanovsky.

"I hope you had a pleasant flight, Mr. Littlejohn."

"Yes, I did Colonel, only I don't think I had enough advance notice to pack everything."

Smiling, Ulanovsky said, "I understand. That is an occupational inconvenience you and I share in our profession."

Ulanovky asked Littlejohn to be seated at a small conference table. Ulanovsky had several documents with him, which he intended to show his guest.

"Mr. Littlejohn, I know you have traveled a great distance, so let me get directly to the substance of your interest. Based on the material and DNA samples provided by CSIS to Major Petrov, we believe that the body you recovered in northern Ontario is that of a Russian citizen."

What fatigue Littlejohn was experiencing after many hours of travel vanished, as he tensed up with alertness. He noticed the FSB Colonel placing a photograph in front of him.

"This is a photograph of Boris Fedorenko," Ulanovsky said. He paused a moment before proceeding, giving Littlejohn an opportunity to study the face that had been detached from the murdered man's body. He noticed it was an elderly man, with graying hair. Even the man's moustache was gray. The eyes were dull gray, and mischievous looking.

"Colonel, who was Boris Fedorenko?"

"Before I answer that, please understand that this is an unofficial meeting between our two agencies. The Russian government shares with your own a deep concern about the proliferation of nuclear materials, so on that premise we will share information with you on a strictly confidential basis."

Littlejohn indicted his understanding, and then listened attentively as Ulanovsky spoke.

"Mr. Fedorenko, who was 68 years old, was a machinist in the nuclear industry of the Soviet Union. He retired on pension a few years ago. He had trouble making ends meet financially, and apparently ran up big gambling debts. Unfortunately, like some other former nuclear technicians who fell on hard times when the Soviet Union disintegrated, he sought to exchange his special knowledge for, shall we say, financial gain far beyond his pension. He came to our attention when we discovered he had gone to North Korea two years ago to work on a special project, which we believe involved nuclear weapons development. When he returned to Moscow, we warned him never to do that again. Six months ago, he traveled to Abu Dhabi in the United Arab Emirates, supposedly to consult on designing nuclear-powered desalination plants. Then, three months ago, he traveled to Switzerland, and has not been heard from since."

"You did say he was a machinist, Colonel?"

"Yes."

"Not a physicist or engineer?"

"That is correct," replied Ulanovsky, who now understood the direction of Littlejohn's question. "I suppose, Mr. Littlejohn, you are wondering why a machinist would be of value in a nuclear project."

"You read my mind, Colonel."

The Colonel began to explain why someone with a professional background that seemed to a lay person so mundane was actually vital in the context of nuclear activity.

"Mr. Littlejohn, let's take a nuclear reactor, as an example. The scientific minds conceive its design, but it is the hands of a skilled machinist that will transform that design into an actual power plant capable of sustaining a chain reaction. One set of skills cannot function without the other."

Littlejohn asked the Colonel if he could shed some light on Fedorenko's work experience. Referring to a document, Ulanovsky proceeded to summarize his career.

"He attended a technical vocational school in Kiev before entering the Soviet Air Force. He was an ordnance technician at a strategic aviation base. After performing his military service, Fedorenko was selected for advanced technical training in nuclear industry fabrication techniques, and then transferred in 1960 to the All-Russian Scientific Research Institute of Experimental Physics. He was there three years, and was then moved to a factory near Moscow that manufactured parts for graphite nuclear power-generating reactors. He retired on pension five years ago."

The Colonel told Littlejohn this was all the information he was authorized to share, however, he hoped that the long journey to Moscow had been beneficial.

◈ ◈ ◈

An old Volvo cleared the security barrier at the CSIS parking lot and pulled into a reserved spot marked "Lazar." An elderly gentleman in his early eighties slowly emerged, clutching his walking stick. He laboriously walked into the headquarters building, telling the security desk he had an appointment with the Deputy Director. He was indeed expected, and was immediately escorted into Dunlop's office.

"Thomas, thank for coming on short notice. Please have a seat. Coffee?"

Dunlop was very solicitous of his elderly guest, who requested plain black coffee, and leaned his walking stick by his chair. His almost transparent white hair contrasted with a jovial face and cheap plastic glasses, which merely distracted from the towering intellect that radiated through the man's eyes. He was Dr. Thomas Lazar, a retired nuclear physicist and consultant to CSIS on nuclear proliferation matters. He came from an old German-Jewish family, which had fled the country after the Nazis attained power, immigrating to Canada. He had majored in Chemistry at McGill University in Montreal, then did graduate and post-graduate work at the University of Chicago in nuclear physics, working with Enrico Fermi. He was recruited during World War II to work on the Manhattan project, which developed the first atomic bomb. He was also the only surviving witness to the first atomic explosion, conducted in the deserts of New Mexico in 1945. Lazar spent twenty years working at the Lawrence Livermore National Laboratory in California, which designed nuclear weapons. Subsequently, he returned to Canada, and taught physics at the University of Toronto before retiring and moving to Ottawa, where he kept active doing governmental consulting work on nuclear matters.

"Alex, you keeping busy?" inquired Lazar in his thick German accent.

"Unfortunately, yes. We have a possible proliferation concern that has arisen. That is why I asked you to come in."

Dunlop explained the matter of the headless body from Lake Abitibi, it's connection to a newspaper editor in Timmins whose vehicle was bombed, the attempt by the Iranian embassy to kidnap the same editor, and other strange coincidences. Continuing, he pointed out, "All these developments in some way seem to connect with this murder victim. We now know he was a Russian citizen, Boris Fedorenko, a retired machinist who worked in the nuclear industry. Henry Littlejohn just returned from Moscow, and the Russians told him a little about his background." Dunlop handed Lazar a sheet of paper summarizing Fedorenko's career.

"As you can see, Thomas, the Russians didn't tell us much. Just an outline, but enough for me to be concerned. Can you possibly fill in the blanks for us?"

Dr. Lazar scanned the summary of Fedorenko's work as provided by the Russians. He muttered softly "eh, huh," several times as he carefully read the report. Handing the paper back to Dunlop, he shared his thoughts with him.

"Alex, I think you have problems," he said in an understated manner.

Dunlop now looked with intensity towards Dr. Lazar, his eyes sharply focused.

"Let me explain, so you understand what you are dealing with," Lazar said. "Most of his working life involved nuclear power plants. The Soviet civilian nuclear industry was not very impressive, so the knowledge he would have acquired there would not be very useful to anyone with special needs. However, during the period 1960-63, he was at the All-Russian Scientific Research Institute of Experimental Physics. That is indeed worthy of note."

Dunlop asked why that would be. Lazar's answer was alarming.

"Because, Alex, that is where the Russians design and build all of their nuclear weapons." Continuing, he added, "It was the Lawrence Livermore of the Soviet Union while Fedorenko was working there. At that time, the head of the Institute was Andrei Sakharov, the father of the Russian hydrogen bomb and, in my opinion, the most brilliant and innovative nuclear weapons designer the Lord God ever put on this Earth."

"Didn't Sakharov eventually becoming a leading dissident in the Soviet Union?" Dunlop asked.

"That is correct, Alex. He came to understand the futility of the arms race and building more than enough nuclear devices to wipe out the human race several times over. He also became disillusioned with having the fruits of his scientific research being used to strengthen a totalitarian regime."

Dunlop asked Lazar to share with him what he knew about the All-Russian Scientific and Research Institute of Experimental Physics.

"It is located near the monastery just outside the town of Sarov, about 400 kilometers east of Moscow, as the crow flies. Even today it is a highly guarded place, but back in the early 1960's it was actually a closed city. You could not find it on any official map published in the Soviet Union. Relatives sending mail to employees of the Institute were only told to put postal code Arzamas-16 on the envelope. It was the code name for the location of the officially non-existent town where the Institute is located, probably because it was 60 kilometers from the city of Arzamas."

"What would a machinist at Arzamas-16 be doing, Thomas?"

Lazar briefly lifted his glasses from his face, using a handkerchief to wipe a speck of dust from them before answering Dunlop's question.

"Let me explain it like this," Lazar said, "there would be guys like me, probably younger like I used to be, who would spend enormous amounts of time formulating complex mathematical equations involving sub-atomic particles like neutrons. They would run laboratory testing and conduct chemical analysis and eventually come up with the design for a nuclear weapon. It would then be the responsibility of the technicians and machinists to fabricate the weapon. A nuclear bomb is a very complex mechanism. There are literally thousands of components that go into a nuclear weapon, and they all must work perfectly, at exactly the right time, measured in nanoseconds, or you end up with a fizzle instead of a big bang. The machinists would be responsible for assembling some of those components, especially involving precision metal fitting."

"My next question, if you can answer it, is what could Mr. Fedorenko have been doing in Canada?"

Lazar did not hesitate in answering. "Well, since this gentleman was killed so brutally in the middle of winter in an isolated area, I think it is fair to assume he was not here on vacation. My hypothesis, and this is why I think you have a big headache on your hands, Alex, is that Fedorenko was assisting in the assembly of a nuclear device."

Hesitating briefly, Dunlop muttered softly, "This is bad, Thomas." Stroking his chin, he was thinking of any alternative other than the most dire.

"Tell me, Thomas, could he have been involved in assembling a radiological dispersion device?"

"You mean a dirty bomb? Well, that is possible, Alex, but highly unlikely."

"Why?"

"Because, it doesn't require any special skills beyond knowledge in handling conventional explosives, and perhaps a basic chemistry background in the properties of certain radioactive isotopes. This guy, Fedorenko, was not a chemist. He was a machinist and had very esoteric skills, which could only be of help in two areas. He could help in the fitting and assembly of components for a nuclear bomb, or he could help build an obsolete, inefficient Soviet-era nuclear power reactor. You decide what is most logical."

Nexus

David Cole was at his desk, reviewing transcripts from intercepted cell phone conversations, when his intercom rang. It was a colleague from north of the border, and he immediately took the call.

"Alex, how's the weather in Ottawa!"

"Probably as chilly as it is in Washington, David."

"But Alex, we have more hot air in Washington."

The cordial frivolities were brief. Dunlop had a deepening concern, and felt it was time for the CIA and CSIS to be in touch.

"David, we have an extremely serious matter of the highest confidence to discuss with you. Is your phone line secure?"

Cole hesitated before answering. "If it's as serious a matter as you're suggesting, it would be better to meet face to face. Would you like me to come up to Ottawa?"

"That's alright, David. It's probably better if I come down to Washington."

The two men agreed to meet at CIA headquarters the next day.

◈ ◈ ◈

A Chevrolet sedan veered into the departure ramp at Ottawa International Airport, and came to a halt at the main unloading entrance. The front passengers stepped out, the driver being a tall man with black hair, dark sunglasses and a narrow, horse-like tanned face. He was Mohammed Iqbal. His wife, Nadine,

62

opened the rear door while her husband opened the trunk and began unloading luggage. The rear passenger was Nadine's father, Dr. Pervaz Khan. Daughter and son-in-law helped carry Khan's luggage into the airport. In the departure lounge, they said their good-byes. Nadine gently hugged her father.

Mohammed Iqbal removed his sunglasses, and stared intensely towards Dr. Khan, as the two men gripped hands in a firm handshake. Khan looked directly at Iqbal with equal intensity, as though in a spell created by the hypnotic gaze stemming from his son-in-law's eyes. In the distance, observing inconspicuously, was Pierre Dextraze. He lifted a miniature video camera and recorded the airport farewell for posterity.

❖ ❖ ❖

At the Timmins RCMP detachment Constable Stevens received a phone call from Littlejohn.

"Constable, we now have an ID on that body you found at Lake Abitibi," Littlejohn said, explaining what they knew, without referring to Arzamas-16 or Fedorenko's nuclear weapons background. He told Stevens it was important to trace Fedorenko's movements in the Timmins area, without, however, raising any undo attention.

"I understand, Mr.Littlejohn. Send me his photo by e-mail and I'll canvass some of the merchants and gas stations in the area and see what we can come up with."

❖ ❖ ❖

Arriving at Dulles International Airport outside of Washington, Alex Dunlop picked up a rental car and headed towards Langley, Virginia. To pass the time, he listened to nationally syndicated radio talk show host Russ Gibbons on the car's radio. As he listened, he asked himself how representative Gibbons' views were of America. One example disturbed him, when Gibbons declared, "...the danger to America, my friends, is not the terrorists, who are being beaten overseas in Iraq, instead of terrorizing us here at home, because we have a President who understands how to wage this kind of war. The danger we face, ladies and gentlemen, is our economy collapsing because of our antiquated FDR-era social security system. It will bankrupt us, and make us a third rate country, like Canada. No, my fellow Americans, this must not happen. The President's plan to privatize social security will save our economy, and keep our country strong. Don't let the liberals fool you into believing anything else..."

After about an hour's drive, Dunlop had arrived at CIA headquarters. Cole met him on the ninth floor, where they warmly shook hands and exchanged greetings, with Cole then showing him into a secure conference room.

The two men sat facing each other, as Dunlop began to relay his dire concern to his American colleague.

"David, both our agencies, and our respective governments, have been keenly aware of the potential nexus between nuclear proliferation and international terrorism ever since 9/11. In the last few days, two separate investigations CSIS has been conducting have coalesced in a manner that suggests the possibility that a nuclear device is in the process of being assembled in Canada by Islamist terrorists."

David Cole could feel his pulse rate accelerate and breath quicken. This was a possibility he had been anticipating, yet the realization of the correctness of his intuitive insight did not, in the least, dampen his sense of horror.

"Alex, before you continue, there is a question I need to ask. In the course of your investigations, has the name of the Lion come up?"

"Why, yes, tangentially it has," Dunlop said. "Is there a reason you would suspect his involvement?"

Cole explained what one of his translators had uncovered in monitoring the website of Al-Assad El-Islamiya. There was increased chatter by terrorists, intercepted by the CIA, boasting of an imminent catastrophic attack on America. "There is also the disturbing fact," Cole added, "that we lost track of the Lion about four months ago. Mind you, most of our analysts at the Intelligence Directorate are convinced he is still in Iraq, staying under cover because supposedly our counter-insurgency campaign has become more effective. I am not as sanguine."

Alex Dunlop proceeded in briefing his counterpart with what was known about the potential threat.

"A few weeks ago, we were alerted by our Department of External Affairs that Dr. Pervaz Khan was entering Canada on a thirty day visa to visit his daughter, who resides in Ottawa."

"Christ, Alex, Khan is the greatest mastermind of black market nuclear materials proliferation in the world!" Cole said with concern resonating in his voice.

"That is why we kept him under surveillance," Dunlop responded. "He departed Canada just a couple of days ago. While he did spend time with his daughter, he also was a frequent visitor to the North Korean and Iranian embassies."

"Both those countries are major customers of Khan's," Cole interjected. "A large part of their nuclear weapons R&D infrastructure was obtained through the Khan network."

"We know that," Dunlop said. "Our original assumption was that Khan would try to purchase dual use technology in Canada that he would later ship to Iran and North Korea. But another development has led us to a radically different set of assumptions. A body was discovered in northern Ontario, which we had trouble identifying, because its head was missing. A small town newspaper published an appeal for information from the public to help in the identification, mentioning the body had a Russian tattoo. Shortly afterwards, an unsuccessful attempt was made to murder the editor, by blowing up his pickup truck with a bomb using explosive compounds only manufactured in Iran. When the editor, in a lapse of judgment, decided to go to the Iranian embassy and confront them, he was kidnapped and nearly spirited out of the country before we were able to rescue him."

Reflecting on what Dunlop had told him, Cole found the series of coincidental occurrences to be more than coincidental.

"What is the possible connection to the Lion?" inquired Cole.

"The coroner found microscopic metal shards in the neck tissue of the corpse we recovered. There were blood samples obtained from the shards that were traced to nine individuals. One of them was the victim. Through Interpol and your FBI, we have positively identified the other eight as being hostages decapitated in Iraq by a terrorist believed to be the Lion."

"That is very disturbing, Alex."

"It gets worse," Dunlop added. "We now know the identity of the body we found in northern Ontario. He is Boris Fedorenko. He was a nuclear machinist in the Soviet Union during the Cold War, and worked for three years at Arzamas-16."

"Arzamas-16! Shit!" exclaimed Cole. "That's the Russian's principal nuclear weapons development center!"

"I share your concern, which is why I felt it was vital that we talk as soon as we learned what we were dealing with," said Dunlop.

Cole asked what time period Fedorenko had been affiliated with Arzamas-16. Dunlop informed him that they had been able to establish that Fedorenko worked there from 1960 until 1963.

"That's almost 45 years ago," Cole said. "Seems strange they would involve someone of that vintage. On the other hand, if he hasn't forgotten anything, that's all the terrorists need. The working assumption we have in the American intelligence community is that if the terrorists were ever to plan on detonating a nuclear device in an American city, it would be of the simplest fission bomb design."

"You mean the gun barrel assembly?" Dunlop asked.

Cole answered in the affirmative. "Provided they can obtain the fissile material, it probably would be within their capability. For the gun barrel design, they would need about forty or fifty pounds of highly enriched uranium, perhaps a little more or less, depending on their skill level. They could also do it with plutonium if they went for an implosion device, but that would require a much higher level of sophistication on their part."

Cole smacked his forehead with the back of his hand, as Dunlop noted the knot-like tension of his facial muscles.

"The horrible nightmare scenario of nuclear terrorism that I have long feared may soon be upon us, Alex."

"I don't want to sound unduly reassuring," Dunlop told his colleague, "however, we have been using new technology at our principal airports and seaports to safeguard against the illicit importation or export of nuclear materials. They don't know this, but the diplomatic baggage of the North Koreans and Iranians has come in for special scrutiny. Up to now, I am reasonably certain no enriched uranium or plutonium has entered Canada undetected."

Dunlop and Cole speculated on the possibilities. They weighed two alternatives. Both involved the terrorists fabricating a bomb in Canadian territory. In one case the required fissile material could be smuggled into Canada at a later date for final assembly of the device. There was another scenario to consider: the bomb could be brought across the border, and then married up with highly enriched uranium surreptitiously brought into the United States. Both men were in clear agreement on one probability, however.

"They may be assembling this device in Canada," Cole said, "but the target lies south of the border. Their intention would be detonate it in a large urban center. I think I know which one."

Cole brought up the warning contained in the Al-Assad El-Islamiya website, emphasizing its message to believers to avoid being in New York City during the middle of March. As he heard Cole relay the dire tone of the Lion's message to believers, Dunlop looked up at a calendar hanging on the wall of the conference room.

"Today is February 5th, David. If there is any substance to that warning, we have five weeks to unravel it."

❖ ❖ ❖

At a gas station outside of Iroquois Falls, a few kilometers west of Lake Abitibi, Constable Stevens parked his police cruiser. The gas station attendant recognized him, as the Constable approached.

"How's business, Ed?" inquired the Constable.

"It picked up over the winter, but now it's slowed down, so things are kind of back to normal, Mike."

The Constable took out a photograph of Boris Fedorenko.

"Ed, we're doing a missing persons search. I'm checking with all the gas stations in the area. Have a look at this photo, tell me if you might have seen this person."

The attendant looked carefully at the photo, studying it for perhaps thirty seconds. "Mike, by any chance, is this guy a Russian?"

"Yes, he is, but what made you ask?"

"Well, I remember now. It was a while back, maybe three months ago, these two men stopped here to buy gas. The driver had dark complexion and this strange narrow face, he almost looked like a horse, and he wore sunglasses, even with the sky being overcast. The passenger looked like the guy in the photo, and he asked me if I could tell them how far they were from the town of Mace. He had a thick Russian accent. I remember this because the guy next to him cut him off, as though the passenger was not supposed to talk. The dark skinned guy then asked me for directions to Mace."

Constable Stevens asked if the attendant recalled the type of car that they were driving.

"Oh, it was a four door something, not sure of the make. All I remember is that it had diplomatic license plates, which struck me as kind of odd for this region."

Heavy Metal

Upon his return to CSIS headquarters, Alex Dunlop met with Dextraze and Littlejohn. He first wanted to set his priorities. "Gentlemen," he told them, "we are now involved in a full-fledged nuclear proliferation investigation involving international terrorism. I believe we have circuitously crossed paths with a plot to build an improvised nuclear device, smuggle it into the United States and detonate it in an American city."

"My sweet Jesus!" uttered Dextraze. Littlejohn sat still as tension filled his veins.

Dunlop informed his intelligence officers that he had discussed this matter with the Director of Counter-Terrorism at the Central Intelligence Agency, and he could only hope that the CIA would treat this as a matter of the highest priority. As far as Canada was concerned, it was imperative that CSIS did everything possible to rapidly track down where this device was being assembled.

"Any possible leads?" asked Dunlop.

"We might have one," Littlejohn responded. "The RCMP detachment in Timmins queried stores and gas stations in the area, showing the photograph we have of Fedorenko, to determine if he had been spotted in the area. They had only one confirmation of his being seen, a gas station attendant near Iroquois Falls. However, the attendant remembered he was with another man, possibly of Middle Eastern or Indian origin. They both asked for directions to Mace, a small town on the north shore of Lake Abitibi."

Dextraze chimed in. "Mace is a very small town, only a few hundred people reside there. I contacted the mayor and all the merchants. The proprietor of the general store told me that a Middle Eastern man would come into his store every other week for the past three months to purchase provisions in fairly large quantities. The man was close-lipped, only mentioning once that the provisions were for a mining surveying group operating near the lake."

Dunlop asked if they had established who this surveying group was, and where it was operating.

"Yes, we contacted the Department of Natural Resources," Dextraze responded, "and they told us that a concession for mining exploration of gold and diamonds was granted to a Japanese company, Takasumi Investments, for an area located about seven kilometers east of Mace, encompassing the lakeshore and underwater, adjacent to an abandoned mining encampment. They obtained visas for an international work force of 40 technicians, geologists and other specialists, and reactivated the mining encampment to provide lodging for the crew."

"There is something important to add," Littlejohn said. "We did some checking on Takasumi Investments. It is actually owned by Korean nationals living in Japan. A funny thing about Koreans in Japan: they are about equally divided in loyalties to either South or North Korea. The Koreans who control Takasumi swear allegiance to Kim Jong-il and the DPRK."

Littlejohn placed before Dunlop a Xerox of an article, which had appeared in *Far Eastern Business Review.* It referred to Takasumi building a new steel plant in North Korea. A photograph showed the CEO of Takasumi shaking hands with the leader of the Democratic Peoples Republic of Korea, Kim-Jong-il, during a visit to Pyongyang. Dunlop took a brief look at the photo.

"We've got to get to that mining encampment, and fast," Dunlop said.

"Here are some aerial photographs an RCMP helicopter took of the encampment a few hours ago. It appears to be abandoned," said Dextraze.

Dunlop determined the next steps. He would be in touch with the Minister of National Defense and the chief of the defense staff. The Director of CSIS, who was already keeping the Prime Minister informed, would contact the RCMP. A joint operation including army, RCMP and CSIS personnel would need to be mounted at the earliest possibility.

"We can't take chances, in the event it is not entirely abandoned. We need to get there with armed force, and with the equipment to deal with hazardous materials, including anything nuclear," Dunlop told his colleagues.

Early the following morning, four Huey helicopters departed the Canadian Forces Base at Petawawa, and headed for the area east of Mace. Aboard were heavily armed soldiers wearing protective suits, gas masks and carrying M-16 automatic rifles. Over Lake Abitibi, two RCMP helicopters joined them, with Dextraze and Littlejohn aboard one of them. Very soon, the mining camp was in sight. One by one the choppers quickly landed and the soldiers disembarked. They ran in groups towards each of the buildings, M-16 rifles drawn. There were six cabins, used as lodgings, and a larger building employed as a workshop. The soldiers entered each structure in assault formation, yelling. But the only response to their threatening utterances were echoes. The encampment was indeed deserted.

Littlejohn and Dextraze entered the workshop, which was completely empty. Joining them was the Major in command of the military detachment, a half dozen soldiers and two RCMP Constables. The Major took off his gas mask. "Looks like not a soul is here," he said to the two CSIS officers.

Littlejohn noticed something in the snow, just outside the entrance to the workshop. He picked it up. It was a discarded cigarette butt, which he vigorously sniffed. "My Indian intuition. This butt was dropped no more than two days ago."

"Henry's nose is more sensitive than any tracking dog," Dextraze responded.

"Then whoever was here left recently, and in a hurry," said the Major. One of his soldiers approached him carrying a Geiger counter, which was clicking ominously. The Major noted that both

71

intelligence officers looked worried. "No need to be alarmed," the Major told Littlejohn and Dextraze. "While it is several times the normal background radiation level, it's still within safe limits. You won't be glowing in the dark."

The Major tuned to his soldiers, telling them to collect air and soil samples.

"It will be interesting to see what those samples tell us, Henry," Dextraze told his colleague.

"I suspect the worst, Pierre," replied Littlejohn.

❖ ❖ ❖

A cab stopped in front of the Banque Suisse building in the center of Zurich, Switzerland. David Cole tipped the driver and stepped out of the cab, looking at the entrance to the building. He quickly looked behind to make sure he was not being followed. He entered the building, and informed the security desk that he was Mr. Donald Smith, and had an appointment with the Vice President for Internal Auditing, Mr. Johanne Kleist. Cole was asked to present his identification, and he removed from his wallet an Indiana drivers license made out to Donald Smith, with Cole's photograph. Satisfied with the identification, security confirmed the appointment with Kleist's secretary. Moments later, Cole was escorted into Kleist's office. Cole noticed that Kleist looked nervous. He was a tall man in his late fifties, slim, and looking every inch a Swiss banker with his navy-blue pinstripe suit and burgundy tie.

"David, you know how difficult your request is," Kleist said after the briefest of handshakes. "I don't feel comfortable giving you this information."

"I know, Johanne," responded an empathetic Cole. "Don't think for a moment I don't appreciate what I'm putting you through. We've known each other a long time. I wouldn't have asked you for this help, and traveled to Zurich, unless it was a matter of the gravest urgency."

Kleist bowed his head, and looked at a photograph of a beautiful young woman on his desk. A teardrop emerged from his left eye, and Cole could feel the sadness of the moment.

"Johanne, I notice you still keep the photograph of your daughter on your desk."

Slowly, Kleist wiped the tears from his eyes and looked towards Cole. "You know, David, she was our only child. I suppose one never gets used to burying your own daughter. It was made more difficult by the amount of time it took to identify the few fragments of her from ground zero."

"A lot of human tragedies were born on September 11th," replied Cole. "One of my translators had a brother who was also killed on that terrible day," Cole said with emotion. "That is why it is so important that every person in the civilized world does all he humanly can to prevent another 9/11 or, God forbid, something much worse."

Kleist nodded his head in agreement. "I know. I have your information. Just please keep my role confidential. If the bank were to discover I was violating Swiss confidentiality laws on banking and providing information to the CIA, my fate would be sealed."

"You mean you would be fired or arrested?" asked Cole.

"Much worse than that. They would transfer me to our branch in Timbuktu."

Kleist flashed a brief smile, which Cole reciprocated.

For the next half-hour, Kleist presented a detailed overview of financial transactions involving secret accounts at his bank linked to an Islamic charity. The CIA believed this charity was sending funds to the Lion and his operation in Iraq. An organization called the Martyr's Fund opened an account at the bank three years ago, and had accumulated and transferred funds in excess of $100 million, mostly raised by radical clerics from wealthy princes and businessmen in Saudi Arabia and the Gulf Arab states. About six months ago, a new account was opened by the Martyr's Fund, and contributions under another name, Holy Jihad, began to flow into that account very fast, and exceeded a billion dollars within a two week period. Just as quickly, $900 million was disbursed from the new account to two separate accounts with different Swiss banks. One account was controlled personally by the dictator of North Korea, Kim Jong-il. Another account was under the control of the Iranian Islamic Revolutionary Guards, known as the Pasdaran.

At the same time, two million dollars was transferred to a third account, set up by a person using a phony name, but who physically resembled the man in the photograph Cole had shared with Kleist, Boris Fedorenko. Three months ago, an additional ten million dollars was transferred to his account. Fedorenko then had one million dollars wired to a casino in Monaco; he apparently lost most of it at the roulette wheel. He must have traveled from Monaco to Mexico a few days afterwards, since he had another $100,000 wired to his hotel in Cancun. There was still nearly eleven million dollars sitting in Fedorenko's account.

"I don't think anyone will be claiming that money, Johanne," Cole said, referring to Fedorenko's demise. He thanked Kleist for sharing information that was important and useful, warmly shaking his hand before departing.

❖ ❖ ❖

Thomas Lazar was back in Alex Dunlop's office. The Deputy Director had asked him to return once the lab results had come in from the soil and air samples that had been collected from the mining camp on the north shore of Lake Abitibi. Dunlop already knew the news was not good, that uranium 235 and plutonium traces had been detected. He handed Dr. Lazar the lab reports.

"Thomas, what I don't understand is how they got enriched uranium and plutonium into the country. Our new detection devices are supposed to be foolproof."

"Maybe the detection devices are not the problem," Lazar said, as his eyes scanned the lab report. "They may have found a source already in the country."

"I don't know of any sources that could exist on Canadian soil. All of the nuclear power generating reactors employ the strictest level of security. The same with our country's research reactors," Dunlop said in response.

Lazar, having finished reading the lab report, placed it firmly on the table, his eyes bulging with concern.

"What is it, Thomas?" inquired an anxious Dunlop.

Lazar momentarily hesitated in responding. In a tone of voice suggesting ominous news, he shared his interpretation of the report.

"Just when I thought things were bad enough," he muttered. Then, speaking more distinctly, he told the Deputy Director what he thought the report meant.

"As you mentioned, Alex, they found at that location samples of the heavy metals essential for any type of nuclear bomb, uranium 235 and plutonium. That in itself is very bad. But what is worse, much worse, and a real surprise to me, is that they also found traces of deuterium and tritium."

Dunlop was perplexed. Though he understood only too well what the implications were of enriched uranium and plutonium as fissile materials, he was not clear on the meaning of the other isotopes mentioned by Dr. Lazar. He asked him to elaborate on their implications.

"As you know, Alex, uranium 235 and plutonium are the key ingredients for making an atomic or fission bomb. Deuterium and tritium are of limited use, and only in a highly developed atomic bomb, and would not even be needed in a simple design. However, they are the essential ingredients in making a hydrogen bomb."

"A hydrogen bomb?" replied a flabbergasted Dunlop. "Are you serious?" he said in disbelief.

"I wish I wasn't," Lazar responded in a melancholy voice. "Unfortunately, the traces of deuterium and tritium leave open no other possibilities. It also makes Fedorenko's involvement much more logical. Alex, the way it looks to me, these people are not about assembling a primitive fission bomb. No, they are much more ambitious then that. They are attempting to put together a thermonuclear device."

"I'm calling the Director," said Dunlop, referring to Samuel Kinkaid, the head of CSIS and Dunlop's boss. He buzzed his secretary, and within moments, Dunlop and Kinkaid were connected. He told the CSIS Director of Lazar's assessment of the laboratory findings related to the samples taken at the abandoned mining encampment. Kinkaid asked Dunlop to hold for a minute. When Kinkaid returned to the phone, he relayed his instructions, which Dunlop passed on to Lazar.

"Thomas, you and I will be briefing the Prime Minister and the security cabinet this evening, at 7:00 PM."

◇ ◇ ◇

The cabinet room on Parliament Hill had only a few of the chairs around the long table occupied: the Prime Minister, Deputy Prime Minister responsible for public safety, Ministers of National Defense and External Affairs and Solicitor General were present. Seated opposite them were Dunlop, Kinkaid and Dr. Lazar. Samuel Kinkaid began the meeting by emphasizing that it was a matter of the highest national urgency that had brought the security cabinet together on such short notice. He then asked Dunlop to update the government officials.

"I know you have been previously briefed on the matters related to the body of the Russian nuclear machinist discovered at Lake Abitibi, the attempted murder and kidnapping of the editor of the local newspaper in that area, and all this coinciding with Dr. Pervaz Khan's recent trip to Ottawa, supposedly to visit his daughter, but also involving numerous side visits to the North Korean and Iranian embassies. All these elements give rise to the possibility that an international terrorist group was in the process of assembling a primitive nuclear device on Canadian soil. I must now tell you that within the last twenty-four hours, our investigation has acquired additional information that leads us to the conclusion that the device being assembled is not a simple, Hiroshima type atomic bomb. We believe that this plot involves building a much more powerful and destructive hydrogen bomb, with the ultimate intention of smuggling it into the United States and detonating it in a major American city, possibly New York."

The Prime Minister's face flushed with near panic, his anxiety replicated by the other members of the security cabinet. They all stared at Dunlop in disbelief.

"This is truly alarming, Mr. Dunlop," the Prime Minister said. "How certain are you of the danger?"

"So we are all clear on the threat this represents, I asked our anti-proliferation advisor, Dr. Thomas Lazar, to join us." Dunlop asked Lazar to address the security cabinet.

"Mr. Prime Minister, Ministers, to enable you to fully comprehend the danger we are faced with, I ask that you permit me to give you a brief physics lecture. I will keep it simple. In order for terrorists to build a nuclear weapon, they must have fissile material. This means elements whose atomic nucleus can be split using conventional explosives, like TNT. The material must be in a sufficient quantity, what we call the critical mass, so that when neutrons are released from the atom's nucleus by the explosives, they bombard other nuclei, releasing more neutrons, which in turn strikes still other nuclei, until a chain reaction occurs and is self sustaining, meaning a vast number of neutrons are released as energy in the form of an atomic explosion. This is a fundamental part of Einstein's theory of relativity, energy equaling mass multiplied by the speed of light squared. In nature, only the nucleus of the heaviest metals, uranium and plutonium, can be split in a chain reaction with conventional explosives. Uranium in its natural state is called uranium 238, and it is not fissile with ordinary explosives. Only enriched uranium, uranium 235, a derivative that is only found in a tiny percentage of uranium that is mined, is suitable for an atomic bomb. Plutonium is not found at all in nature, it must be manufactured from uranium in a very complicated and expensive process. It can also be the byproduct of a nuclear reactor. Both these materials were detected at the mining encampment. There is no doubt about that. The only question is if they have it in sufficient quantity."

The Prime Minister posed a question. "Dr. Lazar, what quantities of either plutonium or uranium 235 would be needed for a bomb?"

"About twenty kilograms of enriched uranium would be sufficient. With plutonium, as little as four or five kilos would suffice. About the size of a grapefruit."

"What is the significance, doctor, of the attempt by the terrorists to build a hydrogen bomb?" inquired the Minister of National Defense.

"Let me first explain the difference between an atomic and a hydrogen bomb. The atomic bomb releases its energy from fission, meaning atomic nuclei are split, releasing neutrons. A hydrogen bomb works exactly the same way as our sun in that its energy is derived from fusion, specifically fusing atoms of the lightest element, hydrogen, to form helium. During this process of fusion, excess neutrons are released as a thermonuclear explosion, which is potentially far more powerful than an atomic blast."

"How much more powerful, Dr. Lazar?" asked the Prime Minister.

"Depending on the design of the weapon, the yield can range from twice as powerful as the bombs used at Hiroshima and Nagasaki, to thousands of times."

"Thousands?" the Prime Minister interjected with both bewilderment and fear.

"Yes, Mr. Prime Minister. To give you an example, the bomb dropped on Hiroshima had a yield of 15 kilotons, or fifteen thousand tons of TNT. I witnessed the very first test of a hydrogen device, in the Pacific Ocean in 1952. Its yield was 10 megatons, or ten million tons of TNT. That is almost 700 times as powerful."

The Deputy Prime Minister wanted to know on what basis Lazar was certain that the device that was being planned was thermonuclear.

"The soil and air samples showed traces of deuterium and tritium, in addition to uranium 235 and plutonium. Deuterium and tritium are the isotopes of hydrogen that are specifically used in hydrogen bombs. I mentioned that unlike the fission of an atomic bomb, in a thermonuclear device the atoms are fused to release energy and create an explosion. However, the conventional explosives that can initiate a chain reaction with fissile materials are nowhere near hot enough to bring about fusion. To accomplish that requires the heat of the sun. There is only one way on Earth to generate such heat, and that is with an atomic explosion. In other words, you must build a fission device as part of a hydrogen bomb - it is the heat of the atomic blast that enables the deuterium and tritium molecules to fuse together, creating an enormous explosion of thermonuclear energy."

The Prime Minister and his colleagues were gripped with fear and anxiety. This was a crisis far beyond their professional training, experience and inclination. That a plot of this character and magnitude could apparently be in such an advanced stage of planning had taken everyone completely by surprise.

"Is there any other rational explanation for the tritium and deuterium being present?" the Prime Minister asked in a frantic, almost pleading voice.

Lazar looked at him with an empathetic gaze. "Unfortunately, there is not, Mr. Prime Minister. Deuterium is the heavy molecule in water, found in a proportion of one in six thousand. Its separation, as you can imagine, is very difficult and expensive. But it is nothing compared to tritium, which is almost unknown in nature, being more a product of the early evolution of the universe. To create quantities of tritium required for a bomb, it must be made by man, in a process even more complex and costly than plutonium, in fact, far more costly. I would estimate that it costs about a billion dollars a liter to produce. The only reason countries like America and Russia go to that expense is because it is indispensable for building a thermonuclear bomb. The one question I have in my mind is how these terrorists could obtain this material."

Dunlop mentioned an earlier conversation he had with Dr. Lazar on tritium. "Dr. Lazar has shared with me some interesting information on tritium. Other than weapons of mass destruction, it is also used in luminous paint for signage, street markers and watch dials. It also decays rapidly for a radioactive material."

"That is correct," Lazar added. "It has a radioactive half-life of only about twelve years. It is really a headache for the world's major nuclear powers. Their stockpile of thermonuclear weapons must have their tritium triggers and components renewed every few years on an ongoing basis, or the weapons become useless". Pausing briefly, he added, "I would presume, however, that the tritium that these terrorists have somehow acquired is fully potent."

❖ ❖ ❖

Later that evening, in his office, the Prime Minister put in a phone call to Washington. A receptionist at the White House answered.

"This is the Prime Minister of Canada. I wish to speak to the President of the United States."

Broken Arrows

Dunlop had returned to Washington D.C. on the instructions of the Prime Minister. The PM had been unable to reach the President, so he had spoken with the Vice President, who agreed to meet with the CSIS Deputy Director the following day. Dunlop knew there would be three other people at the meeting: Cole, Mendick and Larry Braun, Director of the FBI.

His face was chiseled with anxiety as he peered through the porthole of the Boeing 737, observing the Washington landmarks that symbolized American power. The solidity of the Capital Building and Washington Monument seemed to contrast sharply with the vulnerability Dunlop felt was at America's doorstep.

At the airport, Dunlop was picked up by an official limousine, which drove him to the White House. The chauffeur had the radio on, so once more the CSIS Deputy Director endured a sermon by commentator Russ Gibbons. "Don't believe what the liberals tell you about how much you need the government to protect you," he blasted rhetorically. "The liberals are fools! They only stand in the way of progress! It is only through low taxes, the right to bear arms and privatizing social security that our nation can remain strong..."

Arriving at the White House, Dunlop was escorted into the office of the Vice President. Waiting for him, along with the Vice President, were the CIA's Director of Counter-Terrorism, Director of the FBI and Secretary for Homeland Security. All the men were quickly seated and began their meeting.

"I spoke with your Prime Minister the other day," the Vice President said. "Unfortunately, the President could not speak with him; he has been severely preoccupied with legislative matters. However, he has asked me to represent him at this meeting, so that you can brief us, Mr. Dunlop. I understand the Canadian government believes there is a terrorist plot to smuggle a nuclear weapon into the United States?"

"That is correct, Mr. Vice President," Dunlop responded. He summarized the CSIS investigation and its findings to date. "Our conclusion, therefore, is that a radical Islamist group linked to Al-Qaeda and possibly being led personally by the Lion, with the covert support and assistance of certain rogue governments, has used Canadian soil to assemble a highly destructive thermonuclear device with the intention of smuggling it into the United States for use in a mass casualty attack on one of your cities."

Though the tone that Dunlop used was alarmist, the Vice President seemed unperturbed. He turned to Mendik, asking him for his reaction.

"Mr. Vice President, Homeland Security has the situation well in hand. Our experts tell me how difficult it would be for a terrorist organization to build a nuclear bomb. In my opinion, this is just a publicity stunt by the terrorists. We are better off focusing our energies on aircraft hijackings, suicide bombers and cyber attacks on our nation's computers."

While Cole appeared aghast at Mendik's response, the Director of the Federal Bureau of Investigation chimed in. "Bill is absolutely right," Braun said. "There is no basis to speculate on the terrorist capability to build such a weapon. They have none. At most, they can perhaps obtain enough fissile material on the black market for a dirty bomb, but nowhere near enough for a functioning atomic bomb. As for a hydrogen bomb, that is pure fantasy. Frankly, if the Al-Qaeda organization and its offshoots were planning an attack with a weapon of mass destruction, it is far more likely to be chemical or biological. That is where the FBI is allocating its limited resources."

Calmly, Dunlop offered a rebuttal to the comforting conclusions stemming from the operational heads of the FBI and Department of Homeland Security. "The ominous conclusion we have reached, gentlemen, is not the product of paranoia by government officials or the Canadian intelligence community. It is cold, hard scientific judgment based on the solid accumulation of facts and their careful and critical analysis. We are more than willing to pass on all our data to any American specialists you identify for us."

Cole added weight to Dunlop's remarks. "I must concur with the assessment of the Canadian Security and Intelligence Service. It also coincides with credible and growing threats of an imminent and annihilating blow to our country by Islamic extremists, especially the Lion."

Mendik and Braun seemed unimpressed. The Vice President was walking the middle ground. "Mr. Dunlop, our administration appreciates the concern of the Canadian government, and its eagerness to cooperate. After all, terrorism is a threat to our entire North American continent. However, without wanting to cast any aspersions on your scientists, I think we would want to see much more persuasive evidence before we hit the panic button and scare the bejeezus out of the American people. Let me remind everyone that a month after 9/11 an informant told the CIA that Al-Qaeda had smuggled a suitcase nuke with a yield of 10 kilotons into downtown Manhattan, and would detonate it within days. We took the threat seriously, and sent in our Nuclear Emergency Search Team. We tried to keep it quiet, but once the media found out that NEST was in New York City, it threw the entire city into a shitload of panic. The whole thing turned out to be a hoax. The President and I are not going to make that mistake again."

The Deputy Director sought to convince his American counterparts of the seriousness of the situation. "At the very least, Mr. Vice President, please increase the level of scrutiny and surveillance at all the border crossings. We think the bomb is likely still in Canada, however, we have no leads on its location. They are going to try to get it across the border and into your country, and hit you with it. We have a border of more than five thousand kilometers - it is impossible for us to secure it on our own. Even if the odds of their having a functional hydrogen bomb are only one percent, that is far too high a risk to accept, given the catastrophic consequences. Please Mr. Vice President, for the love of God, treat this matter as being of the highest level of urgency."

Dunlop noted, to his distress, that the Vice President's face had skepticism written all over it. Mendik and Braun conveyed a demeanor of studied indifference. Only Cole looked concerned, as well as frustrated. Shortly afterwards, the meeting adjourned.

Cole escorted Dunlop across the White House lawn towards the limousine waiting to take him back to the airport. It was a slow walk, and they had a chance to review the meeting.

"David, where did I go wrong? I obviously failed to convince them of the dire emergency my government believes to exist."

Cole gently slapped Dunlop's back in a gesture of comfort. "You did all you could, Alex. Maybe the failure is on my part. I have not been able to convey to my bosses the sense of foreboding I feel about the next terrorist attack on America. It is as though this administration has its head in the sand, buried in complacency. Their crisis is getting enough votes to privatize social security and keeping the debacle in Iraq out of the headlines."

Dunlop asked his American colleague what they could do. Cole promised to continue to raise the alarm in Washington until they understood the lethality of the threat.

"I have new information on the financing of this plot," Cole said, relaying what he had learned from his Swiss banking contact in Zurich. Dunlop found the news interesting.

"I think, David, based on the timeline of these banking transactions, I begin to see the chronology of this plot. It probably started two years ago, when Fedorenko went to North Korea. Perhaps he was contacted there, or he made the first overture. Six months ago he was in Abu Dhabi, and received a payment. Something must have been exchanged. It's no coincidence that simultaneously the Lion's account also funds payment of hundreds of millions of dollars to the DPRK and Iran. I think we can conclude that this was payment for components of the H-bomb."

"That is my theory as well," said Cole.

"The next payment to Fedorenko occurs when he is in Switzerland. He then heads to Mexico after gambling in Monaco.

The next time he shows up, it is without a head. Can you fill in the gap?" inquired Dunlop.

"I think I can. If they wanted to keep his presence in Canada secret, it actually makes more sense smuggling him into the United States across the Mexican border. Al-Qaeda has a well-established network for infiltrating operatives from Mexico. They also have sleeper cells that could provide him with forged documents for entry into Canada under an assumed name. That way, you would never know he was in your country."

Dunlop paused for a moment, reflecting.

"David, there remain two unanswered questions. What were these terrorists paying Fedorenko to do? If he was merely a machinist, there are plenty of these disaffected and financially broke people around in the former Soviet Union who could have been recruited for far less money."

Cole asked what the remaining question was.

"For the life of me, I have no idea how the terrorists obtained the fissile material we detected at the mining encampment near Lake Abitibi. Our new detection equipment has been deployed at all major ports of entry, including airports and seaports. Since its installation, we haven't detected even the minutest trace quantities of enriched uranium and plutonium. It is a complete and disturbing mystery as to how they acquired this material."

❖ ❖ ❖

Near Iroquois Falls, Dextraze pulled into the same gas station where Constable Stevens had obtained an ID on Fedorenko. He approached the attendant that Stevens had spoken with.

"You must be Ed," Dextraze said in an amiable manner.

"Yes, how do you know me?"

Dextraze pulled out his identification, mentioning he was working in cooperation with the RCMP.

"My Lord, Iroquois Falls never got this attention before," the attendant said.

Dextraze mentioned how helpful he had been in identifying the man in the photo Constable Stevens showed him.

"You mentioned to the Constable that another man was in the car when you saw the same gentleman that was in the photograph.

You said he had a dark complexion. I am going to show you some other photographs. We want to see if you recognize any of these men being that dark skinned man."

Dextraze proceeded to show the attendant several photographs, cautioning him to take his time in looking at each one. He slowly reviewed the first four, shaking his head sideways and apologizing for being unable to make a match. Dextraze then showed him the fifth, and last photograph.

"That's him! That's him!" the attendant exclaimed. "I'll never forget a face like that! Doesn't he look like a horse?"

Dextraze thanked the attendant, then returned to his car, pulling out his cell phone. He reached Littlejohn back at CSIS headquarters.

"Henry, I just received confirmation from a witness that the son-in-law of Dr. Pervaz Khan, Mohammed Iqbal, was seen with Fedorenko just outside of Iroquois Falls."

"That is more than interesting, Pierre. I'll do some digging."

◈ ◈ ◈

Later that day, Dextraze pulled up in front of the MacFarland residence in Timmins, parking behind an RCMP cruiser. Since the mishaps involving MacFarland, he and his family were under 24-hour protection by the RCMP. Dextraze displayed his CSIS badge to the Constable sitting in the parked cruiser, then approached the front entrance to the house. He was invited in by Judy MacFarland, who warmly greeted him. Ironside, the family dog, ran up to him, barking enthusiastically until the MacFarland's daughter, Rebecca, called him away. Vincent MacFarland approached Dextraze, inviting him to have a drink.

"I gladly accept, as long as it's non-alcoholic. After all, I'm on duty."

Dextraze joined Judy and Vincent MacFarland in their living room.

"I suppose I was rather foolish to have made an appointment with the Iranian ambassador right after they tried to blow me up," said a chastened MacFarland.

"That's alright, Vince, we all make mistakes. The important thing is to learn from them," responded Dextraze.

MacFarland told Dextraze that he was now behaving himself, only reporting the most mundane of local trivia in The Weekly Current. He asked Dextraze how long the moratorium on reporting news on the missing corpse would last.

"I don't know how long, but it is still in effect," Dextraze told him.

MacFarland asked if Dextraze knew the identity of the headless corpse.

"Yes, we now have identified the body. You were very helpful in alerting us to the possibility that the victim was Russian. This is indeed the case."

MacFarland asked if there was any information on the victim that Dextraze could share.

"Other then the fact that he is Russian, and worked most of his life at nuclear power stations, I am not at liberty to disclose anything further."

"That's O.K.," MacFarland said. "I think the less I know the healthier I am. Ignorance is truly bliss."

Judy turned to her husband.

"I wonder if that's why he would have been around Lake Abitibi," interjected Judy.

"What do you mean?" her husband inquired.

"Well you know, I'm a science teacher. I'm just more aware of certain environmental issues that you are, honey."

"What environmental issues would you be referring to, Mrs. MacFarland?" asked Dextraze.

"Well, the background radiation level at Lake Abitibi is about four times normal. There are all kinds of theories and explanations. Maybe this Russian was investigating the mystery," said Judy.

Dextraze was intrigued. He asked her what the speculation was.

"Well, Mr. Dextraze, there used to be a lot of uranium mined in this area, so one theory was that an underwater uranium vein was the cause. That's kind of boring. There's another theory that my father has. It's kind of far-fetched, but more creative and interesting. This all happened before I was born, but he told me that many years ago, maybe forty or forty-five, a plane crashed into the lake. It was an American plane. Officially, it didn't have any bombs on board. My father said nobody believed that explanation and he remembers there being search teams that flew into Timmins and headed towards the lake with detection equipment, Geiger counters and all sorts of other paraphernalia. He told me there were American military personnel among the search party. But maybe this is all Northern Ontario's version of an urban legend."

❖ ❖ ❖

The following day, Dunlop was conferring in his office with Littlejohn when Dextraze buzzed the Deputy Director on his intercom. "I have discovered something vitally important," Dextraze said. Dunlop asked him to come into his office immediately.

Clutching photocopies of old newspaper articles, Dextraze appeared in Dunlop's office almost out of breath.

"Here it is, this is why these people were so interested in Lake Abitibi!" exclaimed Dextraze, as he placed a Xeroxed news report from The Ottawa Citizen on Dunlop's desk. Both he and Littlejohn scanned the report, which was dated October 26, 1962.

The headline ran, "American Bomber Crashes into Lake Abitibi."

A B-52 bomber of the U.S. Air Force Strategic Air Command crashed yesterday into Lake Abitibi while on a routine training flight; there were no survivors. Search teams were converging on the area to locate debris from the bomber, which may have washed ashore. The U.S. Air Force, through a spokesman, said that no nuclear weapons were aboard when the aircraft crashed.

"The story claims there were no nuclear munitions on board," Littlejohn said.

"Don't be so sure," responded Dunlop. "It wouldn't be the first time that the Americans have lied about such a matter. We need rapid confirmation."

Dunlop picked up his phone and quickly dialed the CIA headquarters in Langley, asking to be connected to the Director For Counter-Terrorism.

"David, this is Alex, are you on a secure line?"

Cole asked Dunlop to hold a moment, then confirmed he was now using a secure link.

"David, on October 25, 1962, a B-52 bomber of the Strategic Air Command crashed into Lake Abitibi. The press accounts at the time include official U.S. Air Force denials, claiming that no nuclear bombs were on the aircraft. It is imperative that I know exactly what was on or not on that aircraft when it disappeared."

Cole paused briefly, absorbing the importance of the new piece of information, and wracking his brains to quickly identify who could obtain answers for him, and do it quickly. He told Dunlop he would get on it right away. Cole turned to his computer monitor, and pulled up a list of Pentagon contacts and their phone numbers. He saw what he was looking for, the phone number for General Anderson, head of the Air Force Procurement Office at the Pentagon. Within minutes, he made contact with him.

The General knew who Cole was, and had met him on previous occasions. He understood that Cole had the authorization and security clearance to request information from him without restriction. The Director of Counter-Terrorism asked for all classified information that existed on the crash of the B-52 in Northern Ontario, and that priority was extremely high for a quick turnaround on his request.

It took about two hours before General Anderson phoned back with an answer.

"Mr. Cole, I have the information you requested, however, it is too sensitive, sir, to discuss over the phone. Would you be able to come over to the Pentagon?"

Cole told General Anderson he would be there within an hour. He drove at high speed from the moment he departed the CIA headquarters until he reached the visitors section at the Pentagon parking area. Looking stressed and fatigued, he entered the General's office. Anderson invited him to sit down.

"Mr. Cole, I think you'll understand why it is best we discuss this in person. As you mentioned, the news media was informed that no weapons were on board that aircraft when it crashed. We always give them that story if a nuclear-capable aircraft has an accident. It's to protect national security. However, and this is classified to the highest level of secrecy, there were four thermonuclear devices on that aircraft when it disappeared into the lake. Neither the aircraft nor the weapons were ever recovered."

"This is very distressing to learn, General," Cole said.

The General assumed Cole was more worried than the air force professionals were, as civilians would tend to exaggerate the danger.

"Sir, I don't know the reason for your inquiry, but please let me put your mind at ease, and place some context on this matter. We were all young in 1962, but that is the closest the world has ever come to nuclear war. That October the Cuban missile crisis occurred. Until the crisis was resolved, SAC had B-52s in the air constantly, fully armed, so they could nuke the Russians if so ordered. Fortunately, the crisis was resolved so SAC stood down. It was during the missile crisis that this B-52 went down, for some unexplained reason. There was an attempt to recover the aircraft and the weapons, but without success. It probably broke up and got covered with sediment at the bottom of the lake. The bottom line is that bomber, aircrew and weapons were lost without a trace."

Cole asked for an explanation on the dangers posed by thermonuclear bombs that had never been retrieved.

"Mr. Cole, I know the idea of a nuclear weapon being lost sounds dangerous to the general public. However, the danger is greatly exaggerated. The way these weapons are designed, they cannot undergo a nuclear detonation without the precise codes being entered. With the destruction of the aircraft and undoubtedly damage to the bombs, that is now physically impossible to do. The only dangers are from the conventional explosives, which form part of the bomb, and small leakages of radiation. Frankly, leaving them underwater is probably safer than any other alternative."

"You make the loss of four hydrogen bombs sound so routine, General. Is this normal?" asked Cole rhetorically.

"More normal than you might think," the General shot back. "During the Cold War, we and the Soviets each lost several dozen nuclear warheads. Some were lost in accidents involving ballistic missile submarines. Many others disappeared when bombers crashed over water. We actually have a term in the Air Force for this phenomenon; we call them *broken arrows*."

"Broken arrows?" repeated Cole with bewilderment.

"Yes, Mr. Cole. It's actually a very appropriate code word involving any accident or mishap involving an American nuclear weapon. A broken arrow can be a warhead that is destroyed in an accident, or is lost through a mishap. Officially, there have been 11 broken arrows since nuclear munitions entered our military's armories. The actual number is around fifty."

Cole asked General Anderson to provide him with full technical specifications on the weapons that were aboard the ill-fated B-52. He returned to his office late that evening and reached Dunlop at home.

"Alex, I have the answer to your question. It involves broken arrows. I will fly into Ottawa tomorrow morning to brief you. I recommend that you have along your top expert on nuclear weapons."

Mark 41

Alex Dunlop was grim-faced as he sat with Thomas Lazar, being briefed by David Cole. The CIA's Counter-Terrorism Director confirmed their worst fears about the B-52 that had gone down in Lake Abitibi 45 years ago.

"What type of nuclear weapons were on board, Mr. Cole?" inquired Dr. Lazar.

Referring to the specifications sheet provided to him by General Anderson, Cole read aloud the answer. "There were four Mark 41 thermonuclear devices, armed and fused for parachute retarded airburst."

Lazar nodded his head up and down, signaling his familiarity with the weapon. "I know this Mark 41 bomb well, I helped build it when I was at Lawrence Livermore," he said. "Mr. Cole, can you tell me if it was a class Y1 or Y2 version of the Mark 41?"

Cole stumbled at first, not being certain what Dr. Lazar was referring to. However, after briefly scanning the spec sheet, he found the information Lazar was seeking. "It says in the specifications that all four devices were the Y1 class of the Mark 41."

"Gentlemen, the four hydrogen bombs that were lost when the plane went down, and which presumably have been rediscovered by the terrorists, were the most powerful nuclear weapons ever built and deployed by the United States", Lazar said. "The Y2 class was the clean version of the weapon, it had a yield of 10 megatons, with relatively little radioactive fallout. However, the Y1 version of the Mark 41 device was much more powerful, and very dirty. Its designed yield was about 25 megatons, or equivalent to 25 million tons of TNT, with enormous quantities of radioactive fallout created."

Cole and Dunlop stared at each other, stunned. Trying to collect his thoughts, Cole posed a question to Lazar. "During 9/11, Al-Qaeda used our own airplanes as missiles to destroy the World Trade Center and damage the Pentagon. Could it be possible that they are now planning to use our own nuclear weapons to destroy an American city?"

Lazar did not think this likely. He explained why. "Even if they captured an intact nuclear weapon, or bought one which was stolen, it is virtually impossible for an unauthorized detonation to take place due to the safety and security devices consisting of permissive action links, or PALs. This is even more the case with a warhead that has been damaged in an airplane crash. There exists zero probability that those Mark 41 bombs can ever be detonated. It would be much easier to build one from scratch then attempt to repair and make operational the bombs aboard that aircraft."

"Then why go to all that trouble merely to retrieve non-functional nuclear weapons?" asked Dunlop.

Lazar answered without hesitation. "It is actually very logical," he said. "We have been trying to figure out how these terrorists could smuggle in fissile and other nuclear materials without being detected. This is how they do it. Instead of taking the risk of being detected, they merely retrieve the enriched uranium, plutonium, deuterium and tritium that has been lying in that plane wreckage underwater for forty-five years."

"You are absolutely right, Thomas," Dunlop said, absorbing the meaning of Lazar's explanation. "But what about tritium? As you told me earlier, it has a half life of only twelve years."

"That is correct, Alex. The small quantity of tritium and deuterium gas that is used to boost the primary, that is, the fission component of the Mark 41, would need to be renewed. However, the most important use of these isotopes is in the secondary, or fusion stage of the weapon. Instead of pure tritium and liquid deuterium, we created two capsules of Li6D, or lithium-deuteride. It is a solid, so neither the deuterium nor the lithium deteriorates.

When the primary in the weapon ignites, it instantly transforms the lithium into tritium."

"My God," Cole said. "How close are they to having a working hydrogen bomb?"

Dunlop had the same question, which Lazar answered.

"It really depends on three things," Lazar said. "Number one, they would require people with the proper skills to assemble the weapon. At this point, we must presume that they have the right people. Number two, they must have the fissile and other materials. The answer to that question depends on if they succeeded in locating and retrieving those four Mark 41s. I suggest, gentlemen, as a matter of the highest priority, that we seek verification on that point as quickly as possible."

Dunlop asked what the third requirement was.

"Even if they have the assembly teams and the critical materials, there is nothing they can do without a proven design," Lazar pointed out.

Cole asked if there was any possibility that the terrorists could recreate a 25-megaton Mark 41 bomb from the four devices they might have retrieved. Lazar answered in the negative. "Without detailed plans, that is physically impossible. The one thing I am certain of is that they do not have the design of the Mark 41. Even though the weapon is obsolete and was withdrawn from the American Air Force inventory decades ago, the design of the Mark 41 remains one of the most carefully guarded secrets."

Dunlop indicated that he would secure authorization from the highest levels of the Canadian government to mount an immediate search for the remains of the B-52 lying at the bottom of Lake Abitibi.

"While you conduct the search," Cole said, "I will speak with some of my colleagues at the CIA to explore the possibility that the Lion and his gang have surreptitiously obtained the plans for a working thermonuclear device."

❖ ❖ ❖

At CSIS headquarters, Littlejohn shared with Dextraze the information he had accumulated on the son-in-law of Dr. Pervaz Khan. It wasn't much.

"It was an arranged marriage, apparently," said Littlejohn. "Khan's daughter, Nadine, is a microbiologist working for the Canadian Research Council. She is thirty-four years old and, according to her colleagues, never dated men. She had the reputation of being both a workaholic and a loner. She received her Canadian citizenship five years ago. Five months ago she returned to Pakistan to marry Mohammed Iqbal. The two of them returned together to Ottawa four days after the wedding."

Dextraze acknowledged that this was not much of a honeymoon. Littlejohn showed his colleague a recent photograph of Mrs. Iqbal.

"She is rather homely looking, Pierre, wouldn't you say?"

Dextraze agreed that an arranged marriage was probably the only way Khan's daughter was going to be betrothed.

"I understand, Henry, that this is a common practice in Pakistan, where families decide on marriage partners and weddings without any prior involvement of the children."

"This is also an ideal way to gain entry into Canada, if you are a foreigner. As the husband of a Canadian citizen, the gates are wide open," replied Littlejohn.

Dextraze asked Littlejohn what, if anything, was known about Iqbal.

"Not much, Pierre. The documentation he submitted to Immigration stated he worked as a sales representative for a company called Crescent Industries. His father-in-law happens to serve on its board of directors."

"Is that a Pakistani firm?" inquired Dextraze.

Littlejohn informed his colleague that the company was actually based in Kuala Lumpur, Malaysia. He added that the Canadian embassy in Pakistan had been able to add only a few details about Mr. Iqbal. He was known to have gone to Afghanistan after the Soviet invasion, and to have fought with the Mujahadeen against the Russians.

"What do we know about Crescent Industries, Henry?"

Littlejohn relayed details that had been obtained regarding the Malaysian firm. It was a diversified industrial firm, to say the least. It was a partner in a satellite imaging company based in France that aided in geological and mining surveys. It had a plant in Malaysia that manufactured luminescent watch dials. It also had part ownership of several trucking firms in North America, one of which, based in Canada, specialized in transporting hazardous materials requiring special handling.

"I think Mr. Iqbal is clearly a person of interest," Dextraze told his colleague. "It is high time that we spoke to him directly."

"Pierre, this is more than questioning. He is a possible suspect in a murder," replied Littlejohn.

"In that case, let's talk to the RCMP about obtaining a search warrant," Dextraze told Littlejohn.

❖ ❖ ❖

At CIA headquarters, Dobbs's phone rang. It was Amelia Baldwin, with an update.

"Mr. Dobbs, there is an important change on the Al-Assad El-Islamiya website."

Dobbs asked her to immediately report to his office. When she arrived moments later, Dobbs had the website's homepage on his computer monitor.

"Sir, pull up the Message For Believers page," Amelia requested. She helped translate it for Dobbs.

"Oh Moslems, the fourth year anniversary on the Crusaders' calendar is a time to rejoice and not loathe. Fear not martyrdom, for it is the key opening the gates to paradise! Moslems of America! You may prepare for paradise as martyrs of Allah, praise be to him, who uses his instruments to prepare the doom of fire for the greatest Satan."

Dobbs noted that the message was much shorter than the last one. Amelia Baldwin's interpretation was more insightful.

"I believe there are two points that are very significant in this passage. He no longer warns Moslems to avoid being in America during the middle of March, which is in line with recent religious rulings issued by radical clerics who support Al-Qaeda. These rulings have provided a theological justification for launching attacks with weapons of mass destruction in the United States, even if many Moslems are also killed. This implies that there is no longer any restraint on how deadly the next attack on our country will be."

Dobbs asked Baldwin what the other point was.

"For the first time, I believe the Lion hints at a specific date for the next attack on America. In referring to the fourth year anniversary on the Crusader's calendar, he means the Christian calendar. He must be referring to March 20."

"March 20?" Dobbs replied, pausing only briefly. "But of course! March 20th, 2003 is when the United States invaded Iraq. He must be alluding to the fourth anniversary of the Iraqi war." Dobbs told Amelia he would relay the latest change on the Lion's website to David Cole on an urgent basis.

❖ ❖ ❖

It was about 7:00 PM when four RCMP vehicles silently but swiftly headed towards Orleans Street in a quiet residential area of Ottawa. They were followed by an unmarked car, with Dextraze driving and Littlejohn occupying the front passenger's seat. When they reached their destination, the vehicles were soon parked, their occupants taking position around a red brick two-story house. Three Constables, followed by Littlejohn and Dextraze, approached the front entrance and rang the doorbell. A short, Reubenesque-looking woman with olive complexion, coarse black hair and wearing thick plastic-framed glasses answered.

The Constables presented their identification, and asked to speak with Mohammed Iqbal.

"My husband is not home," the woman answered, who identified herself as Mrs. Iqbal.

"In that case," one of the Constables replied, "we have a warrant to search the premises."

"You have no right!" Nadine Iqbal cried out in panic. She was ignored, as the other Constables joined their three colleagues in conducting a thorough search of the entire house.

Littlejohn approached Nadine, asking her where her husband was.

"I don't know," she replied with frustration in her voice. "He told me he had to go on a business trip three days ago. He did not tell me where he was going or when he would be returning."

One of the Constables motioned for the two CSIS intelligence officers to come towards him. In a whisper, he told them, "There are no children in this house, but there are two occupied bedrooms. It appears, based on the bedding, clothing and other items found in each bedroom, Mr. and Mrs. Iqbal were not sleeping together."

"I see," Littlejohn said, absorbing the significance of the information.

"This arranged marriage may be an arrangement without love," Dextraze interjected. "In other words, a marriage of convenience, and not affection."

Dextraze and Littlejohn walked towards a nervous Nadine Iqbal.

"Mrs. Iqbal, I hope you do not think this question is insensitive," asked Dextraze cautiously. Continuing with trepidation, he said, "I ask this without implying any disrespect. Did you and your husband ever consummate your marriage?"

Nadine Iqbal's face contorted painfully. "How dare you insult my dignity!"

"This has nothing to do with your dignity," Littlejohn shot back. "If you consented to a marriage with Mr. Iqbal merely to enable him to enter Canada and not to live with him as his wife, then you have committed a serious criminal offense under the penal code."

"And if Mr. Iqbal has entered Canada with the intention of committing criminal acts," Dextraze added, "you will be charged as an accessory."

Nadine broke down, and tears flowed down her cheeks.

"Mrs. Iqbal, you may be an unwitting participant. If you are, then there is an important decision for you to make," cautioned Littlejohn. "You can talk to CSIS, and we will not disclose your involvement or, if you choose not to cooperate, our colleagues here from the RCMP will probably arrest you and pursue your situation as a criminal inquiry. What is your decision?"

Nadine Iqbal agreed to cooperate. While the RCMP Constables removed clothing and personal effects believed to belong to Mohammed Iqbal, she sat around a small dinette table in her kitchen, responding to questions from the two CSIS agents. She considered herself a loyal Canadian citizen, and was not a deeply devout Moslem. However, she still considered herself a Moslem woman, and felt bound by tradition to total obedience to her father. When Dr. Khan told her about six months ago she had an important duty as the daughter of a Moslem man to return to Pakistan to marry a man she had neither met nor knew, she did as her father dictated. She understood that the marriage was a sham, a subterfuge to enable Mohammed Iqbal to enter Canada as an immigrant married to a Canadian citizen and subsequently create a basis for Dr. Pervaz Khan to obtain a visitors visa from the Canadian embassy in Islamabad. She was otherwise ignorant of what her husband and father were collaborating on in Canada.

❖ ❖ ❖

The following afternoon Dextraze and his colleague reported to Dunlop on what had been learned from the search of the Iqbals's house. The two agents were convinced that Nadine Iqbal was unwittingly used by her father and "husband," having no specific knowledge of what they were up to.

"Mr. Dunlop, we also have the results from the tests run by the RCMP laboratory on Mohammed Iqbal's clothing," Dextraze said in a voice suggesting their seriousness. "There were traces of plutonium, uranium 235 and 238, deuterium and tritium."

"This Mr. Iqbal is clearly a key player in this plot," Dunlop said. "We need to find out who he is and apprehend him."

Littlejohn pointed out that Iqbal was likely not his real name. "The embassy in Islamabad now believes the documents he submitted to obtain his immigrant's visa were forgeries, except for the Pakistani wedding certificate."

Dunlop asked if the embassy had relayed any other details of interest.

"Yes, there are a couple of physical characteristics concerning this gentleman," Littlejohn told the Deputy Director. "The immigration officer at the embassy who met with him recalls that he was left-handed. He remembers that clearly because part of Iqbal's middle finger was missing. He asked him about it, and Iqbal proudly told the officer that it was a war wound he received while fighting the Soviet infidels in Afghanistan."

Dunlop shared with his two agents what was happening on Lake Abitibi since they had verified that the B-52 that had crashed into its waters 45 years ago carried thermonuclear weapons. "Technology has evolved since the crash of that aircraft in 1962. The water depth of Lake Abitibi is actually quite shallow for such a large body of water. The problem is the sediment at the bottom. Due to the force of impact, the aircraft, or what was left of it, was probably swallowed up by the sediment. However, one of Crescent Industries subsidiaries conducts satellite imagery for geological and mining surveys. That technology can differentiate metal from other objects underwater at shallow depths, due to the differential temperatures. We conducted our own imaging of the lake, and believe we have found the possible impact site. It is under about four meters of water. The Department of National Defense brought a team into the area this morning, and they are due to start their excavation and salvage work early tomorrow morning."

Santa Fe

A combined team of civilian workers and military engineers were busy working on a barge on Lake Abitibi, approximately 300 meters from the shoreline. A boat stood moored to the barge, where senior officers and civilian salvage experts were supervising the operation. Underwater, the divers worked alongside the broken remains of the B-52 bomber. The wings were separated from the fuselage, lying crumpled on the floor of the lake. Through a crack in the front of the fuselage, divers entered with underwater TV cameras, which recorded what was being discovered in real-time for the team aboard the boat.

Once the divers were inside the aircraft, they turned toward the cockpit. Still strapped to their seats were the skeletal remains of the pilot and copilot, their flight helmets partially covering exposed skulls. The divers turned away from the cockpit and entered the main section of the fuselage. Debris littered the interior of the aircraft, testifying to the violence of final impact. Through an opening in the floor, the divers penetrated into the bomb bay. They slowly panned their cameras and underwater lights in circular fashion, observing the interior of the bomb bay in detail. It was empty.

Aboard the boat, a senior military officer had been keenly observing the images being transmitted by the divers to television monitors. He picked up a satellite phone and dialed Alex Dunlop at his office at CSIS headquarters in Ottawa. The CSIS Deputy Directory picked up the phone and heard the report he had been expecting, and dreading. "Mr. Dunlop, we have completed our underwater survey of the wrecked aircraft, and I can confirm that there is no ordnance remaining on board."

Dunlop reflected briefly, then put in a call to David Cole. He informed him of the results of the salvage operation on Lake Abitibi. Speaking over his secure line, Cole was grim in his response. "There is no doubt about it now," he said with despair in his voice. "They have all the principle materials they need to build a hydrogen bomb."

Dunlop reminded his CIA colleague of what Dr. Lazar had told them at their meeting. "David, there is still the question of a design for the weapon."

Cole told Dunlop that during the Cold War a number of physicists and technicians who had worked at Arzamas-16 had defected to the CIA. He was trying to track down any defectors still alive who might have known Boris Fedorenko and could possibly shed some light on what weapon designs he would have had access to.

Upon concluding his conversation with Dunlop, Cole turned towards Amelia Baldwin, who was seated in his office. Dobbs had informed him of her latest translation of key sections of the Al-Assad El-Islamiya website, and its disturbing implications.

"Amelia, as you can probably gleam from my conversation with a Canadian colleague, we are facing a terrifying possibility."

Baldwin sat silently, her eyes focused as though staring at an approaching train roaring through a narrow tunnel at high velocity. Cole continued to speak. "I am meeting this afternoon with the Secretary for Homeland Security. I have been unable to light a fire in his gut. I must try again and I want you to join me. Let's hope your insights on the websites and sermons you have been translating compel Mendick to open his eyes before we all live to regret his complacency."

Later that day, Cole and Amelia Baldwin sat in the reception area of Mendick's office. Cole anxiously glanced at his watch. "Our appointment was supposed to start forty-five minutes ago," he whispered to Amelia in frustration. A moment later Mendick's executive assistant, a voluptuous brunette with dark brown eyes, informed the visitors from the CIA that the Secretary was now ready to meet with them.

In Mendick's office, the Director for Counter-Terrorism attempted valiantly to convey the growing urgency of the threat being posed by the Lion. "Since our last meeting with the Vice President," Cole said, "the Canadians have discovered the remains of one of our B-52s that crashed in Northern Ontario forty-five years ago. I was able to confirm through the Pentagon that four high-yield thermonuclear bombs were aboard the aircraft when it went down. The Canadians have conducted a thorough search and inform me that all four hydrogen bombs are missing."

"So," uttered Mendick, his body language conveying impatience.

"Do you realize, Mr. Secretary, that those bombs, even if they are non-functional, contain enough plutonium, enriched uranium and hydrogen isotopes to build a device that can not only heavily damage, but likely totally destroy any one of our largest cities?"

Mendick's reply indicated a lack of concern. He felt this was a Canadian problem, and was assured that merely obtaining components from obsolete bombs heavily damaged in an ancient air disaster was not in itself sufficient for building a functioning nuclear weapon. At this point, Cole asked Amelia to share her analysis of the most recent trends in Jihadist websites and sermons.

"Mr. Mendick, since the time of the Lion's disappearance in Iraq, his website has been predicting an attack on America for sometime in March that would far exceed what occurred on September 11th. Most recently, we have translated sermons from radical Islamic clerics, especially ones known to have connections to Al-Qaeda. These recent sermons provide a theological justification for a mass casualty attack on our country, even if American Moslems also die."

As Amelia spoke, Mendick's eyes lit up as he stared directly at her, giving the impression of absorbing the importance of what she had said.

"Hmm, Ms. Baldwin, that is interesting. Well, maybe we do need to pay more attention to those websites and sermons. Why don't you and Mr. Cole continue to keep me updated," Mendick said with a smile.

◈ ◈ ◈

Littlejohn was briefing the Deputy Director at CSIS headquarters regarding new information concerning Crescent Industries, of which Mohammed Iqbal was supposedly an employee. It transpired that the Malaysian-based company had tentacles reaching into Canada.

"Mr. Dunlop, Crescent has partial ownership of a company called Signar Transport. They specialize in transporting hazardous waste and volatile chemical compounds. Their business includes the shipping of liquid deuterium to nuclear power reactors. They have a subsidiary called Malaya Metals, which purchases scrap metal overseas, and has made several shipments to Canada. Recently, they have been buying up depleted uranium ammunition from the battlefields of Kuwait."

Dunlop was forming a mental picture of what this information added up to. He asked Littlejohn if any other aspects of Crescent Industries were worthy of note.

"There is one other piece of information, sir. They have another subsidiary called the Monsoon Watch Company. They manufacture luminescent watch dials in Malaysia, and shipped a large consignment to Vancouver more than three months ago. The RCMP checked the shipping address, which turned out to be fictitious."

"What would be their motive for sending a quantity of watch dials to a phony address in Canada?" inquired Dunlop. Littlejohn thought for a moment, uncertain of the reason. Then Dunlop realized he could answer his own question.

"You did say those watch dials are luminous, Henry, right?"

"Yes, Mr. Dunlop," Littlejohn responded, now realizing what the connection was. "I think I see exactly what you are alluding to. They use tritium in their watch dials."

◈ ◈ ◈

At the Sheraton Hotel in downtown Washington, Cole met with a senior colleague from the CIA. They shared early evening cocktails, Cole having a gin and tonic while Bernard Hubbard nursed his Manhattan on the rocks. Hubbard was responsible for arrangements for a small army of Cold War defectors from the Soviet Union now residing in different parts of the United States, all under assumed names.

"Bernie, you understand why I need your help?"

"Of course, David. I think I found the right defector," Hubbard told his colleague. "He was at Arzamas-16 from 1959 until 1970 as a technician. He not only knew Boris Fedorenko, he even supervised him at one point."

Cole briefly smiled. It was a piece of good news. "Who is he, Bernie?"

"You know the agency rules on defectors," Hubbard responded. "I'll have to keep his assumed identity under wraps. Let's just call him Mr.Ivanov, for our purposes. He's retired now, living near Santa Fe, New Mexico. When we first brought him here, we had him debriefed at Los Alamos. He was a gold mine of information on Soviet nuclear weapons construction. Afterwards, we set him up with a job at Sandia Laboratories in Albuquerque."

"How soon can you arrange a meeting?" asked Cole with anticipation.

"I have the impression, David, that this is kind of urgent."

"You're damned right it is!" exclaimed Cole in a determined manner.

Hubbard thought he could set up a meeting in Santa Fe in about two days. Besides contacting the defector, he would need to secure a safe house for the meeting.

Cole accepted the arrangement, adding that he would be asking the Deputy Director of the Canadian Security Intelligence Service to join him.

❖ ❖ ❖

At the airport in Albuquerque, Dunlop had just exited from his aircraft carrying an overnight bag, when he saw David Cole waving to him in the arrival lounge. He waved back at his CIA colleague, and the two men soon discussed their itinerary. Cole had a rental car waiting, and they would travel together to a safe house on the outskirts of Santa Fe.

"Alex, I don't know this defector's name, or rather, I'm not supposed to know. We'll just refer to him as Mr. Ivanov."

"I hope, David, he can shed light on what Boris Fedorenko knows," Dunlop replied, feeling acute anxiety about the meeting as the two intelligence men picked up their automobile for the roughly ninety minute drive.

During the journey to Santa Fe, Cole remarked on the desert landscape. "You know, Alex, it was here in the New Mexico desert that the first atomic bomb was built and tested. As I look at the emptiness that surround us, it conjures up the image of how the planet would look after a nuclear war."

Dunlop peered out of the car window, as their vehicle thundered down the interstate at eighty miles per hour. He too noticed the desolate void that enveloped the highway. His impression, however, was somewhat less melancholy than Cole's. "Didn't the artist Georgia O'Keefe spend the latter part of her life in this area, and create some of her greatest paintings here?"

"That's right, Alex. She spent her latter years creating iconoclastic images of the skulls of cows being bleached in the sand."

After about an hour and a half, Cole found the address they were looking for. It was a rented bungalow just outside of Santa Fe, surrounded by poplar trees, overlooking a mountain range. When they rang the doorbell, a well dressed, tall man in his thirties answered. "We've been expecting you," he said. "I'll just need to verify your credentials." After presenting the requested IDs, Cole and Dunlop were escorted to a living room consisting of an armchair and sofa, coffee table and ersatz plants. The security man offered them iced tea, and shortly returned with the drinks and an elderly gentleman of medium height and build, with white hair combed back in the Slavic style. He wore a pair of cotton slacks and a short sleeved tropical sports shirt, with an 18 carat gold Rolex watch worn conspicuously on his left wrist.

Cole and Dunlop stood up with outstretched hands. "Mr. Ivanov, I presume," said Cole.

"I guess you can refer to me by that name, for the purpose of this discussion," replied Ivanov. "How can I be of assistance to you two gentlemen?"

Cole explained that their sole purpose was to learn all they could about Boris Fedorenko while he worked at Arzamas-16.

"I definitely remember him. If my memory serves me correctly, he was at the Institute for three years in the early 1960's." Ivanov spoke with a distinct Russian accent, though his command of English was impeccable.

"What precisely was his job?" inquired Dunlop with unrestrained curiosity.

"He was a machinist tasked with precision metal fittings for bomb assemblies. To be more specific, key components of thermonuclear bombs."

"Did he have any specialized skill?" asked Cole, who was seeking to form an impression of what this man could possibly do for a terrorist organization determined to construct an advanced nuclear device.

"Funny you should ask," said Ivanov with a thin smile. "He indeed had a very important, you might say critical area of specialization. He was responsible for assembling fusion tampers for hydrogen bombs."

Both Dunlop and Cole looked at each other with profound puzzlement. Ivanov noticed their mutual bewilderment.

"I can see from the look on your faces that you two gentlemen are sort of lost in space," Ivanov noted with empathy.

"I suppose you could say that," replied Cole.

Ivanov went on to explain in layman's language precisely what a fusion tamper was.

"I will not bore you with a complex physics lecture," Ivanov told his guests. "I'll presume you know the fundamental basics of thermonuclear weapons design, that is, you have a fission bomb generate massive heat, which in turn ignites the thermonuclear fuel capsules, inducing fusion."

"We're with you so far," Dunlop said cautiously.

"What you must understand is that if fusion occurs too rapidly, the yield of the weapon is much lower. The fusion tamper is a specially constructed metal sheathing that prevents premature fusion from occurring, while simultaneously building up the density of the fuel capsule. That way, the explosive yield is significantly higher." Ivanov paused briefly, then asked laconically, "Does that make sense?"

"I think we get the general picture," Cole said, turning towards Dunlop, who inquired as to the type of metal that the tamper would be fabricated from.

"Well, that all depends on what type of explosion you desire. If the requirement is for a clean weapon, meaning very little radioactive fallout, you ideally would construct the tamper with a metal such as lead. However, if you wish for both a bigger explosive yield and large quantities of radioactive fallout, the fusion tamper must be fabricated with uranium, and that demands even greater skill, which Boris Fedorenko was very accomplished at," replied Ivanov.

Dunlop's mind was racing, compelling him to ask a very specific question. "Mr. Ivanov, if you were to build a high-yield dirty hydrogen bomb, would you need to use enriched uranium for the tamper, as with other parts of the device?"

Smiling widely, and talking in an expansive manner, Ivanov responded with his explanation. "No, you do not need to enrich the uranium in building the tamper. That is the beauty of fusion. The heat generated by the process is so intense that ordinary, garden-variety uranium 238 undergoes fission. At the temperatures involved, it would be a complete waste of money to utilize enriched uranium."

Alex Dunlop stared briefly at David Cole, sweat beginning to emerge from his brow. He turned his gaze back towards Ivanov, continuing his line of inquiry. "Mr. Ivanov, could, for example, depleted uranium be used in the construction of a fusion tamper?"

Ivanov took on the demeanor of a schoolmaster, seeking to enlighten his pupils. "Well, what is depleted uranium? It is uranium that had been used in power reactors that has had all the enriched components, the uranium 235 isotopes, removed. That is why it is called depleted uranium, which really means it is the common element uranium 238. That is exactly what would be used to build the fusion tamper, assuming you want to create a thermonuclear device that is powerful and dirty."

As Cole and Dunlop sought to absorb the information that had been imparted to them, Ivanov briefly glanced at his Rolex. As he did so, Alex Dunlop noticed a familiar tattoo on the defector's left arm. He squinted his eyes to form a sharper perspective, which caught Ivanov's attention.

"I see you are intrigued by my old tattoo," Ivanov interjected.

"I've seen that same tattoo on one other man," Dunlop said. "It was on the arm of Boris Fedorenko."

"Is there something about that tattoo that's significant?" asked Cole, intrigued by the link between the defector and the dead Russian nuclear machinist.

With a look of intense pride, Ivanov elaborated on the symbolic significance of the tattoo. "These two Russian letters, tseh and beh, stand for *Tsar Bomba.*"

"Tsar Bomba?" Cole repeated with an inquisitive grimace on his face.

"Yes, that is Russian for the *King of Bombs.*"

Both Cole and Dunlop shared expressions of bewilderment, which only prompted Ivanov to smile even wider.

"You see, gentlemen," he said, "the Soviet Union had a bankrupt economy. It produced glue that would not stick, door locks that did not lock and trains that never ran on time. But it also designed and produced the world's most powerful bomb, and that, my friends did work as planned."

An even more frightening picture was rapidly forming in Dunlop's mind, as he mentally filled in the missing dots linking Fedorenko to an extremist Islamic terrorist group determined to build a thermonuclear weapon.

"Tell us more about Tsar Bomba," Cole inquired with intensity.

"Well, gentlemen, it was really designed as a propaganda weapon," Ivanov told his guests. "Back in the summer of 1961, the Soviet Union was preparing to build the Berlin Wall. The Kremlin knew this would increase tensions with the West, so to discourage any NATO interference with construction of the wall in East Berlin, the Communist Party Secretary, Nikita Khrushchev, summoned the head of our Institute, Dr. Andrei Sakharov, to meet with him personally. Khrushchev instructed Sakharov to design and build a 100 megaton nuclear device and have it ready for testing within 16 weeks."

Both Cole and Dunlop were mesmerized. They listened almost hypnotically as Ivanov continued his description of this massive weapon.

"As you can imagine, to design such a weapon from scratch and then build it within a very confined period of time was a challenging undertaking. Both the designers and builders had to function in a spirit of close cooperation, working literally non-stop until the device was ready. In fact, we beat Khrushchev's deadline by two weeks; we had the device ready for testing in only 14 weeks. It was quite a feat, especially since the largest yield thermonuclear bomb we had built before that project was only three megatons."

Dunlop asked if the weapon was actually tested.

"That was the whole purpose of building the device, to conduct a demonstration that would intimidate the West. About two weeks after the device, which was code named Tsar Bomba, had been completed, we conducted a test. We were convinced that if the device had uranium fusion tampers installed, the actual yield would be significantly more than what Khrushchev desired, probably in the range of 150 megatons. However, such an enormous blast and release of radioactivity would have caused major collateral damage to populated areas of the USSR, even though the device would be detonated over a remote region. We therefore constructed the fusion tampers out of lead, rather than uranium. We thought that would reduce the yield to 50 megatons. The device was released by parachute from a specially modified TU-95 bomber from an altitude of 10,500 meters over the west coast of Novaya Zemlya Island and detonated at a height of 4,000 meters. What followed was the most massive man-made explosion ever. The fireball from the bomb was visible to a distance in excess of 1,000 kilometers. The blast caused damage over a range of hundreds of kilometers. We later calculated that the yield was far more than we had expected based on the design. The power of the explosion exceeded 58 megatons, or 58 million tons of TNT. It turned out that Boris Fedorenko had constructed the fusion tampers with such skill and precision that its performance exceeded the specifications called for in the original design of the bomb."

As Ivanov was explaining this awesome weapon and the context of its development, the two intelligence officers were simultaneously reminded of what Dr. Lazar had told them; the terrorists, in order to build a functioning thermonuclear device, assuming they had the materials and personnel required for bomb assembly, still required a proven design.

"Mr. Ivanov, would Boris Fedorenko have had access to the entire design and blueprints of the Tsar Bomba?" inquired Cole nervously, as Dunlop grimaced.

Ivanov nodded in the affirmative. "The pressure was intense to design and build this device from scratch. As new calculations were constantly being made and design changes created on the spot, we all took notes and made our own blueprints. It would not have been possible to fulfill Khrushchev's task without all the members of the design and fabrication team being on the same page."

Dunlop directed a follow-up question. "Mr. Ivanov, after the weapon was tested, how likely is it that Fedorenko would have been able to retain his hand written notes and blueprints of the bomb's design?"

"Very likely," Ivanov answered without hesitation. "We were all proud of our achievement, especially those involved in the actual assembly of the weapon, the technicians and machinists. That is why we all got this tattoo, as a souvenir of our project," he said beaming, pointing to the tattoo on his left arm with pride. "None of us, I am certain, discarded our design notes and drawings. Probably due to bureaucratic inefficiency, there was never an attempt made to confiscate them."

"One thing I am very curious about," Cole said with perplexity. "If Fedorenko was so good at his job with the Institute, why was he transferred to work on mundane nuclear power reactors?"

"Ah, your question shows you are not familiar with changes in nuclear strategy and weapons design," Ivanov said with a mischievous look in his eyes. "The Tsar Bomba was totally useless as a weapon. The same thing for very large American hydrogen bombs. They were designed to be carried by big, slow jet bombers that would never have made it to their targets in the face of modern defenses, radars, interceptors and surface-to-air missiles. Both the Soviet Union and America in the 1960's began switching from bombers to ballistic missiles as their primary strategic delivery systems. The great advantage with missiles is that they are reliable; you can count on them to hit their targets. On the other hand, the nose cone of a missile has only a fraction of the volume found in the bomb bay of an obsolete bomber, like the Soviet TU-95 or your American B-52. That meant the conversion to designing and building much smaller thermonuclear bombs, with a fraction of the yield of the earliest generation. However, that is more than compensated for by the ability to deliver far more warheads to their targets, with much greater accuracy. What this meant for a man like Fedorenko is that his specific skills were made redundant, as they were not transferable to fabricating the tampers of much smaller weapons that have yields in only the tens or hundreds of kilotons. I remember when he was notified of his transfer away from our Institute and I recall he was most unhappy with that development."

"I am left with one question," Alex Dunlop asked in a quiet yet ominous tone of voice. "Could Fedorenko have smuggled his copy of the Tsar Bomba design out of Russia?"

"Well, Mr. Dunlop," replied Ivanov, "the Russia of today has much looser security than did the Soviet Union I defected from more than thirty years ago. Yet, I was able to bring out my copy of the Tsar Bomba design without difficulty. It is probably still residing somewhere in the CIA archives."

Tsar Bomba

As Cole and Dunlop drove back towards Albuquerque, grim-faced, they stared forward, silently, for several minutes, until the CIA Counter-Terrorism Director broke the ice.

"David, since we both have some time to kill before our flights, I arranged a brief side trip to Kirkland Air Force Base in Albuquerque. It's the site of the National Atomic Museum. They have exact replicas of actual nuclear weapons. I thought it would be helpful for both of us to see what we are dealing with. At the very least, our understanding of the threat may be less academic."

At Kirkland Air Force Base they stopped at the security gate, and were directed to a parking lot, where a waiting van shuttled them to the museum. At the entrance to the museum an officer was waiting for the two men.

"Good afternoon gentlemen, I'm Major Gleason, and I'll be escorting you through the museum." The National Atomic Museum was an unusual museum, requiring security clearance before being allowed entrance. Once inside the exhibition hall, Cole and Dunlop discovered that they were the only visitors. They followed the Major through a series of replicas representing, in chronological order, America's nuclear weapons development, starting with the "Little Boy" and "Fat Man" bombs that had been dropped on Hiroshima and Nagasaki. They glanced briefly at most of the replicas, pausing somewhat longer while standing in front of the mock-up of a Mark 41 bomb.

"Major, it's not as large as I expected to be," remarked Cole.

"Not large at all," replied the Major, "considering it had a yield of 25 megatons. I think it would fit underneath my dining table."

At the end of the American exhibit, the three men observed replicas to exact scale of the warheads that fit into the nose cone of a Trident missile. Reading the placard in front of the model, Cole and Dunlop noted that eight independently targeted warheads could fit in each missile's nosecone. "I see it has a yield of 100 kilotons, but it could fit in the back of my wife's van," Dunlop noted. "And yet, it is more than five times as powerful as the bomb that leveled Hiroshima," the Major replied. He then pointed towards another exhibit at the other end of the hall. "That's the Russian weapons exhibit."

As they walked towards the Russian exhibit, Cole and Dunlop observed how similar the weapons were in appearance compared to their American counterparts of each generation. Then, towards the end of the exhibit, both men saw a large, cylindrical object with a radically different configuration in contrast with the other weapons in both the American and Russian exhibits. Its dull metallic color gave it a sinister hue. Major Gleason took notice of the direction both Cole and Dunlop had focused on. "That's a new addition to our exhibition, on loan from the Russian Atomic Museum," said the Major with unrestrained pride. "It's the only existing replica of the bomb casing of a device known as Tsar Bomba, or the King of Bombs. Shall we go over and have a look?"

The three men shuffled towards the object, which appeared both massive yet strangely elegant, with a bulbous front and gracefully tapering middle and rear section. From the front, two parallel probes extended outwards. Feeling both awe and foreboding, Dunlop read the placard that stood in front of the replica aloud:

"RDS-220, code named Tsar Bomba (King of Bombs). Most powerful nuclear device ever tested. Number built: 1. Tested: October 23, 1961. Yield: 58 megatons. Weight: 24.8 metric tons, or 27 standard tons. Dimensions: Length 8 meters, Diameter 2 meters. Additional Information: This device was not fully fueled at time of test, to reduce yield and radioactive fallout during testing.

Had RDS-220 been fully fueled, the yield would have been in the range of 100-150 megatons."

"Major, I don't know how large your dining table is," said a shaken David Cole, "but I know this device could fit in the garage of my house in Virginia."

❖ ❖ ❖

Pierre Dextraze had flown to Toronto for a meeting with a trusted source. He was Javid Ali, who ran a lucrative import-export firm. Dextraze took a taxi from the airport to a twelve-story office building on Bloor Street. Carrying a briefcase, he got off on the ninth floor and immediately spotted Ali's inconspicuous office door. Upon entering, the receptionist notified Ali that his visitor had arrived, and escorted Dextraze to his office. Ali, a tall man with thick black hair, graying at the temples, with an eagle-like nose and immaculately trimmed moustache, warmly greeted his guest. He offered him coffee, which Dextraze gladly accepted. They engaged in small talk for a few minutes, asking each other about their wives and children, until the receptionist arrived with their coffees. Ali then instructed her that they were not to be disturbed. Obediently, she closed the office door, and the conversation ensued in earnest.

Ali was a Pakistani expatriate who had immigrated to Canada fourteen years ago. He had come from a distinguished and affluent family, and had served as senior officer in his country's army, being educated at the Royal Military Academy in Sandhurst, England. After rising to the rank of Colonel, he was transferred to the Directorate for Inter-Services Intelligence, or ISI, Pakistan's spy agency. During the nine years he was affiliated with ISI, he became deeply disillusioned. Rather than serving the mission of protecting his country's security, it had become a state-within-a-state, corrupt, stained with drug money, and increasingly in alliance with radical Islamic extremists. His estrangement from the ISI had led to his alienation from Pakistani society, and subsequent self-imposed exile to North America. He was an important source of information for CSIS, and had already met with Dextraze several times.

"Pierre, how can I be of service to CSIS this morning?" Ali asked in a low-key manner.

"We are trying to build a dossier on an individual we believe is a Pakistani national," replied Dextraze, as he pulled out several photographs from his briefcase and placed them in front of Ali. "He entered Canada on an immigrant's visa after marrying a Canadian citizen," he added. "The name he used was Mohammed Iqbal, but we have doubts that this is his true name."

Ali scanned the photographic images, which displayed a man with a narrow face, in most cases wearing sunglasses. He briefly smiled, emitting a shallow burst of laughter as he turned towards Dextraze.

"I do recognize this man, Pierre. And you are right, Mohammed Iqbal is not his real name. He is Aziz Faruqui. A very dangerous man, if I may say so."

Dextraze asked Ali to share whatever information he had on Faruqui.

"He came from the Northwest Province of Pakistan, in one of the tribal areas. Faruqui attended a religious school, what are referred to as madrassas, like most boys in the tribal regions. He apparently excelled in his studies, and, showed an aptitude for science, so he enrolled in a chemistry program at a college in Karachi. He spent three years in the army, and was trained as an explosives expert. After completing his military service, Faruqui obtained a scholarship to attend an advanced chemistry program at a university in the Netherlands. It's kind of ironic how Western institutions are so enthusiastic about granting scholarships to militant Islamic adherents, so they can come over to their universities and learn to how to better kill them later, Pierre."

Nodding his head in agreement, Dextraze asked Ali what he had specifically learned while pursuing his studies in the Netherlands.

"He learned two things of importance, Pierre. He studied the use of advanced explosives for industrial purposes. Then there was the second thing he learned, the important work being done by Pervaz Khan, who was in the Netherlands at the same time as Faruqui."

"Do you mean that Faruqui was in Europe when Khan was also there, establishing his black market network for smuggling illicit and dual-use technology for the secret Pakistani nuclear weapons program?" Dextraze inquired.

"What I can tell you is that Khan recruited Faruqui, who played a leading rule in smuggling centrifuges into Pakistan. It was those centrifuges that enabled the Pakistani military to enrich uranium for building atomic bombs."

Dextraze asked what else Ali knew about the relationship between Pervaz Khan and Aziz Faruqui.

"They became very close. I remember Dr. Khan once telling a group of ISI officers that Faruqui was the son he wished he had. Khan had three daughters, and he ended up treating Faruqui as though he was an adopted son, though his own children never met him. When he returned to Pakistan, Faruqui was recruited by the ISI, and played an important role in assisting the Mujahadeen in fighting the Russians in Afghanistan. He was one of the leading explosives experts in the ISI, and was involved in many covert operations, in both Afghanistan and in Kashmir, against the Indians. However, he always maintained close ties to Dr. Khan, and I know he was involved in helping to build some of the first atomic weapons in Pakistan."

Dextraze was curious about the role Faruqui would have had in assisting Dr. Khan in building nuclear weapons.

"Well, Pierre, I'm no atomic physicist. However, from what I was briefed on, conventional explosives must be carefully designed and situated in order to set off a chain reaction in an atomic bomb. That was apparently the role Pervaz Khan assigned to Faruqui. What he didn't already learn in the Netherlands, I'm certain Dr. Khan instructed him on."

"Tell me, Javid, what was Faruqui's precise role in Afghanistan?" Dextraze asked, as he felt increasing fascination and fear about this enigmatic Pakistani.

"Faruqui was a liaison between the ISI and the most religiously fanatic tribesmen fighting the Russians. His precise role was equipping and training militants in the use of explosives. He was very adept at bomb making, and he had a taste, I dare say a lust, for violence. He personally went on many missions with the Mujahadeen."

Dextraze asked about Faruqui's injury while fighting in Afghanistan.

"He was with some tribesmen infiltrating the mountain passes in Tora Bora when they were attacked by Russian helicopter gunships. Most of them were wiped out, and he lost part of a finger from an exploding rocket. But I can assure you, he got even." Continuing his description of Faruqui, he portrayed a man obsessed with destroying his enemies. "This guy would personally kill every Russian prisoner he lay hands on, after interrogations were completed, of course. He enjoyed killing them by cutting their heads off, slowly, with a knife. He boasted to his friends that it was a knife given to him as a present by the mullah at the madrassa he attended in the Northwest Province."

"Was Aziz Faruqui in any way connected to Al-Qaeda?" asked Dextraze.

"For sure, as was the whole ISI working the Afghanistan operation. They were all in bed with Osama bin Laden and his friends. What is bizarre in retrospect is that the CIA was giving money and weapons to the ISI to funnel to bin Laden's organization. The Americans, in their naiveté, thought that bin Laden and his followers were anti-Communist, when they were actually anti-infidel, be they Russian or American."

The CSIS intelligence officer was eager to know what Faruqui had been up to after the Russians left Afghanistan. Javid Ali indicated that Faruqui was heavily involved in assisting Pervaz Khan in his work in building the Pakistani nuclear weapons program.

"Pierre, what you must understand about Pakistan's atomic weapons program is that it was built entirely on lies, corruption, greed, deception and the black market. Khan was the kind of man who traveled very easily in that world, and Aziz Faruqui was his eager apprentice. Together, they were indispensable. Faruqui was also an important player in the ISI's continuing involvement in Afghanistan. You do know that it was the Pakistani intelligence service that put the Taliban, those medieval bastards, in power in Afghanistan."

Dextraze acknowledged that he was aware of the linkage. The burning question in his mind was what Faruqui was doing in Canada.

"Javid, if you had to guess, what do you think Faruqui is up to in Canada?"

Javid Ali paused for a moment, reflecting. He then proceeded to answer Dextraze's question.

"Pierre, my best guess is that he is using Canada as a way to get into the United States and launch some type of operation, a follow-up to 9/11. He has a pathological hatred of Americans, and is a fanatical believer in jihad."

❖ ❖ ❖

It was late afternoon as Bill Mendick exited his office, carrying his briefcase. He stopped briefly at a receptionist's desk. "Please call my wife and tell her I won't be home tonight. The President has given me a special task that will keep me occupied the entire evening."

The Secretary of Homeland Security walked past the receptionist's desk, pausing only when she called for him. He twisted his head to the rear, grinning with impatience.

"Mr. Mendick, don't you have a 5:30 PM appointment with Mr. Cole from the CIA? He did say it was urgent."

Mendick's face went blank for a moment, then his eyes lit up. "Oh, yes, he called me after scheduling the appointment and decided to cancel it."

"Cancel it?" repeated the receptionist.

"That's right," repeated a harried Mendick, as he swiftly left the office.

An hour after Mendick departed, Cole arrived. He identified himself to the receptionist, who stared at him open mouthed and aghast.

"Mr. Cole, the Secretary left about an hour ago and told me you had canceled the meeting."

Cole was flabbergasted. He yelled "What!" in a voice so loud, it drew the attention of all the nearby secretaries and clerical staff.

Only partially recovering his decorum, he added, "I did no such thing! This is an urgent matter! Where is Secretary Mendick?"

He looked around the office suite, noticing pained expressions on many faces. He then turned towards the receptionist, asking her where Mendick's executive assistant was. The receptionist informed him that she had taken the day off due to illness.

The CIA's Counter-Terrorism Director looked around the office suite, his face red with anger. He spoke in a voice reflecting his deep sense of outrage. "This is supposed to be the Department of Homeland Security! Is there one person in this room who knows how to reach the Secretary in the event of an emergency?"

One of the secretaries spoke hesitatingly. "I have Mr. Mendick's cell phone number, sir. I can try to reach him."

"Please do so now," Cole told her in a voice straining with aggravation.

The secretary pulled up Mendick's cellular number from the rolodex on her computer monitor, and proceeded to dial it. Several blocks away, in the apartment of Mendick's attractive executive assistant, the sound of a ringing cell phone emanated from a suit jacket, which hung lazily over a chair in her bedroom. Below the chair, lying scattered on the floor, were a pair of trousers, socks and underwear. The phone continued to ring, but its feeble sound was overwhelmed by the creaking of the bed, the moaning of the brunette lying in it, and the heavy breathing of the nude Secretary of Homeland Security on top of her body.

❖ ❖ ❖

In his car, tightly gripping his cell phone, Cole frantically dialed Gayle Payne, the President's National Security Advisor. She was at her desk in her office at the White House when she received the call. Payne recognized Cole's voice. Though their contact over the years had been intermittent, there were a handful of occasions when they had met. Normally, David Cole would not be expected to contact Ms. Payne directly, without going through channels at the CIA. In his increasing sense of desperation, normal was no longer an operative situation.

"Gayle, it is vital I meet with you ASAP. It concerns a national security matter of the gravest urgency."

Payne was taken somewhat by surprise. As National Security Advisor, any matter that the CIA deemed grave should have already been brought to her attention. She was not comfortable with the tone of Cole's request.

"David, have you cleared this with Dick Darnell? I think I should hear from him first before meeting with you," Payne said with bureaucratic frigidity.

Cole had to convince the President's senior advisor on national security that it was vital that the two of them meet without delay. He sought to break through her wall of protocol by telling her the unvarnished truth regarding the Secretary of Homeland Security.

"Look Gayle, I've been in Washington a long time, and normally I'm a stickler for following protocol. Dick Darnell is so focused on Iraq and the insurgency there, as you know, that he has pulled himself out of the loop and asked me to report directly to William Mendick on all CIA data and analyses that point to a terrorist threat to the homeland. I am now convinced that our country is facing a catastrophe that is so far greater in scale than 9/11 that if it were to happen the way I think it might, it will eclipse September 11 from the history books. Only I can't get this through to our Secretary of Homeland Security because he thinks it's more important to skip out of a meeting I requested and labeled urgent so he can visit his executive assistant at her apartment."

Payne reflected for a brief moment before attempting to rationalize what had happened. "Let's not get paranoid, David. A lot of sensitive things cross Bill's desk, so he probably needed to meet with his assistant on something important..."

In anger and sorrow, Cole interjected. "Gayle, it is apparently an open secret among the staff at Homeland Security, as I just learned, that Mr. Mendick visits regularly with his assistant, along with additional women, other than his wife, for the purpose of copulation!"

There was a momentary silence on the other end, after which Gayle Payne consented to the meeting, though in a tone of voice suggesting reluctance. Cole drove off immediately, headed for the White House. When he arrived at Payne's office, he stared at her as she stared back. A determined looking African-American woman, she sat behind her desk as though it were a fortress.

Cole respected Payne for her intellect. She had had a distinguished career in academia before joining the President's administration as National Security Advisor. However, he also felt she was very superficial in her understanding of the terrorist threat to America, and more attentive to viewing national security as an expediency to politically assist the Commander-In-Chief, towards whom she felt intense loyalty.

"Gayle, I want to tell it to you straight," Cole said, still standing as he looked directly at Payne. "The worst case scenario we have always had in the intelligence community was an off-shoot of the Al-Qaeda movement smuggling a primitive nuclear device, maybe with the power of a Hiroshima bomb, into an American city and successfully detonating it. That scenario is no longer worst case. I am convinced as much as one human being can possibly be that the Al-Assad El-Islamiya faction of Al-Qaeda has obtained the plans for the most powerful nuclear weapon ever tested, and has built an exact replica of that device. If they should succeed in bringing it into our country and detonating it, it will explode with a force equal to ten thousand Hiroshimas!"

At first, Gayle Payne's reaction appeared to be passive. She continued sitting still, her facial expression stern and her eyes taciturn. It was only her breathing that seemed transformed. Cole noticed that her breaths had suddenly become more rapid and labored, sounding almost asthmatic. Then, she broke her silence. "Why the fuck was I not told about this!"

Payne was known as a very proper woman, and Cole was briefly startled by her unprecedented use of profanity.

"You mean the Vice President never filled you in on the meeting the Deputy Director of the Canadian Security Intelligence Service and I had with him?" responded Cole.

Shaking her head, a flustered Payne said simply "No." She thought for a moment, adding, "Nothing about this even appeared in any of the PDBs." The PDB, or Presidential Daily Briefing, was the highly confidential daily intelligence digest, usually 3 or 4 pages, that was supposed to alert the President to any lurking national security threats. It was prepared by CIA analysts removed from any contact with David Cole, and was approved by CIA Director Richard Darnell and the National Intelligence Director.

"Gayle, you are in a unique position to do something that is vital for our national security," Cole said in an imploring voice. "I urge you, with all the persuasion I can muster, to use your influence in the administration to enable me to personally brief the President on this critical matter."

Payne stared at Cole, her eyes appearing to penetrate through him as they poured out both anger and fear. Without speaking, her lips tightened, she nodded her head approvingly.

"One other request I also deem urgent," Cole added, his body language eloquently communicating his sense of desperation. "It is of the highest priority that I receive presidential authorization to relay to the Canadian Security Intelligence Service a document in the CIA archives pertaining to a Soviet-era weapon known as the RDS-220."

Doomsday

A freezing rain and gray, cloudy sky cast a gloomy pall over Ottawa. Dr. Lazar parked his old Volvo at the CSIS Headquarters parking lot, and exited his vehicle balancing an umbrella in one hand and his walking stick in the other. Laboriously, he proceeded towards the building's entrance, his face conveying a morbid taste of melancholy fortune. Once inside headquarters, personnel solicitously greeted Lazar, taking his umbrella and trench coat, dripping with rainwater, and escorted him to the Deputy Director's office. Behind closed doors, he was soon in conference with Dunlop.

"Thomas, I presume you have reviewed the documents pertaining to RDS-220 that the CIA delivered to us by courier," Dunlop said almost matter-of-factly, though his voice and body language suggested an unendurable dose of tension. "The question I have is this: how bad is it?"

Briefly clearing his throat, Lazar was about to speak, but something made him pause. He looked Dunlop in the eyes, projecting intense sadness. "Alex, I have looked over all the details on the design of this weapon," he said, pausing again before continuing. "The most important thing for you to know is that it is a doomsday device."

"Doomsday?" Dunlop repeated in a low tone of voice, his face looking wearied and lined with fatigue. "I do understand that its potential yield is 150 megatons, but as a layman on nuclear weapons design, I am unable to grasp what a device like this could actually do."

Dr. Lazar nodded his head in a gesture of understanding. He felt it was his duty to ensure that CSIS fully understood the havoc that a nuclear weapon of the magnitude of RDS-220 would wreak on the North American continent. He proceeded to relay that understanding.

"Alex, a nuclear weapon kills in three ways. There is the thermal energy in the form of extreme heat at the moment of detonation. This is followed by a massive blast wave, which causes building structures to collapse due to intense over-pressure. The third means of death is through highly toxic radioactive fallout. If this device has actually been built, and is smuggled into New York City, for example, and detonated there at its full yield, the destruction will be of biblical proportions."

As Dr. Lazar continued his explanation, the look on Dunlop's face was transformed from weariness to one of stark terror. He listened, mesmerized, as though in a hypnotic state.

"I have made some calculations, based on uranium tampers being fabricated for the two lithium deuteride fuel capsules contained in the device," Lazar said, as he lectured Dunlop on what the likely consequences would be if the weapon was detonated in an American city. "Of course, variables such as wind conditions and barometric pressure will affect, to some degree, what I'm about to tell you. However, this is a very likely scenario. In a fraction of second after detonation, a fireball will be created with a diameter of between 35 and 40 kilometers. This would not only cover all of New York City, but substantial populated suburbs in New Jersey, Long Island and Connecticut. Everything within that fireball would be instantly consumed, incinerated to oblivion. There would not even be ruins left. Beyond the fireball, a blast wave will create a zone, where the atmospheric overpressure exceeds five pounds per square inch, which would be at least 120 kilometers in diameter. That means cites such as Philadelphia and New Haven would be severely damaged. The dust and ashes from all this destruction will rise into the atmosphere in the form of a massive mushroom cloud, then fall back to earth as highly lethal radioactive fallout, over the next 24 hours. Depending on wind currents, the fallout will cause mass casualties across a wide portion of the American eastern seaboard and Midwest, and probably eastern Canada as well."

The Deputy Director folded his fists together, elbows resting on his desk. His forehead fell gently on his fists, as he sought to collect his thoughts and impressions. It was as though he wished that when he looked again at Dr. Lazar, this looming catastrophe would vanish. He lifted his head, looking with deep emotion towards Lazar and returned to reality.

"How many people would die, Thomas?"

"The death toll would be influenced by the variables I mentioned," Lazar responded dispassionately. "However, I would conservatively estimate that twenty million people would be killed by the initial thermal pulse and subsequent blast damage. But the real killer will be the radioactive fallout. This weapon produces an almost unbelievable quantity of the most toxic radioactive fallout, and it will fall over a wide area, encompassing major population centers. I would say that within a week after detonation, the final death toll will reach at least 80 million human beings."

"Those numbers are staggering!" exclaimed Dunlop in an anguished voice. "To add to this nightmare scenario, we have no idea where this device is located. I don't even know if it is still in the country, or has been smuggled south of the border."

Dunlop asked Dr. Lazar how certain he was that the terrorists had actually succeeded in building the device. His answer was unequivocal.

"They have satisfied the three main criteria. They have acquired the materials, assembled the fabrication team and procured a design that is not only potent but, more importantly, has been tested and shown to work. The fact that this device was designed by a genius reinforces my belief that it will work to its full potential if the terrorists succeed in detonating it."

"Are you sure that they would have all the materials called for in the design?" asked a desperate Dunlop.

Nodding his head in affirmation, Lazar offered his explanation. "The four Mark-41 bombs the terrorists apparently recovered from

125

Lake Abitibi had ample supplies of lithium deuteride, plutonium and uranium 235, in fact, enough for two of Andrei Sakharov's superbombs, with additional material to spare. They would need fresh tritium for the primary or fission trigger, and those watch dials that were smuggled into Canada by the Monsoon Watch Company have the required quantity of tritium. That subsidiary called Signar Transport has contracts with several nuclear power reactors for shipping supplies of deuterium gas, of which Canada is the world's leading producer. They could easily siphon off minute quantities without it being detected. That would be sufficient for completing the primary stage. They also needed uranium 238 for building the two tampers for the device. The quantities of depleted uranium you have told me Malaya Metals procured in Kuwait are more than enough to meet their requirements."

Dunlop recognized the dire consequences that were staring him in the face. He still mulled over in his mind if there were any aspects to this terrorist project still open to question. He asked Dr. Lazar about the possibility that not all the components had been secured.

"That is doubtful, Alex. True enough, the design requires almost seven thousand different parts. However, that is not significantly more than a Hiroshima-type atomic bomb. The clandestine nuclear industries of North Korea and Iran, with their underground factories, are certainly technically capable of producing these parts, provided they had the proper design specifications. In addition, they could surreptitiously obtain some of the parts that are of dual use nature from European firms. As those parts are not radioactive, or obvious as to their true purposes, it would be relatively easy to smuggle them into the country, I regret to say."

Reflecting on everything they had discussed, Alex Dunlop asked his anti-proliferation advisor how he thought the complex plot to build an exact duplicate of the world's most powerful nuclear bomb would have been organized and coordinated.

"I think it would have evolved through different phases," Lazar told the Deputy Director "We know Al-Qaeda and its offshoots have been trying to buy fissile material and even a complete nuclear weapon, for some time. I think Fedorenko initially approached the North Koreans some two years ago when he was there doing some technical work, probably related to their secret nuclear weapons program. They would have turned it down at first, since it was not a useful weapon for them, being too big to fit on any missile. But they have a relationship with Al-Qaeda and its offshoots and a very strong connection to Dr. Pervaz Khan, who sold them centrifuges and other important parts of their nuclear arms program. They probably passed on the offer to Khan and his extremist Islamic friends, and they must have spent at least a year determining the feasibility of building the device and inserting it into the United States. The main problem they had to solve was how to obtain the fissile and other key isotopes without being detected. It was a stroke of evil genius to figure out that they could mine the thermonuclear bombs of missing aircraft already located in North America to obtain the necessary materials. Once they knew that it was feasible to proceed, they would have bought the design of the RDS-220 from Fedorenko, probably when he was in Abu Dhabi. With those plans, they could provide specifications to Iran and North Korea and have them secretly build the parts, then smuggle them into Canada. They would have been able to recruit the technicians and machinists from those two countries on loan, so to speak, to serve as the fabrication team. They would still have needed to have a supervisor, however, with a high degree of overall knowledge of nuclear physics and weapons design, and that would undoubtedly have been Pervaz Khan."

"But Dr. Khan must have known we would be watching him if he entered Canada," Dunlop said imploringly.

Lazar had an answer buttressed with irrefutable logic. "The supervisor would not need to be standing next to the assembly team, looking over their shoulders, to fulfill his role. He would only need to be in frequent and reliable communication with them. That is probably why Khan made those multiple visits to the North Korean and Iranian embassies. They would have at the embassies secure communications facilities equipped with scramblers so that he could be in touch with his team at Lake Abitibi without risking his instructions being intercepted and monitored by CSIS."

Dunlop brought up the murder of Boris Fedorenko. "Thomas, why was he brought to northern Ontario and why kill him?"

"They had everything else to put the bomb together. However, remember that North Korea, Pakistan and Iran have thus far only designed and built fission bombs. None of the technicians and machinists they could recruit would have had experience assembling a fusion tamper for a thermonuclear device. On the RDS-220 there are two such fusion tampers that must be fabricated to precise specifications. Even the most minute of deviations would severely diminish the bomb's yield."

Absorbing the logic of Dr. Lazar's response, Dunlop could now answer his own question. "Of course! It makes perfect sense. The first payment to Fedorenko was for the design of the RDS-220. The second transfer of money to his Swiss bank account must have been a down payment on the promise of a far greater pay-off once he assembled the fusion tampers. What the greedy fool did not realize is that once he did his job for the terrorists, he became expendable."

Lazar nodded his head in agreement. "As the old saying goes, dead men tell no tales."

Stroking his chin, a grim-faced Dunlop reflected on his growing awareness of the scope and dimensions of the looming terrorist plot. "It appears as though these people have thought of everything, Thomas. This is demonic in its thoroughness."

"Unfortunately, you are probably right," said Lazar. "A cunning and brilliant maniacal mind conceived of all this. They appear to have been meticulous in their preparation. The only aspect that confuses me is having a mixed team of Koreans and Middle-Easterners collaborate on the assembly of the bomb. From past experience, I know how important it is for the technicians and machinists to speak the same language."

Dunlop asked how many persons would be required to assemble the bomb. Dr. Lazar's answer was that fifteen would be the ideal number.

"We know they had at least forty people working on the north shore of Lake Abitibi," Dunlop interjected. "Perhaps they had different roles, such as security and salvage, divided by nationality."

"Maybe you are right," Lazar replied, in a tone of voice suggesting he had his doubts.

❖ ❖ ❖

David Cole was in the White House, waiting to be summoned into the Oval Office. After several minutes had passed, Gayle Payne approached him.

"David, I just came from the Oval Office to provide the President with some background. He is ready to meet with both of us now."

Payne escorted Cole into the President's office. He had only met the President once before and was somewhat surprised at his friendly, almost familiar greeting. Shaking Cole's hand firmly, the President spoke warmly in his distinctive voice resonating from east Texas.

"David, I am so glad to see you!" he said with the aplomb of a politician meeting with a campaign contributor. "Please sit down, can we get you a cup of coffee?"

Cole was focused on what he saw as his mission, warning the President of a clear and present danger to the nation's security. Politely declining the offer of coffee, he began his attempt to thoroughly brief the President. He had just uttered the words, "threat of nuclear terrorism," when the President interrupted him.

"David, just to save us all some time, both Ms. Payne and the Vice President have already filled me in on the concern of the Canadians that some group linked to Al-Qaeda is plotting to build a nuclear bomb and smuggle it into our country. What would you recommend we do about it?"

Startled momentarily, Cole sought to regain his train of thought. "Mr. President, I just want to make certain you are aware that the Al-Assad El-Islamiya, an offshoot of Al-Qaeda, has almost certainly completed construction of the bomb, and it is not a primitive Hiroshima-style device, but a direct copy of the most powerful thermonuclear bomb ever tested."

"I know that," the President said with perfunctory calm. "What do you suggest we all do about it?"

Struggling to retain both his composure and focus, the CIA's Director of Counter-Terrorism sought to formulate the right words to convey the urgency of the situation.

"Mr. President, we must immediately seal all of our borders, including every crossing by land, all airports and seaports open to international travel and shipping. Every person, vehicle and shipping container must be rigorously inspected. The National Guard and army reserve should be mobilized and placed on a war footing. The FBI and every law enforcement jurisdiction in this country, from large city police forces to the smallest county sheriff's office, must be mandated to put aside all other criminal investigations and directed to apply all their resources towards defeating this plot."

The President's demeanor changed from friendly affectation to one of aloof coolness. He looked sternly towards Cole, silent for a moment. "Is there anything else, Mr. Cole, you would have us do?" he said in a voice dripping with sarcasm.

Ignoring the President's skeptical reception of his heartfelt concern for the looming danger, Cole immediately offered one additional recommendation. "Yes, Mr. President, there is one other thing," he told his Commander-in-Chief. "We should fully activate the NEST, without delay."

A puzzled expression emanated from the President's facial features. "NEST?" he repeated, looking first at Cole and then shifting his gaze towards Gayle Payne. The National Security Advisor, recognizing her boss's lack of familiarization with the term, sought to illuminate him in a manner that would not be condescending.

"Sir, NEST is the acronym for Nuclear Emergency Search Team. They are the experts that are called in to search for and disarm a possible nuclear weapon when, for example, the authorities receive a blackmail threat from someone who sounds credible."

"Oh, yes, Ms. Payne. I remember now. When we had that scare shortly after 9/11 in New York City when a CIA informant told us that a suitcase nuke was in lower Manhattan and would be detonated, those are the folks who went in looking for it."

"That's right, Mr. President," replied Payne.

"You both should know that once the media got wind of the fact that those personnel were roaming New York City, they went wild and threw the city into a panic," the President said, turning towards Cole. "And Mr. Cole, we will not do that again. No, not on my watch."

"Mr. President, I offer my recommendations not because I want to throw our nation into a panic. I do so with the conviction that the imminent threat of grave and terrible catastrophe confronts our country."

The President's face briefly tensed up, then relaxed as he flashed a smile. Looking more sympathetically towards Cole, he explained what he did intend to do. "Mr. Cole, I will meet with the Secretary of Homeland Security and the FBI Director, and the three of us will decide on how we will respond. I will tell you that I find the possibility that a ragtag group of terrorists hiding in caves can build a capability that took decades and hundreds of billions of dollars for both us and the Soviet Union to develop, not credible."

Cole looked like a defeated man, something which both Gayle Payne and the President took note of. The President continued speaking, in a more conciliatory tone. "On the other hand, David, I think you have been very diligent in discovering a possible plot to sow panic in our country, maybe using dirty bombs. Let's just make sure that we act in a way that does not help the terrorists achieve their objective. After all, the purpose of terrorism is to sow terror, meaning panic, and shut down our economy. We defeat them by not over-reacting and rushing into decisions that give far more credit to their abilities than is warranted."

Desperate to salvage something tangible from his meeting with the President, Cole attempted to broaden his understanding of the enemy.

"Mr. President, I respectfully disagree with the thesis that the terrorism practiced by Islamic Jihadists is a tactic to bring about panic in our society."

Gayle Payne stared intensely at Cole, her eyes bulging with anger at his attempt to contradict the President. That did not stop him.

"In the past, that was the objective of terrorist groups that had a political goal to achieve," Cole continued. "However, Mr. President, our adversary, Islamist fanaticism, has no political demands to press on us. They are the adherents of a religious messianic ideology that has an uncompromising view of the world. To them, terrorism is not tactics, but strategy. They have no demands to be served by inducing panic and chaos in our society. Their goal is our physical destruction."

The President at this point winked at his National Security Advisor, who then looked directly at Cole. That prompted her to end the meeting. She told the CIA's Director of Counter-Terrorism that the President had a busy calendar and was about to go into another meeting.

"That's right, have some folks from Congress coming over to talk about how we can get more tax cuts and reform our Social Security system," the President said gleefully. "I got a busy day ahead of me."

Transfer Agreement

Littlejohn and Dextraze were at CSIS headquarters discussing Aziz Faruqui, alias Mohammed Iqbal. The principal question was his whereabouts: where had he gone?

"Since Dr. Pervaz Khan departed Canada, Mr. Faruqui has vanished without a trace. I only wish I had kept him under surveillance," said a dejected Dextraze.

"Don't blame yourself, Pierre," Littlejohn responded. "None of us had any idea until recently how pivotal a player he was in this matter. The important thing is that we now know he is a critical piece to this puzzle."

The two intelligence officers looked at their options for attempting to track down Faruqui and learn more about his involvement in what had been transpiring along the shore of Lake Abitibi. They concluded that there was not much more they could do within Canadian borders.

"I think we should recommend to Mr. Dunlop that we bring in the Americans in tracking down Faruqui. If he was an ISI operative in Afghanistan in the 1980's, someone in the CIA must have known him," suggested Dextraze. His colleague nodded in agreement.

The two agents soon joined Dunlop in his office. They could tell by his demeanor and body language that their boss was extremely worried. That only served to reinforce their own sense of anxiety.

"Mr. Dunlop, Pierre and I think the CIA may be able to help us with leads on Aziz Faruqui," Littlejohn said.

"My ISI source in Toronto confirms that Faruqui was in Afghanistan working with the Mujahadeen, simultaneously with the CIA's own involvement," Dextraze added. "They may have someone who knew him and has information that could assist us in our investigation. Otherwise, we are at a dead end."

"Alright, I'll call David Cole right now," replied Dunlop. "I want both of you to put together the most comprehensive file we possibly can on Faruqui, including every photograph, surveillance tape, documents from our embassy in Islamabad, the whole nine yards. But do it quickly, I want to send it out to Washington by courier this afternoon."

❖ ❖ ❖

At the White House, the President had convened a meeting involving the Vice President, National Security Advisor, Secretary of Homeland Security and FBI Director. The topic was David Cole.

"I think Cole needs a vacation," Mendik said. "Sure, maybe some terrorists are planning something from Canada, but not that!"

Larry Braun echoed Mendik's sentiments. "I don't want to put down Cole, he is trying to be alert and do his job. But I do think he is exaggerating what these terrorists are planning. In a worst-case scenario, they may have retrieved some radioactive material from the site of an old B-52 crash, in which case we have to guard against the possibility of a dirty bomb attack. But not a full-fledged nuclear device."

The President turned to the Vice President, asking for his views. In a deliberate manner punctuated with coarse speech, he articulated his perspective on the nature of the threat.

"Mr. President, I start with your own healthy and wise instincts, which is that whatever the terrorists may be planning, their intent is to create a wave of panic in this country, leading to the dislocation of our economy," the Vice President emphatically suggested. "Frankly, these terrorists don't have the capabilities or the balls to do something that is high tech, such as a nuclear attack. When they hit us on 9/11, it was with Swiss army knives and box cutters. I agree with Bill and Larry, maybe some bombings at shopping malls or sporting events will occur, with some plutonium thrown in to create panic and an expensive clean-up job afterwards. I think Cole is putting too much store in what the Canucks up north are telling him. If those weasels in Canada had guts, they would be helping us in Iraq and not trying to scare us about problems with our own borders."

"I couldn't agree with you more, Mr. Vice President," replied the Commander-in-Chief in a mood almost suggesting joviality. "So let's decide what we will do."

Larry Braun indicated that the FBI would step up surveillance of suspected Al-Qaeda sympathizers throughout the United States. The President signaled his agreement, then turned to his Secretary for Homeland Security.

"Bill, do you think we should raise the threat level?" inquired the President.

"No Mr. President, I don't think that is called for. We can quietly improve the readiness level of some of our first-responders, should that be necessary. I can also have our Customs personnel do more inspections of incoming cargo."

"That sounds very good," the President said. "Is there anything else, Bill?"

Mendick thought for a moment, as an idea emerged from the recesses of his mind. "Yes, Mr. President. There is one other thing. I could use my own Arab linguist to help translate some of the intercepts the FBI sends me. Cole has not been very helpful sharing some of those resources with me. He has on staff a translator named Amelia Baldwin, who appears to be good. I would like to have her transferred to me for a few weeks, so I can try her out."

The President immediately signaled his acquiescence. As Gayle Payne looked on nervously, he told Mendick he would call Dick Darnell at the CIA and have the necessary arrangements made.

❖ ❖ ❖

The following day David Cole stood outside his office, awaiting the arrival of Amelia Baldwin. When she appeared, he quickly ushered her into his office, closing the door behind them. He motioned for her to sit down.

"Amelia, I have received by courier important new information from our colleagues with the Canadian Security Intelligence Service. It involves a Pakistani national who entered Canada using a false passport and the fictitious name of Mohammed Iqbal. His real name is Aziz Faruqui." Cole placed before Baldwin several photographs and documents. She noticed an intense looking man, with a very narrow face and strong jaw. In most of the photographs, dark sunglasses obscured his eyes.

"When I found out that Faruqui was in Afghanistan after the Russian invasion, working for the Pakistani ISI," Cole continued, "I spoke with a recently retired CIA field agent who worked there in sending supplies to the Mujahadeen. He knew a little about Faruqui, but more importantly, he gave me this." Cole held up a videotape, which he then passed to Ms. Baldwin.

"Amelia, this is an old training video that the ISI produced for anti-Russian fighters in Afghanistan, volunteers who came from Arab countries like Egypt, Yemen and Saudi Arabia. It's in Arabic, and the instructor is Aziz Faruqui. I have not seen the video, but I am told it is a lecture on manufacturing improvised explosive devices, IEDs."

Amelia grasped the videotape, while looking at the photographs of Faruqui that were arrayed on Cole's desk.

"Do you want me to translate the video, Mr. Cole?" inquired Amelia Baldwin.

Nodding, Cole sought to relay the urgency involved. "Amelia, please put everything else aside and get on this immediately," he said. "So you understand why I am in a hurry to have this translated, be aware that Faruqui was able to gain admittance to Canada using a false passport by affecting an arranged marriage to a Canadian citizen. It just so happens that this Canadian woman is the daughter of Dr. Pervaz Khan."

◈ ◈ ◈

Sitting alone in a conference room at CIA headquarters that was enveloped by audiovisual equipment, Amelia carefully watched the old video David Cole had provided her with. Amid the backdrop of the Pamir mountain range, a tall man wearing flowing robes and a turban lectured in Arabic with a distinct

Pakistani accent. His face seemed shrouded by a long black beard, thick and prickly. Yet, the narrowness of the speaker's face was clearly distinguishable. Amelia looked at several still photographs of Faruqui, comparing them with the figure on videotape. She took voluminous notes as the younger Faruqui conveyed instructions on bomb making during the anti-Soviet campaign in Afghanistan. As she proceeded with her translation, something in the back of her mind bothered her greatly. She was not sure why, but felt compelled to pull out the DVD of hostage executions in Iraq that Cole had earlier provided her with. She paused the image of Faruqui on the video, then loaded the DVD and proceeded to view it. Stopping at a particularly gory episode, she slightly reversed the DVD then replayed it, listening intently to the executioner's words. She did this several times, taking notes with difficulty, as her hands began shaking. She paused the DVD, then again began listening to the videotape. She was no longer taking notes, though her hands continued to vibrate. She then stopped the tape and sat still, absorbing the revelation that had just come upon her.

As her chest began heaving with loud breathing, she could feel a cold sweat on her brow. Wiping her forehead with her hand, she noticed it was shaking more violently. As she attempted to control the involuntary movement of her hands, she fearfully sighed, "Oh, my God!"

❖ ❖ ❖

The next morning, Mr. Dobbs was sitting at his desk when his intercom buzzed. His secretary informed him that Richard Darnell was on the line. Whenever the CIA Director called, Dobbs immediately tensed up. In the past, such calls involved transferring his diminishing pool of Arabic-speaking linguists to Iraq. With bated breath he picked up his phone. Darnell told him that this time only one translator would be leaving the CIA headquarters in Langley and not for Iraq, but for the other side of the Potomac.

"Dobbs, I have worked out a transfer agreement with the Department of Homeland Security. We are going to loan them one of our Arabic-speaking linguists for a few weeks. Arrange to have Ms. Amelia Baldwin relocate; she will be working out of Bill Mendick's office."

Dobbs wanted to know when the transfer agreement would take effect. "Immediately!" was Darnell's reply.

Dobbs reflexively called Baldwin, and summoned her to his office. When she arrived, he told her of the high-level decision that had been made regarding her new posting. He could tell from the look on her face that she was dejected.

"Amelia, you look disappointed. Don't be. This is not a demotion. The Director would not have requested that you specifically be posted to assist the Secretary of Homeland Security unless he knew, as well as I do, how capable you are. Look on this as an opportunity, without having to relocate to Baghdad."

Baldwin was not elated. She was still overwhelmed by what she had learned from reviewing the videotape David Cole had provided to her. "I have been completing an assignment for Mr. Cole that he told me was urgent. Can I speak with him before I'm transferred to Homeland Security?"

"I'm afraid that won't be possible," Dobbs told her. "You need to be at the Department of Homeland Security before noon. Why don't you work up a written summary for Mr. Cole before you leave, and I'll see to it that he receives it today."

It was later in the day when Cole called Dobbs. He had been trying to reach Amelia all afternoon, without success.

"Mr. Cole, I thought you knew," Dobbs said. Cole's startled response on the other end prompted him to add that the CIA Director himself had instructed him to transfer Ms. Baldwin to Homeland Security to provide Arab language translation services for the Department's Secretary.

"Jesus Christ!" uttered Cole in a voice strained with agony.

As he sensed the anger on the other end of the line, Dobbs quickly added something he thought might assuage Cole's anger. "Sir, before she left, Amelia left a memorandum for you labeled highly confidential."

Cole angrily demanded that Dobbs get the memorandum to him right way. He then put in a call to Richard Darnell, trying to reach him so he could have the transfer agreement involving Baldwin countermanded. Darnell was unavailable. He then called Gayle Payne at the White House. When her secretary indicated she was meeting with the Vice President, he told her he would leave an urgent message on Payne's voice mail.

As angry and outraged as he felt, Cole was determined to carefully compose the voice message he was about to leave. He took a deep breath, then spoke when prompted by Payne's recorded voice mail message:

"Gayle, I have warned you about William Mendick's peccadilloes. After meeting with the President, the last thing I expected was that the most capable Arabic-speaking linguist we have at the agency would be taken away from us and placed in the clutches of that unfaithful womanizer. And at a time when she was involved in urgent translation work for me involving the current threat to our country. I am outraged, and personally disappointed in you for letting me down this way. How you could allow this dedicated young woman to be placed in such a dangerous position is beyond words. I will not stand idle. In a few minutes I will head to the Department of Homeland Security and personally rescue Ms. Baldwin from Mendick's lecherous clutches. If you want to avoid a confrontation between myself and Mendick that I guarantee will hit the front pages of the newspapers, I suggest you get there ahead of me."

Cole hung up, then unsealed the envelope containing Amelia's confidential memorandum. He read it carefully, scrutinizing every word. Then, reviewing the last paragraph, he suddenly froze stiff, as if his heart had skipped a beat. His eyes bulging, he uttered to himself, "Good Lord!" He quickly grabbed his coat, and headed for the elevator.

◈ ◈ ◈

At the White House, Gayle Payne emerged from her meeting with the Vice President and headed towards her office. Passing her secretary, she asked if there were any messages.

"Just one," the secretary replied. "David Cole left a message on your voice mail. He said it was urgent."

Her eyes flashing with anxiety, she rushed to her office phone and checked her voice mail. Listening to Cole's frantic warning, she felt intense dismay. Hurriedly, she instructed her secretary to arrange a limousine right away, to take her to the Department of Homeland Security.

◆ ◆ ◆

At a cubicle on the fourth floor of the Department of Homeland Security, Amelia listened to recordings obtained through FBI phone intercepts. Her small head almost obscured by the large pair of headphones she wore, Ms. Baldwin slowly wrote down passages she gleamed from the intercepts, her facial expression betraying their vapid content. A clerical worker from the Secretary's office tapped her on the shoulder, prompting Ms. Baldwin to remove the bulky headphones. "Mr. Mendick would like to see you in his office," she said.

As Amelia headed towards Mendick's office, Gayle Payne's limousine pulled up to the front entrance of the Department of Homeland Security. She opened the door to the front entrance and briefly looked behind, noticing that David Cole had also just arrived and was following in her footsteps. Without pausing, Payne quickly walked towards the elevator. By the time its door opened, Cole had caught up with her. Without exchanging words, they both entered the elevator, Gayle Payne pressing the button for the fourth floor.

When she entered the Secretary of Homeland Security's office, Amelia was surprised to see Mendick standing by the door. His was in shirtsleeves, his tie loosened and shirt opened at the neck. As she walked into the office, Mendick firmly closed the door behind her. She was about to sit down on one of the chairs in front of the Secretary's large, ornate desk when he told her to come over to a small alcove at the side of the office, which had a coffee table with a small sofa and chair. He motioned for her to sit on the sofa, suggesting he would use the chair. Instead, he parked himself next to her on the sofa. Amelia was already feeling uncomfortable, not only by Mendick's proximity to her, but also from the pungent aroma of alcohol mixed with tobacco which was emanating from his mouth.

"So, Amelia, tell me about the FBI intercepts!" he loudly asked, his eyes at first locked on hers, then scanning the rest of her body.

140

"Mr. Mendick, I don't know why you had me transferred here. All the conversations I have overheard involve a bakery in Brooklyn ordering supplies. There is nothing suspicious about them, and I have been pulled away from very important duties at CIA headquarters."

"Call me Bill," Mendick replied, adding that, "those conversations you listened to may sound routine on the surface, but take it from a pro with a lot of experience in law enforcement, there's more to them than meets the eye."

Amelia began to feel tense and fearful, increasingly aware of palpitations emerging from within her body. Insisting on distant formality, she coldly said, "Mr. Mendick, I disagree with you. I am highly trained in Arabic linguistics and have much experience translating and interpreting private conversations that have been secretly recorded. I know for a fact that none of the FBI intercepts I listened to today involves any threat to national security."

Smiling widely and breathing heavily, Mendick's focus on Ms. Baldwin was growing in its intensity, adding immeasurably to her feeling of unease. "Amelia, you just keep listening to those tapes. It will be great for your career." He paused for a moment, then went on. "I can be great for your career. You work well with me and I can open doors for you."

Before even having the chance to absorb the meaning of what Mendick had just said to her, she noticed that the Secretary's left arm was behind her back, his hand stroking the rear of her neck and her left shoulder. She instinctively tried pulling away from him. He responded by pulling her closer to him with his left arm.

"Please let me go, Mr. Mendick," she said in a soft, pleading voice. He smiled, tried kissing her lips and then thrust his right arm through the top of her blouse, his hand reaching under her bra and squeezing her breast.

At that same moment, Cole and Payne arrived in front of the receptionist's desk, asking for Amelia Baldwin. "She's in conference with Mr. Mendick," was her studied reply. As Cole and Gayle Payne looked towards the closed door of Mendick's office, they suddenly heard a piercing shriek, followed by loud cries for help coming from a woman experiencing severe distress. The cries were so loud, they attracted the attention of the dozen or so office workers in the immediate area, as well as several uniformed security personnel. David Cole's fists clenched, while Ms. Payne's face flashed with anger. They both headed towards the door of Mendick's office.

"You can't go in there," the receptionist icily told them, ignoring the panic-stricken cries of Amelia Baldwin that were still clearly audible. "The hell we can't!" was Gayle Payne's response, her voice dripping with outrage. She yanked the door open, and entered the office with David Cole right behind her. With the office's interior fully exposed, staff and security guards clearly observed in stunned mannerism a desperate young woman fighting off an obsessed Secretary of Homeland Security, who was seemingly oblivious to those around him. Only when he saw Gayle Payne's angry face and heard her yell, "Get your hands off of her, you bastard!" did he relinquish his grip on Amelia Baldwin.

Freed from his grasp, Amelia fled from the sofa, running into David Cole's arms. She was distraught, in tears and in a state of shock. She cried uncontrollably, as Cole sought to console her.

Now Mendick looked distraught and fearful. Sweat began pouring from his forehead as he felt intimidated and emasculated by the fierce look of hostility that Gayle Payne was projecting towards him. He lamely got up from the sofa, standing in front of Payne, saying meekly, "It's not what you think, Ms. Payne. I was having a normal meeting when that woman suddenly came on to me. When I refused her advances she threatened to scream and embarrass me..."

"You lying piece of shit!" Payne roared at him, silencing him in the process. She then turned towards one of the security officers, standing at the entrance to the Secretary's office. "Take Mr. Mendick into custody!" she instructed him. "But Madam, he's the Secretary of Homeland Security," the officer replied in defensive bureaucratic fashion. "Do what I say or I'll have you fired!" she shot back.

As Cole stood silently, holding a sobbing Amelia Baldwin in his arms, he observed Gayle Payne taking charge. She firmly told the receptionist to call the Washington D.C. Police Department and report a sexual assault had been committed in the office of the Secretary of Homeland Security. "Tell them the perpetrator's name is William Mendick, he is being detained by security personnel and there are numerous eye witnesses available for the police to talk to."

Payne turned towards Amelia Baldwin, her face transformed from one of anger to sadness and empathy. She then looked at David Cole, betraying a hint of shame. "David," she said sorrowfully, "let's get this poor woman out of this den of iniquity."

Khalifa

Alex Dunlop arrived early at his office, frustrated at the lack of progress in tracking down Aziz Faruqui, or obtaining any leads pertaining to the plot he was clearly a key participant in. Shortly after his arrival, a clerical aide came by his office in a state of excitement, clutching an early edition of the morning newspaper. "Mr. Dunlop!" she said in a loud, choking voice, "I know you would want to see this right now!"

The headline blew the Deputy Director's mind: *U.S. Homeland Security Boss Arrested For Sexual Assault.*

After briefly reading the article, he placed the newspaper on his desk and stared towards the ceiling. He then looked again at the headline, noting that the date was March 1. Somehow, he thought the date significant, marking the beginning of a calamitous descent by the American political establishment. How could it be, he wondered, when a dangerous terrorist threat hung over the North American continent, that the man entrusted with safeguarding America's security had become involved in a sordid affair that was bound to distract attention from far more critical matters? At that moment his phone rang. It was an incoming call from David Cole.

The CIA's Director of Counter-Terrorism sounded fatigued, and Dunlop sensed it was in relation to Mendick's arrest, which he briefly commented on.

"Alex, the Mendick affair is an unmitigated disaster," Cole told his Canadian colleague, "but there is something far more important I need to discuss with you."

Dunlop's ears were riveted to the phone, as he awaited a bombshell from Cole. It was indeed stunning news.

"The information you sent to me by courier on Aziz Faruqui has been far more valuable than you may have realized. One of our Arabic linguists did a comparison of an old videotape of Faruqui speaking in Arabic in Afghanistan with some of the hostage videos from Iraq. There appears to be a match with the Lion."

"Faruqui is the Lion?" Dunlop replied in amazement. "Are you sure?"

"We are as certain as one can be," responded Cole, "pending technical analysis of the voice and biometrics on the photographic images of the eyes. At this point, I can say without the least hesitation that the height and weight appear to be identical, they both have part of the middle finger of the left hand missing, the voices sound alike, and our linguist pointed out that there were specific ways in which Arabic was spoken by the Lion that demonstrate that the individual was a Pakistani with a scientific background, most likely in chemistry, which happens to be a perfect description of Aziz Faruqui."

The pieces of the puzzle were beginning to connect more clearly to both men. Dunlop reminded Cole that fragments from the murder weapon connected the killer of Fedorenko to the perpetrator of the slaughter of hostages in Iraq.

"That would explain, Alex, why he has not been heard from in Iraq for months. He's been here, in North America."

Cole then brought up a sensitive matter with Dunlop. "Alex, I need your help on something that is frankly a humiliation for myself and the CIA. The linguist I mentioned who found the connection between the Lion and Aziz Faruqui was posted to Bill Mendick's office the other day. What I mean to say is, she was the woman who Mendick tried to assault in his office. As you can imagine, she is in shock. Now, the media is hounding her like scavengers, which I suppose is to be expected."

"The poor woman," Dunlop said with sympathy.

"I can't spare her," Cole said bluntly. "Even after what she's been through, with what we're up against, she must continue to work. I want to get her out of Washington and Langley, at least until the worst of this blows over. Would it be possible to post her temporarily at your headquarters?"

Without hesitation, Dunlop agreed, telling his colleague that it was an excellent idea. Amelia would be isolated from the media, and she could still function effectively in a matter that involved both intelligence agencies and their governments working in increasingly close cooperation.

❖ ❖ ❖

An incensed President was conferring in the Oval Office of the White House with his Vice President and National Security Advisor. "Heads will roll!" he shouted. Gayle Payne appeared tense while, in sharp contrast, the Vice President was a model of sublime calmness.

"Why did you have to have him arrested, Ms. Payne! Do you realize the scandal we are now stuck in, like a pig in cold shit?"

Seeking to restrain the vituperative temptations of the President, the Vice President offered a more positive spin on what Payne had done.

"Mr. President, in my humble opinion, speaking just about the political ramifications, I think it is to our advantage that it was your senior National Security Advisor who had Mendick locked up, and not David Cole or one of the Department's staff. This shows we have nothing to hide, and people will focus on that a lot more than on what Mendick did."

Reflecting for a moment on the alternative view of reality that had just been presented to him, the President began to ease up. "I see your point. I guess we are in a no-win situation, no matter what we've done. At least this way, it will appear to Mr. and Mrs. Middle America that we are cleaning up our own mess."

"That's right," the Vice President interjected, adding the steps he felt needed to be done. "The next thing we need to do, Mr. President, is fire the son of a bitch; don't wait for him to resign. Let's do it this morning, we'll call a press conference without answering any questions, make the announcement, and that will take people's minds off our omission to fully vet Mendick."

"That was my call," the President said in an expression of fatalism. "He campaigned with me in Ohio and I really liked him. He came across as a real American hunk, with a tough guy image that I was convinced would make people feel safe. I just thought we could save time skipping all the normal background checks."

"Mr. President, have you given any thought to appointing an interim head of Homeland Security?" asked Payne. "Considering the matters David Cole has apprised us of, I believe that would be the prudent thing to do. We can't afford to have that department rudderless."

The Vice President disagreed. "Homeland Security is a PR package to make the American people feel more secure. In reality, all the different parts of it, the FBI, Customs, Immigration, they'll all continue to function normally as they always have."

The President nodded his head in agreement. "The Vice President is right, Ms. Payne. It will make no difference who runs things there right now. Once burned, twice shy. I want to move real slow on finding a replacement, and I think we need to be very careful politically before we can figure out who should run things there until there's a new Secretary."

Thwarted on her recommendation, Payne then brought up another issue as a way of bringing some focus on her own growing awareness that the plot Cole was investigating posed a very serious national security threat. She mentioned what Amelia Baldwin had been working on before being summarily transferred to work in Mendick's office.

"Mr. President, that remarkable young woman may have discovered the identity of the Lion," Payne revealed. "She thinks it's a Pakistani man the Canadian Security Intelligence Service has been investigating by the name of Aziz Faruqui."

Both the President and Vice President seemed startled at the news. Payne elaborated further. "We were told earlier by CSIS that fragments from a knife used to kill a Russian nuclear technician in northern Ontario had blood samples that were matched by DNA to several of the hostages murdered in Iraq by the Lion. At the time, the Intelligence Directorate at the CIA and Richard Darnell were convinced that the Lion was still in Iraq, in hiding, which is why we have not heard from him in months. But the evidence pointing to Faruqui is persuasive."

"Who is this Faruqui?" the President inquired.

The National Security Advisor provided the President and Vice President with a detailed overview, which she had received from David Cole. She stressed his involvement with Pakistan's ISI, his connections to Al-Qaeda and especially the manner in which he had entered Canada on a false passport, ostensibly for the arranged "marriage" to Pervaz Khan's daughter.

"There could be political benefits in capturing Aziz Faruqui" was the instinctive response from the Vice President. "It would certainly grab all the headlines away from our problems with Mendick."

❖ ❖ ❖

Heading towards Dulles airport, Cole held the wheel of his automobile, while Amelia Baldwin stared forlornly ahead. Noticing the melancholy state of his passenger, Cole sought to comfort her as best as he could.

"I know it's tough what you've had to endure. I'm not sure I could face the world if I were in your shoes. However, we both have a job to do that is vitally important. I think spending a little time in Ottawa with our Canadian colleagues at CSIS will help take your mind off this, at least for a while. More importantly, you can have some privacy away from those damned reporters."

Noticing the time on the car's instrument panel clock, Cole decided to turn on the radio. "It's time for that reactionary, Russ Gibbons. Let's hear what he has to say." Within a minute of tuning in to the conservative commentator, Cole regretted his decision,

"What scandal?" blared the commentator. "The scandal is all in the sick minds of the liberals, who would stop at nothing to bring down the most moral and effective President our country has had in the last hundred years. What did happen? A man was arrested and charged with a crime, which he is innocent of, until proven guilty in a court of law. And who was it that initiated the arrest? It was a senior advisor to the President. So where is the scandal?

The scandal is in the behavior of the unpatriotic, hypocritical liberals. I'm Russ Gibbons, and I'll be back after a word from our sponsor..."

Cole turned off the radio, and glanced apologetically towards Baldwin, "I'm sorry, Amelia, I think you really will have to be out of the country to escape this." He pondered a thought for a moment, then offered a philosophical interpretation on what had transpired.

"You know, Amelia, I think it's in the Gospel of Mathew, when Christ tells his disciples that a prophet has no honor in his own country. Thinking about you and I and how we are trying to warn those in authority who choose not to listen, it seems like the same thing. It might be that your temporary posting to Canada will, in some way, bring more attention to our warnings."

Still staring ahead, a look of sadness frozen across her face, she said in a soft, delicate voice, "I hope you are right, Mr.Cole, because I am scared. Last night I couldn't sleep, not because of what Mendik tried to do to me in his office. I was thinking of my brother trapped in the World Trade Center on September 11, with nobody able to help him. I sometimes feel that I am trapped in those same towers, and no one will hear my cries for help."

◇ ◇ ◇

At a secluded chalet on the outskirts of Zurich, surrounded by an electrified fence, a dark blue Mercedes Benz sedan pulled up to a gate in front of the main entrance. A red and white colored barrier blocked the entrance. Foreign-looking uniformed guards carrying submachine guns stood alertly by the gate. At a booth to the side of the gate, a guard radioed other security personnel located inside the chalet. A multilingual sign by the side of the entrance stated that the premises were the property of the Embassy of the Islamic Republic of Iran and that trespassing was strictly forbidden.

The driver opened his window and handed an ID card to a guard, who carefully scanned all the vehicle's occupants, especially those seated in the rear. He returned the ID card to the driver, then motioned to his colleagues to raise the barrier. The Mercedes Benz passed through the entrance, traveled along a road on the property for a short distance, then pulled into a lot located in front of the chalet. There were already a number of cars parked there, all being various makes of luxury vehicles, including other Mercedes Benz sedans, BMWs and Bentleys. A small group of conservatively attired men, surrounded by gun-toting guards, walked towards the dark blue Mercedes as it stood stationary. One of the men opened the door of the parked automobile as another assisted the first occupant to exit, Sheik Mahmoud Yantissi. The sheik was escorted into the chalet's lounge, where a small group of men were eating sweets from an elaborately arrayed buffet table. Most of the men had beards, all were immaculately tailored, either in expensive Western suits or in traditional Bedouin garb. They all treated Yantissi reverentially, each man personally greeting the sheik and kissing his cheeks.

After twenty minutes had passed, one of the men in the lounge called for order. "Attention please. I know our honored guest is on a tight schedule, so please join me in the conference room."

Once all the required invitees were seated around the conference table in an adjoining room, armed men in mufti closed the door and stood guard. Inside, seated at the head of the table, Yantissi led the group in a reading from the Koran. At the conclusion of the reading, the sheik delivered his message.

"As the most generous and worthy contributors to the Holy Jihad Fund, I consider every one of you seated around this table to be the most righteous of men, worthy of being companions to our prophet Mohammed, may peace be upon him. I also am pleased that past schisms between Sunni and Shiite Moslems have been put aside for the sake of our jihad, as there is only one caliphate of believers in this world, all united in battling the cursed infidel." Yantissi momentarily paused, looking each man seated around the table in the eye, pleased at the intensity and earnestness being manifested.

"It is my duty to let you know that the great task of holy jihad, which we have all striven towards, and of which your almsgiving has been as pleasing to Allah as is the blood of our martyrs, is approaching its climax. The annihilation of the satanic America is within our reach, praise be to Allah. And we shall soon see the day in which Allah's servant, the praiseworthy Osama bin Laden, shall rule all the lands on Earth as the supreme Khalifa, the master of the worldwide caliphate, based on sharia law.

"It pleases Allah that all of you, the generous financiers of the jihad against the far enemy, should profit from your almsgiving. I therefore pass on these instructions, which come from Osama bin Laden himself, may Allah protect him. In advance of the supreme martyrdom operation against infidel America, we want you to begin converting your American dollar holdings to other investments. They may be currencies such as the euro or yen, or real estate in Europe and Asia, or gold and jewelry. We must do this carefully, as we do not want to cause a run on the dollar and collapse its value before we have been able to complete the conversion of your assets. We will be contacting each of you directly over the next several days with instructions. However, and on this point I beg your full attentiveness as pious Moslems, you must dispose of all your dollar holdings before the martyrdom operation has been launched. Afterwards, it will be too late, as the American dollar will be of even less value than the dust blown from the dung heaps of camels."

❖ ❖ ❖

Alex Dunlop was notified that a visitor had arrived. Amelia Baldwin was escorted into his office, and Dunlop offered her a chair and a cup of tea, which he poured for her. He asked her if the accommodations arranged for her during her stay in Ottawa were satisfactory. She replied that they were.

"We have set up a work station for you with all the required internet access, along with a secure line to David Cole's office. Of course, you can communicate with me at any time, and don't hesitate to ask for any assistance you might need." The Deputy Director stopped momentarily, reflecting on the ordeal Amelia had endured. He wanted to say something comforting and at the same time, not remind her of what she had recently and so traumatically experienced. "One other thing I should tell you," he continued. "We at CSIS are honored to have you here with us."

Baldwin thanked Dunlop, then finished her cup of tea. Shortly afterwards, he led her to her new work station, then introduced her to Dextraze and Littlejohn, who had cubicles nearby. He informed her that these two CSIS intelligence officers were directly involved in the investigation of the matter she herself was intertwined with.

"We are glad to have a proficient Arab linguist join us at headquarters," Dextraze warmly said. Referring to his colleague, he told her that Littlejohn was somewhat of linguist himself.

"Unfortunately, my knowledge of Arabic is most rudimentary," Littlejohn told her. "However, I am fluent in French, German, Spanish, Italian, Russian, Korean and my native tongue, Inuit."

"His English is not so bad either," Dextraze interjected, prompting brief laughter from the others at his humor. Restoring a note of seriousness, Dunlop mentioned Baldwin's pivotal role in tying the identity of the Lion to Aziz Faruqui.

Both Dextraze and Littlejohn congratulated Amelia on her role in figuring out the link. "It is you at CSIS who should be commended," she responded. "You are the ones who identified Aziz Faruqui. Without the information you uncovered and passed on to the CIA, I would never have been able to draw the connection."

Dunlop looked sternly at his colleagues. "Having identified the Lion is only a partial success. Without uncovering his whereabouts and apprehending him, we are still scoring zero. Unfortunately, at this point, we haven't the slightest idea where he is."

❖ ❖ ❖

It was approaching midnight as two cars slowly entered the parking lot of a metal works factory on the outskirts of Sault Ste. Marie, a sleepy Ontario industrial town on the northern shore of Lake Superior. The cars parked in the center of the almost empty lot, there being only one other vehicle already parked. Four men exited one of the cars, two carrying AK-47 assault rifles while the other men clutched pistols. They carefully surveyed the area, then one of the men, of Middle Eastern appearance, signaled to his colleagues in the other car. They soon exited their car, three of them, with guns, joining the others in carefully keeping watch over the surroundings. The other man, tall with a narrow face, wearing a cap over his head, looked up at the factory's sign, "Hussein Metal Fabricators." He walked alone towards the factory's entrance, knocking three times on the door. The clanging sound of locks disengaging permeated the otherwise still pitch-black night. A man of average height and weight, with sparse hair and a graying beard, opened the door, smiling at his visitor. "Salaam aleikam!" he said proudly. His visitor flashed a brief smile, and replied, "As-salaam aleikam."

"Come with me!" the owner of the factory, Amad Hussein, excitedly told his visitor, whom he led down a long corridor and into the main area of the plant. There was a section of the plant completely sealed off, with a locked door in the center, and a sign hanging nearby indicating that the space behind was undergoing repairs and renovation. Hussein noisily pulled a set of keys out of his pants pocket, and inserted the correct one into the lock on the door. He opened it with a creaking sound from its hinges, which echoed through the deserted main area of the plant. Hussein and the tall visitor entered the secluded area, which was soon illuminated. The visitor noticed three tarpaulins, two large and one of medium size, covering concealed items. Hussein pulled on one of the large tarpaulins, in a moment exposing a very large metal object. Hussein, beaming with pride, invited his visitor to inspect the structure. As the tall man with the narrow face approached it, Hussein proceeded to unfasten and remove the other two tarpaulins from their concealed objects.

The visitor approached the object slowly, observing its every aspect and feature carefully. He took note of the baked enamel green finish covering most of the object, which was cylindrical in shape and resembled a large machine or mechanical device. He stopped at an inspection plate with a serial number located at the far edge of the contraption. Above the serial number it read, "Manufactured by Davis Industries, Mississauga, Canada. Model 300DN Horizontal Steam Boiler." Attached to it were a pressure gauge, a network of pipes and a control panel affixed to the boiler's front. He smiled, then looked at a duplicate that had also been uncovered. Nearby stood a large rectangular white object.

Amad Hussein looked toward his visitor, who now smiled widely.

"I trust you are pleased with our work, sir" Hussein cautiously said with a voice resonating with humbleness.

"Yes, I am," the visitor replied. "You have built them according to the exact specifications. This is excellent!"

Smiling with pride, Hussein told his visitor in a resolute manner, "It is such a great honor to be of service to the Lion of Islam. May Allah be pleased. What are your further instructions?"

The Lion told Hussein that in exactly 24 hours, the three objects would be retrieved by his men and loaded aboard a truck. He reminded him to continue to keep the items covered and the area cordoned off from the main plant area at his factory.

"Security is vital for our success, brother," the Lion said earnestly. "See to it that you are the only person who has access to this space, and that no personnel other than yourself are present when we next arrive."

Hussein was obsequious in his response. He made it clear that he would be personally responsible for assuring absolute security until the products of his plant's labor were retrieved in twenty-four hours.

"One other thing I must tell you, Amad. Once our operation has been completed, due to its scale, an all-out effort to identify anyone who has assisted us is to be expected. Your role in helping us is likely to be discovered, meaning you will certainly lose your business and all your wealth, and possibly your life."

The Lion looked Hussein directly in the eye, waiting to see how he reacted. He noted that Hussein at first appeared in a serious frame of mind. In a brief moment, as if transformed, he was seized with tranquility, and smiled calmly.

"I tell the Lion I did not come to these infidel lands to make money or live a long life among the heathen and idol worshippers," he said with exuberance. "I am here only to fight the jihad. Your words please me, as I know I will soon be in paradise."

The two men warmly embraced.

❖ ❖ ❖

Early the next morning Amelia Baldwin was at her computer terminal, quickly becoming familiar with her new surroundings at CSIS headquarters. Dextraze dropped by her workstation, offering her a cup of coffee. He returned a few minutes later, noticing that she was engrossed in scanning an Arabic website. Dextraze silently placed the cup of coffee on her desk, seeking not to break her concentration. He stood unobtrusively behind her until Baldwin noticed the puffs of steam being emitted by the coffee. She turned around, apologizing to Dextraze for not taking notice of him.

"No need to apologize, Amelia. Work always comes first around here. I can see you are very focused on that website."

She told him it was the site of the El-Assad Al-Islamiya. "It's the official website of the Lion's organization. For weeks they have been warning that something dire was going to happen to America. As their previous predictions of terrorist incidents have been totally accurate, I take every threat appearing on this site very seriously."

As Amelia clicked onto the page for believers, Dextraze stood over her shoulder, observing. He saw a maze of Arabic script, which he was unable to decipher. He continued to watch as Amelia took note of the latest message on the page, and hurriedly wrote down her translation and impressions.

"I must call David Cole at CIA headquarters right away," she said ominously. Dextraze inquired as to the contents of the website's page that aroused such an elevated level of concern by her.

"The new message to the believers refers to the fatwa that Osama bin Laden issued on February 23, 1998, which was his declaration of war on America. It concludes by boasting that the war will soon end with final victory over America, and the time when Osama bin Laden will be proclaimed the Khalifa is imminent."

Dextraze was unfamiliar with the term Khalifa. He asked Baldwin to explain it to her.

"Khalifa refers to a Moslem of proven piety who is the supreme political as well as religious leader of the worldwide Moslem empire, what is referred to in Arabic as the caliphate. There has not existed a Khalifa for nearly ninety years, when the last sultan of the Ottoman Empire was overthrown."

"What is the significance of bin Laden being proclaimed the Khalifa by this website, Amelia?" inquired Dextraze.

"Not until this message has bin Laden proclaimed himself to be anything other than a modest man fighting jihad for Islam. A proclamation of this extremity by this website, with its pattern of accuracy, suggests a high level of confidence that something will happen soon, very soon, that will neutralize American power."

Bulk Carrier

A dark, noiseless night enveloped the Hussein Metal Fabricators plant on the outskirts of Sault Ste Marie. At first, a gentle breeze blew northward from the frigid shores of Lake Superior. Gradually, another sound permeated that of the wind. The diesel engine of a six-wheel truck became audible. In the otherwise deserted parking lot, Amad Hussein stood expectantly, a solitary figure amidst the nocturnal surroundings. He glanced at his watch, noting that it was exactly midnight. In a matter of minutes, the truck was parked, and three men exited the cab. They opened up the rear of the truck, and five more men emerged. There was a quick exchange of instructions, then Hussein led several of the men into the plant.

In an orderly, precise manner, the dividers inside the main plant area that hid and enclosed the Lion's special items were quickly dismantled. Two large shipping crates and a smaller one were brought into the plant, as a forklift was made operational. Carefully, the two contraptions, identified by manufacturing placards as horizontal steam boilers, were lifted into the two larger crates, as another object, rectangular in shape and resembling a freezer, was also crated.

Outside, the truck was positioned beside the loading dock. Now that all three objects were crated, they were loaded into the rear of the truck. Once the loading was completed and five of the men entered the cargo hold, the rear door of the truck was securely fastened. The three remaining men exchanged greetings

157

in Arabic with Amad Hussein. They all embraced, and spoke of meeting again in paradise.

As the truck's engine roared to life, Hussein looked again at his watch, noting it was now 2:00 AM. He could hear the clutch being let out and gears engaged, as the vehicle slowly moved out of the loading dock. While the truck's engine revved and the vehicle moved more deliberately out of the parking area, Amad Hussein muttered joyfully, "Allahu Akbar!"

❖ ❖ ❖

The President's secretary buzzed her Commander-in-Chief on the intercom, informing him that Glenn Thrush, National Director of Intelligence, had arrived for the morning's intelligence briefing. It was his responsibility to sift through the most current intelligence reports submitted by each of the nation's fifteen separate intelligence agencies, and isolate only the most important elements for the President's attention. It was not easy. The CIA, National Security Agency and a host of State and Defense Department entities compiled a confusing and, at time, contradictory picture. Thrush saw it as his responsibility to exercise his own good judgment. Though lacking previous intelligence or military experience, he had a long and distinguished career in government service, was a cautious man and, for that reason, trusted by the President.

Thrush entered the Oval Office, and sat himself in a chair in front of the President's desk. He was a lean man with a frosty white complexion and jet black hair covering the sides of his head, surrounding a glistening baldpate. He pulled out some notes from his attaché case and proceeded to brief the President, speaking with a crisp delivery.

"Mr. President, there are a couple of items on the threat matrix for this morning that are new. They seem related, but it could all be just coincidental."

The President sat more erect, leaning his head forward, his brow furrowed in concentration. "What are they?" asked the President.

"Last night the National Security Agency reported new movements at the missile test ranges in both Iran and North

Korea. The NSA had satellite images from both sites, and over the last 24 hours there has definitely been a lot of activity. It could be that both the North Koreans and Iranians are preparing for a test firing of their newest long range missiles."

"This is all very important, Glenn," responded the President. "It makes me real glad that my administration implemented missile defense. What do you think the chances are that the Iranians and North Koreans got together on that?"

Thinking on the President's question, Thrush sought to provide a thoughtful answer. "It's hard to say, Mr. President," he said cautiously. "It could be that they chose the same timeframe to conduct a test firing due to atmospheric and weather conditions being optimum in both places at the same time. However, we also know that the two countries have been closely cooperating in the development of an intercontinental ballistic missile."

Shaking his head from side to side and grimacing, the President expressed his concern and skepticism. "I don't like this," the President said. "They're both rogue states. Could be they are planning on testing their missiles to send us a message, intimidate us."

"It's possible," was the reply of the National Intelligence Director. He then proceeded to report on Iraq, listing the number of attacks by insurgents on American forces during the previous 24-hour period. The President displayed no outward emotion as the Director provided the latest casualty figures.

"What about the Lion?" inquired the President. "What does the CIA say on that?"

"Well, Mr. President, the Central Intelligence Agency sort of speaks with two voices on that matter. Their analysts on the ground in Iraq still believe he is there, in country, hiding. Dick Darnell so far is backing them in their estimates. On the other hand, the CIA's voice and biometrics analysts and technicians at Langley have completed their technical examination of the voice patterns and eye images from videos of both the Lion and that Pakistani ISI agent, Aziz Faruqui. Their conclusion is that there is a definite match."

The President seemed confused by the explanation. He asked Thrush how he interpreted the information, and what his recommendation was.

"Well, Mr. President, there is a fifty-fifty chance that each of these competing views is right or wrong," Thrush said guardedly. "My advice is to treat this as a law enforcement matter, and have the FBI look at the information and draw there own conclusions. If the Lion is indeed in Canada and trying to enter the United States, it is up to the FBI to apprehend him."

Thrush's response prompted another inquiry from the President. "Glenn, what about the stuff about nuclear terrorism that the Canadians and David Cole at the CIA are scared stiff over?"

Normally a taciturn man, Thrush emitted a brief expression of laughter, which the President observed and found comforting.

"I don't think we have anything to worry about," Thrush said reassuringly. "I know the words *nuclear terrorism* seize the public's imagination and arouse all kinds of irrational fears. However, the intelligence community, which unlike the public views these things rationally and has access to closed-source information on how nuclear weapons work, assures me that it is absolutely impossible for a terrorist organization, a non-state actor, to design and build a functioning nuclear weapon. Frankly, I believe such a possibility exists only in a Tom Clancy novel."

The President smiled, pleased at the reassurance.

❖ ❖ ❖

On Parliament Hill in Ottawa, Samuel Kinkaid, the Director of CSIS and his Deputy Director were conducting a highly confidential meeting with the Prime Minister behind the closed doors of his office.

"Sir, we at CSIS are convinced that time is running out. If we are not successful in finding the Lion and the thermonuclear device we believe he has constructed, he will succeed in smuggling it into the United States," Kinkaid said with alarm. "That means everything will depend on what the Americans choose to do about it and, so far, they have elected to do nothing."

The Prime Minister looked both worried and lost for words. He wasn't sure how to respond. Dunlop thought he should add weight to the Director's warning.

"Other than the CIA's Director of Counter-Terrorism, who has been crying alone in the wilderness over this threat, nobody in the American government or intelligence community has taken our warnings seriously, Mr. Prime Minister. Unless we can get our American friends off their behinds, a calamity will ensue that will be shattering to the whole North American continent, including our own country."

The Prime Minister placed both hands over his eyes, his contracted forehead giving evidence of the immense stress and strain he felt overwhelmed with. When he uncovered his eyes, both CSIS officials observed a man consumed with fear. Dunlop felt great empathy, for he too was riveted with forlorn worry.

"What should I do?" the Prime Minister asked almost pleadingly.

"Mr. Prime Minister, we are doing all we can in our own country," Dunlop replied. "The RCMP has quietly circulated Aziz Faruqui's photograph and description to Constables in border areas. We have conducted surveillance everywhere we can think of. The armed forces are on call. Our informants have been alerted. However, our adversary is highly skilled and resourceful, as well as being ruthless and determined. The trail is cold and I am not optimistic we will track down the Lion and his nuclear device in time. The only thing we can still do lies south of the border. I highly recommend you do everything in your power to arrange an emergency meeting with the President of the United States."

Sitting still for a moment, consumed with indecisiveness, the Prime Minister seemed seized with psychological paralysis. Echoing his subordinate's advice, Kinkaid added his own verbal reinforcement. "Mr. Prime Minister, I absolutely agree with Alex's suggestion. I see no other option."

"But the last time I tried calling the President, he wouldn't speak with me. I got second tiered to the Vice President. As you both know, the meeting that resulted was not especially useful.

What guarantee can you give me that if I put in another call, the result will be different this time?"

Dunlop was visibly aggravated by the Prime Minister's response. "Sir, I am in a position to guarantee you nothing," he responded in stronger words than he intended, for he had not lost his empathy or respect for the Prime Minister. Continuing, he added, "except for one thing. If we don't try everything in our power to convince the Americans to take this threat seriously, we will all live to regret our inaction."

Kinkaid glanced at Dunlop, concerned he may have overstepped himself. The Prime Minister, however, quickly put his concerns to rest. "You are right, Alex," he told him. "Please excuse me gentlemen, I have an important phone call to make."

❖ ❖ ❖

At a truck stop about ten miles north of Laramie, Wyoming, a physically imposing man, tall and muscular, with bulging tattoo-covered biceps, sat alone in the cafeteria, sipping his beer. He was noticed by another man who had just entered, of medium stature and dark complexion with black hair, wearing a tan leather jacket. The man who had entered walked up to the small table where the other man was sitting. "Are you Mr. Robert Dunn?"

"Yes, you can call me Bob. You must be Mr. Jones."

The other man sat down, looked briefly behind his shoulder to satisfy himself that he was not being observed, than turned towards the heavy set man. "Yes, I am Mr. Jones," he said with an Arabic accent. "I understand you are a very reliable truck driver."

The other man smiled, and offered confirmation of his reputation. "I am independent, and proud of it. Meaning, for the right price, I am very reliable with special deliveries."

Jones looked penetratingly at Robert Dunn. He briefly scanned the tattoos on his arms, noting with satisfaction that several of them had messages that were anti-Semitic.

"Bob, my information is that you will be in Regina, Saskatchewan next Tuesday to pick up a load of biscuits for a customer in Montana. Is that so?"

Dunn confirmed the accuracy of the information. "As I told your associate, it's a run I do regularly every month. The people with Customs on the U.S. border are used to seeing me with the same load. All they usually do is ask to see the bill of lading, then they wave me through."

Mr. Jones was pleased and reassured. Speaking in a low, barely audible voice, he explained the arrangement. His business partners in Regina were in the marijuana growing business. They would arrange to substitute one of the crates of biscuits with an identical crate with one difference; the cartons of biscuits would be substituted with cartons containing cannabis. Once safely over the border, other partners would arrange to pick up their crate, and return the one that was substituted.

Dunn relayed his comfort with the arrangement. He asked for the location of the pick-up in Regina.

"I cannot give you that information here. Once you have loaded the biscuits in Regina, we will contact you by cell phone," Jones curtly replied.

"What about my fee?" inquired the truck driver.

"Yes, we agreed on thirty thousand dollars," Jones replied. He pulled out a wad of cash and handed it to Dunn, who quickly counted it and then placed it in his hip pocket.

"That is a thousand dollars as a down payment. You will be paid the remainder in cash when delivery is completed," Jones told Dunn. He then looked at his watch, and remarked that he had to leave and attend to other business.

Jones and Dunn both stood up, the truck driver extending his hand. As they shook hands, he remarked, "It is a pleasure doing business with you, Mr. Jones."

❖ ❖ ❖

Sitting at his desk at CIA headquarters, David Cole heard his intercom buzzing. He was notified of an incoming call from Alex Dunlop on his secure line. He grabbed his phone immediately.

"David, our Prime Minister finally got through to your President last night," Dunlop informed his colleague. "It took a lot of arm-twisting, but at last and, I must say, reluctantly, the President agreed to a face-to-face meeting."

There was no immediate response from Cole, prompting the Deputy Director of CSIS to ask if he was alright.

"Sorry, Alex. I'm feeling somewhat under siege here. But I heard what you said. It could be our last hope."

Dunlop asked if anyone in Washington was beginning to realize the scale of the looming threat. Cole's reply was not encouraging.

"Alex, I wish I could tell you something positive. But nuclear terrorism isn't even a blip on the radar screen in Washington. In addition to the war on Iraq, social security and the President's proposed tax cuts, there is the scandal over the firing and arrest of Bill Mendik. This morning, Congress announced that they will be conducting hearings into the Mendik affair. There is even talk of subpoenaing Amelia, bringing her back here to testify as to exactly what parts of her body the former Secretary of Homeland Security laid his hands on."

Dunlop couldn't believe the disconnect going on in Washington that Cole was describing to him in such painful detail. "Are they all in Disney World over there?" he asked rhetorically. Then, seeking to buttress hope in both himself and his American colleague, he added, "At least we have a chance with a meeting of the heads of our two governments to get everyone off the dime before time totally runs out."

Cole inquired as to when the meeting was to take place. Dunlop informed him it would happen in two days, at the presidential retreat at Camp David. "I wish it was taking place today," Dunlop added, with frustration in his voice. He informed Cole that he would be accompanying the Prime Minister, along with Dr. Lazar. He mentioned that it was very important that Cole do everything possible to ensure that he was at the meeting.

"By hook or by crook, I'll be there," he told Dunlop. "There is no way in hell that they are keeping the CIA's Director of Counter-Terrorism from attending a high-level summit meeting dealing with nuclear terrorism."

Dunlop asked if there had been any elevation of security measures on the U.S. side of the border. "Our feeling at CSIS is that the attempt to insert the nuclear device across the border is imminent, if it has not already been done," he added.

"I really wish I could be the bearer of good news on that," Cole replied. "Unfortunately, even the modest steps that were to be taken by Customs and the FBI have been placed on hold ever since there has been this unplanned vacancy at the Department of Homeland Security."

❖ ❖ ❖

At the Sault Ste. Marie port entrance, a night watchman sat in a hut by the gate, glancing at the full moon in the night sky, before returning to reading the sports section of his newspaper. The sound of an approaching truck prompted him to stop his reading. He stepped outside the hut and looked towards the headlights of the vehicle, which ground to a halt just before the gate. The driver rolled down his window as the watchman approached.

"Good evening!" the driver said in an exuberant tone of voice, tinged in an accent that sounded either East European or Balkan. The watchman returned the greeting, and politely asked for the driver's identification, which was immediately produced. The watchman returned the identification, satisfied. He then asked what the driver was bringing into the port area.

"I am delivering equipment for the SS Northern Conquest," he said, passing on an invoice listing a steam boiler for the ship's laundry and a freezer for the ship's galley. The watchman wanted to see for himself. Obligingly, the driver stepped out of the cab and opened the rear compartment. Firmly holding his flashlight, the watchman observed a large crate occupying most of the space, with a smaller crate to the rear.

"Can you please show me what's in that crate in back," the watchman asked. Displaying a complete willingness to cooperate, the driver removed the top of the crate, exposing a large freezer.

"I hate to do this, but can you also show me the inside of that larger crate."

"No problem," the driver replied, as he took a crowbar and opened the front part of the crate. The watchman pointed his flashlight probingly at the crate's interior. He was able to discern a large cylindrical object, with pipes and a pressure gauge in front.

"Just as it says on the invoice, a steam boiler," the watchman said approvingly. "I'll open the gate for you."

Within a few minutes, the truck had approached the dock where the SS Northern Conquest was moored. The driver shut off the truck's engine, glanced at his watch, then sat patiently. Moments later, again looking at his watch and verifying that it was exactly 10:00 PM, he stepped out of the cab. In the distance, he observed a swarthy-looking man with a wrinkled olive complexion, approaching him. The men now walked towards each other, stopping with barely a yard's distance between them.

"It is a cold night, and the morning was also cold," said the man who had come from the dock area. "But it was not as cold as yesterday, or the day before yesterday," replied the driver. Without exchanging any further words, the driver opened the rear cargo area of the truck, then closed it after the other man stepped inside, holding a lit flashlight. The driver stood calmly outside, smoking a cigarette while keeping watch.

Inside the cargo bay, the man approached the smaller crate, knocked five times on the top, waited ten seconds, then knocked three more times. He lifted the top of the crate, then removed seals along the top-opening door of the freezer. Once the seals were removed, he slowly lifted the door. As it stood nearly open, Aziz Faruqui sat inside, holding a pistol. A smile formed on his face, and he placed the pistol in a holster hidden by his jacket.

"Jafaar, it is so good to see you, my friend!" Faruqui said with elation.

Beaming with joy, Jafaar replied with equal exultation. "It has been three years since we were last together, fighting the Americans in Falujah. It has been such a long time, my brother."

"I know how hard it has been for you, Jafaar, to have been sent here for three years," Faruqui responded empathetically. "But now, things are nearly completed. You have been sent here for the most joyful of reasons, for the jihad."

With some difficulty, Faruqui lifted himself up, aided by his comrade, and stepped out of the freezer. Jafaar noticed that what looked externally like a large freezer was in fact a concealed living space, albeit one that was exceedingly uncomfortable. There were small air holes concealed on the bottom, with a thin mattress, a small lamp, a copy of the Koran, an AK-47, a box containing food and beverage and a covered plastic container that served as a portable toilet. Jafaar, observing the plastic container, offered to have it emptied and cleaned.

"Thank you for the offer, my friend, but for the sake of security for this operation, I must decline. It is better that I wait until this special cargo has arrived at a more secure location."

Faruqui proceeded to ask Jafaar to brief him on the next phase of the operation, which he would be responsible for.

"The Falujah cell of Al-Assad El-Islamiya consists of eight warriors, including me. We are all crewmembers aboard the SS Northern Conquest, out of a total complement of thirty men. The captain doesn't suspect a thing. I am the chief engineer, and the captain defers to me on all matters involving equipment. I authorized the replacement of the horizontal steam boiler for the ship's laundry and a freezer for the galley. Once our vessel is underway, we will arrange a short circuit in the DC power supply. This will necessitate removing our steam boiler and freezer, along with some other items of equipment for good cover, when we reach our destination, for repairs. Another cell operates an electrical repair facility in Duluth. They will pick you up, send you to your next destination and replace the fake freezer and boiler with the real items, with the identical serial numbers."

Faruqui inquired if everything was still on schedule. Jafaar confirmed that the SS Northern Conquest was set to hoist anchor at 7:00 AM the next morning, as previously scheduled. There were no changes in the weather forecast, meaning the vessel was expected to dock in Duluth, Minnesota about thirty hours from the time they departed Sault Ste. Marie.

"What about security at the port of Duluth?" Faruqui asked.

"No changes to report, my brother," Jafaar said with an air of self-assurance. "Our vessel is a bulk carrier loaded with 20,000 tons of crushed gravel in nine compartments. The security at a Great Lakes port is nowhere near that of an American port on the Atlantic or Pacific coast receiving container shipments from overseas. The Customs inspector will take a quick look at one of the cargo holds, review the manifest and paperwork, and be off the ship in fifteen minutes. They have no interest in any equipment additions or retrofits done to the ship while in a Canadian port."

"Excellent," Faruqui replied, "but what about removing our damaged goods?"

"It is still the same. The only procedure is that a security guard will record the serial numbers of the items we have removed for repair, and verify that when the repaired equipment has been returned, their serial numbers match what was originally taken off the ship."

"You have done well, Jafaar. I am proud of you," Faruqui said with emotion in his voice.

Replying with humility, his comrade said, "It is the greatest honor for me to serve the Lion in doing jihad on American soil. It seems everything is going according to plan."

"Things never go exactly according to plan," Faruqui said in a somewhat pedagogical manner. "We did have a mishap or two, but nothing to worry about. Allah tests our resolve by creating challenges not originally anticipated so that we, as lovers of martyrdom, must use our ingenuity to overcome them. I have already prepared a diversion to deal with the situation and throw the arrogant infidels off our tracks. Listen to me carefully, Jafaar. Nothing, do you hear me, nothing the Americans can do is going to stop us."

Summit At Camp David

In the northern Italian city of Milan, an immigrant neighborhood was barraged with a cacophony of noise, marking the morning rush hour. Among the vehicles traversing a street laced with low rise apartment buildings were three unmarked vans, which parked inconspicuously in front of one of the buildings. They remained parked for several minutes until, at precisely 8:00 AM, the rear doors opened and squads of heavily armed members of the Italian anti-terrorism police leaped out. Wearing helmets and flak jackets and carrying submachine guns, they stormed into the adjacent apartment building and ran up the staircase to the third floor. In front of apartment 307 one of the officers kicked the door open, and his comrades rushed into the apartment.

Four men were in the living room by the door. One of the men pulled out a revolver and aimed it at the police; a rapid burst of bullets ripped his chest open and sent him spiraling backwards, dead. His comrades quickly raised their hands in submission.

A half dozen officers ran into one of the bedrooms, which contained three small beds and a desk by the window with a computer. One man was seated at the computer, attempting to delete files in panicky haste while another man grabbed a Kalashnikov assault rifle. Before he could load a clip of ammunition, a volley of shots ripped into his abdomen, sending his blood spattering on the walls as he cried out in agony. One of the officers ordered the seated man to stop deleting files and stand up with his arms raised. He ignored the command, which prompted several of the officers to pull him away from the computer and wrestle him as he swore at them with a generous dose of profanity.

There was a second bedroom in the apartment, where one of the occupants had started a small fire on the floor and was proceeding with tossing files from a filing cabinet into the flames. Four officers entered the room and shot him dead before he could dispose of any additional files. The police quickly doused the flames and began collecting and boxing the files for removal. In the other bedroom, technicians who had accompanied the anti-terrorism police were already busily working on the computer, restoring the files one of the terrorists had attempted to permanently erase.

Later in the day, a senior officer with the Milan branch of the Italian anti-terrorism police received a call from one of his subordinates. The information being reported to him prompted him to call an assistant into his office, whom he instructed to immediately arrange a secure phone connection with the Deputy Director of the Canadian Security Intelligence Service. Within five minutes, the connection had been affected.

It was late evening in Ottawa, and Dunlop was fighting fatigue, as he was immersed in preparation for the summit meeting at Camp David the following day involving the Canadian Prime Minister and American President. However, the news he received from Milan prompted a rush of adrenaline through his veins. He thanked his colleague in Milan for the information he had passed on and assured him that CSIS and the Canadian authorities would be following up with maximum diligence. He then placed a phone call to Pierre Dextraze at home.

The intelligence officer was playing with his son when his wife answered the phone. When she told him it was Dunlop, Dextraze realized that something of great importance had arisen and that he would be in for a long night. Grasping the phone, he heard Dunlop simply tell him it was urgent that both he and Henry Littlejohn meet with him at CSIS headquarters in half an hour.

Both men arrived at CSIS headquarters simultaneously, and walked briskly to the Deputy Director's office. When they arrived, Dunlop motioned for them to close the door. He then proceeded to share with them new information.

"Earlier today, the Italian anti-terrorism police raided an apartment building in Milan," he told his intelligence officers. "It was being used by an Islamist terrorist cell believed to be linked with both Al-Qaeda and the Al-Assad El-Islamiya organization. This particular outfit was a logistics cell, meaning they supported other terrorist cells with false documents and with money obtained through robberies, drug-trafficking and embezzlement The Italians thought this cell was established to support and fund Al-Qaeda operations in Europe and decided to close it down when they intercepted messages that suggested one of the operations they were funding was about to be launched. However, among the documents and computer files seized were records of money transfers made by this group to a bank in Canada."

Dextraze asked if the name of the bank was known.

"All the Italians were able to pull off the hard drive of a computer they confiscated was an account number, the dates of four money transfers, and indications that the bank is located in Sault Ste. Marie," replied Dunlop. "I will need both of you to head down to Sault Ste. Marie right away and canvass each and every bank in town until we have matched a name with that account number."

Littlejohn asked if the Italian authorities had uncovered any additional information from the raid in Milan that was relevant to Canada.

"Just one other item of interest," Dunlop said. "In the files they seized they found a receipt for payment on items manufactured in Milan that were shipped to Takasumi Investments. The items were labeled as piping for mine exploration activity in Northern Ontario. The Italian anti-terrorism police have informed me that the specifications of these pipes were identical to what is used in nuclear research reactors to control neutron spillation. This means they can also be used in the construction of thermonuclear bombs."

"Good God!" uttered Dextraze.

❖ ❖ ❖

At CIA headquarters, Richard Darnell had just arrived. He stopped by his secretary's desk to wish her a good morning. She returned the greeting, adding that David Cole wanted to meet with him right away.

"Please put him off. Cole is the last person I want to meet with right now," he told her forcefully.

"I'm sorry sir, but it looks like he's going to be the first person you meet with today," she quickly replied.

"What?" Darnell uttered, relaying how inexplicable he thought her reply was.

The secretary explained that David Cole was already in the CIA Director's office; he had insisted on waiting there and she was unable to dissuade him. With a glum expression on his face, Darnell entered his office, visually confronting Cole, who stood facing him, his face flushed with anger.

"Dick, why am I not included with the delegation meeting with the Canadian Prime Minister!" he shouted passionately.

Darnell was not sure how to respond. He stared belligerently at the agency's Director of Counter-Terrorism, attempting through his body language to convey that he had no place at the meeting which was to occur at Camp David later on in the day. Finally, he verbalized a response.

"David, your place is not at Camp David."

"I am the Director of Counter-Terrorism, for Christ's sakes!" Cole yelled. "At a meeting about terrorism, nuclear terrorism, you mean to tell me that I have no place? Where is my place then, Dick?!"

Taking a deep breath, Darnell sought to take the blame off of himself. "It wasn't my call, David," he said defensively. "It was the President's decision, along with the Vice President and National Director of Intelligence. They felt that with me being at the meeting, the CIA was adequately represented."

"Is that all?" Cole asked in a sarcastic voice.

"No, that is not all," Darnell interjected in a forceful manner. "Not a single significant player in the intelligence community agrees with your analysis, let alone that of the Canadians. At Camp David, our objective is to calm them down on this nonsense about Islamic terrorists having a nuclear bomb and attempting to smuggle it into the United States. Instead, we want them to focus on the real threats. You see, David, while you were sleeping last night, the Iranians and North Koreans conducted test firings of a long-range ballistic missile capable of hitting the continental United States. That means once they have developed atomic warheads that can fit on those missiles, and place them in mass production, all of North America will be susceptible to their blackmail."

Shaking his head and appearing dejected, he responded with a melancholy tinge to his voice. "So, I see, Dick. You want to use this meeting as an opportunity to rally the Canadians in support of our missile defense initiative. And as an expert on international terrorism, I just don't fit into the script."

Nodding his head affirmatively, Darnell replied boldly. "I wouldn't have quite framed it so bluntly but, yes, you don't fit our script."

Cole reminded the CIA Director that the Agency's own voice authentication and biometrics experts had confirmed that the Pakistani ISI agent Aziz Faruqui, known to have entered Canada, was the notorious Lion.

"The technical experts can be wrong," Darnell said dismissively. "Our field agents on the ground in Iraq tell me they are certain he is still north of Baghdad, hiding somewhere in the Sunni triangle. Until you can give me more persuasive evidence, I stand by what our people in Iraq tell me."

"I want to go on record as strongly protesting my exclusion from this important conference," Cole told his Director. "You are consumed with a threat from Iran and North Korea that will take at least five and more likely ten years to materialize. The threat both the Canadians and I are terrified of is imminent, meaning not a matter of years or months or even weeks. We are talking about days, Dick! What will it take to convince you and the President that an act of nuclear terrorism targeting an American city is a clear and present danger, right now!"

"Spare me the hyperbole," Darnell angrily responded. "Until I see a mushroom cloud above an American city, nobody is going to convince me that these Neanderthal barbarians have the capability to construct anything more sophisticated than a car bomb."

❖ ❖ ❖

A Canadian armed forces Challenger VIP jet landed at Washington's Reagan National Airport that afternoon and was directed to a secluded area on the tarmac. A Cadillac limousine with accompanying Secret Service and police escort was waiting for them. A few minutes after landing, its passengers disembarked. The Prime Minister of Canada, Alex Dunlop and Dr. Thomas Lazar, the latter clutching his ubiquitous walking stick, walked briskly towards the Cadillac, its rear door held open for them by a Secret Service agent. In a matter of moments, the convoy of vehicles was on its way to Camp David.

During the drive, the Prime Minister asked the CSIS Deputy Director how he thought the Americans would receive them. "With great skepticism," he replied. "They will do everything they can to convince both us and themselves that there exists no imminent threat of nuclear terrorism to their country. Somehow, we must overcome their failure to see the danger that now confronts them."

For most of the drive to Camp David, the three men sat silently in the rear of the limousine, their innermost thoughts impregnated with foreboding. At one point, the Prime Minister asked Dunlop what options would be left should the American administration's senior officials continue to discount the possibility of a terrorist nuclear attack on their nation being in the final stages of preparation. It was a question Dunlop was not at all comfortable answering. "Mr. Prime Minister, should that happen," he said awkwardly, "I think all we could then do is pray for a miracle."

❖ ❖ ❖

Henry Littlejohn stepped out of a bank in downtown Sault Ste. Marie, and entered his rental car parked just across the street. There, he removed his cellular phone from his jacket pocket and called Dextraze, who was in the lobby of another bank.

"Pierre, I just got a negative at the downtown location of Imperial Bank. That's my fourth."

Dextraze reported that he had five negatives, with two more on his list still to visit.

"I have a ScotiaBank branch a block away. I'll check it out and report back to you," Littlejohn told his colleague. He then stepped out of his car, and walked towards the branch. Upon entering, he asked one of the tellers to have the branch manager paged. Moments later, a plump, middle-aged woman appeared. Littlejohn pulled out his identification badge, which prompted a startled expression from the manager. In a low-key manner, he requested a private meeting with her. The manager brought Littlejohn to her office, and closed the door.

"Madame, I'm here on a highly confidential matter involving national security. I cannot divulge the purpose of our investigation, however, CSIS requests your cooperation." Littlejohn withdrew a small piece of paper from his pocket and placed in on the manager's desk. She noticed it was a series of numbers. "I need to know if these numbers match any accounts held by one of your depositors," Littlejohn said. The manager punched the numbers into the computer on her desk, then waited for a response.

"It is not showing up as an active account," the manager told the CSIS officer. "However, there is one other possibility. I'll check our inactive accounts." The manager again entered the sequence of numbers into her computer, and a moment later her hard drive began purring, prompting Littlejohn to become erect with anticipation.

"Mr. Littlejohn, I have a match with an account that was recently closed."

Several minutes later, Littlejohn was back in his automobile when his cell phone rang. Dextraze was reporting that he had another negative from the bank he just visited.

"Good news, Pierre. I just came from the ScotiaBank branch. The account number belonged to an individual who recently closed his account at this branch. I have copies of all the identification this person submitted when he first opened the account. Meet me at the coffee shop on Toronto Street."

About twenty minutes later, the two CSIS intelligence officers were at the coffee shop, reviewing the documents Littlejohn had obtained from the bank manager. They indicated that the account had belonged to a Michael Khoury. A photocopy of the man's driver's license showed a person of average weight and height, dark hair and full moustache.

"I'll bet you dollars to donuts that Michael Khoury does not exist," Dextraze said.

"We should run checks on the address and social insurance number, but I know you're right," replied Littlejohn.

"In that case, let's have the RCMP run the address and other checks on Khoury," Dextraze responded, "while you and I run the photo we have by gas stations in town. If this person lives here, he is bound to have bought gas."

"He also spent money here, and not just on gas, Pierre. Whenever his account got a money transfer from Milan, typically of eight or nine thousand dollars, he was over at the branch within minutes and withdrew all the funds in cash."

❖ ❖ ❖

At the presidential lodge at Camp David, the Canadian visitors had arrived, and were greeted by the Vice President, National Intelligence Director, the Directors of the CIA and FBI and the National Security Advisor. The Vice President warmly greeted the Prime Minister, apologizing for the President being late. "He had an important meeting at the White House with the chairman of the Congressional committee dealing with Social Security. It ran longer than expected, but he should be arriving by helicopter in about forty five minutes."

Dunlop introduced Lazar to the Vice President and other officials as the senior anti-proliferation advisor to CSIS. He then scanned the room, noting the absence of David Cole. "Is Mr. Cole attending this meeting?" he asked hesitatingly. "No," was the brusque reply from the smiling Vice President.

❖ ❖ ❖

Sitting at his office in Langley, Cole's face was a mask of depression and defeat. His forehead was streaked with stress lines, resembling the fatigue cracks on an aging fuselage. He was in a painful contemplation so deep, at first he did not hear his phone ringing. After five rings he was awakened from his depressed mood, and answered the phone. It was Johanne Kleist.

Cole instantly recognized the urgent tone of his friend's voice. This only aroused a higher level of attentiveness in him as he listened carefully to what was being relayed to him from Zurich.

"David, during the last three days, individuals who I know were major donors to the Holy Jihad Fund have been pulling all their U.S. dollar assets out of their Swiss bank accounts."

Pausing momentarily before responding to what Kleist had just revealed to him, he intuitively recognized that these acts were significant, yet he was uncertain as to how.

"How much money are we talking about, Johanne?" Cole inquired.

"So far, about fourteen billion dollars," Kleist said. "They have been converting them to euros, yen and Swiss francs and, in some cases, as collateral for financing real estate purchases in Great Britain, Germany and Hong Kong."

"That's a hell of a lot of money, Johanne. Do you think they are trying to crash the value of the American dollar?"

"No, not at this point," Kleist answered without hesitation. "It does sound like a lot of money, but with trillions of dollars traded every day on the world's currency markets, it's not enough to create more than a blip. Besides, I estimate that collectively the donors to the Holy Jihad Fund have U.S. dollar holdings of about two hundred billion dollars at various Swiss banks. If they wanted to collapse the dollar, all their holdings would have been converted at about the same time, instead of staggering the transactions."

"Very peculiar," Cole said with suspicion in his voice. "They're up to something, it just may not be immediately obvious." He thanked Kleist for the information and requested that he continue to update him daily if these currency transactions continued.

After concluding his phone conversation, Cole sat at his desk in deep thought, attempting to construct the motive underlying the unusual financial behavior of benefactors of the Islamic terrorist movement and Al-Qaeda. At first, the rationale eluded him. Then, in an instant, it all became very clear to him, with frightening implications.

He grabbed the telephone on his desk and rapidly punched in the numbers for Gayle Payne's cell phone. He only got her voice mail. "Damn!" he uttered, realizing that she would have switched off her phone during the meeting at Camp David.

Turning to his computer screen and keyboard, Cole pulled up the phone number for the duty officer at Camp David. It took him only a moment to dial the number. After identifying who he was to the duty officer, he indicated that a matter involving national security of the highest priority had arisen and that it was essential for the National Security Advisor to be paged at once so he could report directly to her. The duty officer complied with his wishes.

Inside the conference room at the presidential lodge, the American Commander-in-Chief had just arrived and the meeting was about to commence. The duty officer quietly entered the conference room. Spotting Payne, he approached her and whispered inconspicuously into her ear. Looking agitated and annoyed, she left the room and took Cole's call.

"What is it, David?" she said in a voice suggesting her antipathy towards the CIA's Counter-Terrorism Director. It took Cole only a moment to respond and for Gayle Payne's demeanor to shift radically.

"You're right, this is very serious!" she said in a voice that was almost shrieking. "The men at this meeting have got to know this. You need to report this directly. I'll arrange for a Marine Corps helicopter to pick you up at Langley and bring you here to Camp David right away."

When the National Security Advisor returned to the conference room, the meeting had already started. The President thanked his Canadian colleagues for taking the time to travel to Camp David, and expressed his appreciation for their spirit of cooperation on addressing the threat of global terrorism. However, it was the unanimous verdict of the American intelligence community that Jihadist groups such as Al-Qaeda and their offshoots, including the Al-Assad El-Islamiya, lacked the scientific and technical know-how to construct a workable nuclear bomb and successfully detonate it, he informed his Canadian guests. On the other hand, rogue states such as North Korea and Iran did pose an immediate danger to both the United States and Canada, he emphasized passionately, calling on the National Director of Intelligence to update everyone on what had transpired during the evening.

Glenn Thrush pulled out a series of 8x10 black and white reconnaissance photographs from an envelope in front of him, and distributed them to the meeting participants. "These are images of the primary ballistic missile test sites in both Iran and North Korea, taken over a four day period. They clearly show that both sites are undergoing preparations for a test launch."

Thrush briefly paused, waiting until the Canadians in the room had seen all the photographic evidence. He then continued. "We now have confirmation that both countries successfully launched long-range ballistic missiles during the evening. This is the first time they have tested these missiles, which we know have been under development for five years. They have sufficient range to reach most targets in the northern hemisphere, including Canada. It is only a matter of time before both of these rogue nations develop atomic warheads for these missiles and begin deploying them."

As the President thanked Thrush for his report, Dunlop whispered into the Prime Minister's ear, "Sir, I think they are trying to pull a bait and switch on us."

The President looked sternly at the Canadian Prime Minister. "You see, Mr. Prime Minister, that's where the real threat lies," he said in a manner that appeared pretentious. "I think this is an opportunity for your country to reconsider its policies in the light of this new information."

Looking tense and somewhat uncertain, the Prime Minister mustered the internal resolve to reply forcefully. "Mr. President, I must respectfully ask that this meeting be confined to the agenda we agreed to during our telephone conversation," he said with passion. "My country has already rendered its decision on missile defense, which is that we do not believe it is in our national interests to join you in this endeavor. Furthermore, this is not the time or the forum to reconsider our decision, especially in light of the terrorist threat that is both immediate and consequential."

"We happen to disagree with you on that point," the Vice President interjected. Turning to the FBI Director, he asked him for his assessment.

"Our joint counter-terrorism task force, involving all governmental and intelligence agencies, has not one iota of reliable information pointing to an elevated threat level to this country," Larry Braun said. "If in fact there was a plot underway, on the scale suggested by our Canadian colleagues, the massive law enforcement and intelligence assets of this government would have detected something. As it stands, no credible information has come our way."

The CIA Director echoed his colleagues, claiming that no information from overseas had surfaced that would lend credibility to the Canadian concern. Dunlop feared that the meeting would deteriorate into a session of ostrich heads being stuck in the sand. In exasperation, he sought to break through the logger jam by addressing a question to the CIA Director.

"Mr. Darnell, if I may be permitted to ask, how many case officers does the CIA have posted overseas?"

Darnell seemed caught off guard by the inquiry from Dunlop. Uncertain if he was authorized to reply, he turned towards the President, who gestured with his head movement that it was alright to answer Dunlop's question.

"We have about 1,100 case officers working outside the United States," Darnell reluctantly answered.

"Well, as I am sure Mr. Braun can confirm, that is fewer than the number of FBI agents who work just in New York City," Dunlop said.

Turning to the his FBI Director, the President asked, "Is that true Larry? Do you have more people in New York City than the CIA has throughout the world?" Somewhat painfully, Braun confirmed the accuracy of Dunlop's statistics.

"I fail to see the relevancy of this," Darnell retorted.

"This is what's relevant, in my opinion," Dunlop interjected. "Out of 1,100 case officers, at least half are posted to Iraq, to deal with the insurgency. Of the remainder, most are detailed to leftover issues from the Cold War, the missile threats from Iran and North

Korea, economic intelligence gathering and activity in China. It is my understanding that a mere fifty CIA case officers are assigned to counter-terrorism duties involving the monitoring of groups such as Al-Qaeda and the Al-Assad El-Islamiya, throughout the world. That includes Europe, the Middle East, Pakistan and the Indian subcontinent as well as Southeast Asia and Indonesia, not to mention Latin America. Since we know that these fifty intelligence agents cannot be expected to work 24 hours a day, that means during any eight hour period the United States of America has between fifteen and twenty CIA case officers covering all four corners of the globe for intelligence regarding the planning and execution of terrorist attacks on your country." Pausing only briefly, Dunlop turned his gaze towards the American Commander-in-Chief. "Mr. President, I ask you in all sincerity, are you comfortable accepting the premise that there is a lack of any confirmation of what the Canadian intelligence community has concluded, based on factual evidence, because the fifteen or so CIA case officers on duty right now monitoring the terrorist threat have failed thus far to discover any corroborating information on their own?"

The President appeared flustered, however, the Vice President spoke. "Intelligence gathering involves much more than cloak and dagger spies wearing trench coats, Mr. Dunlop. The United States has chosen to make its intelligence investments in technology. As we are sitting here at Camp David, at this very moment, our National Security Agency has satellites circling the globe. We are able to intercept phone calls being made anywhere in the world. Technology is impartial and non-subjective. That is the basis for our opinion."

"With all due respect, Mr. Vice President, our terrorist adversary is fully aware of your technical means," Dunlop replied. "They know how to communicate in a manner that is undetectable by your satellites and sophisticated eavesdropping devices. They also know how to plant misleading information."

The President appeared angry, his face turning a discernable shade of red. "If that's the case, then on what basis are you so certain that the terrorists have a nuke?"

"Admittedly, Mr. President, our evidence is circumstantial, however, taken together, it presents a picture that is distinctly clear and frightening," Dunlop responded with firmness. "To help us all see this picture with clarity, I have asked our anti proliferation advisor, Dr. Thomas Lazar, to share some essential information with us."

Before Lazar could speak, Darnell asked what his credentials were. Dunlop briefly described his resume, adding, "Thomas is the last surviving scientist who worked on the Manhattan project."

"The Manhattan project?" the President uttered.

Whispering into his ear, the Vice President informed him that the Manhattan project was the great scientific endeavor conducted during the Second World War that led to the development of the first atomic bombs.

"I am a scientist, gentlemen, a physicist to be specific. Which means I am not an intelligence analyst. However, there is a similarity I should point out. Just as with my colleagues in the intelligence community, a man like myself, by vocation, conducts analytical investigations based on solid data, and not mindless speculation. I want to share with you the data points that lead to my hypothesis."

As Lazar began speaking, both the Prime Minister and the CSIS Deputy Director scanned the conference room. Other than Gayle Payne, all the others appeared stone-faced.

"Data point one, obviously irrefutable, is that a Russian man, Boris Fedorenko, was murdered in the Lake Abitibi region. We know that he worked for three years at Arzamas-16 as a nuclear machinist. Arzamas-16, gentlemen, is where the Soviet Union designed and built its nuclear weapons. That Fedorenko had knowledge on how to construct thermonuclear bombs and had access to their design plans is a matter that simply cannot be disputed. This includes, most significantly, a device the Russians called the King of Bombs, the most powerful nuclear weapon yet constructed.

"Data point two is that Fedorenko left Russia six months ago, making a stop-over in Geneva, and withdrew a large sum of money from a Swiss bank account that had received a substantial transfer from a source the CIA has determined was controlled by Islamic Jihadists. This follows a similar transaction during an earlier trip Fedorenko made to Abu Dhabi.

"Data point three is that a B-52 bomber loaded with four Mark 41 hydrogen bombs, each with a yield of 25 megatons, crashed into Lake Abitibi in 1962. That a well-organized group retrieved the four bombs is beyond question. The materials contained in the four bombs, combined with other components that could be obtained in North Korea, Iran and Europe are sufficient to build a fully functioning duplicate of the Soviet RDS-220 bomb.

"Finally, gentlemen and Ms. Payne, Dr. Pervaz Khan, the world's foremost nuclear proliferation black-marketer, just happened to be in Ottawa simultaneously with all this strange activity taking place at Lake Abitibi. Supposedly he was visiting his daughter and son-in-law, while making almost daily visits to both the North Korean and Iranian embassies. We now know that the marriage of his daughter was a sham, and that his supposed son-in-law is the Pakistani ISI agent and Al-Qaeda sympathizer, Aziz Faruqui, who we now believe to be the Lion. Faruqui is not only a fanatical Jihadist, he also assisted Dr. Khan is building the first Pakistani nuclear weapons."

The President looked towards Dr. Lazar, uncertain how to react. He then turned to the Vice President, asking what he thought of Dr. Lazar's points.

"Admittedly, Dr. Lazar, the information you present is disturbing" the Vice President said. "But you know as an expert how formidable building a workable nuclear device is. Besides, you mention the role of North Korea and Iran in this plot. Surely, both these countries are fully aware that if they were complicit in a terrorist attack on this country involving a nuclear weapon, they face certain and devastating retaliation."

Dunlop stared directly at the Vice President, seeking to covey his impression that he and his colleagues were entertaining dangerous illusions.

"Mr. Vice President, you are describing a geo-political architecture which no longer exists," Dunlop said. "The concept of mutual assured destruction that prevented your country and the

Soviet Union from annihilating each other during the Cold War is not applicable to this situation. Unlike the United States, my country does have embassies in North Korea and Iran, and we have, I think, a better grasp on what motivates the ruling elites in those two tyrannical states than you do. Both the mullahs running Iran and the dictator of North Korea, Kim Jong-il, though espousing different ideologies, share the same fundamental objective, which is survival of their regimes. In their world, the United States of America represents a mortal peril to their continuity. If an event were to transpire that resulted in your country being transformed overnight from the world's sole super-power to a devastated nuclear wasteland, they would consider that existential threat to their survival permanently expunged. The fact that you might retain the ability to initiate nuclear retaliation and kill several million of their civilians is a matter of profound indifference to the rulers of those two regimes. However unpleasant that truth is, I must beg you to believe us."

While her colleagues sat silent and stone-faced, Gayle Payne asked Dr. Lazar why he was convinced that the terrorists planned to detonate a superbomb in an American city. Looking sympathetically towards Payne, Lazar responded in a soft, barely audible voice.

"Ms. Payne, my whole life has revolved around nuclear weapons," he told her, with sadness evident in his eyes. "During the last thirty-five years, nuclear weapons have actually gotten smaller and less powerful, so they could fit on missiles and hit pin-point military targets. A terrorist, however, has a different doctrine. If they ever acquired a nuclear weapon, they would not require it to fit on a missile that could be launched at your ICBM bases, as the Soviet Union may have planned to do at one time, or you yourselves. The Jihadists would use a ship, or shipping container, railroad or truck as their delivery vehicle and not a missile. That means that the size of the weapon is of no concern to them, it is the maximum yield that they are interested in. Furthermore, their objective is purely and simply to create as much carnage as possible. Paradoxically, it is a weapon that was designed more than forty-five years ago that is far more attractive to them than your latest warhead designs. That is the only explanation as to why they have gone to the trouble of recruiting Fedorenko and luring him to Lake Abitibi, where they retrieved the four hydrogen bombs with enough of the critical raw materials to build their own version of the King of Bombs."

"Dr. Lazar, I know you are sincerely trying to help," the President told him in a tone generously hinting at condescension. "We have our own experts here and they have convinced me that the scenario you have described is just not possible. Let's not forget who we are talking about, gangs of primitive barbarians who are on the run! We are winning this war on terrorism! Freedom is on the march!"

At that very instant the duty officer opened the conference room door, through which emerged David Cole. Everyone in the room except for Gayle Payne looked surprised.

"What the hell are you doing here!" yelled an incensed Dick Darnell. Before Cole could answer, Payne spoke.

"David Cole is here on my instructions," she said with firmness. Turning towards the Commander-in-Chief, she said, "Mr. President, David had received only a short while ago information of a critical nature from a trusted source, which has a direct bearing on our deliberations."

The President glared frostily at Ms. Payne, then turned towards Cole. Reluctantly, he signaled Cole to share his information.

"From an unimpeachable source I have learned that principal financial backers of Al-Assad El-Islamiya have begun unloading their American dollar assets. During the past three days, this has amounted to fourteen billion dollars. I expect that this pattern will continue over the next several days and may eventually reach a figure of around 200 billion dollars."

The words that Cole spoke still echoed in the conference room as the demeanor of the participants was radically altered. "Jesus Christ!" Glenn Thrush yelled. "They're trying to crash the dollar!"

The President and Vice President turned towards each other in a puzzled embrace.

"It is not about crashing the dollar," Cole said, pausing as everyone in the room turned towards him with focused attention. "If they wanted to crash the dollar, these financial supporters of the Lion would have immediately dumped all of their dollar holdings. The reason why they are apparently staggering their currency transaction is because they are *anticipating* that something is going to happen that will lead to the imminent demise of the American dollar."

"I don't like this!" the Vice President screeched in an agonizing voice verging on panic. "When it comes to something involving our money, that is serious!"

The President looked towards his CIA Director, wondering if he had any idea as to the implications of what Cole had just described. Darnell, pondering for a moment, said, "While I remain skeptical of what our Canadian colleagues theorize, I must say that what David has learned is deeply disturbing. Based on that information, I am prepared to accept that there is a plot to explode a dirty bomb in one of our cities."

"Than that's what we'll plan for," the President replied. "I'll welcome the assistance of our Canadian friends in thwarting these evil-doers."

Before either the Prime Minister or Dunlop could reply, Lazar spoke. "Gentlemen, you are making a very great mistake," he said passionately. "All the facts contradict that this involves a mere radiological dispersion device, or dirty bomb. If that were the case, all the terrorists would require is conventional explosives and radioactive substances easily obtainable in the United States, under minimal security. Everything we know about what has been done by these people is far too intricate, too detailed and too complex for a dirty bomb. I plead with you, gentlemen. Do not surrender to wishful thinking and dangerous illusions."

A Death In Zurich

The sky was overcast yet the water was calm as the SS Northern Conquest plowed ahead on Lake Superior towards the port of Duluth at eight knots. On the bridge, the captain looked happily at Jafaar, the chief engineer. "Looks like we will arrive in port and weigh anchor at about 1:00 PM, dead on schedule, Jafaar," he told him. "Any mechanical or propulsion issues we need to deal with while we're in port?"

"Nothing major, sir. We did have a minor short circuit affecting the galley and laundry, probably caused by an electrical surge. It did damage to some equipment in those areas such as a press machine and steam boiler, refrigerator and freezer."

The captain looked mildly concerned. He noted that the SS Northern Conquest was due to set sail in two days, after completing the unloading of its cargo of crushed gravel.

"No problem, sir," Jafaar cheerfully told him. "I have already contacted the marine electrical repair service in Duluth, by radio. They will be ready to take these things for repair as soon as we dock and have assured me they will be repaired and returned to our vessel within 24 hours."

"Very good, Jafaar, very good indeed," the captain said.

❖ ❖ ❖

In Sault Ste. Marie, both Dextraze and Littlejohn had come up empty in their visits to gas stations. Not one employee recognized the photograph of the man claiming to be Michael Khoury. In

187

addition, the RCMP had confirmed that Michael Khoury was in fact an alias, as they suspected. The two CSIS intelligence officers met at the café on Toronto street, seeking to explore alternative ways of identifying their person of interest.

"He's obviously not stupid," Littlejohn commented on their suspect. "This person was clearly advised to keep a low profile in town. He probably bought his groceries and gasoline way out of town. It could take us forever to track him down if we have to visit every town and village in the area."

"There may be another alternative," Dextraze suggested. "It's a long shot, but if he ever needed medical attention, there is a good chance he would have used the major clinic in Sault Ste. Marie, since it serves as the regional health center for the whole area. If we are really lucky, he may have had a medical insurance card with his actual identity."

Littlejohn suggested they immediately head towards the clinic. They were there in fifteen minutes, and obtained an immediate appointment with the chief administrator once they identified who they were. They showed her the photograph of Khoury. At first, it did not ring a bell.

"He may have spoken with a Middle Eastern accent," Littlejohn told her, hoping that might stimulate a past memory of the individual.

"Hmm, maybe that does remind me of someone who looks like this person in the picture," the administrator said. "Give me a minute or two to check our files."

The two CSIS intelligence officers waited nervously for several minutes, until the chief administrator returned, carrying a file folder. It turned out that the man who had opened the bank account under the name of Michael Khoury had indeed sought medical attention some six weeks previously. Opening the file folder, the administrator pulled out a Xerox of the man's medical insurance card. Dextraze and Littlejohn noticed that the name on the card was that of Khalil Daoud, with an address in Wawa, a town about 150 kilometers north of Sault Ste. Marie.

"Did he have any photo ID?" inquired Littlejohn.

The administrator handed him another Xerox, which he and Dextraze carefully studied. It was of Daoud's employee identification card, with his photograph. Both men noted that it matched exactly the image on the driver's license of Michael Khoury.

"We always require that new patients present a photo ID along with their insurance card," the chief administrator explained. "I remember that when I asked to see his driver's license, he became really flustered, then said he forgot it. I then asked him if he had any other photo ID and he presented his employee identification card. He was very nervous when I told him I would have to make a photocopy."

"I can understand why," replied Dextraze, as his colleague looked over the medical file in the folder.

"Pierre, it says he received treatment for wounds he incurred from an industrial accident at his place of work," Littlejohn said. "He had lacerations from shrapnel while cutting metal with an acetylene torch. He received first aid treatment and was supposed to return in a week for observation, but never showed up."

Dextraze looked again at the photograph on the ID card, then read the name of the man's employer. It was Hussein Metal Fabricators.

◇ ◇ ◇

At the port of Duluth, a truck from Vector Electrical Repair stopped at the guard post by the exit gate. As the driver rolled down his window, a guard approached. "Hello, Sam," the guard said in a familiar manner. "What is it today?"

"John, I have some items of equipment from the SS Northern Conquest that have electrical damage from a power surge. I'm taking them to our shop for repair," the driver said with a mild Lebanese accent, as he handed an invoice to the guard for his perusal.

"Everything's in order here," he told the driver as he returned the invoice. "I'll just take down the serial numbers for verification. It will just take me a minute."

In a matter of moments, the truck left the port and headed to a desolate area of Duluth, saturated with derelict buildings and abandoned warehouses. As the truck shifted into low gear and slowed down, it took a turn into the driveway of a large building that looked as derelict as it neighbors, save for the men standing in front of a large, open garage at the front of the edifice. A small sign on the building identified it as the premises of the Vector Electrical Repair Company.

Once the truck was inside the building, the garage door was closed, while two men with pistols stood outside, keeping watch. In the interior of the garage, there was a beehive of activity, with a crew of ten men diligently at work. The driver exited the truck, and the rear door was quickly opened. With the aid of a forklift truck, first the horizontal steam boiler and than the freezer were removed and placed on the floor of the garage. Nearby were duplicates of the equipment that had just been unloaded. Working at a feverish pace, several men of Middle Eastern appearance labored to load the identical looking boiler and freezer substitutes into the truck.

One of the men, who appeared to be the leader, walked up to the freezer, which had packing tape around it. He first cut the tape with a pocketknife, then knocked on the top door five times. After a brief interlude, he knocked three more times and then opened the freezer door. Aziz Faruqui slowly stood up, smiling at the man who lent him a hand.

"Good to see you, Omar!" he exclaimed with excitement, as he stepped out of the freezer. Once standing on the garage floor, he began stretching his arms and legs vigorously, working out the kinks in his muscles after days of uncomfortable confinement.

"Welcome to the United States of America, brother!" Omar said with mocking exuberance.

In response, Faruqui emitted a brief burst of laughter, bowed his head towards the garage floor, and spat noisily.

◈ ◈ ◈

At CSIS headquarters, a call came in for Dunlop from Dextraze and Littlejohn. He took their call in his office, anxiously awaiting their report. Dextraze spoke from his car, with Littlejohn seated next to him. "Sir, I think we have a positive ID on the people who received the money transferred from Milan to Sault Ste. Marie." Dunlop rapidly wrote down key elements from their verbal report on a notepad. It was immediately apparent to him that his intelligence officers had uncovered information of the highest importance.

Dextraze relayed their initial finding that the Al-Qaeda money transferred by wire from Milan had ended up in a local bank account under the fictitious name of Michael Khoury. The man had always withdrawn the money in cash shortly after its transfer and had recently closed out the account. By cross-referencing his photo with the identification papers of a patient treated at the regional health clinic, they were now certain that the man who claimed to be Michael Khoury was actually Khalil Daoud, a twenty-seven year old Palestinian man who had entered Canada under a student visa. However, rather than being enrolled at a Canadian university, he was working as a metal fitter at a company named Hussein Metal Fabricators.

"What does this company do?" inquired Dunlop.

"They custom manufacture metal structures, mostly used in construction and manufacturing," Dextraze said. "However, Henry and I were able to speak to one of the employees confidentially. He told us that there was a section of the plant cordoned off until recently, for several weeks. He said none of the regular employees seemed to know what exactly was going on there, but whatever it was, activity was happening twenty-four hours a day."

Pondering the significance of what he had just been informed of, Dunlop asked Dextraze if he knew the identity of the proprietor of Hussein Metal Fabricators. Dextraze told his superior that he was passing the phone to Littlejohn, who had been digging into the background of the owner of the company.

"Mr. Dunlop, Hussein Metal Fabricators is owned by a gentleman named Amad Hussein. He is thirty-eight years old, was born in Amman, Jordan and immigrated to Canada in 1997 and has since received Canadian citizenship," Littlejohn relayed. "Now, sir, this is the interesting part. His original entry visa into Canada had him residing in Kabul, Afghanistan just prior to his emigration to this country. He was sponsored by relatives already living in Canada, who set him up in business."

Dunlop realized the significance of the Afghanistan connection. In 1997, the country was ruled by the Taliban regime, which was in lockstep with Osama bin Laden and Al-Qaeda while they were planning the 9/11 attacks from Afghan territory.

"This connection to Afghanistan really sends red lights going off in my head," he told Littlejohn. "I think you and Pierre may have found a big piece of the missing puzzle. I'll be contacting the Commissioner of the RCMP as soon as I get off the phone with you."

Early the next morning, a dozen RCMP police cars, originating from different directions, converged on the area surrounding Hussein Metal Fabricators. At precisely 9:00 AM, they moved in unison into the parking area in front of the plant as a police helicopter circled overhead. In a matter of moments, twenty Constables with guns drawn entered the factory, quickly rounding up employees and searching offices. Three officers entered Amad Hussein's office, confronting him as he exuded a look of both shock and anger. "Mr. Hussein, we have a warrant for your arrest and to search these premises," one of the officers informed him. As he was being handcuffed, he sneered at the RCMP officers, "I demand to know the reason for this intrusion!"

"You are being arrested on suspicion of aiding and abetting terrorist activity on Canadian soil," the officer replied.

❖ ❖ ❖

At FBI headquarters, Larry Braun was having a meeting with Glenn Thrush. It was decided following the discussions held at Camp David that the Bureau would play the lead role investigating the possibility that Islamic radicals were planning to smuggle a dirty bomb into the United States from Canada.

"The President and I firmly believe that this is a law enforcement matter, Larry," Thrush said. "We are both confident that you have the resources and capability to deal with this matter both effectively and tactfully,"

Braun understood exactly what the National Director of Intelligence meant by his comment. "Don't worry about a thing," he assured Thrush. "We'll make certain nothing leaks to the media."

Thrush emphasized to the FBI Director how critical it was that nothing happened that frightened the American public. "Frankly, Larry, we are far more worried about the economic ramifications from panic than if a dirty bomb actually goes off. So, however you handle this, do it low-key. If, despite your best efforts, a radiological device does go off, we feel we can contain the damage."

Braun told the National Director of Intelligence that he fully understood what was expected of him. He then brought up another matter that was disturbing him.

"I'm glad both you and the President recognize that this is primarily an FBI operation," he told Thrush. "But, what about the CIA?"

"The CIA's job is foreign intelligence. This is strictly a domestic law-enforcement investigation. Dick Darnell understand that," Thrush said.

"Dick Darnell isn't the problem," Braun replied. "I'm more concerned with David Cole sticking his nose into something that is none of his business."

Thrush assured the FBI Director that Cole would be kept in his place.

❖ ❖ ❖

It was about 9:30 AM when two RCMP police cruisers parked in front of a rooming house in the town of Wawa. Four Constables quickly left their vehicles and entered the rooming house. They located the landlady, and asked her where they could find Khalil Daoud. She showed them a locked door on the second floor, telling them she thought he was inside.

One of the officers knocked vigorously on the door, shouting, "Police! Open up, Mr. Daoud."

There was no verbal response, however, the officers could clearly discern noise emanating from inside the room. One of the officers violently kicked the door open while his three colleagues prepared to enter, their service revolvers nervously drawn. Daoud was standing near the door, firmly holding an automatic pistol. He fired several rounds, hitting one of the officers in the abdomen. His two comrades returned fire, striking Daoud with a fusillade of bullets. As the wounded officer groaned in pain, Daoud lay in a pool of blood, motionless.

❖ ❖ ❖

David Cole received another phone call from Johanne Kleist. Peering out of his office window at a deep blue, sunny Virginia sky, the CIA's Director of Counter-Terrorism listened attentively to his trusted source on terrorist financial activity.

"David, in the last twenty-four hours, another eight billion dollars has been converted from American dollars to other currencies and financial assets," Kleist reported. If the numbers alone did not signify the imperative character of Kleist's information, the strained, anxious tone in his voice clearly did.

"It looks like they're picking up the pace of their activity," Cole remarked. He then explained his theory. The benefactors to the Holy Jihad Fund were probably being directed to convert their U.S. dollar holdings in a phased, sequenced manner to protect their wealth. "That leads to only one conclusion," Cole said. He briefly glanced at his desk calendar, noting it was March 10. "Something is being planned by the people these men had so generously funded so that, when it occurs, the value of the American dollar will go into free fall." He added that the scale of the currency transactions suggested that whatever was being planned, it's target date was fast approaching.

"I will continue to keep you updated, David," Kleist told Cole.

Cole realized he was not comfortable with Kleist's offer to continue to seek out information.

"Johanne, please listen to what I'm about to tell you," Cole said in a pleading voice. "You have already gone far beyond the call of duty. I don't want you to put yourself in any further jeopardy."

Kleist was silent for a moment, staring forlornly at the photograph of his deceased daughter on his office desk.

"Johanne, do you hear me?"

"I can't be less brave than my daughter, David," Kleist replied with determination in his voice. "I must continue to help you."

❖ ❖ ❖

Samuel Kinkaid telephoned Dunlop in the afternoon, seeking an update on what had transpired earlier in the day in Sault Ste. Marie. The Deputy Director of CSIS reported that nine suspected members of a terrorist cell linked to Al-Qaeda had been arrested at the Hussein Metal Fabricators plant, including the proprietor, Amad Hussein. Another apparent member of the cell, Khalil Daoud, was killed in a shootout with RCMP officers who attempted to arrest him in the town of Wawa, in which one Constable was seriously wounded.

"Who are these people?" inquired Kinkaid.

"Mostly Lebanese and Palestinians with expired or forged visas, so the police have grounds to hold them in custody pending further investigation," Dunlop told his superior. "It's the owner of the plant I'm most interested in. Unfortunately, Amad Hussein is a Canadian citizen. But if anyone knows something about this plot, it's got to be him."

Kinkaid informed his subordinate that he would be speaking with the Solicitor General about obtaining a security certificate under the nation's anti-terrorism laws, permitting the authorities to hold Hussein in custody indefinitely.

"That is only the first step," Dunlop said. "Our ultimate challenge will be getting Amad Hussein to talk, and soon. The sands of time are rapidly running out."

❖ ❖ ❖

It was 7:00 PM in Zurich when Johanne Kleist completed his daily paperwork and packed his briefcase. He put on his hat and coat and left his office, locking the door behind him. He walked towards the bank of elevators, and within moments entered an elevator car with two other persons, all headed towards the basement garage.

The garage echoed with footsteps and the sound of car doors opening and closing. Kleist opened the door of his Audi sedan, placing his brief case on the passenger's seat as he sat down and closed the door. As if by habit, he placed his car key in the ignition and began turning it.

Near Kleist's car, another automobile had just started its engine. Suddenly, there was an enormous, shattering noise. Smoke rapidly filled the garage, prompting screams from other persons present in the garage. What had been Kleist's automobile was reduced to twisted metal, sheets of flame and smoldering debris.

Extraordinary Rendition

Daniel Rolfe was an attorney with the National Civil Liberties Union, based in Ottawa. He had called an 8:00 AM press conference, and the room was packed with journalists.

"Ladies and gentlemen, this morning the NCLU filed a petition with the Supreme Court on behalf of Amad Hussein, who is being illegally detained by the authorities on a so-called security certificate," Rolfe proclaimed to the media. "Mr. Hussein's family fears that this Canadian citizen, a respected businessman and pillar in his community, will be held indefinitely without charge. This outrageous abuse of our civil liberties must be opposed with every fiber of our being."

◈ ◈ ◈

At CSIS headquarters, Dunlop conferred with Littlejohn and Dextraze on the status of the investigation. They were all aware that the NCLU was challenging the security certificate being used to keep Amad Hussein in custody.

"Has Hussein shown any willingness to talk?" inquired Dunlop.

"He has been uncooperative so far in the interrogations being conducted by the RCMP," Dextraze replied.

Dunlop instructed Dextraze to arrange to meet privately with Hussein in his cell. "Gentlemen, we don't have the luxury of time. Somehow, we must be far more aggressive in finding sources of information on the Lion and the device he has had constructed," he told his intelligence officers. "What about the embassies?"

Both Dextraze and Littlejohn reflected on Dunlop's hint. "I know that all the personnel at the Iranian embassy who would be involved in this plot are fanatically loyal to the mullahs. The true diplomats who might be sympathetic are totally in the dark," Dextraze told his colleagues.

"What about the North Koreans?" Dunlop asked, turning towards Littlejohn.

Pondering Dunlop's query, Littlejohn was tentative in his response. "The North Koreans are very strange, almost as though they reside on a different planet," he told Dunlop. "They are even more fanatical than the Iranians, with the distinction that, instead of the Koran, they worship their dictator, Kim Jong-il, as a living God."

"Maybe this devotion to their so-called Great Leader can be used to our advantage," the Deputy Director suggested.

"I think I get your hint, sir," replied Littlejohn. He went on to explain to Dunlop and Dextraze that the head of security at the North Korean embassy, Han Won-ju, had a weakness for underage boys. The local police had a motel used by teenage male prostitutes, which Won-ju frequented, under surveillance.

"This would be at variance with our organization's standard protocol and ethics," Dunlop said. "However, the urgency of the situation renders those considerations be suspended. As an accredited diplomat with full immunity, he cannot be arrested for such sordid illegal acts, just deported. But, if threatened with deportation, along with full publicity of his immoral acts, he has got to recognize that Kim Jong-il will not exactly greet him with open arms when he is expelled and sent back to North Korea."

All three men recognized that this constituted blackmail. But, under the circumstances, it was a direction that they were willing to proceed on, once the Deputy Director obtained the necessary authorization from higher authorities, a prospect he realized would require intense arm-twisting.

❖ ❖ ❖

Glenn Thrush was at his office, which was located at CIA headquarters in Langley, when his secretary informed him that Cole had arrived for his appointment. Thrush thanked his secretary and personally greeted the Director of Counter-Terrorism, warmly escorting him into his office. When both men were seated, the National Director of Intelligence asked Cole what he could do for him.

"The FBI is not talking to me," he told Thrush in a voice choking with emotion. "We are standing at the edge of a precipice, and Larry Braun won't even return my phone calls!"

Glenn Thrush told Cole to relax. "I'm sure it's nothing personal, David. He's just got a lot on his plate trying to track down that dirty bomb."

Cole asked how he could be effective at his task if he was not coordinating with the CIA, Customs and the Immigration and Naturalization Service.

"Well, David, since our embarrassing vacancy at the Department of Homeland Security, the coordination might be a little spotty, but I know for a fact that Larry Braun is diligently carrying out the President's instructions and doing it in a manner that won't attract unwarranted attention that might induce panic."

❖ ❖ ❖

At ACLU headquarters in New York City, a senior attorney on staff, Harold Tanenbaum, received a phone call from a Canadian colleague, Daniel Rolfe. "I read a report on your press conference," he told Rolfe, complementing him on its success.

"Harold, we both know that the security services in our two countries walk along the same road and harbor an identical disregard for civil liberties," Rolfe said with passionate self-righteousness. "We are seeing unwarranted arrests of Arabs and Moslems in this country. Are you experiencing similar developments south of the border?"

Replying with equal fervor, Tanenbaum confirmed an identical pattern of activity was unfolding in the United States. "We only learned within the past several hours that the FBI, with the connivance of the INS and Customs, is profiling people of Arab or Moslem origin, especially auto and truck traffic originating from

Canada. They have FBI agents at all the major border crossings," he said with dismay.

"I think it is essential, Harold, that both of our civil liberties organizations take a very activist stand in the face of this authoritarian activity being undertaken by our governments," Rolfe advised his American colleague.

"We are preparing a motion that will be filed in Federal District Court this very afternoon, seeking an injunction against FBI harassment of Arabs and Moslems entering our country from Canada" he informed Rolfe with pride.

❖ ❖ ❖

Cole had just returned to his desk when his secretary buzzed him on his intercom, informing him that he had an urgent message from the CIA station chief in Bern, the Swiss capital. Breaking out in a cold sweat, sensing the palpitations from inside his chest, Cole hurriedly contacted the station chief. He grasped the phone tightly as he heard the news he was now dreading.

"Mr. Cole, I have very bad to news to report. I regret to inform you that Mr. Johanne Kleist was killed last night when his car exploded at his office garage. The police suspect it was a bomb."

Cole had already dropped the phone, as his head collapsed into the palms of his hands.

❖ ❖ ❖

At the Vector Electrical Repair facility, the garage door was opened as several men stood by, carefully surveying the area and insuring no trespassers were present. There were two trucks in the garage, the diesel engines of each vehicle running. A hand signal from one of the men outside prompted the driver of one the trucks to engage his clutch and gears, and slowly move out. The truck, with Vector Electrical Repair stenciled in large letters on its side, headed towards the port area in Duluth. Once it had departed, another signal brought movement from the second vehicle, a tractor-trailer rig, with two men in the cab. As the rig slowly departed the garage, its signage was clearly visible to the men standing nearby, Komar Transport. As it moved towards the southern outskirts of Duluth, it picked up speed and entered the on-ramp for interstate 35. It was headed due south on I-35, straight towards Des Moines. The two men in the cab had Caucasian features. There was nothing about their appearance that was in any way conspicuous.

❖ ❖ ❖

At a holding facility for prisoners located near Ottawa, Dextraze was escorted into a small room with two chairs and a table. He stood silently for a moment, tensing up as he heard footsteps, the clanging of metal and then the opening of the door. Two Constables brought Amad Hussein into the room, clad in orange overalls, his hands firmly shackled in front of him. Dextraze motioned for Hussein to be seated, then told the officers that he should be left alone with the prisoner.

"Mr. Hussein, I am Pierre Dextraze, an intelligence officer with the Canadian Security Intelligence Service."

Dextraze noted that the prisoner was staring at him with an intensity that suggested both hatred and deep contempt. Though his eyes spoke, Hussein's mouth remained silent. Seeking to elicit some response from the suspected terrorist, Dextraze tried a different approach.

"Since you don't seem to be communicative at the moment, I'll do the talking for now. We know that you are involved with the Lion in planning a terrorist act in the United States."

Looking carefully at the prisoner's face, Dextraze observed not the slightest stirring of his mouth, only noting an even more belligerent glow from his eyes.

"How can you, as a professed Moslem, participate in an act that will result in the mass slaughter of innocent human beings? The killing of innocents is strictly forbidden in the Koran," Dextraze told Hussein with passion. He was still hoping to facilitate a verbal response from the prisoner, but he succeeded only partially.

For a moment, Hussein sat silent, sneering contemptuously at Dextraze. Then, his face burning with anger and resentment, he blared out, "How dare you lecture me on the holy Koran, you infidel swine!"

Unsure how to react, the CSIS officer sat still, waiting for a further reaction. It was not long in coming. "You read the 22nd chapter of the holy Koran, then tell me how Moslems should deal with unbelievers!"

Dextraze realized that the conversation had come to an end.

◇ ◇ ◇

Back at CSIS headquarters, Dunlop received a call from Kinkaid. "I have bad news, Alex," he informed his Deputy Director. "I have been unofficially advised by a trusted source that the Supreme Court will rule tomorrow afternoon that the security certificate we are using to detain Amad Hussein will be ruled invalid."

Agreeing that this was indeed bad news, Dunlop raised the only other alternative he could conceive of.

"Sam, I know he is directly involved with the Lion. We can't afford to let him on the loose. On the other hand, there is no point in keeping him under Canadian custody, since he refuses to provide any useful information," Dunlop told the Director.

"What are you getting at, Alex?"

Dunlop cleared his throat before uttering the words to Kinkaid. "Extraordinary rendition."

"You mean you want to send him to Jordan?" replied Kinkaid.

"That's his country of origin, Sam," was Dunlop's quick response.

The Director of CSIS remarked that the Jordanian authorities would surely subject Amad Hussein to torture.

"That's exactly why I want to send him there. It is the only chance we still have to get information out of him that is crucial to this investigation. Remember, we are dealing with a plot to commit mass murder with a thermonuclear weapon," Dunlop said with firmness and determination.

The Director pointed out that the removal of Hussein from Canada just prior to the Supreme Court decision would unleash a wave of protests and political hot-water for the government. "On the other hand, Alex, I see your point. We have no choice. The government will just have to bear the heat. Let's get this organized quickly so that when the public learns about this, it will be a fait accompli."

◇ ◇ ◇

That evening, Dextraze returned to the jail cell where Hussein was being detained, accompanied by two plainclothes detectives and a warder, who unlocked the cell. The prisoner, who had been lying down half-awake, was ordered to get up. "We're leaving," Dextraze brusquely told Hussein, whose shackles were briefly removed so he could put on a jacket, as instructed by the CSIS intelligence officer. The detectives then handcuffed Hussein, and escorted him out of the holding facility, to a waiting car in the jail's parking lot.

"Where are you taking me?" the prisoner demanded to know. Dextraze and the detectives remained silent. Hussein was seated in the rear of an unmarked car, a detective on each side of him. Another detective was in the driver's seat, with Dextraze to his right. They left the parking lot, following an RCMP cruiser with red lights flashing and siren wailing. Hussein looked increasingly edgy as the two vehicles traveled at high speed through near-empty nocturnal traffic. In just over fifteen minutes, the cars reached an air force base near the international airport and parked alongside an armed forces executive jet, its engines idling and navigation lights burning brightly. Amad Hussein was quickly removed from the automobile, and made to stand in front of the passenger ramp that was in place for boarding the aircraft. Two men, wearing suits and having a husky build, exited the aircraft and stood in front of Hussein.

"Gentlemen, the government of Canada turns this man, Amad Hussein, over to your custody," Dextraze told the two men, as the prisoner's facial expression was instantly transformed from one of arrogance to another of undiluted terror.

"You can't do this! I am a Canadian citizen!" Amad Hussein protested in a state of panic. The two men who prepared to escort him aboard the aircraft identified themselves as security personnel with the Royal Jordanian embassy.

"Mr. Hussein, you never renounced your Jordanian citizenship and, it turns out, the authorities in Jordan have an outstanding warrant for your arrest. Have a safe flight," Dextraze said sarcastically, as he then turned around, leaving Amad Hussein to his fate.

❖ ❖ ❖

An angry Larry Braun was in conference with the Attorney General over what he considered a disastrous turn of events. A Federal District Court judge had granted an injunction to the ACLU, compelling the U.S. government to cease any activity profiling individuals of Arab or Moslem origin during processing for entry into the United States. The targeted measures that the FBI had undertaken to prevent a dirty bomb from being smuggled into the United States would be derailed, unless the injunction was overturned.

"Don't worry, Larry, we'll file an appeal in the morning with a higher court and seek to overturn the injunction," the Attorney General said assuredly.

"On what grounds?" said an uncertain FBI Director. "We can't base it on the truth, that will undermine the President's concern about not generating panic."

"Well, maybe we can formulate something ambiguous, such as we are reacting to some new terrorist chatter we've been monitoring," mused the Attorney General.

"Damn those liberal lawyer sons of bitches at the ACLU," Larry Braun sighed with exasperation. At that moment, Braun's cell phone rang. He impatiently answered it, as his mind was still absorbed with his dilemma.

The Attorney General noticed that Braun's expression had suddenly been transformed, as he was obviously piqued with interest by what was being relayed to him over the phone. He heard Braun say, "Are you sure?" then a moment later, "Yes, let's move on it."

Putting his cell phone back in his pocket, Braun turned towards the Attorney General, beaming.

"What is it, Larry?" the Attorney General inquired.

"That was our office in Billings, Montana. They got an anonymous tip that sounded credible. A truck carrying contraband is supposed to cross the Canadian border into Montana between 5:30 and 6:00 AM. The tipster didn't specify what the contraband was, he only said that we better have radiation detectors with us."

Taste The Torment of Hell-Fire

Listening to the sorrowful melodies intermixed with static emanating from a country and western radio station, Robert Dunn hummed along contentedly, as he held the large steering wheel of his tractor-trailer. He let out an expansive yawn, noticing the first hints of sunlight. Glancing at his watch, he observed that it was a quarter of six in the morning, as he passed a sign on the highway informing him that the U.S. border lay just ahead. He geared down and pressed on his air brakes, his truck's engine moaning in the process. As he double-clutched, Dunn observed the sign indicating he would soon have to stop at the U.S. Customs entrance on the border.

He had passed this way many times before. Clearing Customs was always fast and routine. He was relieved to see no traffic ahead of him that early morning. Getting through the formality would be a breeze, he anticipated.

He stopped his rig and lowered the window, glad to see a familiar face approach him. This was going to be no sweat, he said to himself.

"Good morning Roger," he said cheerfully to the U.S. Customs officer.

"Good morning, Bob. What are you bringing today?" the officer asked.

"Just a load of biscuits from Regina," Dunn answered nonchalantly.

He expected to be told he could proceed on his way. When, instead, the officer instructed him to step out of the cab and open the trailer's doors for cargo inspection, he instantly felt a jelly-like sensation in his chest, which seemed to drop into the pit of his stomach.

He asked the officer to repeat his instructions, feigning he did not hear them correctly, adding a dash of hope.

The instructions were repeated, and Dunn began to realize that this was not going to be his lucky day.

He stepped out of the cab and then opened the rear cargo van, trying to act calm and cool. His pretense suffered a major relapse when three men and a woman soon joined the Customs officer, each of them wearing a blue jacket with the letters "FBI" prominently displayed, both front and back. One of the FBI men carried a black box with dials, the purpose of which eluded Dunn's understanding. The Customs officer told Robert Dunn that this was just routine, the FBI people were going to take a quick look at his cargo.

With the cargo van opened, two FBI agents stepped inside, surveying the stacked cartons of biscuits. Dunn tried to reassure himself that maybe this was routine, at least these were not agents from the Drug Enforcement Agency. As he nervously watched, a series of clicks began emanating from the black box being carried by one of the FBI men inspecting the cargo. The closer to the front of the rig's trailer the agents approached, the louder and more rapid the clicks became. The meter on their detection device was gyrating wildly. "We have a definite reading!" one of the agents shouted to his colleagues standing outside by the rig.

"You want to tell us what cargo you're really carrying, Bob?" the Customs officer asked Dunn. "Just biscuits, I swear to God!" he fearfully replied.

Inside the cargo van, the two FBI agents thought they had identified the carton that was the source of the readings being detected by their indicator. They carefully lifted the carton, than placed it in a middle aisle of the van. Using a pocketknife, they opened the cartoon, then removed some packing material that lay on top. The limited sunshine entering the cargo van was enough to create a reflection on what appeared to be a metallic cylinder with a mirror-like finish. "We've hit the jackpot!" an agent hollered to his colleagues standing outside.

The female FBI agent turned towards a petrified Robert Dunn. "You are under arrest, Mr. Dunn," she informed him.

❖ ❖ ❖

Near Des Moines, the tractor-trailer rig from Komar Transport took an exit off the I-35 interstate and proceeded along a rural road to an isolated farmstead. Two men stood by the gate at the property's entrance, one of them glancing at his watch while the other relayed instructions through a walkie-talkie he was holding. They opened the gate and the rig entered the property, slowly and noisily negotiating a pathway that led to a large barn, its doors wide open. The tractor-trailer entered the barn and stopped its diesel engine, while some of the men inside closed the barn door.

There were eight men standing inside the barn, their faces reflecting a variety of nationalities. Some looked Middle Eastern and African, others European or American. They were all clean-cut in appearance. One of the men, who appeared older than the others, instructed the crew of the rig to open the rear cargo van. Within minutes, the men inside removed the steam boiler and crate containing Aziz Faruqui's freezer.

With the freezer removed and placed on the barn's floor, the leader knocked on the top door five times, followed by three more knocks. He lifted the door, then helped a tired but immensely satisfied Aziz Faruqui out of his miniature living compartment.

"My friend, Mohammed, it is so good to see you!" said a beaming Faruqui, who embraced the group's leader.

"My brother, I am so honored by your presence," Mohammed replied with emotion. The two men warmly embraced, kissing each other's cheeks. Mohammed then escorted his guest to a quiet corner of the barn, which had stools, and the two men talked.

"The next shuttle will arrive at 7:00 PM tonight, right on schedule," Mohammed advised Faruqui. "You can rest while we are waiting. We will clean and refurbish your living compartment and stock fresh provisions for the next stage of your journey."

"Excellent," Faruqui replied. "Everything that has happened so far reminds me of a well-run military exercise."

"That is because the men are eager to wage the jihad inside fortress America," Mohammed said, manifesting the high level of enthusiasm he witnessed in his own men. "They have trained hard and waited patiently for their orders. The men are now honed to a sharp edge for the battle with the American infidels."

Faruqui smiled, looking with pride at the men in the barn, busily attending to various duties. "They are eager to go and not only because they smell the blood of our cursed enemy, which will soon be shed in quantities he never imagined in his worst nightmares," Faruqui told Mohammed. "They also can taste the sweet scent of paradise that awaits a true martyr of Islam."

Mohammed nodded in agreement, then turned towards the freezer that had been Faruqui's living quarters, which some of his men were cleaning. He then looked sympathetically at Faruqui. "You have truly sacrificed your comfort to exist in that infernal white box," he told him. "Even the Lion has earned a rest. Why don't you let us prepare a bed for you so you can rest until your journey resumes."

Expressing appreciation for the offer, Faruqui politely declined. "Your concern for my comfort is noble, but it is more important that you provide me with a radio. I am awaiting news from the American media that will be much more comforting than any rest."

❖ ❖ ❖

At his desk, David Cole received a phone call from his boss. Dick Darnell's communication with him had been sparse the past few weeks, so it was highly unusual that the CIA Director would initiate a phone call. When Cole answered, he was surprised at how upbeat the Director sounded.

"David, we have very good news," he informed Cole. "It looks like the FBI has rolled up that dirty bomb plot you and the Canadians have been stressing over."

At first stunned at what seemed inexplicable news, he asked Darnell for details.

"The FBI has their dirty bomb. They tried to bring it over the border from Canada and we captured it in Montana," Darnell said. "I can't go into any more details right now, I have to head over to the White House for a meeting with the President. However, the FBI is calling a news conference for 5:00 PM, I suggest you watch it."

After concluding a very short conversation with the CIA Director, Cole put a call into Dunlop at CSIS headquarters. He informed his Canadian colleague of the news that Darnell had just relayed to him.

"This just doesn't make sense," was Dunlop's initial reaction. Cole was in agreement. Perhaps they would both be enlightened once the FBI held its news conference.

"David, I am reminded of what Dr. Lazar has said so emphatically. Everything the Lion and his organization has acquired, plotted and done thus far is too extravagant for a mere radiological bomb," Dunlop told Cole. "I'll wait for the press conference, but I already sense that something about this doesn't add up."

The CIA's Director of Counter-Terrorism was also perplexed. "You're right, Alex, it doesn't add up," he said, pausing while another thought seized him. "That is, unless..."

"Unless what?" Dunlop interjected while a thought was entering Cole's mind.

"Well, Alex, as an undergraduate I played college football. There was a play we had called the Hail Mary Pass. It was a feint to fool the opposition's defense. They'd think the ball was being thrown in one direction and that's where the defense would congregate. The ball could then be passed to the intended player, with our opponent's defense positioned in the wrong part of the field."

Cole's explanation made sense to Dunlop. It fit in with how he rated his terrorist adversary. "This very well could be a Hail Mary play on the part of Aziz Faruqui," he said.

In another part of the CSIS headquarters building, Dextraze walked towards his cubicle, carrying the morning newspaper. The headline was explosive, "Government condemned for Deporting Canadian Citizen to Jordan." He placed the newspaper on his desk, then took his mug, which he intended to fill with coffee.

As he passed Amelia's workstation, he noticed how focused she was in viewing a Jihadist website on her computer. He stopped by her cubicle, offering to fetch her a cup of coffee. She gratefully accepted the offer.

When Dextraze returned with her coffee, he pulled up a chair next to her and asked her a question, which he thought she could illuminate him on.

"Amelia, when I met our suspect, Amad Hussein, during our interrogation of him, I asked him how a professed Moslem could kill innocent civilians. I mentioned that murdering non-combatants is forbidden in the Koran. Not so politely, he basically said I don't know what I'm talking about and that I should read the 22nd chapter of the Koran. Maybe you can give me a better understanding than I could gleam from reading an English or French translation of the Koran."

Baldwin explained as best she could that the Koran, like the sacred texts of other religions, had elements that, from a twenty-first century perspective, were uplifting, while other parts could be construed as intolerant, even barbaric.

"The Jihadists, including Osama bin Laden and his followers, often refer to the 22nd sura of the Koran to justify September 11 and their other atrocities," she told Dextraze. "It's probably the most violent chapter in the Koran, at least in terms of its attitude towards those who follow religions other than Islam."

Dextraze requested that Amelia translate for him the relevant parts of the 22nd sura. She pulled out her Arabic copy of the Koran, taking a moment before finding the proper chapter and verses. She first read it in Arabic, than repeated the words in English.

"Garments of fire have been prepared for the unbelievers. Scalding water shall be poured upon their heads, melting their skins and that which is in their bellies. They shall be lashed with rods of iron. Whenever, in their anguish, they try to escape from Hell, the angels will drag them back, saying, taste the torment of hell-fire!"

As Baldwin placed her copy of the Koran back on her desk, Dextraze sat still, shaken by what he had just heard. Amelia noticed the look in his eyes, which appeared uncomprehending that so violent a thought could permeate a religious text. He struggled for some way to rationalize what he had just heard, failing in his efforts. "Amelia, if this is what Amad Hussein's conscience is fed on, no wonder he can participate in acts of terrorism and mass-killing, without remorse."

"Isn't that the challenge that religious people of all faiths struggle with?" Amelia posed. "I am a Christian, and the Bible has been my guide and my bedrock during the darkest moments of my life. In those terrible days after 9/11, it was those beautiful passages in both the Old and New Testaments that sustained me when I was in grief and despair over the loss of my brother. Yet, I realize that there are verses in this book that I love so unconditionally that, taken out of context, can justify the most appalling atrocities."

Dextraze nodded in understanding. "I am a devoted Catholic," he shared with Amelia. "My faith is the centerpiece of my whole life, my morals and ethics. But I do know that it was Catholics professing a faith as strong as mine that committed the Spanish Inquisition."

"Religion, ours and Amad Hussein's, has had to cope with modernity," Baldwin told her colleague. "In the Islamic world, unlike our own, virtually every country is ruled by a corrupt dictatorship and oligarch. Women are oppressed and the common people feel left behind as the rest of the world has evolved. Men of hate, who live loveless lives, can give legitimacy to that hatred by jerry-picking the Koran. That is the phenomenon of Al-Qaeda, transforming that hate through selective preaching from the Koran, suppressing all its content on tolerance and peace and inspiring those Moslems left behind by modernity to believe that they can have their dignity restored, not by uplifting themselves, but by bringing down all the infidels around them."

◈ ◈ ◈

A portable television set on David Cole's credenza had just been switched on. The CIA's Director of Counter-Terrorism looked at his watch, noting it was just a minute before 5:00 PM. He stood watching the television screen and soon heard the announcement that regular programming was being pre-empted due to a press conference being held at FBI headquarters. A moment later, Larry

Braun appeared in front of a podium, with the Attorney General at his side. Flashes occurred in rapid sequence as cameramen congregated in front of the podium. Braun smiled, then began speaking.

"Ladies and gentlemen, earlier today the FBI made an arrest and confiscated a device, which we believe was a radiological or dirty bomb," Braun said with glee, pausing as some of the journalists expressed shock and surprise. "The man we arrested, Mr. Robert Dunn, aged 37, of Casper, Wyoming, is suspected of being a senior Al-Qaeda operative. The radiological dispersion device is currently being examined by experts from the Department of Energy, however, our initial reports are that the bomb contained about fifty pounds of conventional explosives and a small quantity of plutonium."

Several of the journalists attending the news conference echoed the word "plutonium," in surprise, prompting Braun to elaborate, so as not to induce panic.

"A microscopic amount of plutonium was found in the bomb, not enough to kill anyone, just induce panic, which is the goal of the terrorists." The FBI Director then called on the Attorney General to make a statement.

"The arrest of Robert Dunn removes a suspect we believe to be a dangerous Al-Qaeda operative from our midst," said the Attorney General in a judicial sounding voice. "His capture and the discovery of the dirty bomb, long before it could deployed and detonated by the terrorists, once again demonstrates to the American people that they can have total confidence in the vigilance, skill and effectiveness of their law enforcement guardians.

"This development also affirms the unrelenting commitment of this administration to never compromise in its efforts to protect the safety of the American people."

As the press conference was underway, a radio located in a barn outside Des Moines carried the broadcast live to its occupants. Aziz Faruqui seemed aroused with joy as he listened, his smile being replicated by all the other men standing nearby. Turning to Mohammed, Faruqui said with ardent conviction, "We've done it! Praise be to Allah, the infidel is a blind fool!"

Mohammed turned off the radio, then approached Faruqui, embracing him as he chanted, "Bismillah allahu akbar - in the name of God, God is great!"

❖ ❖ ❖

Robert Dunn was seated in a small, cramped conference room at a jail in Billings, Montana. Two beefy FBI agents were with him in the room, while several others observed what transpired through a one way mirror. Dunn, wearing slacks and a white T-shirt encrusted with perspiration stains, his eyes bloodshot, was shaking with trepidation as he underwent interrogation.

"You want a lawyer, Bob?" one of the FBI men asked.

"I can't afford a lawyer," a frightened Dunn responded.

"Well, you know the court will appoint one for you. But you're a smart man, Bob," the other agent interjected. "You know that you get what you pay for. Chances are, you will get a nitwit for a lawyer. And with the new anti-terrorism legislation, you could be liable for the death penalty!"

Looking desperate, Dunn spoke pleadingly to his interrogators. "Please, I'm no terrorist! Please!" At that point, Dunn broke down. This appeared to be what the two FBI agents were hoping for.

"Look, I want to be helpful, Bob," an agent told a sobbing Dunn. "But, you've got to give me something to work with. My best advice to you is to tell us the truth, right now. You'll never have a better shot at a deal than at this moment. I know the DA in this area, he's the go-for-the-jugular type. If we tell him you are being cooperative right from the start, I know he'll go easy on you. But, if we tell him he's going to actually have work to do on this case, well, I hate to phrase it this way, but you're shit out of luck, pal."

"I'll tell the truth," Dunn said sorrowfully. In a crying voice, he explained that he had been contacted by anonymous persons, who set up a meeting in Laramie with a Mr. Jones, who offered him thirty thousand dollars to smuggle marijuana across the Canadian border. In Regina, after picking up his load of biscuits, he was contacted by cell phone and directed to a deserted warehouse, where men wearing masks placed the carton in his rig. He had no idea what his final destination was. He was instructed that half an

213

hour after crossing the U.S. border he would again be contacted by cell phone. He concluded by affirming that he had told the whole truth, then he again sobbed uncontrollably.

The two FBI agents looked contemptuously at their prisoner. "I am very disappointed in you, Bob," one of the FBI agents angrily told him. "This is the biggest bunch of bullshit I've ever heard in my life."

Blackmail

A special-forces team assigned to the U.S. 10th Mountain Division carefully surveyed the terrain surrounding a cave in the Tora Bora mountains astride the Afghan-Pakistan border. It was evening, and through their night vision goggles, the American soldiers had a half dozen Taliban warriors under observation, sitting near a campfire outside a cave. The officer in command of the special-forces team looked at his watch, tension flowing from his eyes. "Let's go!" he commanded. In an instant, all hell broke loose.

The Taliban fighters were literally ripped apart in a hail of automatic gunfire. Within seconds, a dozen American soldiers stormed through the cave's entrance. Their night vision devices enabled them to pick out five more Taliban militants, rendered blind by the absence of light in the cave. Another series of salvos from assault rifles snuffed out their lives.

Their adversaries dead, the solders methodically searched the cave, shining their flashlights into every nook and cranny. Scattered in various corners were stacks of rifles, mortar and rocket rounds, and belts of machine gun ammunition. One of the soldiers noticed an object that was distinctly non-military in appearance: a filing cabinet. Concerned that it might be booby-trapped, the soldier very slowly and carefully opened one of the file drawers. Once opened, he pulled out a file folder, surprised at its contents. Rather than files, the folder contained photographs.

❖ ❖ ❖

Early morning at CIA headquarters, David Cole took a call from Colonel Magnus, an intelligence officer with the 10th Mountain Division.

"Good morning sir," the Colonel said cheerfully.

"How's the weather in Kabul?" asked Cole.

"Well sir, with the weather, it's hot during the day and cold at night. But I got some G-2 for you that is hot all over."

Cole's interest was aroused. He let the Colonel know that he was all ears.

"Sir, we raided a Taliban hideout in Tora Bora and killed some of the enemy. We thought the hideout was being used as an ammo dump, but apparently it was also being used as a photographic archive for Al-Qaeda."

"Please continue," Cole said excitedly.

"Most of the photographs are snapshots of buddies who attended Al-Qaeda training camps together, looking tough for the cameraman. However, one photograph we found I know will be of great interest to you, sir. I just e-mailed it as an attachment and wanted to alert you that it's on its way."

David Cole profusely thanked Colonel Magnus, than hurriedly pulled up his e-mail inbox on his computer monitor. The e-mail had indeed arrived and he hastily clicked on it and opened the attachment.

For a moment, Cole's heart seemed to skip a beat, then stop altogether. His eyes bulged with foreboding as his mind raced to absorb the implications of what he had just observed. Breathing heavily, he swiftly called Alex Dunlop at CSIS headquarters, advising him that he was in the process of forwarding an e-mail attachment that he considered urgent.

Within five minutes, Dunlop had returned Cole's phone call. "This really does tie it all together, David," Dunlop told him.

"They say a picture is worth a thousand words," Cole replied.

"I am looking at the photograph as we speak," Dunlop commented, as he nervously eyed the clear color image of three men standing amid the backdrop of a mountainous range in Afghanistan. The man in the center was tall, with an imposing presence and conspicuous, long, dark beard with streaks of white. He was the most recognized man in the world to any intelligence officer involved in the anti-terrorism field: Osama bin Laden. To his right stood Dr. Pervaz Khan and, to the left, Aziz Faruqui.

Cole told his colleague that the photograph constituted documentary evidence that bin Laden had personally discussed something of great importance with the two men. It was obvious to both intelligence officers that Dr. Pervaz Khan would only have traveled to Afghanistan for a meeting with the leader of Al-Qaeda to discuss an operation involving his area of specialization, nuclear bombs.

"I think you and I have to disregard this nonsense about a barely literate redneck truck driver being an Al-Qaeda mastermind of a dirty bomb plot," Cole told Dunlop, "even if my own government has surrendered to wishful thinking."

"We're fighting the clock, David."

"I know that, Alex," sighed Cole, with deep frustration manifest in his voice. "Information is what we need. That is our only salvation."

Dunlop informed Cole that he had received confidential authorization from the highest levels of the government to do something that was unprecedented in the history of CSIS. He explained to him that the head of security at the North Korean embassy in Ottawa was a pedophile and that CSIS was going to use his perversions to induce him to turn over everything he knew about Faruqui's plot.

"That might be an important breakthrough," Cole said, wishing his colleague luck. "But the man who ultimately knows the most, other than Aziz Faruqui, is his mentor, Pervaz Khan. Unfortunately, the U.S. government won't touch him. They have accepted Pakistani assurances that he is no longer involved in nuclear arms proliferation, in exchange for their support of our war on terrorism."

"I should think that what we now know invalidates those assurances," Dunlop angrily said.

"You would think so, but this administration, which I serve, will go out of its way to indulge in self-deception," Cole said with resignation. "I'll do what I can on my end, Alex, but I may need your help."

"You've got it," Dunlop said without a trace of hesitation.

❖ ❖ ❖

At a military base outside of Amman, Jordan, a van escorted by jeeps with machine guns mounted on them parked in front of a closely guarded stockade. Under heavy guard, Amad Hussein was dragged out of the van, his legs restrained by irons and his hands bound behind his back. Amid yells and curses in Arabic, he was roughly escorted into the prison compound. A senior army officer confronted Hussein as he was brought inside.

"Amad Hussein, you are going to tell us everything you know," the officer told the prisoner in a threatening tone. "You will talk, have no doubt about that. The only thing at issue is if you are wise enough to make it easy on yourself, or foolish enough to suffer first. The choice is yours, I personally do not care." Concluding his menacing tirade, he contemptuously dismissed Hussein as he was led away, his face betraying not a hint of emotion.

❖ ❖ ❖

At the Claremont Inn on Rideau Avenue in downtown Ottawa, a Chevrolet Impala bearing diplomatic license plates pulled into the parking lot. Out of the vehicle stepped a short, thin man wearing a beige raincoat and black, polyester suit. He was of oriental appearance, with severe-looking eyes, shielded by thick, plastic-rimmed glasses. His black hair was neatly combed but greasy, shining as brightly as his patent leather shoes. He looked nervously in several directions, as though he feared being followed. Then, walking with rapidity, he entered the Claremont Inn and walked up to the check-in counter. No other persons were in the lobby, with the exception of a solitary clerk standing on duty at the counter. The Asian man approached the clerk. Not a single word was exchanged, as the oriental gentleman removed several twenty-dollar bills from his pocket and passed them to the clerk, who then stuffed the money into his pants pocket. In exchange, the clerk provided his patron with a room key. The Asian gentleman immediately headed towards the bank of elevators in the lobby, waiting impatiently for an empty car. He looked repeatedly at his watch until the elevator bell sounded, and he entered the car for the short ride up to the third floor.

Leaving the elevator on the third floor, he walked swiftly towards a room he was more than familiar with. Removing the key, he looked behind his back, satisfied that he was alone. He then entered the room, closed the door, and stared with intense anticipation at a teenage male with long blond hair and an athletic build, who stood at least four inches taller than him. He was now breathing heavily. He walked towards the teenager, looked him over from head to toe, than withdrew several twenty-dollar bills, which he passed to the adolescent male. The object of the man's affections calmly placed the money in his pocket, and then stood impassively as the Asian gentleman began stroking his blond hair and rubbing his shoulders.

A sharp cracking sound ensued, as the door was brutally forced open, almost being torn from its hinges. Four uniformed policemen rushed in, yelling loudly, "Police!"

"Fuck!" yelled the teenager, as he was handcuffed and led out of the room, spewing torrents of profanity. The Asian man was obviously frightened, as he was also handcuffed. He was led out of the room, screaming in a high-pitched voice in broken English, "Me diplomat! Me diplomat! Have immunity!"

Ignoring the protestations, the police led the diplomat to the room next door. One of the officers knocked on the door, which was swiftly opened by Henry Littlejohn. He instructed the officers to bring the diplomat inside. "You can remove his handcuffs" he told them, adding that he would be meeting alone with the diplomat.

"Just let us know if you need anything, we'll be right outside," one of the officers said. They stepped out of the room, closing the door behind them.

To the surprise of the diplomat, Littlejohn began speaking to him in fluent Korean. He politely invited the diplomat to remove his coat and sit on one of the chairs. Littlejohn took note of the lapel on the diplomat's jacket, which contained a gold-framed portrait of the dictator of North Korea, Kim Jong-il.

219

"Mr. Won-ju, I'm intelligence officer Littlejohn with the Canadian Security Intelligence Service, and I'm here to be of help to you."

Won-ju's facial expression gave evidence of total befuddlement. Littlejohn continued speaking Korean, providing the diplomat with a more complete awareness of his predicament.

"I can understand that you, as a man far way from his country, with a very important and stressful job, needs time to relax and work off some steam," Littlejohn said straight-faced. "Regrettably, the ways you have found to, shall we say, get your rocks off, are contrary to Canadian traditions. More seriously, having sex with an underage adolescent prostitute is highly illegal in this country, and is considered statutory rape."

"I have full diplomatic immunity!" Won-ju shouted defiantly.

"That makes the situation far worse," Littlejohn said, as the diplomat grimaced with perplexity. "You see, if you were not a diplomat, we would just send you to jail, you would serve your sentence, and then that would be the end of it. But unfortunately, it is due to the fact that you have diplomatic immunity that this is a very messy problem. You see, we are not dealing with a mere crime, your status has transformed this matter into an international incident. It will create complications in the relationship between our two countries."

Won-ju seemed unable to comprehend what those complications might be. Littlejohn sought to enlighten him.

"This is what will probably happen. Because the police are involved, this will become a public matter, meaning the media, television and newspapers, will heavily publicize this incident. The politicians will get involved, the opposition parties will call for a public inquiry, which will further arouse the people's hostility towards the Democratic People's Republic of Korea. Of course, you will be expelled from Canada and sent back to North Korea. Finally, our ambassador in Pyongyang will personally deliver an official protest to Kim Jong-il, and hand him some incriminating information, asking him if this is how representatives of the Great Leader behave when they are guests in a foreign land."

Littlejohn took hold of an envelope lying on a desk, withdrew several photographs and handed them to Won-ju for his perusal. The North Korean diplomat was visibly shaken, as he observed several candid shots of him involved in compromising activity with an under-aged minor. Ashen faced, he handed the photographs back to Littlejohn, who placed them back in the envelope, taking note of the violent tremors in the diplomat's hands.

"Please, Mr. Littlejohn, you must help me! If my government and the Great Leader find out about these pictures, it will be very bad for me and for my family. Especially my family!"

Littlejohn gently slapped Won-ju's shoulder, expressing his understanding. "I'll do what I can to help you, Mr. Won-ju," he told the diplomat. "As you can appreciate, it won't be easy. It would require the squashing of all police records on this matter. To be honest with you, the only chance I see of being able to accomplish that is if you help me to help you."

When Won-ju asked for an explanation of what was required, the CSIS intelligence officer was ready with an answer.

"It would have to be what we call a quid-pro-quo. In other words, I need from you something that would be so helpful and valuable to the Government of Canada, so that out of gratitude, they would have no choice but to remove this difficulty that hangs over you."

Shrugging his shoulders and looking puzzled, Won-ju asked what he could possibly do that would be construed as helpful.

"Well, as an example, Mr. Won-ju, you serve as the head of security at the DPRK embassy," Littlejohn said, with the diplomat nodding his head in agreement.

"That means you would be knowledgeable of any foreign visitors entering your embassy, correct?"

Won-ju confirmed the accuracy of Littlejohn's assessment.

"Well, Mr. Won-ju, throughout the month of January we cataloged seventeen visits to your embassy by a gentleman named Dr. Pervaz Khan. What was the purpose of his visits?"

Simultaneously with Littlejohn pronouncing Khan's name, the diplomat's body stiffened as a look of fear overcame him. "I do not know about this person," Won-ju protested.

"I don't believe you," was Littlejohn's abrupt response.

Obviously frightened and speaking with hesitation, the diplomat said pleadingly, "Please Mr. Littlejohn, it is very dangerous for me to talk to you about this man."

Littlejohn stood up, taking firm grasp of the envelope containing the compromising photographs. He approached the door, preparing to open it. With his hand on the door knob, he turned his head towards the diplomat, saying, "I'm very sorry, Mr. Won-ju. I really wanted to help you, however, since you refuse to cooperate with me, there is nothing further I can do for you. I'll have the police take charge of this matter."

Won-ju yelled desperately that he would indeed cooperate with Littlejohn. He asked for assurances that his government would not learn of his disclosure of information to a foreign intelligence service.

"I can give you an absolute guarantee that not a word will leak out concerning the source of the information you share with us. However, I need assurances from you, that you will answer all of my questions truthfully, and not hold back on any information."

Won-ju replied that he would offer his assurances that he would speak the truth.

"I'm afraid that your verbal assurance is not sufficient," Littlejohn advised. "I need something more reliable than that." He opened the door and signaled for Won-ju to follow him. They only had to walk to the room just across from their own. Once inside, Won-ju's eyes exuded surprise when he observed that another man was present, standing by a machine alongside a chair.

"Mr. Won-ju, that is a polygraph machine. It will let me know if you are answering all of my questions truthfully. If the technician advises me that even one of your answers is untrue, my offer to help you becomes null and void."

❖ ❖ ❖

At the farmstead near Des Moines, the darkened sky silhouetted the men standing by the entrance. They observed the headlights of the approaching tractor-trailer rig before they could hear the raucous whine of its powerful diesel engine. As the rig came to the entrance, one of the men looked at his wristwatch, noting with satisfaction that it was exactly 7:00 PM. The rig was waved through, and it began negotiating its way along the path leading to the barn, its doors already fully opened, with several men standing by, looking alert. The signage on the trailer was clearly visible even with the minimal illumination. It read, "Alliance Transport."

❖ ❖ ❖

Gayle Payne was at her office in the White House when Cole reached her by phone. He was frantically raising the alarm, while the remaining decision-makers within the American intelligence community wanted to stand down, in light of the arrest of Robert Dunn in Montana.

"Gayle, you surely don't believe that an independent truck driver in Montana is an Al-Qaeda front man?"

The National Security Advisor shared Cole's skepticism, yet she felt constrained by her jurisdictional limitations.

"It doesn't matter, David, what I believe or don't believe. This is a domestic law enforcement matter, and falls outside my authority, and yours, too," she admonished him.

"Terrorism is a national security issue," David Cole protested, "so unless you have moral certitude that this plot only involved a dirty bomb and one Robert Dunn, Aziz Faruqui alias the Lion is still in Iraq, the men who seized those H-bombs in Northern Ontario are merely souvenir hunters and Dr. Pervaz Khan was only making goodwill visits when he dropped in on the Iranian and North Korean embassies in Ottawa, you not only have jurisdiction, but the responsibility to do everything in your power to aid me."

"I go to church for my sermons, David," Payne tersely replied.

Pausing for a moment, taking a deep breath, Cole then apologized for pontificating. "I didn't mean to lecture you, Gayle, I'm just desperate, and afraid."

"You don't need to apologize, David. You're doing your job. It's just that some people around here believe you're too vigilant."

Cole mentioned that he had forwarded an e-mail attachment to her marked urgent, and inquired if she had viewed it.

"I'm sorry David, I've been inundated. The latest reports from the National Security Agency seem to indicate that the North Koreans and Iranians are planning another long-range missile test. The President has asked me to prepare a paper identifying policy options for our administration."

"You do realize that these North Korean and Iranian missile tests are just a diversion?" Cole said, adding, "Just like the dirty bomb the FBI was anonymously tipped-off about."

The National Security Advisor was not submissive to Cole's argumentation. "We happen to believe that long-range ballistic missiles in the hands of rogue states pose an existential security threat to this nation," Payne maintained with self-assurance. "That's why this administration has placed the development of an effective missile defense as our number one national security priority."

"Gayle, we can spend hundreds of billions of dollars on missile defense, and be helpless to stop one single rusty, old ship or innocuous looking truck from delivering a nuclear device to Washington D.C., or anywhere else in this country."

As Cole was talking, Gayle Payne pulled up the e-mail attachment on her computer monitor and opened it. She was flabbergasted at what she saw. "My God!" Cole heard her exclaim.

"What is it, Gayle?" Cole asked.

For a brief moment, Payne was oblivious to Cole on the other end of the line. She stared at the photographic image showing Osama bin Laden, flanked by Dr. Pervaz Khan and Aziz Faruqui.

"This can't be!" Payne repeated to herself, her voice reflecting the shattering impact of the graphic image that was only too clear in its meaning.

"David, when we agreed with the Pakistani government not to push for Dr. Khan's extradition to stand trial before an international tribunal, they not only promised to end his lucrative nuclear black-market proliferation activities, they assured us that he had only dealt with states and not terrorist organizations. They specifically affirmed that he never had dealings with Al-Qaeda, and guaranteed he would not do so in the future."

Cole reminded Ms. Payne how the photograph had been acquired, meaning that there could be no questioning of its authenticity. He then confronted her with the implications raised by the photographic image. "You know what my interpretation of this photograph is, Gayle. But in case I am overreacting, you tell me how you think we should read it."

The National Security Advisor took another look at the image on her computer screen, knowing instinctively what the implications were, yet trying to suppress the most dire probabilities.

"David, I want to fight you tooth and nail on this, but unless I suspend all my faculties of judgment and reason, I'm left with only one conclusion. I know Dr. Pervaz Khan would not have traveled to Afghanistan to pay a social call on bin Laden. He's a serious man, and he was there to discuss serious business, an operation by Al-Qaeda involving the use of a nuclear weapon."

Cole felt a sense of relief that a senior staff person in the White House, one of the few he still held in high regard, was finally absorbing the big picture. Yet he felt empathy towards her, recognizing she now would be haunted with the same formidable fears he had been bearing for the past several weeks.

"Now that we both are certain of the looming catastrophe that confronts us, I need your help and intervention in exercising the one option that may still enable us to thwart this plot, if we aren't too late," Cole said in a soft voice to his colleague over the phone.

Gayle Payne asked what that option was.

"We need to get our hands on Khan, that is the last card we have to play with," he told her.

Payne's initial reaction was that this was not feasible. "David, you know that the Pakistani government would never agree to turn him over to us, or even allow us to interrogate him on their own soil. He's a revered figure in Pakistan, a national hero. No government in that country cold survive if they were seen by their public as exposing him to American pressure."

"I recognize that fact," Cole replied. "I'm not thinking in terms of a formal request to the government of Pakistan, that's clearly a waste of time, which we can ill afford. What I have in mind is securing Pervaz Khan through..." He paused briefly. "Through covert means."

The National Security Advisor took a deep breath, weighing in on the seriousness of Cole's proposal to her, with its attendant consequences and risks. "I don't see how this administration could approve such a thing. It would destroy our relationship with Pakistan, a country that is crucial to our war on terrorism. Also, and I tell you this off the record, the Vice President is a personal friend of the President of Pakistan. To say that he would be in opposition to such a step would be an understatement."

"I don't give a damn about Pakistan right now," Cole said bluntly. "If this plot involves a thermonuclear bomb, as I believe it does, I am prepared to sacrifice our friendship with the entire world, if that's what it takes to prevent a holocaust on American soil!"

Uncertain how to proceed, Payne asked the Director of Counter-Terrorism if he had discussed such an operation with the Director of the CIA.

"Gayle, you know that's futile," he told Payne firmly. "Dick Darnell is convinced that it's only a dirty bomb plot we confronted, and that the FBI has defeated it. He's not going to approve such an operation, unless the National Security Council, which you chair, overrules him. I am asking, I am even pleading, Gayle, that the NSC recommends to the President that he authorize a covert CIA operation to apprehend Dr. Khan, so he can be effectively interrogated once he's in our custody."

Payne was breathing nervously, manipulating a ballpoint pen between her fingers in a none-too-successful attempt to diminish the intense pressure she felt bearing down on her. "Let me think on this, David. We'll talk again in the morning."

❖ ❖ ❖

A very early morning conference was held at CSIS headquarters involving the Director and Deputy Director, Pierre Dextraze and Henry Littlejohn, the latter participant distributing a verbatim transcript of his session with Han Won-ju, held the previous day at the Claremont Inn. As the men around the table reviewed the transcript, each page of which was labeled "Top Secret," Dunlop asked Littlejohn to summarize the outcome.

"Won-ju confirms that a highly secret intelligence operation was underway at the North Korean embassy, which revolved around Dr. Khan's visits. He told me he was not privy to exactly what the operation entailed, only that it was approved by and involved the highest levels of the North Korean government. He himself reported directly to the head of military intelligence for the North Korean Peoples Army, who in turn directly reports to the dictator, Kim Jong-il. The operation was so secret, not even the North Korean ambassador was informed of what was occurring in his own embassy."

"What was Won-ju permitted to know about this operation?" asked Samuel Kinkaid.

"He was told that a group of twenty North Korean technicians had traveled to the mining camp near Mace under the cover of working as mining surveyors and geologists for Takasumi Investments and that his mission was to ensure that Dr. Khan had a secure and reliable communications link, including video capability, from the embassy to the mining camp. He also made available to Khan, on demand, a senior Korean intelligence officer serving under diplomatic cover as the embassy's science attaché, who acted as his interpreter. He was specifically instructed that no one else in the embassy was to know the purpose of Khan's visits, and that an elaborate communications room was to be made available for his use at any time. He was also warned that his life would be forfeit if the communications link to Mace was not impervious to interception."

Dunlop inquired if Won-ju had any intimation as to what this operation entailed.

"He was told personally by the head of military intelligence that a big operation against the United States was in the works, but nothing more. He understood that this matter was a state secret of the highest order, and it would be dangerous for him to ask questions. He's a true Nuremberg type, just following orders and doing what he's told."

"What about the Iranians?" asked Dextraze.

"According to Won-ju, while he knew that Dr. Khan was also visiting the Iranian embassy during his stay in Ottawa, he was not aware of what was transpiring there. He was instructed by his superior not to have any discussions with his peers from Iran's embassy," Littlejohn explained.

"This information confirms what we have already hypothesized, to some extent," Dunlop pointed out. "However, Won-ju doesn't seem to have any information on the type of device being constructed at Lake Abitibi. More importantly, he is unable to tell us how the device was to be smuggled into the United States, and confirm the identity of its target."

Littlejohn pointed out that there was one other piece of information gleamed from his interrogation of Won-ju. "He told me that, in addition to his role facilitating Khan's ability to communicate with the Koreans working at Lake Abitibi, during this time the head of military intelligence also instructed him to provide a large sum of cash, in American dollars, to a North Korean espionage agent based in New Jersey."

"How much money was involved?" inquired Dunlop.

"Around $200,000," Littlejohn replied.

Kinkaid asked if Won-ju had any intimation that the agent in New Jersey was involved in something connected to what was happening at the mining encampment.

"He doesn't know for sure," Littlejohn said. "However, he did tell me that this was out of the ordinary. Normally, North Korean agents working in the New York metropolitan area receive funding through cash drops left by members of Pyongyang's delegation to the United Nations. The fact that military intelligence was involved, and the money was transferred on Canadian soil, suggests to him that this agent was involved in an operation so important and secret, the North Koreans wanted to be absolutely certain that the Americans would be unaware that a large sum of money was being made available to a senior agent operating near New York City."

Turning to Kinkaid, Dunlop said that the information provided by Won-ju had filled in some gaps, and that the connection with a North Korean agent in New Jersey could be significant. However, there were still too many imponderables. "Amad Hussein is still not talking to the Jordanians," Dunlop said with frustration in his voice, "no matter how hard the Jordanians work him over."

"The Prime Minister is taking a beating on the Hussein deportation," Kinkaid said. "There's a mass protest demonstration in support of Amad Hussein taking place today on Parliament Hill."

"I don't have the luxury of being sympathetic towards Mr. Hussein," Dunlop said with a hint of impatience. "And we don't have the luxury of waiting until he cracks. I'm certain that factory of his built some contrivance that was used to smuggle the nuclear device into the United States. I just can't, for the life of me, make even an educated guess of what it might have been."

"Maybe we can approach this from a different angle," Dextraze suggested. "Hussein's plant is located in Sault Ste. Marie, which happens to be a major Great Lakes port."

Everyone in the room seemed to jump on what Dextraze had just introduced into the conversation.

"Pierre, I think we have been staring at the trees without realizing there's a forest in front of us. You're absolutely right," Dunlop told his colleagues. "That must be how they planned on getting the bomb into the United States."

Littlejohn pondered the possibility, trying to put himself in the shoes of the terrorists. "There's one problem with that scenario," he pointed out. "Wouldn't it be logical for them to use a shipping container, since the Americans only inspect four percent of them? If they used a container, that doesn't fit in with a Great Lakes port."

Kinkaid agreed with Littlejohn's observation. "Henry's point is valid," he said. "Only bulk carriers ply the waters of the Great Lakes. Most of the ships coming out of Sault Ste. Marie are ore-carriers. The cargo is placed in open holds. I just can't imagine a nuclear bomb being buried under thousands of tons of iron ore, or copper or gravel, without protection."

Littlejohn added that a complex device such as a nuclear bomb would be literally crushed in the cargo hold of a bulk carrier. "If the bomb was encased in anything protective, how could it be unloaded without detection, since the mineral cargoes are literally scooped out of the hold in broad daylight, in full public view?"

Dextraze reflected on the obstacles that stood in the way of the terrorists using one of the Great Lakes bulk carriers to transport their nuclear device into the United States. Putting himself in

Aziz Faruqui's place, he constructed a plausible means in his own mind. "What if they didn't smuggle it in as shipping cargo?" he said.

Dextraze captured the attention of his colleagues. Continuing with his train of thought, he fleshed out his hypothesis. "Suppose that whatever Amad Hussein's factory was constructing in that sealed off area of the plant, it was some form of equipment that was part of the ship, that could be off-loaded in an American port for servicing or repair."

Littlejohn, along with the Director and Deputy Director, suddenly stared at Dextraze, than at each other. It was as though they were all struck by lightening. Intuitively, they each recognized that Pierre Dextraze had just figured out for them how the Al-Assad El-Islamiya mastermind had probably inserted the nuclear device across the border, in a manner that defied even the remotest possibility of detection.

"Pierre, you are correct, that is how they must have done it," Dunlop said. "Now, the challenge is, what form of shipping equipment, and at which port did they unload?"

"That could be like trying to find a needle in a haystack," Kinkaid indicated with a note of skepticism, "especially since we are running short of time, unless the Jordanians can get Amad Hussein to talk."

Dunlop felt that at least they could begin tracking down all shipping movements out of Sault Ste. Marie in the past several days destined for American ports on the Great Lakes. However, he recognized that they would still need the cooperation of the American authorities.

"How do I convince the Americans to investigate shipping activity in their Great Lakes ports when they have convinced themselves that they have already found Aziz Faruqui's so-called dirty bomb?"

Hoboken

The sound of roosters crowing coincided with the breaking of dawn across the Iowa countryside. At the farmstead outside of Des Moines, work was underway inside the barn. Two tractor-trailer rigs, one bearing the moniker of Komar Transport, the other of Alliance Transport, were receiving their final mechanical checks. At a far corner in the barn, Faruqui huddled with the three men who would be the drivers and crew on the next leg of his journey. Two of them had a Caucasian appearance, one with light blond hair and the other with neatly groomed brown hair. They were both clean-shaven and with skin of light complexion. The third man's skin was brownish; he had short black hair and a thin moustache, with a distinctive Latin look.

Faruqui peered over each of these men with composed scrutiny. He marveled with satisfaction at the look of determination chiseled into the faces of each of these men.

"My brothers, you have the responsibility of bringing me, and the instrument of Allah's wrath on America, to our final destination. I have selected you for this honor, not only because of your fealty to Islam and the cause of jihad for the sake of Allah," Faruqui said with a voice exuding power and purpose. He stopped momentarily, insuring each of his words permeated the very essence of each of the men. "You have also been chosen because of your appearance. This operation demands that you do not look like a Moslem, at least in the way our enemies believe a Moslem man should look. Now, let us do a final documents check."

231

The three men pulled identification papers out of their wallets, and placed them on the ground in front of them. They included credit cards, drivers and operators permits and licenses, Teamsters union membership cards, photographic snapshots of girlfriends and business cards from various bars located in several Midwestern states. Faruqui perused the names indicated in the different forms of IDs; Ronald Parker, Jack Burns and Martin Lopez. He looked up at Martin Lopez, and smiled at the crucifix he wore around his neck. He then turned to Ronald Parker, the driver with blond hair, who would be the leader of the crew. "Let's go over the itinerary one more time," Faruqui directed.

"We have a load of three horizontal steam boilers and four large-capacity freezers," Parker answered obediently. "Our first stop is in Chicago on March 15, for delivery of one horizontal steam boiler to a dry cleaning plant and a freezer to a high school cafeteria. On March 17 we arrive in Cleveland, first delivering a freezer to a restaurant, and then at a hospital we drop off a freezer for the cafeteria and a steam boiler for the laundry. Finally we arrive at our last destination, Hoboken, New Jersey on March 18 and unload our final deliveries."

Faruqui patted Parker's arm, smiling in satisfaction. He then again faced all three men, speaking with a sobering voice. "Brothers, it is important that you not only look like an American infidel, you must also act that way. As you have already been instructed, and of which I remind you of, stop at truck stops that are known for their rowdy bars, strip clubs and brothels. Act the way you would expect an American truck driver to behave in these places. Do not arouse even a hint that you are pious Moslems embarked on jihad. I know how difficult a sacrifice this is for virtuous men who adhere to religion as a bee does to honey. When you feel that doing these things violates all you cherish and hold dear, remember that you are doing these things for Allah's sake, and it pleases Allah that you fight for the jihad against satanic America. By making these sacrifices, you are assured of entrance into a martyr's paradise."

The three men stood at attention, their rigidity conveying their desire to carry out Faruqui's instruction with exactitude. "One last thing I must tell you," Faruqui continued. "Nothing must stop us from arriving in Hoboken. If anyone stands in our way, be they a man, woman or child, they must be slaughtered without pity. Do you all understand?"

The three Jihadists stood still for a moment, unflinching. Then, with a rapturous voice, Parker yelled out, "Allahu Akbar!" His two comrades joined in with equal fervor, their chants echoing across the rafters of the barn.

◈ ◈ ◈

At FBI headquarters, the Director reluctantly took a phone call in the morning from David Cole. The Director of Counter-Terrorism for the CIA was passing on information he had just received from CSIS that Aziz Faruqi's bomb was probably smuggled into the country aboard a bulk carrier that had departed the Canadian port of Sault Ste. Marie on Lake Superior.

"Cole, we've got the damned bomb. I presume you watched our press conference," Braun told him with ample condescension.

Sensing he was up against a brick wall, Cole tried vainly to arouse concern on the part of the FBI. Only they could initiate a search of ships that had recently arrived in American Great Lakes ports that had embarked from Sault Ste. Marie, as the CIA was legally barred from conducting any domestic investigations. "Sir, please consider the possibility that the dirty bomb you confiscated in Montana was planted for you to find, as a diversion. We have nothing to lose by checking out the possibility that the Canadian theory is correct."

"I've had as much as I can take from you, Cole!" Braun angrily yelled over the phone. "The FBI does not take instructions from the CIA. We have conducted our own investigation, and are satisfied that we have the Al-Qaeda suspect and his dirty bomb in custody."

"Have you asked yourself, Mr. Braun, what motivation a truck driver named Robert Dunn would have in smuggling a dirty bomb across the border?" Cole asked.

"I don't give a crap about motivation!" responded an incensed Larry Braun. "It's the job of the DA to identify motive. For all I know he's a convert to Islam, or a member of a rightwing militia group that sympathizes with Al-Qaeda. All I care to know is that the plot was foiled, end of story. I'm warning you, Cole. You keep trying to interfere in FBI matters and I'll get a hold of Dick Darnell, and demand he cut you off at the knees!"

At that point, the FBI Director angrily slammed his phone.

Cole sat at his desk, uncertain as to what his next move would be. He stared out the window, observing an ominous-looking weather front unfolding, allowing only a feeble remnant of the morning's sunshine to penetrate the cloud cover. Then, his phone rang. He instantly answered the incoming call. It was Gayle Payne.

"David, I called an emergency meeting of the National Security Council earlier this morning," she informed Cole. "It was contentious, but I finally convinced them to approve a recommendation that we surreptitiously take Dr. Pervaz Khan into custody."

David Cole smiled for the first time in weeks. He thanked the National Security Advisor for what she had been able to accomplish.

"I am afraid that is premature," Ms. Payne warned. "Ultimately, the President has to grant his authorization before we can proceed. First, I will need to get the Vice President to sign off on this. If he doesn't, the President won't even give consideration. As I explained to you last night, the Vice President is not likely to agree to this."

"You must try, Gail, somehow, to convince him that this is absolutely essential for our country's safety and security," Cole pleaded with her.

Payne told him she would do her best, however, the tone of her voice suggested to him that she was not sanguine over the prospects of success.

❖ ❖ ❖

Among the vehicles proceeding south on Washington Street in downtown Hoboken was a four door blue Pontiac sedan with New Jersey license plates. The street ran parallel with the banks of the Hudson River, the skyline of Manhattan clearly visible on the far side. At the intersection with Borden Street, the Pontiac made a right turn and proceeded for half a block, stopping while a parked car began pulling out of its space. Shortly afterwards, the Pontiac was parked in the recently vacated space. A man in his mid-twenties stepped out of the car. He was an Asian gentleman, immaculately groomed and attired. He wore a brown cashmere coat, unbuttoned at the neck, revealing a designer silk tie, pinstripe suit and white button-down shirt. Whistling to himself, he walked a short distance to an empty storefront on Borden Street, where another man, of middle age, stood waiting for him, carrying a briefcase. His name was Lou Tremonti, and he was a realtor, specializing in commercial real estate in New Jersey.

"Good morning, Mr. Kim!" Tremonti said with elation, as his hand warmly grasped and shook Kim's. "Shall we step inside?" he urged his client.

Tremonti took out a set of keys and opened the glass door that led into the deserted storefront, save for a counter that stood facing the front window. As the two men stood by the counter, Tremonti removed a set of documents from his briefcase.

"Mr. Kim, I have the rental agreement, including the permit and wavers for you to do the necessary construction work," Tremonti advised his client. Kim reviewed the paperwork and signatures, noting that the agreement had his name spelled correctly, Mark Kim.

"Everything appears to be in order, Mr. Tremonti," Kim said with satisfaction, the New England refinement of his accent belying his relative youth and Asian ethnic origin.

"Congratulations, Mr. Kim, you are now officially in business," Tremonti said, again shaking his client's hand.

"Well, not exactly official yet," Kim interjected. "It will take six weeks to complete the construction work and renovations, so we won't be officially opened until early May, if we stick to our schedule."

"One thing I'm curious about, Mr. Kim, we already have approximately thirty cleaners and laundry establishments in Hoboken. What convinced you that you could compete successfully at this location?" inquired the realtor.

"Well, my family in South Korea is in the dry cleaning business, so this is in my blood," Kim patiently explained. "They loaned me the capital so I have strong financial backing. Also, I completed my MBA at Columbia Business School, and as an assignment

235

for one of my classes I created a comprehensive business plan and marketing survey for establishing a successful dry cleaning business in Hoboken. One of the things I discovered while doing my research is that while there are, as you said, thirty similar businesses in Hoboken, only two of them have a dry cleaning plant on their premises. I will be installing the equipment for an on-site plant, and offer my customers same-day service."

Lou Tremonti nodded his head approvingly. "That's very savvy of you," he complemented Kim. "Also, you can't beat the location. You're just a block from the train station that goes to Manhattan. You'll catch the commuters, both morning and evening rush-hour."

"That was a key element in my decision to lease this property," he told Tremonti. "It costs a lot more in terms of the lease, but I like the proximity to Manhattan. I just have to walk half a block to Washington Street, and the Manhattan skyline seems so close you can almost touch it."

❖ ❖ ❖

The Vice President was informed that the National Security Advisor had arrived for her hastily scheduled appointment with him. He remained at his desk , maintaining a glum countenance as Gayle Payne seated herself. Her face was riddled with fatigue, giving expression to the pessimism she harbored on the prospects of convincing the Vice President to go along with the recommendation the NSC had approved for the President's consideration.

"Ms. Payne, there's no way in hell either I or the President will go along with this. Not even considering the obstacles that stand in the way of successfully abducting Dr. Khan, you of all people know what this would do to our relationship with Pakistan," the Vice President stubbornly postulated.

"I understand the risks and the impact this would have on our cooperation with Pakistan in the war against terrorism," Payne said. "However, I am now coming along to David Cole's position, at least to the point of believing it is a possibility that the Lion's organization is attempting to bring a nuclear device into the country."

Shaking his head from side to side, he said, "You're an astute woman, Gayle. The FBI found the bomb, and it was a crude radiological device. David Cole is so worked up over his doomsday scenario, he just can't let go."

Payne asked if that meant that the NSC recommendation was now a dead letter.

"I won't allow it to come across the President's desk," he said with uncompromising firmness. She knew at this point that it was futile to continue the conversation, at least for now.

When the National Security Advisor returned to her desk, she immediately called David Cole, to relay the unfortunate, though not unexpected news.

"I thank you for trying, Gayle," he said in a submissive tone.

Payne asked Cole how much time remained before the terrorists would strike.

"Amelia Baldwin believes that the website of the Al-Assad El-Islamiya has already delivered a solid hint that whatever they are planning to do in this country, it will coincide with the fourth anniversary of the invasion of Iraq."

"That's March 20th," Payne replied, looking at her office calendar, displaying today's date, March 14. "That's less than a week!"

"We have six days left, if Amelia is right," he said with gloom. "And the FBI won't even investigate the CSIS theory that the bomb was smuggled into the country through one of our Great Lakes ports." He paused, reflecting on the plight he felt the nation was facing in total ignorance of its appalling consequences. Then, in a voice riddled with despair, he added, "This might sound rhetorical, Gayle, but sometimes I wonder whose side God is on."

❖ ❖ ❖

A private executive jet landed at Tehran's Imam Khomeni Airport on the outskirts of the Iranian capital. It taxied past the glass and steel main terminal building towards a group of cars, both unmarked and police. A ground crew was waiting near the aircraft as it came to a halt, setting up a gangway for it passengers to disembark.

A group of dignitaries stood by, waiting to greet an important person who had been on board the private jet. They were a diverse group; senior clerics in the leadership of the Islamic Republic of Iran wearing traditional robes and turbans, senior officers from the Islamic Revolutionary Guard or Pasdaran and a retinue of bodyguards wearing civilian clothes and carrying submachine guns. Shortly after the aircraft's door opened, Sheik Yantissi stepped down the gangway, to be warmly embraced by the awaiting delegation. Cheeks were kissed in reverence to the esteemed visitor, who was escorted into a waiting Mercedes Benz limousine with smoked glass windows to assure the privacy of its occupants.

A convoy, including Yantissi's car and police escort, soon left the airport and proceeded along the Tehran-Qom highway at a high rate of speed. Approximately a half-hour after departing the airport, the cavalcade of automobiles came to a dirt road exit, which they took and continued traveling on, until reaching a restricted military base operated by the Pasdaran. An electrified fence and barbed wire surrounded it, with guard towers located along the perimeter every 100 meters. At the entrance to the base, the convoy had been expected and the sentries on duty swiftly removed the barrier and allowed the cars to enter.

Several minutes later, Sheik Yantissi and his entourage arrived inside a closely guarded building and sat around a mahogany conference table festooned with flowers, trays of fruit and pitchers of water. On the walls of the room hung paintings of the Ayatollah Khomeini and various religious leaders serving in the senior leadership of the Islamic Republic of Iran.

The men around the table engaged in social conversation. There was a mixture of traditional religious garb and full dress military uniforms. As the conversations died down, all eyes turned towards Sheik Yantissi.

"We are all privileged to be present at the dawn of a new era," Yantissi said, stroking his beard as he scanned the determined faces sitting around the conference table. "In a matter of days, Allah willing, the world shall again witness the cleansing tide of Islam, as it devours wickedness and abolishes the minions of Satan from the face of the Earth."

The sheik poured himself a glass of water, clearing his throat in the process, as each man at the table had his eyes glued on him.

"Islam means submission to the inalterable word of Allah, as witnessed in the holy Koran and infused in the breasts of man by his divine messenger Mohammed, may peace be upon him," Yantissi pronounced. "Those who refuse to submit are declared by Allah to be *kaffirs*, unbelievers and infidels. It is the presence of those unbelievers upon the Earth that compels us, as Allah instructs, to wage jihad. Our enemies seek to portray us as fanatical, emotional and hateful, seized with hysteria as we slaughter the enemies of Allah. This shows with clarity how the American infidels, in particular, do not understand Islam. It is not blind hate or rage that propels us to seek martyrdom as the means towards their destruction and doom. Without emotion, without temper and without sentiment, we rationally and scientifically adhere to the words of the Koran, the divine instructions of Allah, and execute them in blind submission as true Moslems."

A brief silence filled the room, followed by a round of applause for the sheik, who acknowledged the response to his words by humbly bowing his head. He then turned towards one of the senior Iranian military officers, attired in an ornate uniform. "May I call on Rear Admiral Avad Ali Zamkhoni of the Islamic Revolutionary Navy to brief us on some forthcoming measures that will aid in the final execution of our mission?"

The Rear Admiral ran his fingers across his moustache and adjusted his eyeglasses, which had slipped down his nose. Smiling, he shared what he felt was pertinent information. "My esteemed comrades, on March 18 we, in coordination with our partners in the Democratic Peoples Republic of Korea, will commence the second series of ballistic missile tests. We are confident that this will totally absorb the attention of the Americans, so that they will be in total ignorance of what is soon to come."

❖ ❖ ❖

Peering with total concentration at her computer monitor, Amelia Baldwin was once more reviewing the Al-Assad El-Islamiya website, as she had become accustomed to doing several times each day as a matter of routine. On the Message for Believers

Page she once more observed an updated message in Arabic. The message was short, yet its content was so powerful, Amelia stared at it for several minutes as if frozen by its words. She pulled out her copy of the Koran, placing it on her desk as she quickly found the chapter and verse which the Lion's message had made reference to. After reading the verse, her face manifesting horror and revulsion, she hastily dialed David Cole's number.

"What is it, Amelia?" answered Cole, sitting at his desk at CIA headquarters in Langley.

Before Amelia answered, she noticed that both Alex Dunlop and Pierre Dextraze were standing behind her work station, sensing she had something of importance that affected them as much as David Cole.

"Sir, I believe the final message from the Lion to his followers has just been posted on their website," she told Cole, her voice betraying her sense of fear and foreboding.

"What does it say, Amelia?" Cole asked. Before answering, she briefly turned around, looking at Dextraze and Dunlop, who observed a woman experiencing an acute state of fright and helplessness.

"Mr. Cole, the message begins by saying that the Lion, as befits a martyr, has prepared his will and last testament. That's a statement a Jihadist makes when he expects his own death in battle to be imminent."

Cole asked Baldwin what else the message had to say.

She initially hesitated in replying. She then spoke, slowly and deliberately, though her words were spoken in a voice that was clearly shaken.

"Sir, the message concludes by reminding the Lion's followers that Osama bin Laden had personally warned the American people that if they continued to allow their government to engage in policies that were harmful to Moslems, they would all be responsible in the eyes of Allah, and would suffer divine punishment as prescribed in the Koran. The final sentence says simply that the prophecy contained in the 17th sura, 16th verse of the holy Koran will be fulfilled on the fourth anniversary on the infidel calendar of the criminal invasion."

"That must be another reference to the invasion of Iraq, March 20," Cole said in frantic despair. "Amelia, what exactly does that verse in the Koran say?"

Dextraze and Dunlop both noticed with concern that Amelia was shaking, tears forming in her eyes. She whispered to them that Cole wanted her to translate the 17th sura for him, though she wasn't sure she had the strength to do it.

Dunlop looked at her with empathy, and spoke gently. "Amelia, it is hard for all of us. But you must do as David asked you. However painful, we need to know what the final words are from Aziz Faruqui to his followers."

Amelia Baldwin, with trepidation flowing from her heart, turned towards her copy of the Koran, and began reciting it to Cole in Arabic, then again in English:

"When we resolve to annihilate a people, we first warn those of them that live in comfort. If they persist in sin, we rightly pass our judgment and utterly destroy them."

All Points Bulletin

Rolling down interstate 80 heading east, the rig from Alliance Transport had just passed the last exit for Davenport. Traffic was extremely light, the highway almost deserted as night fell. In the cab, Ronald Parker was at the wheel, his eyes appearing to glisten from the reflections stemming from the headlights of oncoming traffic. Martin Lopez, seated behind his two comrades, tapped Parker on the shoulder. "Would it be safe for us to take a bathroom break?" he requested.

Parker noticed a pebble-encrusted clearing on the side of the highway up ahead, apparently for emergency use. "I think we can, there's very little traffic tonight," Parker said in response.

The tractor-trailer geared down, its air brakes squealing. As they prepared to pull over to the side of the highway, all three men noticed a black four door Dodge immobilized at the front of the clearing. Its lights were off, the engine not running and it appeared, to all three men, to be deserted. "Must have broken down," Jack Burns commented with equanimity.

Once the rig was parked in the clearing, Lopez walked towards the forest, in search of a suitable spot to relieve himself. His two comrades opened the rear of the trailer, and Parker leaped in, walking towards the front, where the freezers had been loaded. He knocked on the door of one of the freezers five times, followed by three more knocks. Parker then slowly lifted the freezer door open, as Aziz Faruqui lifted himself up.

"We've just stopped for a few minutes for a call of nature," Parker informed Faruqui. He lifted himself out of the compartment, yawning with exhaustion. He asked Parker if the area was secure.

"Just an abandoned car, my brother. Otherwise, the area is deserted."

Faruqui told his comrades that he would stretch his legs and get some fresh air inside the trailer, with its doors left open, while the crew attended to their needs. Parker stepped out of the trailer, joining Burns and Lopez in the trees. Other than the periodic roar of a passing truck on the highway, the area was eerily silent.

Inside the black Dodge, in the back seat, an eighteen-year-old high school senior was lying on top of his girlfriend of similar age. Almost no words were spoken as they kissed with fervor and embraced with frenetic energy. They were totally absorbed with themselves, and oblivious to their surroundings.

"Let's go all the way, Susan," the young man whispered to his girlfriend.

She kissed him on the lips, smiled, and then shaking her head from side to side, said "No."

"Why not?" the young man asked, kissing her cheeks.

She told him how uncomfortable she was with the prospect of making love in the back seat of a car parked on the side of a public highway.

The young man sat up in disappointment, then looked through the windshield of his automobile, noticing the truck parked further up along the clearing, with its lights extinguished and rear trailer doors open. "Look there, Susan!" he said excitedly, pointing towards the truck.

She asked her boyfriend what he thought.

"The drivers are probably sleeping in the cab," he said. He turned towards his girlfriend, smiling widely, and she responded with a flurry of giggling.

"Are you thinking what I'm thinking?" he asked her with a mischievous tone to his voice. Nodding her head in affirmation, she again giggled. A moment later, they left their car, and walked stealthily towards the open doors of the rig's trailer, holding hands.

They stopped briefly, standing in front of the trailer's open doors. The young man then leaped up into the trailer, turning around to lend a hand to his girlfriend. Once inside, the two teenagers walked slowly towards the front of the trailer, navigating the narrow aisle between the steam boilers and their protective packing.

"What's that noise?" the young woman asked worriedly, as she thought she heard a sudden, shuffling sound emanating from the front of the trailer.

His mind distracted by a more immediate pursuit, the young man simply said, "I didn't hear anything."

They took a few more steps forward, then froze in petrified rigidity as they were suddenly confronted by a tall figure shining a flashlight at them. Their eyes were involuntarily squinting from the glare of the flashlight, however, they began to make out the outline of a tall, powerfully-built man with a narrow, horse-like face infused with anger, though the lips were still.

"Sorry sir, we got lost, but we'll leave," the young man clumsily said, his words made choppy by the fear-induced shaking that now convulsed his body. He and his girlfriend quickly turned around, preparing to make a hasty exit out of the trailer. Their hearts froze in terror, as Ronald Parker and Martin Lopez now entered the trailer, and moved towards them.

Outside, cars and trucks sporadically sped down the interstate highway. The black Dodge appeared forlornly empty. There was a slight breeze which, combined with the noise from the modest evening traffic, almost drowned out the cries of "No! No!" stemming from a male voice, reflecting mortal peril, along with the anguished pleas of mercy from a teenage female. There followed a bloodcurdling series of screams that seemed almost animal-like in their expression of torment and agony, interspersed with yells from a panic-stricken female desperately crying out, "Oh my God!"

❖ ❖ ❖

Early the following morning, a state police vehicle was cruising along interstate 80 when it spotted the abandoned black Dodge in the clearing near the Davenport exit. There were two state troopers

244

in the vehicle, and one mentioned to his colleague that the car seemed to match the description of the automobile driven by one of the two teenagers from the nearby town of Dixon who had been reported missing. "Let's pull over and check the license plate number," one of the officers suggested. Moments later, the police cruiser was parked behind the Dodge. They called their dispatcher over the radio, asking for verification of the license plate number of the missing teenagers' car. A moment later, the numbers were reported to them, which they noted matched the Dodge's license plate. They reported to the dispatcher that they had found the car, apparently abandoned near the Davenport exit on I-80, and would investigate on the scene.

The state troopers left their police cruiser, firmly slamming the doors behind them. They cautiously approached the black automobile from both sides, looking first at the rear seat. There appeared to be two human forms lying on the floor, however, it was not immediately discernable if they were asleep or dead. Slowly, they moved towards the front of the passenger compartment, then looked inside. They stared at what confronted them in stark horror, than at each other.

"Christ almighty! What monster would do something like that?" one of the officers asked his comrade, seething with revulsion.

◈ ◈ ◈

The state police had contacted the FBI office in Des Moines. The authorities believed they were dealing with a possible serial killer, an area that the Bureau specialized in. The District Director for the FBI contacted the coroner's office by phone, alerting them of what had happened near Davenport, and that the two bodies were being brought in by helicopter for an immediate autopsy. He asked to speak directly with the coroner, and discuss the urgency of the situation.

"Doctor, I don't know if the perpetrator is a sex maniac, or just plain sadistic, but we have a very dangerous killer on our hands. I need you to give me as many forensic clues as possible, as quickly as possible."

The coroner asked the FBI District Director if there was anything noteworthy about the slaying that had been observed.

"There sure was," the FBI man said. "Those poor kids had their heads cut off. The savage who did it left them on the bucket seats of the car, as though they were there for decoration."

❖ ❖ ❖

In Islamabad, Pakistan, a phone call came in to the American embassy from CIA headquarters in Virginia. The man answering was Vernon Barnes. Officially, he was the agricultural consul, however, that was merely diplomatic cover. In actuality, he was the CIA station chief.

"Vernon, this is David Cole, are you on a secure line?"

Barnes confirmed that he was.

"Vernon, I have a request that is top secret. No one, not even other colleagues from the Agency, must know about this. Can you confirm the present location of Dr. Pervaz Khan?"

"David, he is usually confined to a residential compound just outside of Karachi, under tight security," Barnes replied.

Cole emphasized to his CIA colleague that he had to know definitively if he was in fact still at his compound. Barnes told Cole he would contact a confidential source within the Pakistani Army general staff and get back to him.

❖ ❖ ❖

A Mercedes trailed an unmarked police car at a high rate of speed on the outskirts of Karachi, slowing down as it approached the exit for Jinnah International Airport. Several minutes afterwards, the two vehicles came to a halt in front of the departure terminal at the airport. There was a flurry of activity as several bodyguards exited the two cars, carefully checking the surroundings through their dark sunglasses. As one of the bodyguards held open the rear door of the Mercedes, Dr. Pervaz Khan stepped out. He was escorted into the terminal, with his bodyguards continuing their vigilant watch as he approached the Malaysia Airlines ticket counter.

❖ ❖ ❖

Larry Braun was at his desk, dictating a memorandum to his secretary, when his phone rang. His secretary answered the incoming call, and informed her boss that is was the FBI's District Director in Des Moines, calling about an urgent matter. Braun took the call, displaying no outward signs of alarm. "Urgent" phone calls from District Directors were routine for him, occurring several times a day. He expected this one to be no different. It took less than a minute for Braun to comprehend that this urgency was anything but routine. His secretary noted with alarm the worried expression that came over his face as the call ended and he hung up. "Mr. Braun, shall we proceed with the memorandum?" she asked.

Braun seemed temporarily oblivious to his secretary's presence. Then, regaining some composure, he instructed her to immediately connect him with the Vice President.

◈ ◈ ◈

At the U.S. embassy in the Pakistani capital, Vernon Barnes called David Cole on his secure line. Cole immediately answered, anxiously awaiting confirmation regarding the location of a man he considered a linchpin in the terrorist plot that his own government was adamantly in denial over.

"David, my source informs me that Dr. Khan left Pakistan earlier today, and is traveling abroad."

"Where is he headed?" Cole excitedly asked.

"To Kuala Lumpur, Malaysia," Barnes replied.

"What for?"

"He is supposedly attending a meeting of the Board of Directors of Crescent Industries," the CIA station chief told his colleague.

◈ ◈ ◈

Gayle Payne was buzzed in her office at the White House and told that the Vice President wanted to meet with her immediately. She stepped out of her office and walked rapidly through a long corridor. When she entered the Vice President's office, she was surprised to see him standing in front of the open door, pacing nervously. He closed the door firmly as she entered, and started talking even before he seated himself at his desk.

"We have a disaster on our hands," he said with astonishment. "Larry Braun just told me about a murder that occurred in Iowa last night. Two teenagers had their heads decapitated. The FBI thought they were dealing with a serial killer, but the medical examiner found something far more disturbing than that."

As the Vice President paused, breathing heavily, Payne pondered why a murder in a Midwestern state, albeit of a gruesome character, would warrant an emergency meeting with the National Security Advisor.

"What did they discover, Mr. Vice President?" inquired Payne.

"The medical examiner pulled microscopic particles of metal out of the victims' throats," he panted. "There were traces of DNA found on the metal particles that came from nine other persons, five of them Americans who had their heads cut off in Iraq by the Lion."

Gayle Payne stood motionless, seeking to weigh in her own mind the significance of this information. She looked directly at the Vice President's anguished face. Before she could respond, he shouted at her, "Larry Braun dropped the ball. He really fucked up royally!"

In contrast with the tumultuous reaction exhibited by the Vice President, Gayle Payne was a model of calm fortitude. "Mr. Vice President, this clearly means that the plot being pursued by the terrorists is still in process, and must be responded to, accordingly," she said in a deliberative tone. "Under the circumstances, I feel obliged to urge that you reconsider my earlier request that I be authorized to submit to the President the NSC recommendation."

The Vice President sat still, momentarily silent. Then, in a tone reflecting his reluctance, he said, "I still have my doubts about the wisdom of that course of action, but I agree that the President should have the opportunity to make a decision. I'm calling an emergency meeting of senior cabinet officers responsible for national security matters and the President for this evening, we can decide then."

There was one other imperative in Ms. Payne's mind, which she relayed to the Vice President. "I also recommend that we place the National Emergency Search Team on standby," she told the Vice President.

"I am still convinced that we are dealing with a dirty bomb, Ms. Payne," he said in a tone of voice that suggested his certainty.

Payne told him that even if they were facing a radiological dispersion device and not a full-fledged nuclear weapon, NEST would still be an indispensable asset in trying to track it down. "Remember, sir, that NEST exists right now only as a paper organization. It would require at least 48 hours to mobilize and deploy the first teams. That is why I think it would be prudent to at least bring it to standby status."

As the National Security Advisor looked on expectantly, the Vice President's demeanor gave hint of his uncertainty on the matter. He hesitated for a moment, than told Gayle Payne that the issue of the National Emergency Search Team could be deferred for deliberation at the evening meeting.

❖ ❖ ❖

It was nearing afternoon as the Alliance Transport rig slowed down on the I-80, and veered to the right as it came to the exit ramp for Chicago. Burns was driving, with Parker to his right and Lopez seated behind them. "Let's check the local news," Parker said, noting on his watch that it was three o'clock. He switched on the radio and heard the first item on the local news station.

"In the headlines for this hour, the FBI has been called in to assist in tracking down the killer or killers responsible for the savage slayings of two teenagers, both 18 years old, on interstate 80 near the Davenport exit. In other news, it is reported in Washington that a Congressional committee looking into the William Mendick scandal will begin holding public hearings next week. Mendick, the former Secretary of Homeland Security, was fired by the President after he allegedly assaulted a female employee on loan from the CIA..."

Parker turned off the radio and stared through the windshield, his face devoid of expression. His two colleagues also stared ahead, focused entirely on completing their mission.

❖ ❖ ❖

In Ottawa, the CSIS Deputy Director was contacted over the phone by David Cole. He began by reminding Dunlop that he would likely need his help. That was in fact the case, and he explained what he had in mind. Cole informed his colleague at CSIS that Pervaz Khan was in Kuala Lumpur for a meeting of the board of Crescent Industries.

"I don't know how long he's there, and we both know that the sands of time are running out. This may be our only chance to take him. The odds are that the CIA can't do this on its own. I need you to help us pull this off, Alex."

Dunlop asked Cole if he had authorization to arrange a kidnapping of Dr. Khan. The CIA's Director of Counter-Terrorism told him that there was an emergency meeting taking place at the White House that evening, at which point a final decision would be made.

"Alex, the National Security Council has already submitted a recommendation to the President that the CIA takes Khan into American custody. Let's both pray that he makes the right decision."

"Be frank with me, David," Dunlop asked with trepidation. "Given the reticence displayed so far by the administration, how hopeful are you that the President will buy in to the recommendation on grabbing Khan?"

"Speaking frankly, Alex, until a few hours ago, I didn't think I had a snowball's chance in hell of getting authorization," Cole responded with forthright candor. "However, something has happened that has improved the odds in our favor, though in a horrifying manner."

Dunlop inquired as to what had occurred that would have transformed the situation from the perspective of the White House.

"There were two teenagers brutally murdered along interstate 80 near the Iowa and Illinois state line," Cole said. "They were both decapitated, and you know whose trademark that is. But that's now established as fact, not opinion. The FBI forensic laboratory confirms through DNA analysis of blood samples found on fragments of the killer's knife that the weapon used also matches five victims of the Lion in Iraq."

As Cole relayed this information to Dunlop, the Deputy Director recalled the time he had first learned of the forensic results from the headless corpse found along the shores of Lake Abitibi. Though that had occurred only a few weeks ago, it now seemed that an eternity had elapsed since that moment in time.

"David, I will also need authorization from my government," Dunlop informed his colleague.

"I know that Alex, but please hurry. We must make this happen tomorrow, if we are to have any chance of pulling this off. The logistics for this type of operation are very complicated, and I must get started now, and assume that I will receive presidential authorization."

Dunlop assured David Cole that he would move on this immediately. As soon as the conversation was concluded, he walked down the hallway and entered Samuel Kinkaid's office. The CSIS Director, seated at his desk, looked up at Dunlop. He instinctively recognized that his Deputy Director would have entered his office without a scheduled appointment only on a matter of urgent priority.

Dunlop explained the request for assistance that he had received from the Director of Counter-Terrorism at the CIA.

"What is your recommendation, Alex?" asked Kinkaid.

Without hesitation, Dunlop was emphatic in stating his view that CSIS should do everything possible to assist the CIA in grabbing Pervaz Khan. "Time is running out, Mr. Kinkaid. Our only and last hope for tracking down Aziz Faruqui's nuclear device is by enabling the Central Intelligence Agency to capture Dr. Khan, so he can be thoroughly interrogated."

Kinkaid pointed out that even if the Americans had Khan in their grasp, there was no guarantee he would talk. "Look at Amad Hussein, the Jordanians have had him in their custody for several days, without the encumbrances of the media, lawyers and the Red Cross. He still hasn't talked."

Agreeing with his boss that there was no certainty that even if Khan were grabbed, he would divulge the information being sought, he simply added, "But what are our choices, sir."

Nodding his head in understanding of the unassailable logic of Dunlop's simple definition of the stark choices that now confronted them, Kinkaid buzzed his assistant on his intercom. "Connect me with the Prime Minister," he commanded.

◈ ◈ ◈

Inside a posh hotel room in Bahrain, a man with the physique of an NFL quarterback, lightly tanned skin, with wavy brown hair and a thick brown moustache with streaks of gray, lay on his bed. He was fully clothed, and occasionally grabbed a glass of whiskey on the nightstand, sipping it sparingly. A phone rang on his desk, and he placed the whiskey back on the nightstand and lazily lifted himself out of bed, walking over to the desk. He had four different cell phones arrayed on his desk, and it took him a moment to determine which one was ringing. Before answering, he knew where the call was originating from.

"This is Foster," he answered in a dull, monotone voice, devoid of any expression. Charles "Chuck" Foster, a former special forces non-commissioned officer in the U.S. Army's Green Berets, had also spent time as a field agent with the CIA, specializing in covert operations. He was now a private entrepreneur, his unique product and service being the arrangement of difficult operations for a variety of clients, including his former employer. The special service he provided for the CIA was choreographing snatch and grab operations, which involved stealthy kidnappings of individuals of great interest to the U.S. government, in situations where it was deemed more prudent to have the task performed by a private enterprise, not directly linked to a governmental agency.

"Chuck, this is David Cole," answered the voice on the other end of the conversation. It was a voice instantly recognizable to Foster.

"What do you need, Mr.Cole?" responded Foster.

"We have a package that needs to be picked up."

The request aroused not the least confusion in Foster's mind. He knew exactly what Cole was looking for.

"Where is the package located?" asked Foster.

"In Kuala Lumpur, Malaysia."

"How secure is the package?" Foster inquired.

"The package has bodyguards with him on a 24 hour basis," replied Cole. "We are working on an arrangement to place the package in a foreign embassy, so he will be isolated from his security detail."

Foster asked if presidential authorization had been received. Cole informed him that the President would make a decision within a few hours, and if approval was granted, he would forward to him full details on the target to be grabbed, through secure data-link.

"Where is the final destination for delivery of the package?" Foster asked in a matter-of-fact tone of voice.

"Still awaiting final arrangements before I can confirm where package is to be delivered," Cole said. "There is a high probability that the location will be in Central America."

◈ ◈ ◈

In the Oval Office, the President was conferring with the Vice President, Attorney General, National Director of Intelligence, Directors of the CIA and FBI and National Security Advisor. Having announced with grandiose fanfare that an Al-Qaeda linked plot to smuggle a dirty bomb into the United States had been foiled, Larry Braun was now in the hot seat. He knew he had egg on his face, and sought somehow to mitigate the damage to his reputation.

"Mr. President, let's look at the bright side. We got Robert Dunn and the dirty bomb he had in his possession. It might be that his was the only dirty bomb, which was to be delivered to the Lion," Braun said defensively. "Without a bomb, it might be that he's now just on the rampage, seeking to kill randomly and sow panic."

"If it leaks out to the media that the Lion has left Iraq and is now decapitating teenagers on the highways of America, this administration is going to look fucking ridiculous," the Vice President said with anger. "We are just lucky the mid-term elections were last fall."

The President looked troubled, and asked his associates for their advice on how the administration should respond.

"Unfortunately, I see no way we can keep Aziz Faruqui's presence in the United States hidden from the media, assuming he is the Lion," the Attorney General said in response. "It would be better for us to go public and show we are being proactive, so we can put our own spin on this whole situation."

Nodding his head in agreement, the President turned towards his FBI Director. "Well, Larry, what do you think?"

Unsure of himself, Braun thought it best to show he was prepared to take action and not be passive.

"Mr. President, I agree with the Attorney General. We should launch a nation-wide manhunt for Aziz Faruqui," Braun told the President. "We can have all the FBI offices alerted, press releases distributed to the media, and an all points bulletin issued to all the major police jurisdictions in the area."

While the President nodded approvingly, the Vice President expressed his concern. "We might look like keystone cops if we tell the American people that the Lion was able to sneak into the country, right through our fingers."

"I don't see a problem with that," Glenn Thrush interjected. "It all depends how we communicate it. I think we can legitimately say that due to our effectiveness in Iraq, the Lion can no longer operate safely there so he snuck into the United States. Law enforcement is on top of it, which is why we have gone public after discovering he was in the country."

"I like that," the President said, expressing his comfort with the recommendation. He then turned his gaze towards Gayle Payne, noticing the cold, discordant look she was exuding. "What's the matter, Ms. Payne?" he said, recognizing her concerned demeanor.

"Mr. President, I am very worried that the device the FBI confiscated in Montana was not the only device that was smuggled into the country."

The President stared at Payne for a moment, then scanned the faces of the other senior officials in the room, noticing that not one of them displayed any reaction to Gayle Payne's concern. He then looked again at his National Security Advisor.

"What do you recommend we do, Ms. Payne?" the President calmly asked.

With a trace of anguish in her voice, suggesting the extremity of the situation as she perceived it, she told her Commander-in-Chief that the only responsible course of action was to prepare for the possibility of a worst case scenario, that there was one additional device brought into the country, and it could be a full-fledged nuclear bomb.

"That is nonsense, Ms. Payne!" the Vice President interjected, exploding with anger. "You have been talking to David Cole too much for your own good! All the experts who understand how nuclear weapons work agree that cave-dwelling terrorists lack the know-how to build an atomic bomb that would actually detonate."

The President indicated basic agreement with the Vice President. He told Payne, however, assuming that the Lion had a remaining dirty bomb in his possession, the administration should do everything in its power to find it. He asked Gayle Payne how that could be accomplished.

"Our only chance to find the device, Mr. President, is by following the recommendation that the National Security Council has placed on your desk for your consideration," Payne said passionately.

"You mean kidnapping Pervaz Khan?" the President asked. Dick Darnell raised his eyebrows in response to the President's remark.

Looking worried, the Vice President raised his objections. "Mr. President, you know what a disaster such a move would be for our relationship with Pakistan. How can we wage our war on terrorism if we alienate our most important ally in the Moslem world?"

Reflecting for a moment, the President initially responded with caution. "The Vice President raises a valid point," he said "On the other hand, if what Ms. Payne has said turns out to be the case, even if it's just a dirty bomb we're talking about, and we haven't shown the American people that our administration will stop at nothing to protect them, there could be grave political ramifications. I have an ambitious domestic agenda, and I don't want it jeopardized by our opponents in Congress getting people sidetracked by making allegations that we aren't doing enough to protect the homeland. We're already taking heat because of the Bill Mendick affair."

Looking directly at Gayle Payne, the President asked if she had any other thoughts on the matter.

"Mr. President, I believe it would also be highly prudent for us to call the National Emergency Search Team to operational readiness," Payne suggested.

"Operational readiness? What do you mean?" the President asked, with a puzzled look upon his face. "Aren't these people all set up and ready to go?"

"No Mr. President. On paper, there are 600 scientists and other experts who serve on the NEST," Gayle Payne explained. "However, because their skills are so specialized and vitally needed in the defense sector and nuclear energy industry, they all serve in regular jobs related to their fields, and can only by mobilized to actively serve in the NEST by presidential order. It's essentially a reserve force, Mr. President, like the National Guard, and is only activated if there is deemed to be a national emergency that warrants such a measure."

❖ ❖ ❖

A full moon hung over a black Virginia sky, its reflection casting its subtle light on the windows of David Cole's office at CIA headquarters.

Cole's phone rang, and he immediately answered the incoming call. It was Gayle Payne.

"David, the meeting at the White House just adjourned. You have a go to proceed with attempting to grab Dr. Khan, provided there is plausible deniability of official American involvement."

"That won't be easy," Cole said, "but somehow I'll manage it. I do thank you, Gayle. I'll get right on it, there isn't a moment to lose."

"There is one other thing I need to tell you. I know you won't be happy to hear this," Payne told Cole, the tone of her voice ill-disguising her unease. "They decided to go public regarding Aziz Faruqui being in the country. An APB is going to be circulated to the major police departments around the nation."

"It's sheer madness, Gayle!" Cole reacted, with concern. "Whatever small chance there might have been of Faruqui making a mistake and showing his face will vanish once he knows we're looking for him."

"I know that," Payne said with fatalism. "That means, David, you must capture Dr.Khan and somehow make him talk. At this point, no other options are on the table."

Global Salafist

Alex Dunlop and Samuel Kinkaid sat facing the Prime Minister in his study at the official residence on Sussex Drive. A crackling noise emanated from an ornate marble fireplace, lending an ambience of formal tranquility to the room. However, the discussion was anything but tranquil.

"I absolutely refuse to have one of our embassies serve as the staging ground for a kidnapping!" declared the Prime Minister in a voice infused with righteous indignation.

The two senior officials from CSIS looked at each other in frustration, understanding the ethical context underlying the Prime Minister's adamancy, while recognizing that a new universe had supplanted the one that the head of the Canadian government was still functioning in.

"Mr. Prime Minister, Alex and I would never have made this recommendation unless our country, and indeed the whole North American continent, was facing dire jeopardy. That is in fact the situation, Mr. Prime Minister. Unless we are prepared to think outside the box and not be constrained by a normalcy that no longer exists, we must accept unspeakable consequences."

Dunlop observed the Prime Minister closely as the CSIS Director made his case, and noticed to his dismay that he seemed impenetrable. His thinking was focused on other concerns.

"Mr. Kinkaid, Mr. Dunlop, do you gentlemen realize the wrath from public opinion that has been unleashed on me since I allowed you to talk me into approving the extradition of Amad Hussein to Jordan?"

Dunlop glanced nervously at his watch, realizing that a narrow window of time was rapidly eroding. Unless he could find a way to convince the Prime Minister of the vital necessity of assisting the Americans in kidnapping Pervaz Khan, a looming catastrophe would be inevitable, he told himself.

"Mr. Prime Minister, please do not think for a moment that Mr. Kinkaid and I don't understand the predicament you are in. The decision to extradite Amad Hussein was very difficult and courageous. It was also the correct decision, under the circumstances," Dunlop said. "The circumstances that compel the two of us to make this understandably troubling request are even more acute. Please hear me out, so that your decision will be based on all the relevant factors."

Talking in an imploring and, at times, emotional tone of voice, the Deputy Director described the weapon that CSIS was now positive had been constructed along the banks of Lake Abitibi. First relaying the technical details of the weapon and its yield, he then began describing its destructive power in human terms.

"Sir, Dr. Lazar is of the opinion that if this weapon is detonated, it will explode with the power of 150 million tons of high explosives. That number is so staggering, it defies human comprehension. It would be as if ten thousand bombs identical to the type that leveled Hiroshima were detonated simultaneously, at one location."

Dunlop paused for a moment, observing that the Prime Minister was attuned to his words, his face betraying a hint of disbelief, as though a weapon with that magnitude of power was inconceivable.

"The Russians code named this weapon the King of Bombs for good reason," Dunlop continued. "In the entire history of human civilization, there has never been a device as destructive as this. Dr. Lazar informed us that, at the moment such a weapon explodes, for a brief fraction of a second, it will release the power equivalent to six percent of all the energy generated by the sun."

Both Kinkaid and the Prime Minister seemed startled by the frightful comparison being postulated by the Deputy Director.

"Imagine, Prime Minister, if six percent of the power of the sun was released in the form of an explosion, converging on a single urban target. Contemplate, sir, if that power was unleashed right in the heart of New York City. Try to think what world we will wake up to the following day," Dunlop said with eloquence and feeling. "I ask you, sir, to think along those lines, because if we fail to find and disarm Aziz Faruqui's bomb, than our next meeting will be to wail over the aftermath of such an apocalyptic event."

As the Prime Minister took a deep breath, cold sweat emerged on his brow, reflecting the roaring light emerging from the fireplace. Dunlop and Kinkaid briefly glanced at each other, than turned towards the Prime Minister.

"How certain is CSIS that this bomb will explode?" the Prime Minister asked in a hushed tone of voice.

"We have total confidence that it will detonate at full yield, unless we and the Americans find it in time," Dunlop responded forcefully.

"What if we don't find it?" the Prime Minister interjected.

"In that case, Prime Minister, we need to plan for mass casualties on Canadian soil, and the catastrophic break-down in the social order of our American neighbor, which can only contribute to the suspension of the way of life we have grown accustomed to in our country, probably for the next century, at least," Kinkaid grimly forecast.

Buttressing the CSIS Director's melancholy prophecy, Dunlop shared with the Prime Minister Dr. Lazar's belief that the King of Bombs would kill, at a minimum, eighty million Americans. Furthermore, the radioactive fallout likely to afflict eastern Canada, encompassing the nation's major urban centers, including Toronto, Montreal and Ottawa, would likely doom five million Canadians to a gruesome and agonizing death.

"That is the frightful reality we face, Prime Minister," Dunlop said in a somber tone. "That is, unless we can discover this device before it's too late. Dr. Pervaz Khan, we believe, was an indispensable ringleader in the planning and preparation of this plot. That is why we must help the Central Intelligence Agency apprehend him."

Both Dunlop and Kinkaid sat still, their eyes fixated on the stony features of the Prime Minister's weary face, anticipating a response that they were desperately awaiting.

◈ ◈ ◈

Cole's office looked like a war room, with maps and charts affixed to his walls and scattered all over his desk. His shirt soiled by perspiration and his tie hanging limply, he made notations on one of the charts as his phone rang. Answering it, he recognized he was about to receive a response to an issue that hung over him like the sword of Damocles.

"David, it's Alex. We just finished our meeting with the Prime Minister," Dunlop said, pausing briefly to catch his breath. Cole could sense his colleague's exhaustion, and his own inner tension. "We have authorization to co-operate on the matter involving the Canadian High Commission to Malaysia, in Kuala Lumpur."

"Thank God!" exclaimed Cole, not in the least seeking to suppress his feeling of relief.

The Deputy Director told Cole that the Prime Minister had personally called the First Secretary at the Canadian High Commission, Ms. Rita Paddington, and informed her of the pending operation. She would be the point person for the CIA's operatives to contact and coordinate arrangements.

◈ ◈ ◈

Just outside the town of Elkhart, Indiana stood a ubiquitous-looking truck stop with an adjacent motel. Inside one of the nondescript motel rooms, a tired-looking blond woman wearing a garter belt and a skimpy black nightgown counted a hundred dollars in small bills as she stood next to the bed. In front of the bed, facing a wall-mounted mirror, Ronald Parker finished buttoning his shirt. He tightened the belt around his khaki pants, then turned towards the door and left, not exchanging a single word with the woman he had spent the last hour with. He walked silently towards the lot in front of the truck stop, looking at the tractor-trailer rig he was responsible for. As it loomed closer, he noticed a newspaper vending machine, which contained the early edition of the morning paper. The sky was still pitch black, it being early morning. He glanced at the front page of the newspaper, displayed in the machine. What he observed prompted him to pull some change out of his pocket and purchase the paper.

He approached the Alliance Transport truck, and leaped into the cab. Both Burns and Lopez were awake, though drowsy. They rubbed their eyes, then sat still, transfixed on one of the newspaper headlines, which Parker displayed for them. "You'd better tell the Lion," Burns said.

Burns left the cab, with Parker following behind. The trailer doors were opened by Burns momentarily, enabling Parker to enter, grasping the newspaper and a flashlight, with his comrade then closing the doors behind him. The Jihadist walked to the freezer in the front of the trailer, knocked five times followed by three, then slowly opened the top door.

Faruqui sat himself up in his cramped compartment, with a weak light emitted by the lamp mounted in his claustrophobic living quarters, reinforced with the beam of light being projected by Parker's flashlight.

"I thought you should see this sir," Parker said, as he held the newspaper up for Faruqui to read. On the lower right side of the front page, he read the headline, "FBI Searching For Aziz Faruqui, Alias Lion Of Iraq, Inside U.S."

Betraying no emotion or hint of concern, he simply told Parker, "I am only surprised it has taken them this long to know I am in their midst." He grasped Parker gently by the arm, smiled, and emitted a brief, sharp laugh, prompting his comrade to also smile.

"My brother warrior of Islam, the infidel will be looking in all the wrong places, stop all the wrong vehicles, question all the wrong people, while we continue on our journey, undisturbed," Faruqui said boastfully. "It is too late for the far enemy to stop our rendezvous with destiny."

❖ ❖ ❖

At ACLU headquarters in New York City, Harold Tanenbaum was briefing the media on its latest legal submission before Federal District Court. Seething with indignation, speaking with unrepressed fury, he lashed out at what he perceived as a grave injustice.

"Our organization, in partnership with the National Council of American Moslem Associations, has jointly filed suit in Federal District Court to halt the government's outrageous conduct directed against our fellow Moslem citizens and residents. Using the manhunt for Aziz Faruqui as a pretext, law enforcement agencies have begun a witch-hunt directed at Moslems and Arabs living and working in the United States. The reports we have of racial profiling are so prolific, they give evidence of a clear abrogation of the constitutional rights of many of our Moslem citizens. Homes and businesses owned by Arab-Americans and Moslems have been raided, trucks and commercial vehicles are being stopped and searched by the police on our nation's highways, solely on the basis of the ethnicity or religion of their drivers. This outrageous conduct by the government must cease and desist!"

One of the reporters present at the briefing directed a question and Tanenbaum. "Mr. Tanenbaum, the Attorney General claims that the government has detected a spike in chatter by Al-Qaeda and its affiliated groups, which it says may point to a heightened threat level coinciding with the detection of Aziz Faruqui, who may be the notorious Lion of Iraq, in our country. If these reports are accurate, don't they point to a need by our law enforcement agencies for heightened vigilance?"

"Absolutely not!" Tanenbaum passionately pronounced. "The fundamental rights of individual citizens are under assault, not from Al-Qaeda or other terrorist groups, but from our own government. That is where the danger lies!"

❖ ❖ ❖

A twin-engine turboprop aircraft feathered its engines as it approached a small airfield, its landing gear lowered in preparation for touch-down. Within minutes, it was parked on the side of the small runway, with a military jeep standing in wait. The airfield was located in the eastern jungle region of El Salvador, close to the border with Honduras. As the aircraft's passenger door opened, David Cole emerged, wearing a safari jacket and straw hat, his eyes bloodshot from lack of sleep. Once he had his feet on the ground, he motioned to the soldiers in the jeep that he was ready to embark on his short journey. He seated himself next to the driver, indicating the haste he was in. Confirming his destination, he told the driver, "Pronto!"

After traversing a network of bumpy, poorly surfaced roads and jungle clearings, the jeep arrived at a tobacco plantation, it's manicured patches and colonial style stucco house contrasting with the well-rusted barbed wire entanglements which enveloped the property. The jeep stopped at the entrance, where a husky man wearing peasant garb and holding an M-16 carbine approached as Cole peered upwards at the sign beckoning above the entrance, "Guzman Tobacco S.A."

One of the soldiers simply said "Senor David Cole," which the man with the carbine acknowledged by nodding his head. He quickly announced that the expected guest had arrived over his walkie-talkie, and waved the jeep through. It drove into the plantation until coming to rest in front of the stucco villa. Cole stepped out of the vehicle and turned towards the villa's balcony, observing a man of medium height standing, his hands resting on his hips. Cole recognized the man's features, greasy black hair combed back, thinning in the middle. He had a gray moustache, dark, foreboding eyes, a wrinkled face and scarred chin. The man looked harsh, exactly as Cole remembered him.

The CIA intelligence officer walked up towards the balcony, each step seeming insufferable to him. He disliked the man he was about to meet. His name was Ernesto Guzman, currently the proprietor of a lucrative tobacco plantation. When Cole was more familiar with him, Al-Qaeda did not exist and the major national security threats to the United States were deemed to be Spanish-speaking Marxist rebels in Central America. That period now seemed to Cole to belong to an epoch from ancient history. Yet, it was one of those relics of a long-forgotten conflict who was now intersecting with the most imperative requirements of the war on terrorism. The last time David Cole knew him, Ernesto Guzman was a Colonel in the El Salvadorian national army, responsible for interrogating captured rebel prisoners and suspected Marxist sympathizers. Guzman was not known for his delicacy in following the rules of the Geneva Convention. In fact, he once boasted to Cole that he never even bothered to read the protocols written in Geneva. His job was to get accurate, timely information out of people who otherwise would never divulge what Guzman's superiors needed to know. The Colonel was none too subtle in his methods, and Cole profoundly disliked him for that. Yet, undeniably, he was supremely effective in achieving results for his superiors.

Cole hated himself for having to make this journey, feeling even more self-loathing as he gazed at the man waiting for him on the balcony. He reminded himself, however, of the criticality of the situation he was confronted with. There was no choice, he told himself. Attempts at gentle persuasion would not induce Dr. Pervaz Khan to reveal what he knew of the location of Aziz Faruqui's superbomb. Any non-coercive measures would be futile and doomed to failure, with ghastly consequences. It was not good enough to merely abduct Khan - he had to be made to talk. David Cole knew that there was only one man on the face of the Earth who could possibly break Pervaz Khan. The question was, would he do it, and at what price?

Without smiling, and sensing Cole's feeling of near-contempt for him, Guzman weakly held out his hand for Cole to shake. "I hope you had a pleasant journey to El Salvador," Guzman said in a flat voice, devoid of any trace of warmth or emotion. Cole answered in a perfunctory manner, and Guzman directed him into the villa, where they sat alone in a small living room. They got right down to business.

Guzman reminded Cole of what he had done for the CIA in helping to quash a leftist uprising in El Salvador. "In those days, I was a hero, Mr. Cole, I even once received a letter of commendation from President Ronald Reagan," Guzman said with a hint of nostalgia. "But once the Cold War was over, I became a pariah. I was barred entry into the United States, even to visit my relatives. So-called 'human rights' organizations attempted to have me extradited to stand trial before an international tribunal in Europe. Your country could not have won the Cold War without people like me, yet America abandoned me. And now, after nearly twenty years, when I have retired from the military and, through the sweat of my own labor, built a successful business, you come knocking on my door. Why should I hear what you have to say?"

Though initially appalled at himself for even having to be in the presence of Guzman, Cole, to his surprise, found he harbored a reluctant respect for Guzman. He told him that he was not going to lie to him, this was not a mere social call, or an apology for the Agency having coldly discarded him when it felt it had no further requirement for his special and unique skills.

"I'm not going to deceive you, Guzman, I am only here because I have no choice," Cole bluntly said.

Ernesto Guzman's eyes flashed with anger and resentment, and Cole thought he was about to unleash a tirade. Instead, he merely asked what Cole wanted from him.

"If everything goes according to plan, we expect to have in our custody Dr. Pervaz Khan, the father of the Pakistani atomic bomb and mastermind behind a network of black market nuclear weapons technology suppliers, in the next several hours," Cole explained.

Though Guzman did not know Khan personally, he was familiar in a general way with what he had been involved with. He asked Cole what information he was seeking to learn from Khan, and why the urgency. Cole shared with him, in simple words, his belief that Khan was allied with Jihadists linked to Al-Qaeda, and had helped them assemble a nuclear bomb. It was almost certain that the bomb had been smuggled into the United States, and would likely be detonated within a few days in New York City, unless the location of the device could be discovered in time. Dr. Pervaz Khan had to know the location.

"My niece lives in New York City with her husband and small child," Guzman said, briefly displaying a hint of emotion, which instantly dissolved into a demeanor of ruthlessness. He asked Cole how positive he was that Khan knew the location of the bomb. Cole was adamant that Dr. Khan had to know the location of the nuclear device, since he clearly played a key leadership role in the conspiracy.

"Then, I will agree to interrogate him," Guzman said. "I do this not out of any affection for the CIA, whose abandonment of me remains a bitter wound. However, I am a professional, who took a lot of pride in doing this dirty but necessary work well. You have presented me with the ultimate challenge, literally saving the world. It must really hurt, Mr. Cole, that it is in my despised skills that you must travel such a long distance to seek salvation."

Cole could sense that Ernesto Guzman relished the moral contradiction he had entered. Looking directly at Guzman, who could see his weary eyes, he told him that necessity was truly the mother of invention, prompting the retired Colonel to flash a brief smile.

"When do you expect Dr. Khan will arrive here as my guest?" asked Guzman. Cole informed him that Khan would be delivered in about 24 hours.

"Once Dr. Khan is welcomed here, to receive my special hospitality, I will accept no interference from the CIA or any other arm of the American government. This must be handled my way, with no restraints imposed by you, or anyone else, or I will decline to assist you. Do you understand?"

Cole nodded his head in affirmation. He then asked Guzman about his fee.

"Mr. Cole, I will make you the deal of a lifetime," Guzman said with a hint of guile. "If I fail to extract the necessary information from Dr. Khan, you owe me nothing. However, if I succeed in my mission, my fee is twenty-five million dollars in gold."

Cole wasted no time in agreeing to Guzman's terms. There was nothing further to discuss, and without even the cordiality of a handshake, the CIA's Director of Counter-Terrorism departed for the long journey back to Langley.

❖ ❖ ❖

In downtown Hoboken, a truck was parked in front of the storefront on Borden Street being leased by Mark Kim. The side of the truck identified the vehicle as belonging to Garden State General Contractors, Inc. A large cardboard sign had been posted in the window facing the street, announcing to passing pedestrian traffic that "Kim Brothers Dry Cleaning and Tailoring is pleased to announce its grand opening on May 12. We will be offering a ten percent discount in appreciation for your patronage."

Inside, in shirtsleeves, Kim was directing some of the workers in setting up ceiling-mounted revolving hangers for the hundreds of garments that would be awaiting customer pick-up once the cleaning establishment had opened its doors for business. In the rear of the storefront, there was a small kitchen with space reserved for installation of a freezer. Behind the kitchen was a large area, with two employees of the general contracting firm engaged in carpentry work, in preparation for the installation of large items of machinery.

❖ ❖ ❖

Nadine Iqbal, dressed in her nightgown, was in the process of preparing her morning coffee as part of a light breakfast before getting ready for work. Her doorbell rang unexpectedly. She left her kitchen and approached her door, noticing through her peephole that two RCMP Constables were present. Worried and uncertain, she opened her door. The Mounties informed her that CSIS had learned that her life was in grave danger, and that a special security certificate had been issued to place her in protective custody. They would take her to a secure location, where she would be under 24-hour protection until the danger had lapsed. She was instructed to get dressed, and pack enough clothing and toiletries for at least four days.

While Nadine Iqbal was being attended to by the RCMP, Henry Littlejohn had an appointment with the president of St. Mary's Hospital. Upon his arrival, he was escorted into the president's office, where he presented his credentials.

"Sir, CSIS requests the cooperation of your hospital and its staff on a matter involving national security," Littlejohn solemnly informed the hospital's president who, in response, unhesitatingly offered his full and complete cooperation.

"I need to have a private space set up in your hospital that is patched into your telephone switchboard. There is a particular incoming call we expect your hospital will be receiving from overseas; it is urgent that this call be immediately transferred to me," the CSIS intelligence officer said.

❖ ❖ ❖

Dominating the skyline of Malaysia's capital were the majestic Petronas Towers, tallest office buildings in the world. In one of the towers, Crescent Industries had its corporate offices, where its board of directors were convening in the conference room. A secretary knocked on the closed door. One the directors opened it a crack, and heard the secretary whisper a message that prompted an alarmed look on his face. He in turn came up to Dr. Pervaz Khan, who was one of twelve board members seated around the table. He whispered into Khan's ear, compelling him to immediately get up and leave the conference room. He followed the secretary to a phone, which he picked up to take an urgent call for him.

"Dr. Khan, this is Rita Paddington, I'm the First Secretary at the Canadian High Commission," the woman said, pausing briefly upon identifying herself. Khan asked in a perplexed voice why she was calling him.

"I regret to have to inform you, Dr. Khan, that your daughter was involved in a serious car accident."

A worried look came upon Khan's face, prompting him to inquire about her medical condition.

Paddington informed him that she was alive but unconscious and in critical condition. She had been taken to St. Mary's Hospital in Ottawa, and would require immediate surgery, if her life was to be saved. "Under Canadian law, if a patient is incapacitated, written authorization from a recognized legal guardian is required before surgery can be undertaken," Paddington informed Khan. "The hospital has not been able to locate Nadine's husband, so as her father you would be recognized as having guardianship."

"Of course, I give permission," Pervaz Khan told the First Secretary. She said in response that written authorization was required.

"Why not have someone take the forms to my office, and I can sign them here," Khan said in reply.

In a sensitive voice, Rita Paddington explained that for a faxed authorization, originating from overseas, to be accepted by the hospital, it needed to be signed in the presence of a Canadian consular official, who would co-sign as a witness. She apologized for the requirement, but her hands were tied by the legal stipulations.

Pervaz Khan hesitated for a moment, than his thoughts turned to his daughter. He asked Paddington for the location of the High Commission. It was on the fifteenth floor, in the Menara building on Jalan Razak Avenue, which he knew was only a few minutes by car from the Petronas Towers. He told Paddington he would be over at the High Commission in a few minutes.

He was about to make arrangements to get over to the High Commission, when an instinctive reaction caused him to freeze. Standing still, as his mind filled with suspicion, he came back to the phone and dialed the overseas operator. "I want to be connected with admissions to St. Mary's Hospital in Ottawa, Canada," he demanded.

In the main switchboard office at St. Mary's, a receptionist received the operator's call from Kuala Lumpur. The call was instantly transferred to Henry Littlejohn, located in another part of the hospital. "St. Mary's Hospital, admission's department," he answered.

A voice responded, which the CSIS agent recognized as belonging to Pervaz Khan. "Is a Nadine Iqbal a patient at your hospital?"

"One moment, please," Littlejohn said in a manner suggesting routine. A moment later, he came back to inform the caller that there was a Nadine Khan who had been admitted following a morning automobile accident.

"How is she?" a worried Khan inquired.

"I'm sorry sir, we are not allowed to give out that information unless you can identify yourself as being next-of-kin," Littlejohn replied in a script-like manner.

Khan had nothing further to say. He had hung up.

❖ ❖ ❖

Just over the Ohio State line, on I-80 heading east from Indiana, a police roadblock had been established. Every commercial vehicle with more than six wheels was being pulled over to the side of the highway for inspection. Among the vehicles that had been flagged was the tractor-trailer rig from Alliance Transport, which was parked over on the side behind a medium-sized truck from Ahmed Provisioners, which was in the process of being inspected.

A state trooper demanded the operating permit from the driver, a middle aged man of Middle Eastern appearance. There was a young man seated next to the driver, and the policeman asked who he was.

"He is my son," replied the driver, who identified himself as Tareq Ahmed, owner of the business, and that his son was employed by him.

"And what is your business?" the trooper inquired with suspicion. The driver explained that Ahmed Provisioners supplied grocery stores throughout northern Ohio.

"Get out, both of you, and open your rear doors for inspection," the trooper said in a threatening tone of voice. The two men complied in robot-like fashion, and soon three members of the Ohio State Police were busily looking over loads of vegetables and canned goods, as Ronald Parker and his two comrades viewed what was unfolding through their windshield, their faces reflecting profound disinterest.

The driver and his son had hoped that their ordeal was over when the three troopers were finished with their cursory inspection. Instead, they were informed that they were being taken into custody for further questioning, and that their cargo was being impounded for more rigorous inspection. They protested loudly that they had done nothing wrong, and that their business would be jeopardized by this action, as another state trooper approached the Alliance Transport rig.

"Good morning, officer," Parker said through the rolled down window of the door of his cab.

"Good morning, sir, may I please see your operators permits," the policeman requested.

Parker handed the three permits to the officer, who quickly perused them, briefly scanning the faces of the three men before returning the documents.

"May I ask what you're carrying in your rig?" the officer politely requested.

"We're hauling a mixed load of laundry and cafeteria equipment," answered Parker.

Smiling, the officer said, "Thank you for your cooperation. You may proceed on your way, have a pleasant day."

Parker thanked the officer, let out the clutch, placed the transmission in gear, and with a lurch, the massive rig began gaining momentum, while Tareq Ahmed and his son continued to argue in vain at what they perceived as the injustice of their detention, and confiscation of their goods.

❖ ❖ ❖

On the fifteenth floor of the Menara building, adjacent to Kuala Lumpur's business district, the receptionist at the Canadian High Commission paged the First Secretary, informing her that Dr. Pervaz Khan had arrived. When she indicated to Rita Paddington that two men had accompanied Khan, she realized he had brought his bodyguards with him. She told the receptionist she would greet Pervaz Khan momentarily.

A heavy-duty steel door, locked electronically, barred the way into the High Commission. Paddington, a woman of average height, light skin and shoulder-length red hair, emerged from the armored door, which opened with a drone-like noise. She introduced herself to Dr. Khan, who mentioned that two of his associates were with him.

"I'm sorry Dr. Khan, but we have strict security protocols at the High Commission, and we can only allow specific individuals having official business access to the High Commission."

The two bodyguards were about to object, when Dr. Khan signaled through a hand gesture that there was nothing to worry about, and that they could wait in the reception area. He stood up, and Paddington escorted him into the High Commission offices. They walked passed a suite of small offices and cubicles, towards a remote area near the back of the High Commission, near a door marked "Fire Escape." Paddington opened the door to a large office, and had Pervaz Khan follow her in. The door was left open, and Paddington told her guest that the necessary documents were on her desk. She passed them over to Dr. Khan, telling him it was important that he review and read them very carefully before signing them, as it involved a life-or-death decision for his daughter.

Paddington watched Khan carefully, as he took out his reading glasses and began perusing the documents. Suddenly, without warning, an intense noise, resembling an explosion, occurred. Almost immediately, electrical power in the building failed, as lights went out amid cries of panic. Black, acrid smoke began pouring out of the air ducts.

Paddington and Khan looked at each other, unsure of what had happened, until a klaxon began sounding on the building's intercom system. This was followed by a male voice identifying himself as the Menara building's fire safety director. He advised the tenants that an explosion had occurred in the building's electrical utility room, and that the city's fire department had been notified and was on their way. Fire wardens on each floor would be organizing an evacuation in small groups, and tenants should not panic but follow the instructions of the wardens. Almost as soon as the announcement ended, an athletic looking man with black hair appeared in Paddington's office, informing her that he was the fire warden for that area of the High Commission, and that she and her guest should follow him. The First Secretary and Khan obediently complied, and left the smoke-filled office, heading to the nearby fire escape, where four men and a woman were standing in wait. The warden opened the fire escape door, and directed the group to follow him down the stairs. Paddington led the way, followed by Khan and the rest of the group. They quickly ran down several flights, panting, as smoke wafted throughout the fire escape. Soon, the sound of fire engine sirens could be heard, contributing to the sense of emergency.

The group appeared to be almost out of breath when Rita Paddington noticed two men in fireman's rescue uniforms, running upwards. One of the firemen carried an ax, the other an oxygen tank with breathing apparatus. The group stopped, and the firemen asked if any of them required assistance. One man in the group said he needed some oxygen. The First Secretary pointed out that Khan was an elderly gentleman, and should be the first one to receive oxygen. The fireman agreed, and removed his oxygen tank, handing the connecting breathing mask to Pervaz Khan. The fireman instructed Dr. Khan to place the breathing apparatus over his face. Coughing profusely, he complied with the instructions. Once the mask was securely fastened on Khan, the fireman turned on a valve in the oxygen tank, and almost immediately a panicked look took hold of Pervaz Khan. Reflexively, his hands reached for the mask, in a frantic attempt to remove it. As Rita Paddington stood by, several members of the group grabbed Khan's arms and legs, immobilizing him until, a moment later, he lapsed into total unconsciousness. The man who had presented himself as the fire warden turned towards Rita Paddington, thanking the First Secretary for her cooperation. "You can return to your office, then join the other employees who are evacuating through the other fire escape. We'll take it from here."

Several minutes later, an ambulance sped away from the Menara building, as additional fire engines were approaching it. Inside the ambulance, Khan was strapped to a gurney, still unconscious. A woman dressed as a medical orderly pulled out a syringe, which she then injected into Khan's right arm. She turned to her two colleagues in the rear of the ambulance, telling them that Pervaz Khan would be sleeping for at least the next twelve hours.

Just past a sign indicating twenty kilometers distance to the international airport, the ambulance's siren was switched off, and it took a side road with sparse traffic. It pulled into an abandoned garage, where two cars were waiting. One of the vehicles was a BMW, the other a Toyota sedan. The driver remained in the BMW, while three well-dressed men emerged, and removed Khan from the gurney. They carried him to the rear of the BMW, and removed a large suitcase. Khan's ankles and wrists were tied together, reducing his form to that of a human ball. He was then placed into the suitcase, and loaded into the automobile's trunk. Within minutes, the BMW was traveling at high speed towards the airport. The accomplices who had been in the ambulance abandoned it, leaped into the Toyota, and headed in the direction of downtown Kuala Lumpur.

Less than an hour later, the luggage from the BMW was loaded aboard an executive jet, joined by the car's occupants.

Within minutes, the flight crew received clearance for take-off, destination Honolulu. Unknown to the flight controllers at Kuala Lumpur International Airport, that was not the final destination for the most important item of cargo on board the aircraft.

❖ ❖ ❖

Amelia Baldwin was seated in Alex Dunlop's office. The Deputy Director continued to be perplexed at the lack of comprehension by America's intelligence and law enforcement community of the imminent and cataclysmic danger that faced them. He told Amelia that only his colleague at the CIA, David Cole, knew exactly what they were up against.

"Amelia, we have recommended to the FBI that they trace all shipping traffic that landed at American Great Lakes ports after loading on the Canadian side. Instead, they have ignored our advice and are focused on a manhunt, intimidating every Arab or Moslem-looking truck driver on the interstate highways. I don't understand why there is such obtuseness. Not only will this tactic fail, it will alienate anyone in those communities who may have relevant information, and be otherwise well-disposed to provide assistance."

The young linguist was equally dismayed, but thought she understood why so many in her country's intelligence and governmental leadership had so misread the facts on the ground.

"Mr. Dunlop, conducting racial and ethnic profiling in such an insensitive and cavalier manner just illustrates how myopic our nation's leaders are in the war on terrorism. By stopping and harassing Arab-looking men, sending informants into mosques and conducting surveillance on taxi drivers from Pakistan who lead pious lives, they are actually doing what these Islamist terrorists so desire. In their eyes, such concentration of effort by their enemies assures them of success."

Dunlop asked Ms. Baldwin why that was so.

"That is because the core of the radical Islamist terrorist movement, including men such as Osama bin Laden and Aziz Faruqui, are actually part of the Global Salafist Jihad, which has its own unique rules on how to fight what they refer to as the far enemy, meaning the infidels of Europe and America."

275

Sheldon Filger

Intrigued, Dunlop asked Baldwin to elaborate on the Global Salafist Jihad.

"The name is derived from the Arab word *salaf*, meaning ancient one, the companions of the prophet," Amelia explained. "A salafist is the most extreme among radical Islamists. He believes that the ends justify the means, and therefore, to destroy the Dar al-Harb, or house of war, the lands where infidels dwell, all means of trickery and deceit are not only acceptable, it is a religious obligation that they be practiced. That means the men who are working with Aziz Faruqui have likely shaved their beards, adopted an American appearance in dress and mannerisms, drink alcohol and eat pork. The last place they would be found at is a mosque, or in an Arab neighborhood."

"That was exactly the modus operandi of the hijackers who perpetrated 9/11," Dunlop remarked. "From what you are telling me, the FBI and police are looking in all the wrong places."

"Unfortunately they are, Mr. Dunlop," Amelia said in a dejected tone of voice. "They would be far more likely to find Aziz Faruqui and his network by looking in brothels and seedy bars. Instead, they have fallen for his diversionary tactics."

A Candle Burning at Both Ends

The Vice President was seated at his desk when an aide entered his office, informing him that Professor Jack Welles had arrived from Boston for his scheduled appointment. The Vice President instructed the aide to bring Professor Welles into his office immediately, making it clear that they were not to be disturbed. Within moments, a man of short height, moderately overweight, with a full head of silver hair and wearing black-framed spectacles and a blue suit, entered the office of the second-highest ranking leader in the executive branch of the American government. Professor Welles, chairman of the nuclear physics department at the Massachusetts Institute of Technology in Cambridge and a leading consultant to both the nuclear power industry and Defense Department, also held a position that was virtually unknown, the exception being a handful of senior government officials. He served as Director of the National Emergency Search Team, and it was in that capacity that the Vice President had sent for him.

Once Welles had seated himself in front of the Vice President's desk, he received an explanation as to why he had been summoned.

"Professor Welles, as you have heard in the media, a terrorist linked to Al-Qaeda and involved in the insurgency in Iraq, Aziz Faruqui, may be operating in the United States," the Vice President stated. "While we succeeded in foiling a plot to smuggle a dirty bomb into the United States a few days ago, we cannot rule out the

277

possibility that there is a second radiological device that Faruqui has in his possession."

"I see," Welles said in a low-key manner, as he reflected momentarily before directing a question at the Vice President. "In the event Faruqui has such a device, do we have any intelligence as to his intended target?"

Welles was informed that hints found on a Jihadist website some weeks ago pointed to New York City. "But that could be a diversion," said the Vice President. "My own gut feeling is that Washington D.C. is a far more appealing target to the terrorists, since it is the hub of government," he said. He wanted NEST to be mobilized and begin searching for a possible radiological dispersion device in those two cities.

"Are you sure just New York and Washington, or as a precaution, should I call in additional teams and resources and activate them in other large metropolitan areas, such as Chicago, Los Angeles, Houston and San Francisco?" inquired Professor Welles.

"Just Washington and New York City," the Vice President insisted. "We are convinced that the main goal of the terrorists is to promote a state of panic, that will result in major upheavals in our nation's financial markets. It is crucial that we avoid a repeat of the fiasco that occurred shortly after 9/11, when we flooded New York City with your teams due to a false lead about a possible suitcase nuclear bomb being hidden somewhere in Manhattan. If the press gets wind about NEST being present in our nation's capital and New York, both the stock market and the value of the dollar will tank big-time. We must avoid scaring the public, at all costs."

"I understand, sir," Welles compliantly said. "We'll be as low key as possible." The professor went on to explain that forty-eight physicists and technical experts on call to NEST would be mobilized, forming two teams of 24, and be deployed in the two cities identified by the Vice President as potential targets. Each team would utilize three unmarked vans containing radiological detection equipment.

"When will the teams become operational?" asked the Vice President, displaying a hint of anxiety.

"Well, Mr. Vice President, these people are all over the country, involved in very detailed scientific research, military and industrial activity," the professor explained. "It will require no less than forty-eight hours before the two teams and their required equipment can be assembled and actively deployed."

The Vice President's facial expression gave evidence of his unease at the time factor Welles was indicating to him as being realistic. However, he suppressed his inner feelings, and merely remarked that it would be March 19 when NEST could begin searching for a possible dirty bomb.

"That is correct sir, March 19," Welles confirmed. "Does the intelligence community have any leads on when such a device might be detonated?"

The Vice President told Welles that Jihadist websites had pointed to March 20, the fourth anniversary of the American invasion of Iraq, as a possible date, adding that he was skeptical about the claim, believing it was likely just propaganda or misinformation.

"That may be so, Mr. Vice President, however, in the eventuality that there is some substance to that date, and given we can only begin our search on March 19, I suggest that, with regards to New York City, we concentrate on just the island of Manhattan, and leave out the outer boroughs and suburban areas."

The Vice President heartily agreed. He mentioned that it simply did not make sense for the terrorists to detonate a dirty bomb near the Bronx Zoo.

"If there is in fact a second dirty bomb, and the terrorists manage to bring it into Washington or New York, what are our chances of finding it?" inquired the Vice President.

Professor Welles seemed initially hesitant to answer the question. It was as though his delayed response was his way of communicating his inability to provide absolute assurances that his teams would find any radiological devices that were hidden in one of the two cities. Choosing his words selectively, he seemed to at least verbalize a response that satisfied the Vice President. "Sir, if we are dealing with an unsophisticated group, they are unlikely to have the capability to shield their device sufficiently so as to thwart our radiological detection equipment. It is only in the event that they have a level of skill equal to our own that they could shield their bomb in such a manner as to neutralize our detectors."

The Vice President nodded his head, reflecting his own self-assurance. He was convinced that the opposition was primitive, and lacked the sophistication to defeat the superior prowess of American technology.

"One last question, Professor Welles. Assuming you do discover the location of a dirty bomb, will you be able to disarm it?"

"Sir, as you know, the National Emergency Search Team has never before discovered an actual nuclear or radiological device. Every previous situation where NEST has been deployed turned out to involve pranksters with more than average knowledge of nuclear physics and faulty intelligence leads."

"I know that," the Vice President shot back. "I'm still looking for an answer. Suppose you do find a bomb? What then?"

Somewhat clumsily, Welles attempted to respond to the Vice President's question. "We do have a databank of foreign and domestic nuclear weapons designs, both full-fledged fission bombs and dirty-bomb designs, either posted on the Internet, or obtained from Al-Qaeda documents seized in Afghanistan. Hypothetically, if we find a radiological bomb that fits a design pattern we know and understand we should be able to dismantle it. Otherwise, it is a leap in the dark."

The Vice President was not comfortable with the answer provided by Professor Welles. Accordingly, he sought to provide his own reassurance.

"Well, Professor Welles, fortunately we are dealing with a dirty bomb, and not a nuclear weapon that will explode with a chain reaction. I suppose, in a worst-case scenario, where you discover a bomb but are unable to dismantle it, we can just organize an evacuation of a few city blocks around ground zero. Afterwards, we can decontaminate the area."

❖ ❖ ❖

The Alliance Transport rig was parked in the loading dock area in the rear of Cleveland General Hospital. The three men who crewed the tractor-trailer were busily manhandling a steam boiler and freezer that had just been unloaded. Sweating profusely and breathing heavily, the men took a short break by the rig. Lopez fetched bottles of Coke from the cab, which he passed on to his comrades. As they sipped the beverage, Parker glanced at his wristwatch. Turning towards Lopez and Burns, speaking softly, he told them matter-of-factly that, "We're dead on schedule. We should be arriving in Hoboken tomorrow evening, exactly as planned."

◈ ◈ ◈

Though the day was getting late, construction work was gathering momentum at what would eventually be Kim Brothers Dry Cleaning and Tailoring. Amid a cacophony of noises emanating from a variety of power tools, including drills and buzz saws, interspersed with frequent hammering, Mark Kim seemed oblivious to his surroundings. With disciplined concentration, he reviewed blueprints detailing the layout of equipment that was in the process of either being installed or delivered. Peering over the plans, he checked off with a pencil various items of equipment that had already been set in place. With his finger, he made a mental note of two vital items still to be delivered; a freezer for the laundry's kitchen and a horizontal steam boiler to be installed in the rear of the premises.

The sound of vigorous knocking on the front door refocused Kim's attention away from the blueprints. He observed a slim man with light brown complexion, clean-shaven with neatly cut black hair, and higher-end casual clothes, standing in front of the storefront's door. Kim looked at his watch and gave a contented look, suggesting the man had arrived at precisely the time he was expected.

Placing the blueprints across the counter, Kim approached the door, which he swiftly unlocked and partially opened. "Sir, we won't be opening until May 12," Kim told the visitor, with a steady cadence.

Speaking with a thick Arabic accent, the man said, "That is too bad. I was hoping you would be open on March 20."

Without further delay, Kim held the door completely open, and the visitor entered, introducing himself as Walid Nasrallah.

He approached the counter, and Kim pointed to the blueprints. "The work is proceeding on schedule," he told the visitor. "We should have everything completed by the time the last equipment delivery arrives."

Smiling broadly, the Middle Eastern man told Kim that the five other members of his team would be arriving in the morning, fully prepared for receiving the final items of equipment necessary for their joint business enterprise.

❖ ❖ ❖

With a thunderous roar from its massive turbofan engines, a Boeing 767 airliner, devoid of markings, lifted off the runway at Hickam Air Force Base, near Honolulu. Ascending at a steep incline, it cleared Hawaii's airspace as it headed in a south-southeasterly direction. After several minutes had elapsed, the aircraft gradually leveled off as it approached its cruising altitude. In the cockpit, the captain directed the co-pilot to check on the latest weather report for San Salvador International Airport.

In the passenger compartment, Pervaz Khan gradually regained consciousness. Still groggy, he opened his eyes and observed the blurred images of several men watching over him, most of them wearing holsters mounted with hand guns. As his vision became sharper, the blurred figures became singularities. Khan's awareness of his surroundings was now enhanced. Turning to his right, he noticed a porthole window that had been blocked by a screen. The ambience, noise and occasional bumps from air turbulence established in Khan's mind that he was on board an aircraft. He noticed that a seatbelt was firmly fastened around his waist, with his hands manacled in front. To his left sat "Chuck" Foster, eyeing him attentively.

"How are you feeling?" Foster asked in a solicitous manner.

Replying in a voice laced with sarcasm, Dr. Khan asked, "Where are you taking me? To Abu Ghraib? Or, to Guantanamo Bay, Cuba?"

"Sir, I am not authorized to provide you with that information," Foster said reflexively. "I can only confirm that we will eventually land somewhere, at a final destination."

Foster noticed that his prisoner, while somewhat edgy, betrayed no outward sign of fear or apprehension. He asked Dr. Khan if he wanted anything to eat.

"American mercenary, why should I concern myself with nourishing my body, when it will soon be subjected to abuse and torment at the hands of your colleagues?" Khan responded, in a manner suggesting the refinement of a man originating from an upper class Karachi family, highly cultured and having received his graduate education at an elite university.

Feeling a modicum of respect towards his prisoner, Foster told Khan that he had personally arranged for halal food to be brought on board the aircraft, adhering to the strictest dietary requirements of the Islamic religion.

"What are you serving?" Dr. Khan asked.

"Chicken kabobs with rice," replied Charles Foster.

"In that case, why not," Pervaz Khan said with resignation. "At least, it will keep me from getting bored on this flight."

❖ ❖ ❖

At the ministry of defense building in Amman, Jordan, a high-ranking army officer, Major Abdul-Tal, telephoned Alex Dunlop, who had just arrived at his office early that morning. Dunlop picked up the receiver, and when he heard the Major introduce himself, he realized he was about to receive important news that he had been anxiously waiting for.

"Mr. Dunlop, Amad Hussein finally talked. I apologize for the delay, but we now have some answers to your questions," the Major informed the CSIS Deputy Director. "The relevant details from the interrogation have been sent to you by telex, and you should be receiving them in a few minutes."

It did not take long after Dunlop's conversation with the Jordanian army officer for him to receive the telex, which prompted him to ask both Dextraze and Littlejohn to join him in his office. With the two intelligence officers seated before him, Dunlop shared what he had just learned.

"Under interrogation, Amad Hussein confessed that he secretly constructed replicas of three objects," the Deputy Director informed his colleagues. "Two of the objects were horizontal steam boilers, and one was a large capacity freezer, of a type used in restaurants or cafeterias."

"What is a horizontal steam boiler?" Dextraze asked.

"I used to work in a laundry to pay my way through university, so I'm very familiar with them," Littlejohn said. "They are usually found in large laundry operations that do dry cleaning on their own premises, rather than sending the garments to another outlet. Dry cleaning requires a lot of steam, as do the laundry presses. The steam boiler does what its name suggests, it generates the steam that is necessary for both cleaning and pressing garments."

Stroking his chin, his face a manifestation of pensiveness, Dunlop was putting two and two together in his mind. "Henry, what do these steam boilers generally look like?" he asked.

Littlejohn described steam boilers as being typically cylindrical in shape. "They tend to be long and narrow," he said.

"I think we just discovered how Aziz Faruqui smuggled his bomb into the United States," Dunlop told his two subordinates. "Based on the dimensions of these two boilers as disclosed by Amad Hussein to his interrogators, and the configuration Henry just described, it would be a perfect fit for concealing the nuclear device I believe was built at that encampment on Lake Abitibi."

"Why two boilers?" inquired Dextraze.

Dunlop wasn't sure why, speculating that perhaps one of the boilers was used as a ruse, in the same manner that the dirty bomb found in Montana had probably been employed. He also shared with the two CSIS officers the information gleamed from Amad Hussein that the object resembling a freezer was actually equipped as a living compartment, ideal for smuggling a person across the American border.

"That must be how Aziz Faruqui is traveling to his American target," Dextraze told Littlejohn and Dunlop. "It means, even with their decision to go public and issue APBs, there isn't a snowball's chance in hell that the FBI will catch him."

"You can depend on it," Dunlop said with dismay. "We are not only confronted with a diabolical mass murderer, he is a thoughtful and methodical planner as well."

Amad Hussein had disclosed during his interrogation that the two steam boilers had factory identification plaques with identical serial numbers, Dunlop told his intelligence officers. "Hussein couldn't recall the serial numbers, but he remembered that the identification plates indicated that these objects were manufactured by Davis Industries in Mississauga. We need to follow up on that immediately."

Dextraze pointed out that it being Sunday, the company was probably closed for the day. The Deputy Director realized that the weekend posed an obstacle for their investigation, but that they could not afford to sit idly until Monday. "Try to track down the owner of this business, or a senior executive, even a janitor, as long we can check their records and find anything that points towards Aziz Faruqui and his cohorts."

❖ ❖ ❖

The President was at Camp David, exercising his dog on a grassy meadow, under the watchful gaze of several secret service agents. He had just thrown a stick, which his dog was in the process of fetching, when an aide ran up to the President, telling him that Glenn Thrush was on the line for him on an important matter. Fifteen minutes later, a Marine Corps helicopter arrived at Camp David to pick up the President. Shortly afterwards, he had arrived back at the White House, and was at his desk in the Oval Office, still wearing the casual clothes he had worn at Camp David. Seated in front of his desk was the National Intelligence Director.

"Mr. President, we detected these missile tests in North Korea and Iran just over two hours ago," Glenn Thrush informed the Commander-in-Chief. "They were definitely coordinated, the two launches occurred less than thirty seconds apart."

The President had a worried expression on his face. He asked Thrush what he thought the implications were.

"These missile tests say two things to us, loud and clear," Thrush said with alarm. "First thing to recognize, they have now successfully demonstrated intercontinental range with their new missiles. That means the entire American mainland will soon be vulnerable. Secondly, we must infer that Iran and North Korea have been jointly developing these long-range ballistic missiles, pooling their resources. That suggests we must drastically shorten our estimate on the time they will need to place these missiles into mass production, and start deploying them with nuclear warheads."

Looking both puzzled and worried, the President asked the National Intelligence Director for his estimate of when the two countries would have the capability to launch a missile attack against the United States.

"I would say, in as short a time as two years, Mr. President."

"We need to have an emergency meeting of key officials, both cabinet members and senior advisors involved in national security, to decide on our response," declared the President in a decisive manner.

Thrush suggested to the Commander-in-Chief that the meeting be scheduled for early Monday morning.

"It is important that the Secretary of Defense be at this meeting," the President replied. "Right now, he is visiting our troops in Iraq, and is not scheduled to arrive back in Washington until tomorrow evening. If we recall him from Iraq ahead of schedule, the press is going to make it out that we are in a panic over what the Iranians and North Koreans are doing, and were caught off guard."

The President paused, took a deep breath, then made his decision. "Glenn, another day won't make a big difference. We'll call this meeting for Tuesday morning. Meanwhile, you get with the CIA, NSA and our other intelligence agencies, and tell them to get me as much information and analysis as possible before our meeting. Make it clear to them that this is our number one priority, even if we must put everything else aside."

"Yes, sir," Thrush replied obediently. He quickly departed the Oval Office, prepared to execute the President's instructions without delay.

❖ ❖ ❖

Both Dextraze and Littlejohn diligently sought to identify and contact anyone connected with Davis Industries who would have access to the company's records. After several hours of Internet searches and long distance phone calls, Littlejohn finally connected with Peter Warren, the company's chief financial officer. Littlejohn, apologizing for disturbing him on a Sunday afternoon, informed Warren that a sensitive national security matter required CSIS to request that recent purchase orders for one of the company's products be checked. Warren asked Littlejohn for a description of the product, which he indicated was a steam boiler, relaying the dimensions that Amad Hussein had revealed during his interrogation.

"That must be our model 300DN horizontal steam boiler," Warren said. "It's a heavy-duty product, designed for industrial laundry applications. Typically, we manufacture and ship out 60 units of that model each month, about three quarters for export to the United States."

Littlejohn asked him how long it would take to check his records for the past month for the 300DN model. Warren told him he could be at the plant in about forty-five minutes, and it could take him another hour before he ran through all the purchase orders. The CSIS officer asked Warren to call him and let him know each and every purchase for that time period, in detail. He then touched base with Pierre Dextraze, letting his colleague know that he had made a connection with Davis Industries, and it could be a couple of hours before they learned anything definitive.

"Henry, it looks like we are frozen until the CFO from Davis Industries calls back," Dextraze mused.

"Pierre, it's like being in the army: hurry up and wait."

❖ ❖ ❖

At the entrance to the Guzman S.A. tobacco plantation, a half dozen armed men, some carrying M-16s with others having revolvers and pistols only partially concealed in their pockets, stood alert. From the distance, in the thickness of the tropical jungle, a van noisily negotiated the torturous road that led to the plantation. As the van's engine became louder, the men who were to form a reception committee stood to the sides of the entrance. Within minutes, the van pulled into the entrance and stopped. The rear doors were opened, and two armed men in military fatigues held up their solitary passenger, a middle-aged man wearing a blindfold, his arms immobilized behind his back by tightly fitting handcuffs. Pervaz Khan could not yet see his surroundings, but he was certain he had just arrived at his last destination on Earth.

The men outside the van assisted their uniformed comrades who had accompanied Khan in removing their captive from the vehicle. Two men grasped Dr.Khan by his shoulders, and slowly led him towards the stucco villa where Ernesto Guzman resided. Guzman stood on his balcony, wearing dark sunglasses, his hands on his hips, while he surveyed the blindfolded man whom he would soon begin interrogating. One of his employees stood with Guzman on the balcony, also eyeing the prisoner.

"Senor Guzman, he looks like a man who has always led a sedentary life. He's in poor shape, and it should be very easy for him to crack."

Still staring at Khan as he was awkwardly led on his walk towards the villa, Guzman contradicted his employee's perspective. "You are wrong, in my opinion," he said. "Based on what our CIA client has told me, time is on this man's side. He needs to hold out for two days, that is all, and he has won, even if he dies. He knows that. In his physical condition, if I exert too much pressure on him, he will die. This interrogation will demand a level of finesse and careful calibration that we could have dispensed with if this man were young and physically vigorous."

❖ ❖ ❖

At the National Security Agency headquarters located in Fort Meade, Maryland, cryptologist Morris Tate placed an urgent call to David Cole. Lying on a cot at his Langley office, Cole had been taking a short nap, until interrupted by the sound of his phone ringing, which roused him to his desk. Upon answering, Tate identified himself, and first shared troubling news.

"Mr. Cole, I wanted to alert you that all the NSA cryptologists who had been monitoring Al-Qaeda and related signals have been told to cease that activity."

"What!" exclaimed a confused and angry Cole.

Tate explained that a directive had come down from on high to shift priorities due to the simultaneous ballistic missile tests that had been conducted earlier in the day by Iran and North Korea

"Everyone in my section that had been monitoring known Jihadist cells and training camps, from Yemen to the Afghan-Pakistan border, have been redeployed to monitor the communications grid for Iran's missile development program. There is an emergency security meeting scheduled for Tuesday at the White House. The big brass has made it clear that this is their number one concern right now, and they want us to gather as much information as possible in preparation for that meeting."

The Director of Counter-Terrorism was aghast at such a decision. He knew that what had occurred was part of a well-orchestrated deception program. To his dismay, the men making the key decisions in Washington were falling into a trap that, to Cole, was transparent.

"There is one other thing, sir," Tate informed the Director. "Until I got redirected to watching Iran, I noticed that there was a spike in chatter by the Al-Qaeda cells until Friday. Then, the chatter diminished dramatically, dropping to almost nothing by the time I was pulled away from watching it."

David Cole did think this anomaly was intriguing. He asked Morris Tate how he interpreted this phenomenon.

"Sir, it's identical to the pattern before 9/11, when there was a spike in chatter in the weeks leading up to that date, until just a few days before the attacks when the chatter almost went silent."

Cole's memory was stimulated by Tate's observation. "You are absolutely correct, the chatter did decline markedly just a few day before September 11," he said thoughtfully. "History just may be repeating itself. The calm before the storm."

❖ ❖ ❖

Dextraze and Littlejohn sat like sentinels around a small conference table at CSIS headquarters, surrounded by a bank of phones, fax machines and portable computers. When the phone finally rang, it was already early evening. Littlejohn answered and engaged the speakerphone, so his colleague could hear the conversation. Peter Warren was on the line, and he had uncovered a mountain of documents, which now he and the two CSIS agents had to sift through and make sense of. It took them more than an hour to accomplish that. Upon completion, they entered Dunlop's office.

"Mr. Dunlop, Pierre and I have been wading through a paper trail at Davis Industries, but we think we are beginning to connect some dots," Littlejohn informed the Deputy Director. Both he and Dextraze proceeded to elaborate on what they had been able to deduce from the purchase orders.

"We proceeded on the theory that a bulk carrier departing Sault Ste. Marie would be the most likely means of smuggling Faruqui's device into the United States," Dextraze told Dunlop. "It turns out that there was a purchase order for a 300DN steam boiler for the SS Northern Conquest, but very strange, after an invoice had already been generated in preparation for final shipment, the order was cancelled at the last moment."

Dunlop agreed with Dextraze that this was indeed peculiar. Littlejohn then added a detail that thickened what was already a murky transaction. "Davis Industries was contacted by a company based in Dearborn, Michigan, Ace Industrial, which supplies laundry and kitchen equipment for institutional customers. They already had two 300DN boilers on order, and said they had an urgent need for a third boiler. They had learned through a contact in the shipping industry of the cancellation of the order from the SS Northern Conquest, and asked if that boiler was still available. It was, so it was shipped to Ace Industrial along with the two others."

Dunlop's mind was accelerating, along with his pulse. Though feeling an almost unbearable load of pressure, somehow the pieces of the puzzle were coming together. He asked his intelligence officers if they had obtained the serial number of the boiler shipped to Ace Industrial; they confirmed that they had it.

"I have a feeling, gentleman, that the serial number you received from Davis Industries will match exactly a model 300DN boiler that is already installed in the SS Northern Conquest's laundry," Dunlop told his subordinates. He asked if the present location of the SS Northern Conquest was known. Dextraze replied that it was docked in Sault Ste. Marie, but was scheduled to depart early Monday morning.

The Deputy Director immediately grabbed his phone, and dialed the private extension for the Commissioner of the Royal

Canadian Mounted Police. As Dextraze and Littlejohn listened with evident tension, Dunlop informed the Commissioner of the latest meandering twists in the investigation of the Lake Abitibi matter.

"Commissioner, it is imperative that the SS Northern Conquest be impounded ASAP. There is probably an Al-Qaeda or Al-Assad El-Islamiya cell on board, so every crewmember must be questioned. Most importantly, CSIS must know the precise serial number of a model 300DN steam boiler, manufactured by Davis Industries, installed in the vessel's laundry. Please make this happen quick, Commissioner. Right now, we are a candle burning at both ends."

❖ ❖ ❖

Early Sunday evening in Hoboken, few cars were parked on Borden Street. Ronald Parker was at the wheel of the Alliance Transport tractor-trailer as it made the wide turn off of Washington Street. Lopez pointed to a vacant spot in front of the storefront leased by Mark Kim, long enough to accommodate their rig. They slowly maneuvered their large truck into the space, as Mark Kim stood behind the counter. He glanced at his watch, noting it was 6:30 PM. He then turned around and proceeded to the rear of the premises, where the carpentry work had been almost completed. Standing in front of him were Walid Nasrallah and five men of Middle-Eastern appearance, all clean-shaven and wearing nondescript clothes. Kim simply told Nasrallah and his men, "They're here."

Speaking in Arabic, Nasrallah energetically told his men that it was now time to go to work. Within moments, a beehive of activity consumed the space in front of and behind the storefront. Several members of Nasrallah's cell combined with the tractor-trailer's crew in unloading the steam boiler and freezer, and conveying them into the incomplete cleaners and tailor shop.

With the aid of a forklift truck, the boiler in its protective packing was maneuvered to the rear of the building, and brought through the rear loading doors of the establishment. Amid grunts of intense physical exertion, the boiler was situated in the rear of the establishment.

After it was secured, the freezer was carefully carried into the kitchen, as drapes and levers were pulled and lowered to conceal the interior of the establishment from external observation.

Walid Nasrallah approached the freezer, removed protective taping, and then knocked five times on the door. He waited momentarily, than knocked three more times. Then, in a thrusting gesture, his arms pulled the door open, and Aziz Faruqui emerged.

Nasrallah lent Faruqui a hand, as several members of the cell smiled with pride and admiration. Faruqui stepped out of what had been his confined living space for more than a week, and warmly embraced his comrade.

"Walid, my brother, it has been a while since we were last together, hunting infidels in Falujah!"

Deeply moved, Nasrallah looked into Faruqui's penetrating eyes as his own shed tears. "My fondest wish since then has been to share a martyr's death with the Lion," he said with intense feeling. They both smiled.

Paradise Express

Late Sunday evening, a column of police vehicles and unmarked SUVs descended on the port of Sault Ste. Marie, their dome lights extinguished and sirens silenced. At a synchronized moment, dozens of RCMP Constables, many of them equipped with flak jackets and automatic weapons, descended on the SS Northern Conquest. Within minutes the ship was in the process of being thoroughly searched, with several crewmembers, including the chief engineer, taken into custody. About an hour later, the RCMP Commissioner contacted Dunlop, and briefed him on the results of the raid on the suspect vessel. Following their conversation, Dunlop called Dextraze and Littlejohn into his office.

"As I anticipated, the steam boiler on the Northern Conquest matched the serial number of the unit they had originally ordered, then cancelled," the Deputy Director informed his intelligence officers.

Littlejohn asked what the implications of such a bait and switch were.

"The implications are this," Dunlop said with certainty. "A cell working for Aziz Faruqui had infiltrated the vessel's crew and was led by the chief engineer, who ordered the steam boiler, informing the ship's captain of its purchase. He then cancelled the order, this time without telling the captain. He still had the original invoice, which was used to get the fake boiler, concealing the nuclear device, through port security and loaded aboard the ship. When underway to Duluth, the chief engineer reported to the captain that an electrical short had damaged the new boiler, so it would need to be off-loaded at Duluth for repairs. They apparently had another terrorist cell in Duluth that supposedly repaired the boiler. What they actually did was swap boilers."

Littlejohn and Dextraze looked at each other, coming to the same realization. "Sir, what you are telling us is that the steam boiler that had been shipped to Ace Industrial in Dearborn, supposedly for one of their customers, was actually sent back on board the Northern Conquest," Littlejohn said.

Continuing Littlejohn's train of thought, Dextraze told his colleagues, "Which means that the phony boiler with a nuclear bomb inside was retrieved in Duluth, and sent on its way, to its intended target."

Dunlop added that the fake freezer, which was in fact a concealed living compartment, would have been used in the same manner to smuggle Faruqui into the United States, alongside his superbomb. Based on the murders of the two teenagers in Iowa off the interstate highway, the Deputy Director theorized that the bomb and Faruqui had been traveling in a large truck or tractor-trailer along the I-80 interstate highway, which ran straight to New York City.

"Mr. Dunlop, do you think they've arrived at their destination?" Littlejohn asked with a hint of trepidation.

Nodding his head in affirmation, looking dejected, Dunlop expressed his certitude that their nemesis had already succeeded in bringing his death-dealing cargo to its final destination, where he actually intended to detonate it.

Dextraze asked his boss if the Americans were doing anything to try to find the device.

"The bare minimum, aside from David Cole's efforts to get information out of Pervaz Khan" the Deputy Director said with melancholy forthrightness. "They still believe they are just dealing with a dirty bomb, so there is no sense of urgency. They have, somewhat late, begun the process of deploying one of their National Emergency Search Team units to New York City, but it will not be until sometime Monday that they begin searching for a possible radiological device, which is all they are worried about.

Based on what Dr. Lazar told me earlier today, I don't think they have any chance of detecting the device."

Littlejohn asked Dunlop to relay what Lazar had told him.

"The technology used by NEST to detect nuclear devices is based solely on sensing radioactive emissions, in other words, detecting alpha, beta, gamma and other highly radioactive particles. Unfortunately, according to Dr. Lazar, the bomb casing of the device we believe Faruqi and his collaborators built is sufficiently thick to preclude normal detection, unless the detectors are located no more than two meters distance from it."

"But sir, don't the devices we use at major Canadian airports and seaports use a more advanced technology?" inquired Dextraze.

"That is correct," replied the Deputy Director. "Our devices use a type of neutron bombardment, which creates a particular type of gravitational anomaly found only in plutonium and highly enriched uranium. It can detect those materials from as far away as 100 meters. The government did offer to share the technology with the American authorities, but they rejected our offer"

Rubbing his cheeks, Dunlop looked with intensity at his two agents, noticing through the look in their eyes that they were as weary as he was. "Gentlemen, you are both exhausted, I want you to go home and get some sleep."

Both men protested that the urgency of the situation demanded that they remain on duty. Dunlop felt great admiration towards his men for their devotion. However, as the Deputy Director, who could contemplate what might occur 48 hours into the future, he recognized that, with all that was unknowable, there was the certainty that his men must be alert and focused.

"I am ordering both of you to go home to your families, and sleep. We will reconvene in my office at 6:00 AM. The next 24 to 48 hours will be very hard on all of us. You must be well rested, so that you can endure what might very well be unendurable."

❖ ❖ ❖

In the basement of Guzman's villa, Pervaz Khan sat on a wooden chair, shirtless, his arms and legs bound tightly to it. The basement was an archaic mixture of pitch-black darkness, intersected by harsh beams of light emitted by bare, high intensity incandescent light bulbs. Breathing heavily, though the air was foul and damp, he already could feel numerous points of soreness scattered across his face, shoulders and chest, which were pockmarked with bruises and angry welts. Guzman stood a few feet in front of him, his face glacial, yet strangely passive.

Near Khan's chair stood a small table with a cup of steaming coffee. Guzman took a sip of the coffee, pronounced it too bitter, then said to his prisoner, "Maybe you would like some coffee?" He approached Dr. Khan, placing the cup and saucer in front of his parched lips. Then, with a sudden movement of his wrist, he spilled the entire contents across Khan's face, which prompted him to utter a loud, agonizing scream as the scalding liquid singed his cheeks.

Guzman stood silent for a moment, allowing his captive a chance to recover, before speaking to him.

"Dr. Khan, even though several members of my family are living in America, I don't hold that against you," Ernesto Guzman said, without any hint of anger or feeling towards the prisoner. "You are a man who has principles, like me, and is willing to fight and die for them. That is commendable." He paused, observing Khan carefully, noticing his heavy breathing, suggestive of fear and suffering, juxtaposed with the firmness of his jaw and coldness of his eyes, which were indicative of courage and defiance.

Guzman lit a cigarette, as he continued talking. "You see, whatever is happening here, it is nothing personal. This is strictly business. If you don't talk and tell me what my client is so eager to know, I won't get paid and that means I have wasted my time. Being a businessman who understands that time is money, that is not an acceptable proposition for me."

Looking more sternly at Khan, Guzman withdrew the cigarette from his lips, allowing circular puffs of tobacco smoke to flow from out of his mouth. Holding the lit cigarette between his fingers, he slowly moved it towards his captive's face, and held it still in front of his left eye, which now abandoned its defiant look for one of terror.

On the balcony of the villa, two of Guzman's men stood guard duty, clutching their assault rifles. The stillness of the night was suddenly broken by a piercing, shrieking yell that sounded half-animal, half-human, which emerged from the basement. One of the guards remarked to his comrade, "It appears that the Colonel has gotten off to a slow start this evening. It seems he's going easy on him, for now."

❖ ❖ ❖

In the rear of the Kim Brothers establishment, ten men bowed over their prayer rugs, in the direction of Mecca, as they recited Koranic verses. It was past midnight, and Mark Kim lay asleep on a small cot behind the counter. At the conclusion of the devotionals, Aziz Faruqui gathered Ronald Parker, Martin Lopez and Jack Burns together for a final chat. The three men were about to depart, and the Lion wanted to review their final arrangements.

"My brother, we will leave in five minutes, and in about half an hour our rig will be abandoned at a field outside of Jersey City," Parker told Faruqui. "A car driven by a comrade from the Jersey City cell will pick us up, and take us to Newark International Airport. We are all booked on separate early morning flights to Europe. From there, we should all arrive in Yemen in about 24 hours."

Lopez turned towards Faruqui, tears forming in his eyes. "I only wish we could all be with you for the end of this operation, so we too can be martyred," he said earnestly.

Faruqui patted Lopez on the shoulder, then looked with pride at all three men. "Do not be envious of those of us who will remain here, my brothers," he told the men in a reassuring tone of voice. "It is the will of Allah that some of us are destined to die earlier than others, but none are less worthy if they struggle, without wavering, for jihad."

Faruqui walked up to each of the three men, embracing them in turn. As he took his final leave of them, he told them that when they were in Yemen, after news of the operation had become publicly known, they should say prayers for the Lion and his companions, and rejoice that they would be waiting for their other comrades to eventually join them in paradise.

❖ ❖ ❖

297

Cole had spent another night at his office. His alarm woke him at five in the morning. He lazily pulled himself out of his cot, and took a few minutes to freshen up and change his clothes. When he returned to his office, he noticed the message light on his secure line was blinking. He immediately retrieved the message from his voice mail. It was Ernesto Guzman, asking Cole to call him for a progress report. From the tone of Guzman's message, the Director of Counter-Terrorism could easily guess that Pervaz Khan was nowhere near the breaking point. He rapidly dialed the number to Guzman's tobacco plantation, and when he was connected with the retired Salvadorian army Colonel, he soon had confirmation that his guess was correct.

Guzman warned David Cole that the interrogation would be a close-run thing. "He will talk, of that I am certain, but not until the last possible moment," Guzman said. "When he does break, it will be with very little time to spare, so you must be prepared to move fast, once I get you the information you are seeking."

Cole asked Guzman for his assessment of Khan. "He is a very intelligent, very thoughtful man, even under extreme duress," Guzman relayed with admiration. "He has been deliberately trying to provoke me into subjecting him to greater pressure than his body can endure, so that he will die before talking."

Cole hung up after receiving Guzman's update, feeling even greater discouragement. Reflecting on what his other options were in the event Guzman did not succeed in breaking down Pervaz Khan's will to resist or die, he decided to call Alex Dunlop, and share with him the status of the interrogation of Dr. Khan.

Dunlop, like his CIA colleague, had also spent the night in his office. Wearily, he answered his phone, apologizing to Cole for feeling and sounding fatigued. Cole told him there was no reason for an apology, as he felt just as worn down. He then proceeded to relay what Guzman had just told him concerning the interrogation of Pervaz Khan.

"David, while getting Khan to talk would be our greatest break in tracking down Faruqui and his device, we should not put all our eggs in that one basket," Dunlop told his American colleague. He mentioned that Dr. Lazar had told him that the equipment being utilized by the NEST unit in New York City would be incapable of detecting Faruqui's bomb unless, due to some miracle, they were within a few feet of it.

"You have a far better chance of winning the lottery than of that occurring," Cole replied.

The CSIS Deputy Director than explained that a far more advanced detection methodology was being employed in Canada. "Our machine can detect traces of plutonium and uranium 235 from a distance of up to three hundred feet, even if it is shielded by thick metal," Dunlop said. "We could loan one of our machines to NEST."

"Unfortunately, I don't see any way the administration will agree to accept the machine, and admit that our own technology is inferior," Cole sadly said. "Right now, they think they are dealing with a dirty bomb, which in their myopic world is a minor nuisance compared to the Iranian and North Korean missile threat, which is what they are all wrapped up about."

There was an interval of silence as both men struggled to conjure up ideas and strategies that would increase what they saw as the slim odds of averting a calamity of cosmic proportions.

A thought then began to permeate Cole's head. As his ideas began forming, he also recognized that he would have to violate his own agency's strictest rules, and urge his Canadian colleague to do likewise.

"Alex, suppose you send your own CSIS agents to New York City, with your detection machine."

Taken off-guard by Cole's idea, Dunlop responded without yet fully grasping what the CIA's Director of Counter-Terrorism had in mind. "Do you think you have time to get authorization from your government, and have them formally request our help?" Dunlop asked, somewhat doubtfully.

"You and I both know there is no time for dealing with this on a formal basis," Cole shot back. "By the time the ink was dry on the first memorandum, Faruqui's bomb would have already been detonated."

Dunlop now recognized exactly what Cole was alluding to. "You want me to send CSIS intelligence officers to New York, with our detection equipment, without your government being formally notified?" Dunlop inquired, caution ringing in his voice.

David Cole confirmed that this was exactly what he was requesting. "Alex, my anti-terrorism portfolio at the CIA gives me no jurisdiction to conduct any operations on American soil, even an operation to prevent a nuclear holocaust. I have no resources or operatives to draw on inside the United States. All my powers to influence the course of events exist overseas. Otherwise, I would gladly ask you to loan me your detection machine and I would go out and try to find this bomb on my own."

Dunlop recognized that what Cole was asking him to do defied all norms and regulations on how CSIS should operate. It had no mandate to infiltrate its spies into the United States, yet that was exactly what his CIA colleague was urging him to authorize. As Dunlop pondered Cole's plea for an unprecedented form of assistance, he came to the realization that the extraordinary confluence of forces beyond his control compelled him to accede to his colleague's request.

"Obviously, we must do this very carefully," Dunlop said. "However, I see this from the same vantage point as you." He told his colleague he would give thought as to the most propitious method of doing what Cole had convinced him needed to be done.

❖ ❖ ❖

Acting on an urgent tip from CSIS, the Detroit FBI office teamed up with a SWAT team from the local police department in executing a search warrant on the premises of Ace Industrial in Dearborn, Michigan. It was early morning, yet rush hour had already begun, as workers departed their homes for the morning factory shift. Amid the traffic, the FBI and police vehicles circled the fence surrounding Ace Industrial. The parking lot was deserted, and no lights were on in the building.

Several heavily armed law enforcement officers approached the main entrance, which was padlocked. An FBI agent holding the search warrant rang the intercom several times, with no response. "Break the door down!" he yelled to several officers standing near him who were firmly grasping crowbars. In a matter of minutes, the doors were removed and teams of FBI agents and police roamed throughout the premises. The shouts of the officers echoed off the walls and long corridors of the building. They were the only noises to be discerned. Ace Industrial was totally deserted. Its filing cabinets were empty, its computers disconnected and, presumably, purged of their data.

"It looks like whoever occupied this space left in a hurry, taking everything with them, including the kitchen sink," remarked one of the FBI agents to his colleagues.

◈ ◈ ◈

Dextraze and Littlejohn arrived in Dunlop's office just after six in the morning. They both observed the bags that seemed to have formed under the Deputy Director's eyes. He obviously had not received much sleep, and the lines on his forehead were now more pronounced, reflecting his deep anxiety.

Dunlop told his intelligence officers that he required them to perform an urgent and also dangerous task. He explained that it would involve their surreptitious insertion into New York City and utilizing an advanced nuclear materials detection system, in an attempt to find Aziz Faruqui's bomb. "Gentleman, this mission requires us to do something unprecedented in the history of our organization, conducting an operation on American soil, without the official knowledge of the government of the United States. It may also expose both of you to extreme danger. For that reason, I cannot morally order you to undertake this mission. I am therefore requesting that you volunteer to do this for our country, as well as for our most important ally." Dunlop paused, almost allowing his emotions to let go, then steeled himself to make clear what his men needed to know. "Both of you have families. If you volunteer for this assignment, the dangers you face are unknown, but very real. I want you to take ten minutes to think it over, then let me know your decision. If you decide not to volunteer, I promise you there will be no recriminations."

"I don't need ten minutes to decide, Mr. Dunlop," Littlejohn spontaneously interjected. "This is what I get paid for."

"Sir, I feel the same way as Henry. What are your instructions?" Dextraze added.

Dunlop almost wept, he was so profoundly moved by the devotion of his men. However, as the Deputy Director for operations at CSIS, he knew he did not have the luxury of being emotional. He thanked his intelligence officers for volunteering, than proceeded to discuss what needed to be done.

"You will both be traveling to New York on official business of the Canadian government, with diplomatic credentials. Officially, the purpose of your trip will be to inspect security arrangements at the Canadian Consulate in New York. We will also ship to New York our D70 gravity anomaly detection machine, which will be installed in a rental van. You will receive a quick training session from a technician on how it operates," Dunlop told his agents.

"Do we know where to search?" inquired Dextraze.

Dunlop explained that no precise intelligence existed on where the device was concealed. Barring any breaks, they should begin their search in Manhattan, than expand to the outer boroughs if the D70 machine did not detect any anomalies, he told his agents.

"What do we do if we find Faruqui's device?" Littlejohn asked.

The Deputy Director was momentarily stymied before he could conceive of a response. "The Americans have deployed a NEST unit to New York City. It includes experts who supposedly know how to disarm a nuclear bomb. We'll have to notify them ASAP once you have discovered the bomb."

❖ ❖ ❖

At the Federal Emergency Management Office in the Federal Building in lower Manhattan, Professor Jack Welles was conducting a meeting behind closed doors. Security guards stood vigilantly in front of the conference room's doors, while on the other side, Welles began briefing the NEST personnel who had arrived in New York.

"This team, and another one also forming in Washington D.C., have been tasked by the executive branch of our government to find a possible radiological dispersal bomb, located somewhere on the island of Manhattan," the professor told about twenty physicists, chemists and technicians who were present. "The authorities in

Washington have stressed to me the importance of not arousing unwarranted alarm, so as you conduct your sweep of Manhattan, do so in as inconspicuous a manner as possible."

Proceeding with the briefing, Jack Welles mentioned that several members of the team responsible for New York City had not yet arrived, but should be available by early afternoon, when the search would begin. Using three unmarked vans crammed with detection gear, they would be conducting atmospheric sampling at ground level at various points, to determine the presence of any one of a number of radioactive isotopes that could be part of a dirty bomb. The search pattern would involve two of the vans traversing the streets and avenues on either side of Central Park, working their way south. A third van would begin its search at Battery Park on the southern tip of Manhattan, and conduct a similar sweep pattern, moving in a northwards direction. "It might be necessary to repeat the sweeps several times, and there should be frequent samples checked for indications of radioactivity, so any change from normal background radiation can be detected," Welles advised.

One of the technicians attending the briefing at FEMA asked Professor Welles what they should do if they in fact detected signs of a dirty bomb.

"Under no circumstances should you attempt to disarm the device on your own," Welles warned the members of the search team. "Alert us here at FEMA, and I and the experts on the team charged with that responsibility will travel to your location as quickly as possible."

◈ ◈ ◈

At the Kim Brothers establishment on Borden Street, a truck had parked nearby. Several members of Nasrallah's cell were assisting the truck's drivers in unloading equipment, including laundry presses and electrical equipment. In the rear of the establishment, hidden from public view, Mark Kim conferred with Aziz Faruqui. "The activity we are doing today will be the continuation of the construction and installation that would be necessary for a new dry cleaning and tailoring business," Kim told Faruqui with a note of reassurance.

"That is very good," Faruqui said. "It is important that passers-by don't even take a second look at this place. Tonight, while the infidels of Hoboken are asleep, we will get the device prepared, just as we always planned."

Kim nodded with satisfaction, as a thought crossed Faruqui's mind. "I don't mean to pry into your affairs, but I am curious about one thing," Faruqui told his Korean partner. "My men and I know that we are certain to enter paradise, when we complete our task. What do you have to gain for your forthcoming sacrifice?"

At first, a look of mystifying perplexity overcame Kim's face. In a quick metamorphosis, calmness was restored and he formed an innocent smile. "What I have to gain, Mr. Faruqui, is immortality, as a hero to my fatherland and our Great Leader."

Though their motivations appeared worlds apart, Faruqui nodded in understanding. After all, he said to himself, they were united in a common desire to vanquish, once and for all, their common foe.

❖ ❖ ❖

At CSIS headquarters, a technician showed Littlejohn and Dextraze how the D70 detection system operated. A rack containing a series of modular boxes, with dials, knobs and bar graph meters formed a confusing visual array. However, the technician assured the two intelligence officers that the machine was actually simple to operate. "Everything on this machine has been carefully calibrated, so don't touch anything," the technician said in an admonishing voice. The only exception was a single switch to turn on the machine. He then pointed to a particular meter that would register first a yellow, then a red bar graph if plutonium and enriched uranium were detected within a distance of 100 meters. After the briefing was concluded, the technician informed the two agents that the D70 machine would be traveling to New York City, and be waiting for them at the Canadian Consulate in mid-town Manhattan, sometime in the late afternoon.

While Dextraze and Littlejohn were familiarizing themselves with the D70, Dunlop had called Amelia Baldwin into his office, to inform her that the two intelligence officers would be traveling to New York City to help track down Faruqui's device. "It is very possible that they will need an Arabic translator, depending on what they encounter. For that reason, I want to set up a satellite phone link, so that they can be in instant communication with you."

"Mr. Dunlop, suppose the communication link breaks down due to technical problems?" Baldwin interjected. "They need me in New York City, not here."

Shaking his head from side to side, the Deputy Director explained why he felt he could not have her accompany his agents. "Amelia, I cannot in good conscience have you do that," Dunlop said, and he began talking in a hushed tone of voice. "This may very well be a kamikaze mission. It is only because I believe we are all standing on the brink that I have made the painful decision to send two brave men on a dangerous journey, confronting a nemesis who would kill them without pity. In God's name, I can't expose you to such a fate."

Amelia stared directly into Dunlop's eyes, though she saw images of her late brother, who had died on 9/11. "Mr. Dunlop, if Aziz Faruqui succeeds in carrying out his threat to annihilate my country, I have no reason to live. You can't protect my safety by keeping me here. Henry and Pierre need me. My place is with them."

The Deputy Director looked with empathy at the linguist, who had already demonstrated her commitment and value, though exposed to duress and pressures that would have broken a less courageous human being. He was momentarily frozen in thought, unsure what to do. He then told her that he respected her bravery, but felt it was not for him to make the ultimate decision to accede to her wishes. David Cole would have to make that call. In her presence, he phoned the CIA's Director of Counter-Terrorism, and explained the situation to him. Cole asked Dunlop to place him on speakerphone, so Amelia could hear him.

"Amelia, I must tell you in all candor: Alex is right, joining the CSIS agents in New York City could mean walking into a death trap. If anything were to happen to you, I could never live with myself," Cole said in an emotionally charged voice.

"Mr. Cole, if I don't join them in New York, and do everything I can to assist them, then I could never live with myself," Amelia said in response, her voice reflecting deep emotion and cast-iron determination.

Both Dunlop and Baldwin could hear Cole's agonized breathing over the speakerphone, as he struggled to make a decision. With trepidation evident in his voice, he said, "Alex, it may go against my better judgment, but after hearing what Amelia just said, how can I possibly say no?"

The decision was made. Amelia Baldwin would be joining Pierre Dextraze and Henry Littlejohn in a desperate search for Aziz Faruqui's deadly device. Dunlop told her to join the two intelligence officers in about half an hour for a final briefing in the conference room with Dr. Thomas Lazar.

◈ ◈ ◈

Dextraze, Littlejohn, Baldwin and Dunlop sat around a small conference table, with Thomas Lazar standing by a board with drawings and charts, which stood next to a video monitor. The Deputy Director explained that though the CSIS agents were aware, along with Amelia, that Faruqui's plot involved detonating a nuclear device in New York City, he had thus far kept confidential any details as to specifically what type of device was involved. They must now learn the frightening details, so they were clear on what they were confronting. He referred to the tattoo that had been found on the arm of the decapitated Russian nuclear machinist, Boris Fedorenko. Dunlop drew the link so that everyone now understood that Faruqui's bomb was likely a carbon copy of the King of Bombs device, built and tested by the Soviet Union in 1961.

"Before I have Thomas brief you on the basic facts about this superbomb, we'll first view a short video I obtained on loan from the Russian Atomic Museum, courtesy of a friend at the Russian embassy," Dunlop said, as he stood up and turned on the video monitor. "What you are about to see is footage of the actual test of the King of Bombs, conducted by the Soviet Union on October 23, 1961."

The video was silent, so there were only grainy images as the sound of breathing intermixed with an occasional cough from the persons present in the conference room. The individuals around the table viewed the stationary image of a long, bulbous, cylindrical object, dark gray in color, sinister-looking, with fins at the end and two probes in front. Seconds later, the object was seen falling out of the bomb bay of a large, ancient-looking turbo-prop bomber, a prominent red star emblazoned on its tail. A few seconds of free-fall preceded the release of a large parachute, which retarded the bomb's descent. The film was briefly interrupted, then a wide-angle view of the distant sky was visible. In an instant, the sky turned a bright red and orange, of an intensity that seemed not of this world. Neither Amelia nor her colleagues had ever before seen such a violent explosion and mixing of intense colors. They all shielded their eyes, as though having inadvertently stared directly at the sun.

"The view of the explosion you have just observed was taken from a Soviet observation aircraft, flying 200 kilometers distance from ground zero," Dunlop commented.

The video concluded, Dunlop observed the facial expressions of the two men and one woman seated at the table. They were identical in each case, a look of stunned horror fortified with profound amazement. "My God!" uttered a shaken Dextraze.

Dunlop took his seat as Dr. Lazar prepared to brief the agents on the terrible, ingenious weapon of mass destruction that they were assigned to help track down.

"I want to keep this as simple as possible, as I know you don't have much time," Lazar said thoughtfully. "Let me begin by saying that most nuclear weapons fall into one of two categories, fission and fission-fusion. Fission bombs are basically atomic bombs, the Hiroshima and Nagasaki devices being prime examples. Fissile materials in these bombs undergo a chain reaction, initiated by a conventional explosion, resulting in the nuclei of either plutonium or enriched uranium being split, releasing explosive energy. Their destructive yield is measured in kilotons, or thousands of tons of TNT." Lazar paused briefly, observing the mesmerized look being projected by his captive audience.

"A fusion device, or thermonuclear weapon, is more commonly known to the general public as a hydrogen bomb," Lazar continued. "It functions the way our sun does, as a furnace that fuses together the heavy isotopes of the element hydrogen, forming helium. To do that requires immense heat, far hotter than the conventional explosives used to set off an atomic bomb can generate. So, to create the fire to fuse the hydrogen atoms, we must first set off an atomic device as part of the thermonuclear weapon's physics package. That is why we refer to a hydrogen bomb as being technically a fission-fusion weapon. The atomic explosion creates a thermal temperature of fifty million degrees centigrade, causing the thermonuclear fuel to undergo fusion, releasing vast quantities of neutrons, leading to a massive expulsion of energy in the form of an even bigger explosion."

Lazar paused again, asking if what he said thus far was understood. The two intelligence officers joined their CIA linguist colleague in nodding their heads, indicative of their comprehension. Lazar continued his briefing.

"During the Cold War, there were a small number of devices created that are referred to as fission-fusion-fission weapons. It is to this latter category that the King of Bombs belongs," Dr. Lazar explained. "If we go back to a simple atomic bomb, because of the limited heat produced by conventional explosives, only highly enriched uranium is susceptible to fission, and there is a fixed limit on the explosive yield, irrespective of the quantity of plutonium or uranium 235 contained in the weapon. With fusion, however, new possibilities arise. The capsules in the bomb that contain the thermonuclear fuel are constrained by a metal sheathing, referred to as a tamper. Its role is to extend the generation of fusion, meaning delaying its onset by about a tenth of a millionth of a second, while greatly increasing the capsule's density. The purpose of this is to substantially enhance the weapon's explosive yield. At the moment of detonation, the thermonuclear pulse reaches a temperature of 300 million degrees centigrade, several times hotter than our sun. If the fusion tamper is constructed out of uranium 238, the common form of uranium, that heat will cause the tamper to undergo fission, with no restrictions on its yield, apart from the quantity of material that is used in the tamper. This is what we refer to as a fission-fusion-fission bomb, which is exactly the kind of weapon we believe Faruqui and his colleagues have created, a direct copy of the King of Bombs, the most powerful nuclear device ever constructed."

Dextraze, Littlejohn and Baldwin were fixated on Dr. Lazar, their eyes wide open as though in a trance. Lazar continued his discourse, pointing to a diagram providing a skeleton view of the King of Bombs. He noted at the far end of the device, near its tail fins, was a small sphere of plutonium, enveloped by a plastic bonded explosive composition, which served as the primary stage of the weapon. There were also channels of deuterium and tritium and a beryllium reflector, which would boost the yield of the primary stage. Using a laser pointer, the doctor made note of what he referred to as the radiation channel, fabricated with polystyrene foam, which directed a flood-tide of photon gas from the primary trigger towards two separate capsules of lithium-deuteride, the second capsule being significantly larger than the first. A cocoon of pure uranium surrounded each capsule.

"When the bomb is detonated, the conventional explosives will compress the plutonium sphere, which will implode and undergo fission. A fraction of a millionth of a second afterwards, photon gas, reinforced with enriched uranium, causes the radiation channel to become ionized. A blast of heat is channeled towards the two thermonuclear fuel capsules, which in turn become super—heated, while the uranium tampers undergo ablation, meaning they prevent, for another ten millionth of a second, a premature explosion, while compressing the capsules. In that brief interval of time, the two lithium-deuteride capsules are reduced by the tampers to $1/30^{th}$ of their original volume, while the density increases by one thousand times. The lithium is converted into tritium, it fuses with the deuterium to form the element helium, and vast quantities of excess neutrons are released as an explosion, with a yield measured in megatons, or millions of tons of TNT."

Lazar paused momentarily, observing the stunned expressions written on the faces of the agents he was briefing. Continuing his description of the weapon, he noted that the bomb tested by the

Russians in 1961 employed lead tampers instead of uranium, so as to reduce the yield. That meant it functioned as only a fission-fusion bomb, though its still exploded with a force of 58 megatons, ranking it as the most powerful nuclear bomb tested thus far, by a very wide margin.

As Dunlop looked directly at Dr. Lazar, he then described in a solemn voice the one distinction between the original RDS-220 device and Faruqui's copy. "The information we have, based on soil samples and intelligence, makes it clear to me that Faruqui's bomb has uranium tampers installed for both lithium-deuteride capsules. That means, in about a millionth of a second after the thermonuclear fuel has undergone fusion, the uranium tampers will then be subjected to fission, on a vast scale. This will result in two things: a titanic explosion with a yield that will reach 150 million tons of TNT in power, and massive quantities of alpha, beta and other highly toxic radioactive emissions being generated, and falling back to earth over a wide portion of the North American continent."

The CSIS intelligence officers and their CIA colleague were shaken to the very core of their souls by what they had just learned. There was stunned silence in the room, which spoke more vividly of the apocalyptic power of the weapon they now were entrusted with searching for, than any words they could conceive of.

◈ ◈ ◈

At the Detroit FBI office, the regional director, Bruce Conway, received a call from an old friend. David Cole was a desperate man, requesting a desperate favor. The CIA's Director of Counter-Terrorism had learned of the raid on Ace Industrial in Dearborn, which revealed that the recent occupants had vacated the site in great haste.

"Bruce, I need a big one from you. You've got to track down someone, anyone connected with Ace Industrial, who would know about recent shipments."

Though his relationship with Cole went back many years, Conway was hesitant to assist him. "David, everyone in the Bureau knows that Larry Braun hates your guts, and that you're off-limits as far as cooperation goes. If I do as you ask, I might as well take early retirement, since my career will be over."

Fully aware that the sands of time were running out, and confronted with a surreal world where no one but him and a handful of others had any realization of the cataclysm that was looming, Cole struggled to convince Conway that he must help.

"Bruce, I know you have been told that there may be a dirty bomb loose in New York City, and that was the reason for the Bureau authorizing the raid on Ace Industrial. I want to tell you in the strictest of confidence that I have solid reasons for believing that the device is not a dirty bomb, but a full-fledged nuclear weapon."

"What?!" exclaimed Bruce Conway.

"You have two choices in front of you, my friend," Cole said, with a voice reflecting strain and suffering. "You can either conclude I'm off-the-wall, in which case, you have every reason not to jeopardize your career. Or, on the other hand, you can decide that I'm telling it to you straight, in which case, I know you'll do the right thing."

Conway thought through what Cole had just shared with him before responding. "I've known you too long, you old S.O.B., to believe you would tell me something this serious that you didn't have good reason to believe was accurate," the FBI regional director said with feeling. "I'll see what I can do."

❖ ❖ ❖

The Air Canada jet circled over Manhattan prior to landing at LaGuardia Airport. Littlejohn, Dextraze and Baldwin looked through the aircraft's starboard side window, taking in a late afternoon view of Manhattan. The broad expanse of skyscrapers seemed like an image taken directly from a post card.

Having already cleared U.S. Customs and Immigration at the international airport in Ottawa, upon landing they entered a waiting car parked by the curbside outside of the main terminal building. They sat silently in the rear of the automobile, deep in thought and reflection, almost oblivious to the urban canyons that surrounded them, as their car traveled on the Long Island Expressway towards Manhattan.

About forty-five minutes after departing LaGuardia Airport, Amelia and her two colleagues arrived at the Canadian Consulate, where a technical consultant on loan from CSIS was waiting for them. He informed them that their van was parked in the building's garage with its equipment already installed. There was also a message for Dextraze and Littlejohn to call Alex Dunlop on a special line with speakerphone, set up in a private office. With Amelia left waiting with the technician, the two intelligence officers entered the office, shutting the door behind them before contacting the Deputy Director. Both men noticed a package on the desk, marked for the two men.

When Dunlop answered, he mentioned that he was aware that the two agents were fully qualified in the use of small arms. "You know that we are normally unarmed at CSIS when we conduct our investigative and surveillance work," Dunlop reminded them. "But this situation is uniquely different. The package on the desk contains two Browning automatic pistols and ammunition. From now on, you are both to undertake your mission fully armed, and are authorized to use deadly force, if necessary. Understood?"

Both men indicated that they fully comprehended Dunlop's instructions.

Several minutes after receiving their latest directive, Dextraze and Littlejohn joined Baldwin and the technician in taking the elevator down to the garage, where an innocuous looking white Ford van was parked. The technician opened the van's doors, and quickly demonstrated the layout of the D70 detection machine in the rear compartment, and special communications gear up front, enabling them to be in real-time communication with Alex Dunlop at CSIS headquarters. The vehicle was also equipped with a GPS navigational system. The technician, having completed his work, wished his three colleagues good luck, and then departed. The two men and one woman entered the van, Dextraze at the wheel, Baldwin beside him and Littlejohn in the rear compartment. They had little luggage, as they expected to be at their task throughout the night, not stopping until they met with either success or failure. Dextraze engaged the ignition, placed the transmission in reverse, and then slowly backed the van out of its parking space. A moment later, the vehicle was moving forward, out of the garage, and into the density of midtown Manhattan.

❖ ❖ ❖

On Lower Broadway, another unmarked van, blue in color, was traveling north from Wall Street. There were four men in the van, all part of the NEST unit deployed in New York City. In the rear compartment, two men operated a bank of detection gear. Next to the driver, a physicist held a Geiger counter. He asked his colleagues in back if they had detected anything remarkable.

"Just normal background radiation," was said in response.

The physicist suggested to his colleague driving the van that they take a side street going west. "I don't know Manhattan very well, but maybe that next street," he said as he pointed.

Reflexively, the driver made a left turn on Chambers Street, and almost immediately it became apparent to the vehicle's occupants that they had made a wrong turn on a one-way street. Before comprehending their predicament, a yellow taxicab rammed into the front of the van. Within seconds, several doors were opened and slammed shut, as a battery of car horns exploded in rage. The cab driver and passenger approached the blue van, their faces livid with rage.

"You fucking asshole!" the cab driver swore at the van's occupants.

In a panic, the physicist seated up front grabbed his cellular phone, and called Professor Jack Welles at FEMA. "Jack, I'm sorry to have to report this, but we just had an accident. Our van is out of commission."

❖ ❖ ❖

At the ministry of defense headquarters in Tehran, Sheik Yantissi was seated at a desk bedecked with flowers and bowls of fruit. Behind him stood a bookcase stacked with Koranic texts and commentaries. An adjutant in crisp military fatigues entered the sheik's office, informing him that a special phone call had just come in for him on the secure phone line. The sheik thanked the adjutant, as he picked up the phone, simply saying, "Yes."

On the other end, in Hoboken, New Jersey, in the rear of a cleaners and tailors shop due to open in several weeks, was Aziz Faruqui. Using a disposable and untraceable cell phone, he simply said, "The paradise express will depart on time," then hung up.

In the Iranian capital, Yantissi gently placed his phone down, then turned towards his adjutant, smiling broadly. "It happens tomorrow, precisely on schedule, Allah willing," the sheik said, with a note of quiet satisfaction. "In twenty-four hours, the United States of America, the great Satan, will exist only in the obituaries and history books."

Fission or Fusion

Sitting in the basement laboratory of his home, surrounded by test tubes, flasks, burners and racks of electronic analyzers, a tired looking Thomas Lazar had been working since three in the morning. He was deeply troubled by something that had gnawed away at him during the night. Sipping strong, black coffee, he put in a call to Alex Dunlop at his office. As the Deputy Director answered the call, he glanced at a wall clock, noting it was 6:00 AM, Tuesday morning, March 20.

"Alex, I believe we have another big headache to worry about," Lazar informed Dunlop. "It concerns Faruqui's background. He is a highly trained explosives expert who also knows how nuclear weapons are assembled."

"What are you concerned about, Thomas?" the Deputy Director asked, nervously.

"The improvised explosive devices he is believed to have designed in Iraq are known to be virtually tamper proof."

Without delay, Dunlop absorbed the significance of what had aroused Lazar's anxiety.

"Is it your belief, Thomas, that he has ensured that once the RDS-220 device is armed, any attempt at disarming it will cause it to immediately detonate?"

"I'm afraid so," Lazar replied with a note of alarm. "In other words, if the NEST team, which has never before actually attempted to dismantle an armed nuclear device, tries to do that

315

for the first time with Faruqui's bomb, the result will still be a detonation, with a chain reaction."

"Are you telling me that it will be impossible to stop that bomb from exploding!" exclaimed a frantic Dunlop.

"We must never abandon hope, Alex. Nothing is impossible. I have studied the plans of the RDS-220 since early this morning, and I am working on an answer that will bypass anything Faruqui may have done with the arming mechanism. I just need a few more hours to figure it out."

"Please hurry, Thomas," Dunlop pleaded. "I don't even know if we have a few hours to spare."

◈ ◈ ◈

In Guzman's basement, two husky men carried a large electrical dynamo down the staircase and placed it near the chair that Pervaz Khan was bound to. They began rapidly unwinding wires and plugging the dynamo into a wall outlet, as another man carrying a rifle stood guard.

Ernesto Guzman watched his men, then glanced at the stooped figure of Dr. Khan. His body had accumulated numerous bruises, both his eyes were black and swollen, and lips badly cut. His face was lowered as he struggled to breathe the sordid atmosphere of Guzman's basement.

"Let's do a circuit test before we work on the good doctor," Guzman commanded in a firm voice. Obediently, one of the men placed two probes together, both attached to wires emanating from the dynamo. Instantly, fierce sparks were created, their crackling noise permeating the still air of the subterranean confines below Guzman's villa. "Everything checks out," another man said, monitoring a meter attached to the dynamo.

Guzman quickly glanced at Pervaz Khan, then turned towards his subordinates. "Let's get to work, then," he said in an authoritative voice. "Remove his trousers."

◈ ◈ ◈

The Ford van driven by Pierre Dextraze had just passed 42nd Street, moving south on Second Avenue. Littlejohn had been monitoring the D70 machine, without noticing any indication of a nuclear weapon. "Pierre, this is our third sweep of Manhattan," he told his colleague. "Maybe it's time to expand our search to the other boroughs."

Dextraze agreed, but wasn't sure which borough to proceed to. He turned to Amelia, seeking her suggestions. "I know this is a superficial criteria, but I can't think of anything else. Are there any areas of the city that have a large Arab or Moslem population?"

"The Atlantic Avenue area of Brooklyn has a significant Middle Eastern community, the majority of them immigrants," she pointed out. "We can get there by taking the Brooklyn Bridge, near City Hall."

Dextraze and Littlejohn agreed that it made sense to drive through the neighborhood along Atlantic Avenue, since no other localities in the city loomed as obvious haunts of Al-Qaeda or Al-Assad El-Islamiya.

Dextraze told his colleagues that he was somewhat tired, and asked Littlejohn if he would take the wheel. "No problem, Pierre," he replied. The van briefly halted so that Dextraze could move to the rear, taking over the task of monitoring the D70 detection machine. With Littlejohn now at the wheel, the Ford van continued on its journey, heading towards Brooklyn.

◇ ◇ ◇

A hint of sunshine penetrated an otherwise overcast sky that had formed over the lower Hudson River, shrouding Manhattan and the Jersey suburbs on the opposite bank. In Hoboken, there were the first stirrings from morning commuters boarding the trains and ferries for Manhattan. On Borden Street, Mark Kim carefully observed pedestrians walking past the storefront of his establishment. In the rear, hidden from view by a curtain extending the width of a wide corridor, was the horizontal boiler facade, now coming undone. Already, several chunks of sheet steel had been removed from the phony contrivance, and laid neatly to one side of the large space it had been confined to. Nasrallah, with meticulous attention to detail, supervised three of his men, as they worked diligently with oxyacetylene torches. They wore protective helmets and visors, giving them the appearance of astronauts, as super-heated flames poured forth from their torches. With noisy electrical arcing, causing metallic sparks to dart erratically in a multitude of directions, more flanks of the artificial steam boiler peeled off its structure.

Nasrallah briefly turned towards Faruqui, who observed the dismantlement of the boiler with undisguised delight. "The Lion should be pleased, we are exactly on schedule," Nasrallah advised his leader.

"It is not I, Walid, but Allah who should be pleased," Faruqui replied. "In a few hours, we will give those American infidels something they can really chew on."

❖ ❖ ❖

Gayle Payne was in her office, reviewing briefing papers in preparation for a meeting of key administration officials at the White House, due to start in about an hour. The simultaneous ballistic missile tests conducted by Iran and North Korea had become the center of gravity for the President's national security agenda. All other considerations, including the war on terrorism and hunt for Faruqui's dirty bomb, were of marginal concern. Except for Gayle Payne. When David Cole called her that morning, she was hoping beyond hope that the interrogation of Pervaz Khan had been successfully concluded, and the location of the nuclear bomb disclosed.

"Gayle, Dr. Khan has not yet cracked," Cole informed the National Security Advisor.

Gayle told the Director of Counter-Terrorism that she was extremely worried. "David, in an hour a meeting is going to begin here at the White House involving decision makers who are deaf, blind and dumb to the real threats. Getting Pervaz Khan to talk is our only hope. Will he break?"

Cole could sense Payne's apprehension, only exceeded by his own. He answered her question as honestly as he could. "I can't guarantee he will talk. The only thing I am certain of is that if he does break, it will be with little time to spare to act on his information."

The National Security Advisor felt that this required the ability to make a quick executive decision once useful information from Khan became available. "The one advantage of this meeting convening at 8:00 AM in the Map Room is that all the key actors in the executive branch will be present at one location, here at the White House."

She told Cole that since she would be attending the meeting, her own office would be vacant. "David, I'd like you to run your operation from my office. That way, if anything breaks with Dr. Khan, you are here at the White House. You will just need to walk down a long corridor to the Map Room to alert us."

Cole complemented Gayle Payne on an excellent idea. He told her he was on his way, and would be at her office, with his necessary communications gear, within the hour.

❖ ❖ ❖

A deluge of freezing rain, intermixed with hail, began devouring the sidewalks and streets of Brooklyn. Littlejohn gently pressed on the accelerator of the Ford van, lurching forward with the thick column of cars and commercial vehicles crossing Atlantic Avenue. Dextraze kept his eyes glued on the dormant meter attached to the detection machine.

"Are you picking up any reading at all, Pierre?" inquired Littlejohn.

"Negative, Henry, the meter still shows no indication of fissile materials."

Amelia Baldwin observed the sidewalk traffic along the small side streets that ran perpendicular to Atlantic Avenue. Even though the weather was inclement, shopkeepers were busily removing the padlocks and gates from their storefronts in preparation for opening. Signs in both English and Arabic heralded the Near Eastern complexion of the neighborhood. She noted in passing that the Damascus Coffee Shop was full of early morning patrons.

"What is it, Amelia?" Littlejohn asked, noticing a puzzled look on her face.

"It just seems so normal out there, like a regular work day," Baldwin commented. "There's no way I can be absolutely positive, but my gut feeling is that if a major terrorist event was going to be unfolding in this close-knit neighborhood, somehow the word would get out on the street, and people would not be acting in such an unconcerned manner."

"Amelia is right," Dextraze said. "It was only a hunch on my part, anyway, that this area might be worth scanning. Let's try a different section of Brooklyn."

Littlejohn asked Amelia Baldwin if she had any suggestions. "Let's investigate the Greenpoint section," she suggested. "It's an old industrial area, so there are a lot of abandoned factories and warehouses that Faruqui could have used to conceal his bomb."

Littlejohn and Dextraze agreed with the recommendation of their CIA colleague. They changed direction, and proceeded towards Greenpoint.

◈ ◈ ◈

At 8:00 AM sharp, a meeting convened in the Map Room at the White House. The President presided over the meeting, the Vice President seated to his right and National Intelligence Director to his left. Looking down a narrow table, the President observed his CIA Director, National Security Advisor, the Secretary of Defense, James Murray and the Chairman of the Joint Chiefs of Staff, General Robert Maude. The President began the conclave by summarizing what had been observed by the U.S. intelligence community on Sunday involving North Korea and Iran. He then called on the Vice President to share his thoughts.

"Mr. President, it is my conviction that the Iranians and North Koreans have done us a great favor. On Capital Hill, the opponents of our plan to greatly expand missile defense have so far succeeded in filibustering every attempt we have made to have our supplemental budget package approved. If we play our cards right, maybe with a presidential broadcast to the nation, public opinion will be so stirred up, no one in Congress will oppose us - if they want to be re-elected."

The President, smiling, said, "I like the Vice President's thinking on this matter. It shows real creativity."

◈ ◈ ◈

A NEST van driving east on 72nd street parked for a brief period so that air samples could be tested. The driver switched on the radio while his three colleagues took instrument readings just outside the van. Russ Gibbons was on the air, delivering his morning commentary.

"My fellow Americans, this is Russ Gibbons. Don't be fooled by the liberals," Gibbons began in his robustly belligerent style. "The most dangerous threat to America's security right now is taxes. Our safety as a nation is enhanced and fortified by the unencumbered spirit of free enterprise, represented by the businessmen and women of America. We must reduce the burden of taxation on America's most productive people. Which is another way of saying, the taxman from the IRS is the real terrorist threat in America today."

The driver turned off the radio as his colleagues reentered the van. "We appear to have a reading coming from a source about half a block up ahead," one of the physicists said.

"What category are the emissions?" inquired the driver. "X-rays," replied the physicist.

"There, my meter has a solid reading, it must be the next building," another member of the van's team said. A few seconds later, the van stopped at the location of the strong and constant source of X-rays. A bronze sign above the building's entrance read, "St. Luke's East Side X-Ray Diagnostic Center."

❖ ❖ ❖

Sitting in Gayle Payne's office in the White House, Cole's heart skipped a beat as his special phone hook-up to his office at the CIA rang. He was hoping it was Ernesto Guzman. It was not.

"David, this is Bruce. I think I have something for you."

The FBI regional director in Detroit told Cole that the Bureau had tracked down a woman who had worked at Ace Industrial until it had shut down several days before. The woman had been employed in the shipping department. She was a clerk, apparently unconnected to any terrorists. Conway explained the significance of what she knew.

"Her job was to make sure that the paperwork on all shipments to customers was in order," Conway explained. "It turns out that included ensuring warranty forms were forwarded to the original manufacturer, prior to shipping out any items of equipment to their purchasers."

David Cole was absorbed by every word being enunciated by Bruce Conway, who told him that the warranty forms required that the serial number and customer address be included on every warranty form. "David, this woman had a new baby, so she only spent a half-day at the office, then she would take a computer disc with her and work from home. We checked one of her discs that she still had in her possession, with a record of warranty forms recently completed. It has a record of the Davis Industries horizontal steam boiler with the same serial number as the one found on board the SS Northern Conquest."

"Bruce, where was it shipped to?" Cole asked with extreme anticipation.

Conway told his CIA friend that the boiler was shipped to Khalil's Dry Cleaning, 745 Henderson Avenue, in Hoboken, New Jersey.

"Bruce, God bless you!" Cole exclaimed with intense gratitude. He hung up, then quickly connected with Alex Dunlop at CSIS headquarters.

"Alex, I think God in his mercy has given us a break," Cole excitedly informed his colleague, relaying the information that he had just received. Sharing in his excitement, Dunlop told Cole he would patch in his agents in New York.

In the Greenpoint section of Brooklyn, the Ford van plowed the rain-swept streets, as an amber light flashed on the vehicle's communications gear, simultaneously with the emission of a beeping sound. Littlejohn switched it on, engaging the microphone and speaker.

Dunlop informed his agents and Amelia that David Cole had received a possible lead on the location of the nuclear device. Cole came on line, and read out the name and address of the dry cleaners in Hoboken. Amelia Baldwin turned on the GPS device, and punched in the address. "It looks like the quickest way there is through the Holland Tunnel," she informed her colleagues.

"Get there as fast as you can!" Dunlop said with emphasis.

"When you have a confirmed reading on your detection machine, let Alex and I know right away," Cole added.

Littlejohn acknowledged that they were on their way to Hoboken as he made a wide turn, causing the van's tires to squeal in protest. His foot vigorously depressed the vehicle's accelerator as it headed back towards Manhattan.

After issuing their instructions to Littlejohn, Dextraze and Baldwin, Dunlop advised Cole of what Lazar had told him regarding the likelihood that NEST would be unable to safely disarm Faruqui's bomb. "Hopefully, David, Thomas will figure out how it can be done. I know he is moving heaven and earth to come up with a solution."

Cole realized that with all the careful preparation Faruqui and his comrades had thus far demonstrated, it had to be assumed that he would apply his advanced knowledge in explosives towards thwarting any attempt at disarming his superbomb. "I just pray with you that Dr. Lazar has the answers, or we're all dead."

The two colleagues agreed that, in any event, the National Emergency Search Team should not be advised to send its personnel to Hoboken until the D70 detection machine had delivered a conclusive reading.

❖ ❖ ❖

On Borden Street, work seemed to be proceeding apace at the Kim Brothers dry cleaners. Mark Kim stood in front of the counter, leaning over a set of blueprints, as two men worked on installing metal fittings and brackets behind him. One of the men operated an oxyacetylene torch while another utilized a power drill. To the side, a curtain hid a wide corridor. Behind that curtain, a different world, radically dichotomized from the one that Kim could observe through the window of his establishment, was rapidly forming.

In the rear area on the other side of the curtain, numerous metal plates and fabricated forms lay against the walls, as though they formed some bizarre pattern of decoration. In the center, amid the stupefied gazes of the men surrounding it, was a large, dark gray tubular shaped object. It was six feet in diameter, and twenty-four feet in length. It sat on a wooden platform, its tapered appearance suggestive of its deadly elegance. In front of the device, wires from two probes that extended from the bomb's bulbous front connected to a rack containing a box with a series of digital

323

readouts. The first digits were fixed at 11:00 AM, below was the current time, 9:59 AM. Below the current time the readout just showed a series of dashes, with a keyhole underneath. Faruqui stood in front of the rack, holding a bronze-colored key, as Nasrallah and three of his men stared at him, their eyes exuding eager anticipation. In a deliberate manner, a look of determination and hatred manifesting from his narrow face, Faruqui inserted the key into the box. He waited until the center readout showed the exact time as being 10.00 AM, then he turned the key fully clockwise. At that moment, the bottom readout displayed sixty minutes and zero seconds, than fifty nine minutes and fifty nine seconds.

Faruqui took his hand off the key, then looked towards his comrades, his look of hatred transformed into an expression of transcendental joy. "The bomb is now armed, and will detonate in one hour, at eleven o'clock exactly!" he cried out blissfully.

His comrades gathered closely towards him, silent at first, a look of piety written on their faces. Then, in unison, they all began chanting, "Allahu Akbar! Allahu Akbar! Allahu Akbar! Allahu Akbar!"

As the chants to the greatness of Allah grew in fervent intensity, Aziz Faruqui joined in, the tendons of his neck straining as he sang out his praises with the full force of his lungs.

◈ ◈ ◈

Littlejohn did his best to negotiate the mid-morning traffic of Manhattan, made worse by the periodic spurts of freezing rain. Dextraze noted that it was 10:00 AM, and suggested that Amelia turn on the radio for the latest newscast. "I wonder what else is happening in the world today," Dextraze said.

Amelia switched on the volume and tuned the radio to a local AM news station. The three listened wearily as the announcer began with the lead item.

"In today's headlines, a senior staff attorney with the ACLU, Harold Tanenbaum, announced that his organization will file suit in federal district court today, challenging the constitutionality of all the government's special legislation designed to help prevent another 9/11 from occurring in the United States. He claimed, in a special press release, that the possibility of future terrorist attacks in the United States involving mass casualties has been wildly exaggerated by the government, and that it is an administration that seeks to limit individual civil liberties which is the true terrorist threat to the American people. In other news..."

Amelia switched off the radio, as she and her colleagues continued on their desperate journey towards Hoboken, New Jersey.

◈ ◈ ◈

From his basement laboratory, Thomas Lazar appeared fatigued but excited. He was about to pick up his phone, when his wife yelled that it was time for him to take his medication. "Honey, forget about the medication. I'm very busy and must not be disturbed," he shouted with exasperation.

He dialed Dunlop's direct line and informed him that he had come up with a solution to disarming the RDS-220 device. The Deputy Director brought David Cole into the conversation through phone hook-up, who informed Dr. Lazar that the CSIS intelligence officers and Amelia Baldwin were headed towards a suspect location in Hoboken.

"As soon as they have secured the area and have access to the bomb, they should contact me immediately, and I will instruct them what to do," Lazar said imploringly.

"How certain are you, Dr. Lazar, that your solution will work?" Cole asked with a note of trepidation.

"Mathematically, everything works out," replied Lazar. "But there is only one way we will know for sure."

◈ ◈ ◈

The Ford van had finally entered the Holland Tunnel, which ran underneath the Hudson River between Manhattan and suburban New Jersey. Dextraze, Littlejohn and Baldwin were headed towards Jersey City, moving somewhat more rapidly in the tunnel, as traffic began thinning out. The clock on the van's instrument panel indicated that it was 10:25 AM.

Within minutes of entering the tunnel, the van emerged above ground, on the New Jersey side of the Hudson River. It traveled into the heart of Jersey City until it reached Henderson Avenue, where Henry Littlejohn made a right turn. They were now headed north, towards Hoboken.

As they passed a sign informing them that they had just entered Hoboken's city limits, with the additional anecdote that this was the town where Frank Sinatra was born, Amelia looked attentively though her passenger's side window, noting address numbers. She told her colleagues they had just passed the 600 block on Henderson, and that the dry cleaning establishment they were seeking had to be only a few blocks away. Henry eased off the accelerator, slowing down the van so they would not miss the address they were looking for. "Any reading on the D70, Pierre?" he asked Dextraze.

"Nothing so far," Dextraze replied.

"There it is!" Amelia yelled out, pointing her finger forward.

"I see it," Littlejohn responded, as he stopped the vehicle beside a parked car, directly in front of the red brick building housing Khalil's Dry Cleaners.

"Still no reading," Dextraze informed his colleagues.

"That's odd," replied Littlejohn, as all three carefully observed the establishment's storefront window. There appeared to be a customer with a folded garment on the counter. Facing the customer from the opposite side of the counter were a man and a woman, both apparently in their mid fifties. The woman wore a traditional Moslem head covering, as did a younger woman behind them, sorting clothes suspended on hangers that were attached to a rotating mechanism built into the ceiling.

The advertising on the window proclaimed a variety of services that were offered to the residents of Hoboken: dry cleaning, alterations, shirts laundered, household fabrics cleaned and tailoring done on the premises. There was the promise of same day service on all dry cleaning. Below the advertising, in smaller letters, Fouad Khalil was identified as the proprietor of the business. Dextraze noticed a copper plate hanging above the counter, containing Arabic writing in a calligraphy style. He asked Amelia to translate it for him.

326

"It means, there is no God but Allah, and Mohammed is his messenger," she informed her colleagues. "It's a signpost commonly found in the homes and businesses of devout Moslems."

The customer inside Khalil's Dry Cleaners had just departed. The three individuals inside the van needed to make a decision. Though the D70 machine provided no indication that pointed to Faruqui's bomb being concealed at 745 Henderson Avenue, the information relayed to them by Cole and Dunlop seemed definitive. "There's got to be some explanation why we aren't detecting anything," Littlejohn advised his two colleagues.

"I think we have no choice," replied Dextraze. "Let's go in."

Littlejohn, Dextraze and Baldwin departed the van, slamming its doors behind them. They entered the dry cleaning establishment together, standing in front of the counter. Facing them was Fouad Khalil, who politely asked them, "Please, how can I be of service to you?"

Dextraze and Littlejohn pulled out their Browning automatics, pointing them directly at Khalil and the two women standing behind him, who shrieked with fear.

Frightened, more for the two women than for himself, Khalil told the agents, "You may take my money. Just please don't harm my wife and daughter!"

Khalil's wife grasped her arms protectively around their daughter, who began crying, as her body pulsated with fear.

Dextraze and Littlejohn looked at each other, exchanging puzzled glances. Firmly gripping his pistol, Littlejohn now stared directly at Khalil, demanding to know where he kept his steam boiler.

Terrified, yet also perplexed at the question being posed so belligerently, he immediately answered that it was located in the rear of the shop, behind the laundry presses. "Keep a close watch on them," Littlejohn advised his colleagues, as he walked towards the rear of the establishment. He found an alcove behind the laundry press, which contained a steam boiler. The CSIS intelligence officer bent over, inspecting a plate that identified the manufacturer as Tompkins Limited, of Peoria, Illinois. The date of manufacture was September, 1977. Littlejohn knocked his fist against the boiler,

327

verifying that is was not hollow, while sensing the heat permeating its metal structure. He placed his pistol back in his holster, and walked back towards the front of the establishment.

"Pierre, what we're looking for is not here. It must have been false information," Littlejohn said in a subdued voice.

Returning his pistol to his concealed holster, Dextraze apologized profusely to the Khalil family.

"I am so sorry that we have disturbed you in such a manner. We are agents involved in an anti-terrorist matter, and apparently incorrect information concerning your business was given to us. Please, I beg you to forgive us," Dextraze said with great remorse.

"We love America!" Fouad Khalil shouted, his face simultaneously betraying anger and sorrow. His wife and daughter retained their looks of terror. Littlejohn noticed that Khalil had turned towards a framed photograph, mounted prominently on the wall near the entrance. Dextraze and Baldwin now also observed the photograph, which the shop's proprietor stared at obsessively, tears forming in his eyes. It was a portrait of a young man in the dress uniform of a lance corporal with the United States Marine Corps. The face had the firm, uncompromising gaze of a committed marine. Next to the photograph hung a small American flag.

Turning towards the three intruders who had moments ago held him and his family at gunpoint, Khalil said to them, "That is my son!"

Amelia told the family that they must be very proud of their son. Mrs. Khalil began crying, while speaking emotionally in Arabic. Amelia replied in her language, talking softly and with respect. Turning to her colleagues, she told them, "He was their only son, and was killed last summer in Iraq, by a roadside bomb."

Both Dextraze and Littlejohn bowed their heads, feeling intense shame. Fouad Khalil wanted them to know that they should not feel that way. His eyes still clouded with tears, he held his head up high. "I am so proud to have given my only son to America! This is our country! We would sacrifice everything to protect her!" He then apologized for both him and his family being frightened.

"We were just robbed two weeks ago. The robbers threatened to do terrible things to my daughter, I was scared."

Dextraze reiterated the acute regret he and his colleagues felt over their unwarranted intrusion into the lives of the Khalil family. Littlejohn asked them if they knew of any other cleaners in Hoboken that provided same day service, and would have a steam boiler on their premises. Fouad Khalil replied that there was only one other dry cleaners in the city offering that service, Centerpoint Cleaners on Main Street.

"What about the new place that will be opening soon?" interjected Fouad's daughter. She then exchanged words in Arabic with her mother, which Amelia translated for her colleagues.

"She says there is a place that will be opening sometime in May, on Borden Street, just off of Washington Street," Baldwin informed the two CSIS agents. "She thinks its called Kim Brothers Dry Cleaning and Tailoring."

"Kim Brothers?" Littlejohn repeated. "Kim is a Korean name."

Dextraze and Littlejohn stared at each other with alarm. Intuitively, they recognized the significance of the ethnicity of the supposed owner of the soon-to-open cleaners. "We've got to get there fast!" exclaimed Dextraze.

As the three individuals departed Khalil's establishment, Amelia, holding the door open, turned towards the family, saying a few words in Arabic before catching up with her colleagues.

"What did you tell them?" inquired Dextraze, as they began boarding their van.

"I told them I feel blessed to have met such a patriotic American family," Baldwin replied.

Littlejohn wasted no time in starting the engine and shifting the vehicle's transmission into drive. He floored the accelerator, as Amelia fed him directions from the GPS device. Within five minutes, they had reached the intersection of Washington and Borden.

"I'm getting a reading!" Dextraze shouted, his eyes fixated on the D70 machine's bar graph meter, which was displaying yellow. Littlejohn made a left turn onto Borden Street, proceeding slowly until all three occupants of the van spotted the storefront of the

Kim Brothers establishment, noting the sign indicating it was undergoing renovation and construction prior to its opening for business in May.

Littlejohn stopped the van, then turned towards Dextraze, who told him in a solemn tone, "the bar graph is now red."

Engaging the microphone on the van's communications gear, Littlejohn reached Dunlop at CSIS headquarters, with Cole patched in from Gayle Payne's office at the White House. He informed the two men of the false information concerning the location on Henderson Avenue, but alerted them to the fact that they now had a definite reading on the D70 detection machine from another dry cleaners, this one at 125 Borden Street.

David Cole told his colleagues that he would immediately see to it that the National Emergency Search Team unit in New York City was alerted and dispatched to Hoboken. Dunlop instructed his agents to attempt to determine the exact location of the bomb, "But be careful," he stressed vociferously. Littlejohn acknowledged the instructions, then gently tapped the accelerator of the van, creeping forward just enough to have a full view of the entrance and storefront window of the establishment before shifting the transmission into park.

The three agents carefully and inconspicuously scanned the shop's window and glass door, observing a man behind the counter, and two workmen in the rear installing equipment. "The gentleman behind the counter must be Mr. Kim, he looks Korean," commented Littlejohn.

"But where the hell is Faruqui's bomb?" Dextraze remarked with concern.

Littlejohn told his colleagues that somehow, they must find a way to look inside. Dextraze turned to Amelia, saying, "I think you and I will have to play the role of a couple that is new to Hoboken and got lost. Let's ask Mr. Kim for directions," Dextraze said, with Amelia nodding affirmatively. Baldwin opened the passenger door, and as she and Dextraze exited, Pierre advised Henry Littlejohn to keep a sharp eye on them.

Dextraze and Amelia walked up to the entrance, and attempted to open the door. It was locked, and Mark Kim observed them from behind the counter. The CSIS agent waved to Kim, signaling for him to open the door. Mark Kim, nodding his head side to side in refusal, pointed his finger to a sign posted on the window, indicating the establishment would be opened in May.

"Amelia, we'll have to discard the lost couple routine," Dextraze told his colleague. "Let's try something else." The intelligence officer withdrew his identification badge from his inside jacket pocket, and with a menacing look on his face, waved it at Kim. Through the glass door, the Korean proprietor could view an official looking photographic ID, with Dextraze's face prominently displayed, though the fine print was unreadable from behind the counter.

He approached the door, as Dextraze placed the ID back into his pocket. As Mark Kim unlocked the entrance and opened the door just a crack, Dextraze told him, in an official sounding voice, "We are with the Hoboken Fire Department, and noticed you did not display your fire safety occupancy permit."

There was a brief look of puzzlement on Kim's face. Then, speaking calmly, he told them that he had the required permit. "We're not due to open for business until May, so I thought it was not necessary to post the permit while the premises are still under construction."

In a firm manner, Dextraze advised him that it was a city regulation that occupancy permits be posted from the moment construction and renovation work proceeded. Kim assured him he would take care of the requirement right away.

"Sir, before we leave, I will need to verify that you in fact have an occupancy permit," Dextraze said with determination.

"Of course," Kim replied, with a slight suggestion of nervousness, as he opened the door for Dextraze and Baldwin. Kim got behind the counter, and began sorting through a folder containing documents and invoices. "It's somewhere in this stack," he said nonchalantly. The two agents cautiously scanned the rear of the establishment, noting a wide curtain concealing what appeared to be a hall or corridor. To the rear of Kim, the two workmen continued their installation activity, though occasionally glancing at the two agents with perturbed hostility.

331

"There, I found it," Kim said with relief, as he placed the permit on the counter so Dextraze and Baldwin could view it.

At that precise moment, a barely audible chorus of male voices could be heard, emanating from behind the curtain. In a whisper strained with agitation, Amelia told Dextraze, "Pierre, that's Arabic. They're chanting prayers for men about to die!"

Due to his proximity, Kim could distinctly overhear Amelia's warning. For a fraction of a second that seemed to endure for an eternity, his eyes locked menacingly with those of Pierre Dextraze. In a sudden movement, Kim's hand reached into his pants pocket and withdrew a revolver, as Dextraze pulled Amelia down on the floor. A shot was discharged, while Dextraze lay atop Amelia, shielding her. Kim's bullet penetrated the glass door of the establishment. Littlejohn, who had seen Kim remove his gun, withdrew his Browning automatic and fired repeatedly towards the Korean man. The bullets shattered both the passenger's window of the van and the storefront's glass door, slamming into Kim's chest, blood spurting both in front and behind him. Littlejohn leaped out of the van, amid the panicky screams from pedestrians, firmly holding his pistol. Dextraze lifted himself up, also clutching a Browning automatic. The two workmen in the rear had dropped their tools, and grabbed Kalashnikov assault rifles that had been hidden nearby. Dextraze aimed at one of the men who had just disengaged the safety catch on his weapon, firing two quick rounds, which impacted the terrorist's forehead, drilling neat, red-colored penetration holes. The man fell dead, his rifle dropping to the floor. The other terrorist aimed his AK-47 at Dextraze, just as a series of noises flowed from Littlejohn's pistol. The bullets perforated the terrorist's abdomen and chest. He cried out, than collapsed into a lifeless form. Littlejohn grabbed his rifle, while Dextraze retrieved the other casualty's Kalashnikov. With Amelia right behind them, the two agents passed through the curtain, rushed down a corridor and entered a large space with a view that stunned and horrified them.

Time seemed suspended as a massive steel object seared their consciousness. They instantly recognized it as a copy of the King of Bombs that they had viewed on video at CSIS headquarters only the day before. What seemed like minutes were actually nanoseconds, as they became aware that five desperate and fanatical men surrounded the bomb. Three of them ran towards the entrance from the corridor, where AK-47s were stacked against a wall, while two others pulled out pistols from their pockets. A burst of automatic fire from Dextraze's Kalashnikov mowed down three of the terrorists just as they retrieved their weapons. Nasrallah and Faruqui both fired their pistols, a bullet from the latter's gun grazing Amelia's head. A burst of fire from Littlejohn's AK-47 struck both of them, as they toppled to the ground, moaning briefly before they were silenced.

The three agents quickly surveyed their macabre surroundings. Four of the terrorists were definitely dead. Dextraze knelt by Faruqui's body, recognizing his distinctive narrow face. He squeezed Faruqui's wrist, checking for a pulse. "He's barely alive, and unconscious," he informed his colleagues. "He's probably dying," he added, as he stood up, noticing Littlejohn was inspecting the rack containing a box with digital readouts, positioned just in front of the nuclear device.

"It's already been armed," Littlejohn told Dextraze and Baldwin. "It's set to detonate in just under fifteen minutes!"

Dextraze pulled out a cell phone that gave him instant access to Dunlop's office. He informed the Deputy Director of what they had discovered, prompting Dunlop to order them to standby for instructions from Dr. Thomas Lazar.

❖ ❖ ❖

Gayle Payne received an urgent text message on her cell phone from David Cole, as the meeting in the Map Room had degenerated into a dull and mundane critique of Congress and how it had dropped the ball on missile defense. She immediately left the room and returned to her office, confronting the CIA's Director of Counter-Terrorism.

"I have a confession to make," Cole told the National Security Advisor. "To supplement our own NEST unit in New York, on my own authority, I authorized the Canadian Security Intelligence Service to send two of their agents with an advanced nuclear detection system, to New York, to search for Faruqui's bomb."

333

Payne appeared livid, and was about to lash out at Cole. Before she could speak, Cole told her, "They found the bomb."

Payne's demeanor was instantly transformed, as Cole relayed the details to her, including the location of the device at 125 Borden Street in Hoboken, New Jersey. She immediately grabbed her phone, reaching the White House switchboard. "This is a matter of national emergency!" she instructed the operator. "Connect me with Professor Jack Welles at FEMA in New York City. Make it quick!"

At FEMA, in the special operations room set up by NEST to coordinate its search activities, Welles picked up the urgent call that had just come in from Gayle Payne at the White House. His colleagues noticed that his usually placid face had become red with excitement and worry. Putting down the phone, he told them in a voice saturated with anxiety, "We have confirmation on the location of the dirty bomb! It's in Hoboken, on the other side of the Hudson River!"

Recovering somewhat from his initial shock, he told his colleagues the exact address where the device was located. "We need to have FEMA arrange for a helicopter to lift us there immediately," he told them. One of the physicists in the room looked outside through the windowpanes, observing a sky that was still overcast.

"Jack, I don't think anything is flying in this weather," he advised the NEST leader.

"Shit," Welles muttered in response.

❖ ❖ ❖

Thomas Lazar was patched into the CSIS communications network, so that Dextraze could speak to him directly. He was now standing with Littlejohn in front of the detonator control module, and advised Dr. Lazar that there was only thirteen minutes left prior to detonation. From his basement laboratory, Dr. Lazar began issuing instructions.

"Don't try cutting any wires, or firing bullets into the bomb. If you try anything like that, the device will instantly explode, at full yield," Lazar emphasized, with Dextraze acknowledging his firm warning.

"There is only one way we can safely disarm the bomb. We need to find a heat source that generates a flame of not less than 3,000 degrees centigrade," Lazar told Dextraze, who repeated the instructions for Littlejohn.

Scanning the room, Littlejohn noticed an oxyacetylene torch lying by one of the dead terrorists, near the entrance from the corridor. He told his comrade to check with Lazar if such a tool would create the required level of heat. Responding to Dextraze's query, Lazar replied hopefully. "Normally such torches operate at a temperature of 3,480 degrees centigrade, so that is perfect." Lazar then proceeded to instruct Dextraze on what he had to do to render Faruqui's superbomb harmless.

According to Lazar, the only means of safely rendering the bomb incapable of sustaining a chain reaction was to ignite the lithium contained in the thermonuclear fuel capsules. This would create a flash fire of intense heat, vaporizing the primary fission trigger of the device before the conventional explosives would detonate and set off a chain reaction.

"This is how you will do it," Lazar explained. "You must burn a perforation underneath the device on the center-line, about one and half meters from the front. Too far back and you risk detonating the primary. To far forward and the detonation mechanism will detect an attempt at disabling the bomb, and immediately set it off. It should take about eight minutes to penetrate the bomb casing. At the moment of penetration, the lithium will reach a temperature of 850 degrees centigrade, causing it to boil and become gaseous. Simultaneously, the tamper will arc, creating sparks that will ignite the gas and generate a flash fire. Any questions?"

Dextraze replied that he understood Lazar's instructions. Laying his Kalashnikov beside the bomb, he put on protective goggles, which he had found nearby, and Littlejohn handed him the oxyacetylene torch. Within seconds, he was underneath the nuclear device, where the wooden deck that held it up terminated. At exactly the point described by Dr. Lazar, the intelligence officer went to work. The torch emitted a bright, powerful flame underneath the bomb, generating sparks that clustered over the floor, as his two comrades nervously watched.

❖ ❖ ❖

Jack Welles was in van approaching the Holland Tunnel, with five other members of his team. It was their responsibility to disarm what they believed to be a radiological dispersion device. As they took the last exit to the tunnel, they found themselves subsumed by a massive traffic jam, with police and ambulance dome lights flashing furiously up ahead. "It looks like an accident," the driver told Professor Welles.

"This is ridiculous," Welles told his colleagues. Grabbing his cell phone, he called the Director at the FEMA headquarters in New York, explaining to him that his team was caught in a traffic jam at the entrance to the Holland Tunnel. "Look, weather or no weather, you've got to get me a helicopter, or else prepare to deal with mass contamination and evacuation," Welles said with exasperation.

"It looks like the weather front will clear in another fifteen minutes. We can fly then," replied the FEMA Director.

❖ ❖ ❖

Dextraze had been burning a hole underneath the front of the bomb for nearly four minutes, when his torch suddenly went out. Removing his goggles, he uttered, "Merde!"

"Pierre, I saw another torch up front, I'll grab it," Littlejohn said hurriedly, as he rushed towards the corridor, leading to the front of the establishment.

Dextraze heard a moan from Faruqui, who opened his eyes and looked directly towards him. "I will tell you how to disarm the device," he said suggestively. He then coughed, and spoke much softer, telling Dextraze he would need to come closer, as he had difficulty talking.

Wearily, the CSIS agent walked up to the prostrate Lion, who was now speaking so softly, his words were inaudible to Dextraze. As Amelia observed with a worried expression on her face, Dextraze crouched down to better hear Faruqui. She saw a flash of light reflected from a swiftly moving metal object, followed by a loud piercing shriek of agony from Dextraze. Almost immediately, the intelligence officer toppled onto his back, his body still, as torrents of blood flowed out of his throat.

"My God! Pierre!" cried Amelia in shock and horror, as Faruqui smiled at her, clutching his bloodstained knife. Baldwin ran towards him, kicking the knife out of his hand. With a violent burst of energy, Faruqui grabbed Amelia, and pushed her backward with such intense force, she collided with the far wall next to the corridor. The Lion of Islam, his strength seemingly renewed and fortified despite his wounds, lifted himself up and leaped towards the side of the bomb, where Dextraze had laid his Kalashnikov. He grabbed the weapon and swiftly disengaged its safety catch.

In the front of the establishment, Littlejohn had just found another oxyacetylene torch, which he was retrieving, when he suddenly heard the sound of rapid gunfire. He immediately ran back through the corridor, pulling out his Browning pistol. As the rear of the shop came into view, he witnessed with stunning pain the sight of his colleague Dextraze, obviously dead, his throat grotesquely cut open. Nearby, parallel to the bomb, lay Faruqui's body, ripped like a sieve by numerous entrance wounds from an assault rifle, an AK-47 at his side. Littlejohn turned to his right, and observed Amelia Baldwin, her eyes reflecting pain and suffering, her diminutive, quaking body almost dwarfed by the Kalashnikov she held firmly in her grasp. She had been able to grab one of the terrorist's weapons that had been laid against the wall near the corridor, and by a split second, was able to fire first, before Faruqui could pull his trigger.

"Henry, he murdered Pierre! But I killed him!" Amelia cried out, as Littlejohn told her she had done the right thing, and was very brave.

Though grieved at the loss of his friend and colleague, Littlejohn realized that neither he nor Amelia had the luxury of mourning. He ran up to Dextraze's body, removed his cell phone, and connected with Lazar, with Cole and Dunlop listening in. "This is Henry, I'm taking over, tell me what to do," he said with firmness.

"What happened to Pierre?" Dunlop asked.

Littlejohn simply said, "He's gone." Dunlop felt as though he was being stabbed as Lazar repeated the instructions for Littlejohn. The intelligence officer put on the protective goggles, got underneath the bomb, and switched on the torch. While sparks flew in every direction, he asked a still sorrowful and shaken Amelia Baldwin to monitor the detonation module, and let him know how much time remained before the device would explode.

"There's less than four minutes!" Amelia informed him, her voice reflecting with alarm the narrow window of time remaining. As Littlejohn continued to use the torch to burn into the bomb's thick steel casing, he could hear the sound of his own heart palpitating.

"Just under three minutes, Henry!" Amelia yelled with intense anxiety. The CSIS intelligence officer knew there was no other alternative but continue his task, until success or failure. Then, a large piece of steel fell off the bomb casing, and hot gas poured out of the perforation. Littlejohn dropped the torch and rolled over to the side of the bomb, as a sheet of flame began pouring out of the front underside of the device. He grabbed the cell phone and hurriedly reconnected with Dr. Lazar, telling him what had just transpired.

"Dr. Lazar, what do we do now?" he asked,

"What do you do?" responded Lazar with surprise. "Run like hell!"

Grabbing Amelia by the arm, he told her excitedly, "We've got to get the hell out of here."

They ran through the corridor, past the front counter and out the door of Kim Brothers Dry Cleaning and Tailoring. In the background, police sirens could be heard, responding to previous reports of gunfire. If they had looked behind them, the two agents would have observed police squad cars with dome lights flashing. However, their eyes were glued on Washington Street, and the Hudson River that ran alongside it.

They ran across Washington Street, both almost out of breath, when a loud, shattering noise enveloped them, resembling the concussion stemming from a volcanic eruption. They were both thrown some distance, as debris fell over them and thick smoke congealed. The noise seemed to endure forever, with nothing but thick blackness surrounding them. Amelia, in pain from lacerations incurred due to the blast, wondered if she was still alive, or had departed from her earthly existence to an empty void.

Slowly, the black smoke began to dissipate. She could first make out her hands, then next to her, Littlejohn, who lay flat on the ground. The smoke was now clearing, and she could clearly see Littlejohn beginning to move. The CSIS agent pulled himself up, then turned towards Amelia, asking her if she was alright. She nodded her head in a tentative gesture, as Littlejohn took her gently by her hand, and helped her up. They both stood rigidly, facing the Hudson, as smoke formed in front of them, shrouding the horizon with a thick smog. As the smoke blew towards the south, Amelia and her colleague began to make out the distinct and ubiquitous skyline of Manhattan. The sky had also begun to clear, as the clouds receded and sunshine brightly glowed, bathing the skyscrapers of New York City in a golden hue.

"Look, Amelia, there's a rainbow over Manhattan!" Littlejohn said excitedly. Amelia had noticed it too. She turned towards Henry Littlejohn, as she wept, though also smiling.

"Henry, I can see in that rainbow the spirit of Pierre, and also of my dear brother!" she told her colleague with great emotion. Seeing the tears in Amelia's face, Littlejohn threw his arms around her, as the two became locked in an unbreakable embrace.

◈ ◈ ◈

Gayle Payne re-entered the Map Room, David Cole right behind her. Their entrance startled the President, Vice President and senior officials. "What's going on, Ms. Payne?" the President demanded to know.

"Mr. President, a short while ago, two agents from the Canadian Security Intelligence Service and a staff member from our own Central Intelligence Agency discovered Aziz Faruqui's bomb in Hoboken, New Jersey. We believe they were able to successfully disarm it, but we're awaiting confirmation from the National Emergency Search Team. They're on their way now, and we should be receiving reports from them shortly," she advised the Commander-in-Chief and other top administration officials.

The revelation from Gayle Payne transformed the agenda of the meeting. There was now concern expressed over what had actually happened, and whether or not the administration would look bad, and be attacked in the press for its negligence. "The FBI screwed up again," the Vice President uttered sardonically.

David Cole suggested that the speakerphone in the Map Room be patched into CSIS headquarters in Ottawa, to ensure proper coordination as more facts regarding developments in Hoboken became available. Without enthusiasm, the President reluctantly acquiesced to the arrangement.

◇ ◇ ◇

Several FEMA helicopters had landed astride Washington Street in Hoboken, as emergency vehicles converged on the area where the blast had occurred. Professor Welles and members of his NEST unit were on the scene, surveying the area and taking atmospheric readings. One of the physicists assigned to NEST motioned for Welles to view one of the analyzers that had been deployed, which was issuing readings of an entirely unanticipated character. Welles took one look at the analyzer, then cried, "Jesus Christ! Where did they get this idea of a dirty bomb? I've got to contact the White House right away!"

◇ ◇ ◇

A call now came into the Map Room from Professor Welles in Hoboken. As those present in the room listened, joined by Dunlop and Lazar in Ottawa, the chief of NEST delivered an alarming revelation. Speaking directly to the Vice President, he relayed his findings.

"Mr. Vice President, I don't know the source of your intelligence about the terrorists' weapon being a dirty bomb, but the device was a full-fledged nuclear bomb," Welles informed the Vice President and his administration colleagues. "And not just any nuclear bomb, but an exceptionally powerful one," he added.

Momentarily, everyone in the Map Room was silent. The President and Vice President looked at each other, exchanging awkward glances. "How do you know that, Professor Welles?" the Vice President asked.

The Director of NEST explained that their equipment had detected the presence of fissile materials in the air. "But that's not all, Mr. Vice President. There's enough tritium and deuterium that's been detected to have constructed a high yield thermonuclear bomb!"

"My God!" uttered the Director of National Intelligence, a look of anguish mixed with embarrassment written on his face. The CIA Director sat still, his face impassive.

The Vice President inquired about the yield of the weapon. Welles informed him that it was impossible to tell at this stage, but based on the nuclear materials that had been detected, it probably was in the range of several dozen megatons. "Thank God those Canadians were able to disarm the nuclear component of the device, or I would not be speaking with you now, and we would have to bury millions of dead Americans, not to mention clearing the debris of New York City."

As the officials seated around the table in the Map Room exchanged looks tinged with acute embarrassment and bewilderment, David Cole asked about the condition of Amelia Baldwin and the CSIS agents.

Responding to Cole's concern, Welles told him that both Amelia Baldwin and Henry Littlejohn had sustained cuts and abrasions due to the blast from the flash fire that had destroyed the nuclear component of the weapon. They had also been exposed to radioactivity. "Fortunately, they were both evacuated swiftly to a hospital, and received immediate decontamination treatment. Their short-term prospects are good, but of course, with radioactivity, we can't be sure of the long-term impact on their health," Welles added.

Dunlop asked about Pierre Dextraze, already knowing the answer, yet hoping the worst had not happened, despite all evidence to the contrary.

"I can confirm that unfortunately the CSIS intelligence officer, Dextraze, was killed," Welles informed him.

"He was a very courageous man," Cole added, prompting Dunlop to tell him that all three agents had displayed uncommon valor, and that both nations owed them a great deal.

Ignoring the comments of Cole and Dunlop, the Vice President thanked Welles for his work, and asked him to keep the White

House apprised of further developments. Having concluded the conversation with the NEST Director, the Vice President suggested that the communications link with CSIS headquarters could now be terminated. The President concurred, thanking Dunlop for his organization's assistance and telling him that the administration would be in further contact with the Canadian government as the situation warranted.

The speakerphone now silent, the Vice President introduced a new item on the agenda. "Gentlemen, and Ms. Payne, let's discuss how we inform the American people that, owing to the vigilance and effectiveness of this administration's anti-terrorism policies, we thwarted a deadly plot by Al-Qaeda and Al-Assad El-Islamiya, saving millions of lives."

The meeting continued, as several of the participants brainstormed on public relations strategies, while both Payne and Cole sat silently. Midway through the conversation, an aide entered the Map Room and whispered a message into the President's ear, prompting him to stand up.

"Excuse me, I have the governors of New Jersey and New York on the line in the Oval Office," the President said. "It looks like we'll have to declare the region affected by this morning's events as national disaster areas. You can all carry on while I talk to the governors."

Several minutes after the President departed the Map Room, the Vice President called one of his aides on the phone. The aide appeared several minutes later, carrying a platter with glasses and a bottle of champagne.

"Colleagues, I normally don't partake in libations this early in the day," the Vice President said gleefully. "However, under the circumstances, I think a little celebration is in order, considering how God, in his infinite mercy, has just delivered us from evil."

He poured champagne into each of the glasses, which were distributed around the room, with only Cole and Payne declining to partake in the toasting which followed. They both sat stone-faced, disbelieving the frivolity that seemed to dominate the senior officials who had apparently escaped a disaster, abetted by their own miscalculations, by the skin of their teeth.

Amid the laughter and toasts, David Cole's cell phone rang. He pulled the phone out of his jacket pocket, and placed it firmly against his ear.

"Mr. Cole, this is Ernesto Guzman. Dr. Pervaz Khan finally talked. I can reveal his information to you, and I must warn you, there is no time to lose."

The call startled Cole. He had almost forgotten about Dr. Khan. Amid the surreal flurry of laughter and self-congratulation that surrounded him, he told Guzman that the nuclear device had been found and rendered safe.

"And would that device have been located in Hoboken?"

"Yes," Cole replied, with a growing sense of uncertainty.

"And was it set to detonate at 11:00 AM, Eastern Standard Time?" Guzman asked.

Again, and with heightened unease, Cole confirmed the accuracy of what Guzman relayed from his interrogation of Pervaz Khan.

"Then, Mr. Cole, I congratulate you on uncovering one of Aziz Faruqui's bombs," Guzman said, without even a trace of irony.

Instantly, Cole's face had turned ashen white. Payne noticed his appearance with alarm, though her administration colleagues continued with their bantering.

"What do you mean, one of his bombs?" Cole asked fearfully.

As more information was relayed to him, David Cole took on the appearance of insufferable agony.

"Are you sure there is a second bomb?" Cole asked in a desperate tone of voice. As he did so, the frivolity in the Map Room instantly dissolved, as everyone seated around the table now had their eyes and ears glued on him.

Guzman provided additional information, which prompted the Director of Counter-Terrorism to ask if that was all the information Pervaz Khan had knowledge of. He then told Guzman he understood the situation, and would have to contact him later. As several pairs of eyes stared at him, he hung up, placed the cell phone back into his jacket pocket, than glanced at an antique clock, which sat on a mantelpiece. He turned towards the Vice President, and shared his agony.

343

"Under interrogation, Dr. Pervaz Khan disclosed that two copies of the RDS-220 device were constructed at Lake Abitibi. They realized that to totally destroy our country, one bomb alone would not be sufficient. Their goal was to detonate two such devices, one on each coast, at locations where wind currents would guarantee the widest possible dispersion of toxic radioactivity across the continental United States."

There was not a single person present in the room who did not feel intense shock and unbridled fear. The Vice President asked tensely where Khan revealed the bombs had been placed.

"He told Guzman that one device was located in Hoboken, and the other in Glendale, a suburb of Los Angeles."

Glenn Thrush shrieked in panic, feeling stunned. "God help me! My daughter and grandchildren live in Glendale!"

Secretary of Defense Murray asked Cole when the bombs were supposed to detonate. Cole informed him that Khan claimed the Hoboken device was to have exploded at 11:00 AM, which they now knew was accurate. "According to Khan, the nuclear bomb in Glendale will detonate at precisely 10:00 AM, Pacific Time."

With those words, everyone's eyes stared at the clock on the mantelpiece. "That's one o'clock our time, just forty-five minutes from now!" shouted Dick Darnell.

Shaking, almost losing control of himself, a desperate Vice President asked if Khan had revealed the exact location of the bomb in Glendale.

"Unfortunately not, Mr. Vice President," Cole sadly told him. "Khan selected the general areas where the devices were to be placed, Hoboken and Glendale, based on urban concentrations, weather patterns and wind currents. However, he instructed Aziz Faruqui to pick the specific locations, without informing him, so that in the event he was captured and tortured, he would have no information to reveal."

A feeling of fearful hopelessness permeated the Map Room. "There's no way in hell we can find that bomb in forty-five minutes, let alone evacuate Los Angeles!" yelled the Vice President.

Gayle Payne turned towards Cole, asking him if he had any ideas. Looking dejected, he told her that he had no solutions, but if any man on the planet did, it was Dr. Thomas Lazar. Hearing Cole's comment, the Vice President ordered the communications link with CSIS headquarters restored, and he himself briefed a shaken Alex Dunlop of what had just been learned from Pervaz Khan's interrogation. Without delay, Dunlop patched in Lazar from his home laboratory, and shared the nightmarish news.

"Dr. Lazar, is there any chance Khan might be bluffing?" the Vice President desperately inquired.

"No, Mr. Vice President, it should be obvious from his confirmation of the details in Hoboken that he is telling the truth about the second device," Lazar answered dispassionately. "Furthermore, until this revelation, the mixed team of North Korean and Middle Eastern nuclear experts working together on bomb assembly at Lake Abitibi did not make sense to me, owing to language difficulties. But it is very logical if they had two separate assembly teams, divided by nationality and language, each responsible for its own bomb. Also, the materials they recovered from the four Mark 41 hydrogen bombs, and additional materials we know they obtained from other sources, are sufficient for two RDS-220 devices."

"Dr. Lazar, given the awful predicament in terms of time factor, do we have any options?" David Cole asked, knowing he was requesting a miraculous solution that seemed unobtainable in the real world.

"There is a solution," Lazar said, defying the expectations of the petrified officials seated around the table. "It would be completely effective, if implemented without delay. Unfortunately, it will also be very painful."

Fearing the worst, yet grasping for any hint of salvation, the Vice President asked Dr. Lazar what he would propose should be done.

"Since we only know the general locality where the second nuclear device is situated, and not its specific location, Glendale must be completely destroyed by a tactical nuclear weapon," Lazar informed a horror-stricken Vice President.

"Dr. Lazar, that is too horrific to contemplate!" the Vice President painfully uttered, as his colleagues looked on morbidly.

"I know, Mr. Vice President, but you don't have much time, so listen to me carefully," Lazar pleaded. "If Faruqui's device is allowed to detonate, it will explode with the force of 150 million tons of TNT, and spread deadly radioactivity across half of your country, rendering those areas uninhabitable for centuries. Its impact will be almost identical to the results of an explosion in the metropolitan New York City area, and I would predict a minimum of 75 million fatalities. If you adopt my solution, probably a half million people will be killed instantly by the blast and thermal pulse, and another half million in the following week from the effects of radiation poisoning, with the bulk of radioactive fallout restricted to the Los Angeles area. I admit both outcomes are horrifying, but clearly distinguishable. What it boils down to, Mr. Vice President, is that there will be a nuclear detonation on the West Coast. You can do nothing to avert that from happening. The only alternatives you have, sir, are whether the nuclear explosion is fission, or fusion."

General Robert Maude introduced himself to Dr. Lazar as chairman of the Joint Chiefs of Staff. "What is the minimum yield required to be placed on the target?" he asked Lazar, who responded that 45 kilotons would be sufficient. Turning towards the Secretary of Defense, he informed him that the B61 bomb in the air force arsenal would do the job. Speaking without a trace of emotion, he informed the Secretary, Vice President and his colleagues that, "The B61, in the Mod 4 version, is a boosted implosion-fission device, with an exact yield of 45 kilotons."

"Can we get it to the target on time?" the Vice President inquired, with anxiety ringing in his throat.

General Maude quickly glanced at his wrist chronometer, making swift mental calculations before responding to the Vice President's question. "Sir, we maintain a stockpile of B-61s in that modified version at Luke Air Force Base, in Arizona, where the 944th fighter wing is deployed. We now have 40 minutes until the terrorists' nuclear device is set to detonate. Provided I give the order now, it would take ten minutes to arm and load a B61 bomb onto an F-16 fighter, fuel and prepare the aircraft for take-off. It will take another 25 minutes for the aircraft to reach the target area. That gives us a window of five minutes. As you know, sir, the pilot will require presidential authorization before he can actually release the nuclear weapon to strike and destroy its target."

Nodding his head in understanding, the Vice President directed General Maude to proceed with issuing the necessary orders. As the General got up to attend to his onerous duty, the Secretary of Defense joining him, the Director of National Intelligence burst into tears, wailing uncontrollably.

The Vice President stood up, telling his fellow administration officials that he now had the most painful burden to bear in telling the President that he must issue an order that would result in most of Los Angeles being destroyed, with frightful casualties resulting. Before departing the Map Room, he turned around, displaying a face that revealed a broken man. "We fucking blew it!" he screamed, as he kicked the wall in frustration and anger, before departing for the Oval Office.

Glenn Thrush continued to weep, as Gayle Payne watched over him with empathy. David Cole also observed the sorrowful figure that the Director of National Intelligence had been reduced to. He then looked at the Director of the CIA, who tried desperately to avoid eye contact with him.

"Dick, you told me you would not believe that the terrorists could build a nuclear bomb until you saw a mushroom cloud over an American city," Cole angrily reminded Darnell. "Well, Dick, before this day is done, you will get your damned mushroom cloud, one way or another!" he yelled, as the CIA Director lowered his head in a gesture of abject self-pity.

❖ ❖ ❖

At Luke AFB, the wing commander received an urgent call from the chairman of the Joint Chiefs of Staff. "Colonel, this is General Maude, do you recognize my voice?" After the Colonel replied affirmatively, the General relayed an order that struck with stunning disbelief. The Colonel requested that the General repeat the order.

"This is not a drill, Colonel. You will scramble an F-16 with sufficient fuel for a high-speed dash to Glendale, designated target area, in the Los Angeles metropolitan area. The ordnance to be carried is a fully armed B61, Mod 4 tactical nuclear device, set for airburst. The aircraft is to be in range of the target area no later than 09:55 A.M. Pacific Time, and standby for presidential authorization to launch the B61 and destroy the target. Please acknowledge that you understand the order I have just given you," Maude enunciated with crisp military detachment.

The Colonel acknowledged the order, and within seconds, klaxons blared out noisily at Luke AFB, as an F-16 was being prepared to be scrambled, and ordnance technicians began the process of arming and fusing a B61 nuclear bomb for its intended task.

◇ ◇ ◇

His face engulfed with trepidation, the Vice President entered the Oval Office. The Commander-in-Chief was still engaged in his conference call with the governors of New York and New Jersey. He laughed aloud, bantering with his political colleagues. The conversation had obviously shifted from the dire predicament of radioactive decontamination to more trivial political matters. The Vice President approached the President's desk, whispering that an urgent matter had arisen. The President politely ended the phone conversation, informing the governors that the Vice President had a matter he wished to discuss with him. He hung up and looked directly at the Vice President, who was standing stiffly erect, rather than seating himself, as he would normally do.

With the President smiling, his number two man in the administration struggled to find the words to communicate the most terrible message he would ever deliver. Failing at finding a formula that evoked eloquence, the Vice President just poured out the convergence of hideous outcomes, making the case for selecting the one which was least appalling.

"Mr. President, this is the most awful day in our country's history. Pervaz Khan finally broke and revealed what he knew about what we thought was a dirty bomb, and disclosed that there was not one, but two nuclear devices smuggled into the United States. The worst part is this: the intelligence community, this administration, myself included, all thought it was a slam-dunk that this device was only a dirty bomb, at worst."

The President's smile had vanished, replaced by an uncontrollable nervous tick afflicting one of his eyes, as the Vice President continued to relay his foreboding message.

"Mr. President, I have to tell you now, everything David Cole and the Canadians have been telling us is accurate. Each bomb individually is so powerful, it can wipe out half the country. The terrorists' objective was to annihilate the United States entirely, by detonating two bombs. Only one of them was discovered and rendered safe, the device in Hoboken. Khan revealed that there is a second bomb, just as deadly, in Glendale, California. It will detonate in less than thirty-five minutes. We don't know where it has been hidden, and there is no hope we can find it in time."

The Vice President briefly paused, observing the change in the President's facial expression. He appeared puzzled and bewildered, giving the impression that what the Vice President was telling him was inexplicable, and could not be an accurate reflection of reality.

Painfully, and displaying profound sorrow, the Vice President continued his difficult task, knowing he was constrained by the sands of time.

"Mr. President, we have consulted with Dr. Lazar, and he has given us the one and only solution that will prevent a holocaust from wiping out half of our nation. I must warn you, it is frightful, but absolutely necessary. We must destroy Glendale ourselves, with one of our own nuclear weapons."

The President's demeanor was now one of extreme uncertainty, as he looked at his Vice President, exuding child-like fear.

"I have ordered the chairman of the Joint Chiefs of Staff to launch an F-16 fighter, armed with a tactical nuclear weapon," the Vice President tearfully informed his Commander-in-Chief. "It will be in range of the target area in just under half an hour. As you know, the weapon cannot be launched without presidential authorization. I am asking you to make the most difficult and vital decision of your presidency. Please issue the order right now to destroy Glendale."

The Vice President stared at the nation's leader and head of state, whose tortured face revealed a man who recognized that his own grotesque ineptitude would result, inevitably, in an irreversible, monstrous calamity. As the Vice President repeated his pleas to issue the required authorization to destroy an American city with one of the nation's own nuclear weapons, the President's jaw began moving erratically, simultaneously with his lips vainly attempting to pronounce words. However, not a single audible syllable emerged from the President's throat.

"Please, Mr. President! You must make this terrible but necessary decision!" the Vice President implored the Commander-in-Chief. "America is just like a body suffering from a dangerous disease, like cancer. We must cut off a limb and stop the cancer from spreading, so the body can live! You must amputate one of our cities so that America does not die!" the Vice President tearfully pleaded.

The President could no longer hear the words being desperately unleashed at him by his Vice President. He placed his right hand with outstretched fingers across his mouth, in a fan-like configuration of concealment. His face was a bloodcurdling image of a man oppressed by profound guilt and remorse. His eyes revealed a life in politics that had now culminated in the tragedy of failure, only sanctified by the realization of doom.

Printed in the United States
108470LV00004B/200/A

9 781420 860559